MADE OF FIRE AND STEEL AND THE GUTS OF MEN, AN ISLAND WORLD WITH A SPECIAL PRIDE

To her captain, she was the reward for a lifetime of dedicated service.

To the young lieutenant, she was his first taste of command.

And to the six hundred brave young men in her company, she was the greatest ship of all time.

H.M.S. *Antigone*
THE CRUISER

Also by Warren Tute
Published by Ballantine Books:

THE ROCK

THE
Cruiser

Warren Tute

© 1955 Warren Tute

BALLANTINE BOOKS • NEW YORK

First published in England in 1955 by Cassell & Company Ltd.

© 1955 Warren Tute

All rights reserved. Published in the United States by Ballantine Books, a division of Random House, Inc., New York.

ISBN 0-345-29573-0

Manufactured in the United States of America

First Ballantine Books Edition: August 1956
Second Printing: July 1981

Author's Preface

This is a story about the Royal Navy, a story about professional men—the RN—the men whose career it is. I stress the word 'profession' because to me it is significant. A profession is neither an enthusiasm nor a hobby. It is not something embarked upon in an emergency, however necessary at times that may be. A profession is something to which you give your whole life.

The Royal Navy is exactly that to its Regular Officers and Men. For the British the Navy has always had a special position. The Preamble to the Articles of War which first bore the signature of Charles II read — 'It is upon the Navy, under the good Providence of God, that the Safety, Honour and Welfare of this Realm do chiefly depend.' Whether those words apply now — I do not know. At the period of this book they were certainly true.

In stressing the professionalism of the Royal Navy, however, I wish in no way to detract from the RNR and the RNVR. At the start of a war, volunteers pour into the Navy with fresh ideas and a healthy scepticism of all that is 'RN'. By the end of a war they are indistinguishable from their 'regular' shipmates. In some cases, indeed, they become more 'RN' than professional Naval Officers.

But that this is possible presupposes that there is something about being 'RN'. It assumes a style—a mystique if you wish—which the regular sailor possesses, something a little rare, something the amateur values while retaining his right to jeer at certain of its aspects.

I believe this to be so. I believe that it cannot be said to apply in anything like the same degree to the other two Services. It is something nearly impossible to define. There may be 'something about a sailor', but it dodges out of sight as soon as you make an attempt to catch it.

The jolly, rather hearty, 'decent' Naval Officer known to the reader of fiction is very often a figure of fun. He has superficialities which are easy to caricature and qualities which he prefers to disguise. It is also embarrassingly easy to sentimentalize about the Silent Service, to over-value the dramatic properties of the Navy's day-to-day life. To the professional sailor the sea is never cruel. It is simply the medium on which he works.

But there are other sentimentalities about our brave boys in blue which are just as deep-rooted and just as dangerously false. They all add up to what might be labelled the *Boys' Own Paper* outlook on the sea, a curiously unadult outlook where everything is black or white, where jolly ripping adventures are the order of the day and where nobody ever goes to bed with somebody else's wife.

The truth is, of course, that like all human beings, the regular sailor is a compound of ordinary virtues and faults. He is a human being first and a naval entity second.

I would like to explain why I have focused this story on a cruiser. Every man-of-war is a compromise built for a special purpose—an agreed mixture of speed, armour, offensive and defensive weapons, seaworthiness and living accommodation. A battleship has huge guns, is heavily armoured but is usually slow. A destroyer has no armour, light weapons and is very fast. Mid-way between the two stands the cruiser—to me almost the ideal ship.

A cruiser is the smallest of the major war vessels. She has all the essentials and a number of the frills. She carries a Surgeon, a Chaplain and a detachment of Royal Marines. She is an independent command in the charge of a four-ringed Captain RN.

Her spick-and-span, spit-and-polish appearance and routine, while lacking the pomposities of a capital ship, are very far removed from the roll-top sweater and oil-stained cap of the sloop or corvette. From one point of view a small maritime township; from another a most effective expression of naval power, a cruiser is comfortable to live in and is perhaps the most versatile warship the world has seen.

I must end with the usual reminder that *all* characters in this story are imaginary. Where real events are mentioned they are brought in because this is a story set in a particular time and the historical events of that time are, of course, its unchanging background. So far as names are concerned, if I have used any real person's name who might perhaps have been connected with the Navy at the time—then I apologize in advance and assure him or her that it is purely accidental. I would like at the same time to acknowledge a debt of gratitude to my friends Peter Norton and Peter Moore without whose sardonic help I would long ago have been lost in a literary sea.

HMS *ANTIGONE*

Main Characters

COMMANDING OFFICER
Captain Colin Trevesham, DSC, RN
  Captain's Secretary: Paymaster Sub-Lieutenant D. L. Marsh, RN ('Scratch')
  Captain's Coxswain: Petty Officer Vincent

EXECUTIVE OFFICER
Commander W. E. Hatchett, RN ('Stubby')
  Chief Bos'n's Mate: Chief Petty Officer Arthur Penniwick ('Chief Buffer')
  Commander's Writer: Able-Seaman Clarke ('Nobby')

EXECUTIVE DEPARTMENT
First Lieutenant and Quarterdeck Division: Lieutenant-Commander J. Collard, RN ('Number One')
Foc'sle Division: Lieutenant Cravenby, RN
Top Division: Lieutenant Crawford, RN
Senior Gunroom Officer: Sub-Lieutenant Darbigh, RN ('Sub')

GUNNERY DEPARTMENT
Gunnery Officer: Lieutenant-Commander (G) T. Brasson, RN ('Guns': 'Honest Tom')
Gunner: Mr Legg, RN

TORPEDO DEPARTMENT
Torpedo Officer: Lieutenant-Commander Fossingham, RN ('Torps') afterwards Lieutenant John Casper RN
Gunner (T): Mr. Partle, RN

NAVIGATING DEPARTMENT
Navigating Officer: Lieutenant A. Spratt, RN ('Pilot': 'Aggie')

Chief Quartermaster: Chief Petty Officer Bowling ('Chief QM')

COMMUNICATIONS DEPARTMENT
Signals and Observer Officer: Lieutenant Peter Osborne, RN
Chief Yeoman of Signals: Petty Officer J. Mellish ('Chief Yeoman')

AIRCRAFT
Pilot: Lieutenant (P) A. Grey-Bennett, RN ('Marcel')

ROYAL MARINE DETACHMENT
Officer Commanding: Captain Taw-Street, RM ('Bullock Major')
Colour-Sergeant Forrester, RM ('Forky')

ENGINEERING DEPARTMENT
Engineer Officer: Commander (E) ('The Chief')
Senior Engineer: Lieutenant (E) J. S. Meldrum RN ('Senior')

ACCOUNTANT DEPARTMENT
Accountant Officer: Paymaster-Commander ('Pay')
Central Storekeeping Officer: Paymaster-Lieutenant Hale, RN ('CSKO')

MEDICAL DEPARTMENT
Medical Officer: Surgeon-Commander ('PMO': 'Doc')

METEOROLOGICAL AND INSTRUCTOR
Instructor-Lieutenant ('Schooly')

MISCELLANEOUS
Master-at-Arms (Senior Rating on lower deck): Petty Officer Kirby ('Crusher' or 'Jaunty')
Petty Officer Cook Jenkins
Leading-Seaman Battersby
Marine Parker ('Nosey')
The Three Fat Men of the Sea—ABs Kavanagh, Rillington and Clarke.

CHAPTER ONE

Commander William Edgar Hatchett, Royal Navy, rolled up his napkin, threw the morning paper on to a chair and went out into the hall. It was twenty minutes to nine and in a brisk quarter-of-an-hour he could be down at the office in the shipyard five minutes before anyone might reasonably expect him to be there.

'Back about one,' he called out to his wife as he picked up his bowler hat and then, with a private snort, put it back on the hat stand. He had an acute dislike of that hat, and as it was Saturday morning he felt he could dispense with its services for once. In March 1938 the shadow of the Bowler Hat was receding from the professional Navy, but it was still a symbol with many unpleasant associations for executive officers.

Hatchett had been a midshipman at the end of the Great War. He had seen the Geddes axe and other reorganizations sweep away the majority of his Term into what he called 'bowler hatterdom'. But Hatchett had survived. The 'twenties had gone on their way. Four years ago he had been promoted Commander and was now appointed Executive Officer of HMS *Antigone*, a cruiser of the 'Leander' class completing at Messrs Harland and Wolff's shipyard. Those were facts, but in moments of reflection he still found them surprising.

He won his daily tussle starting the Morris-Cowley, and in a few moments had swung out of the gate of Fernlea into Cushendall Avenue. It was a fine morning and he whistled through his teeth as he pressed on down into Belfast. He did not like the house they had rented. He was always glad to be out of it and away to the ship. However, madame was content and that was all that really mattered. They had let their own house near Havant while he stood by the ship, and Fernlea with its hideous brickwork

1

and derelict garden was only a temporary home. He and Alice were fully used to packing up one home and setting up another, be it in Hong Kong or Malta or now, as it seemed likely, Bermuda.

HMS *Antigone* was to join the America and West Indies Station and in 1938 Bermuda still boasted a dockyard on which the Eighth Cruiser Squadron was based. Hatchett was not sure he could afford to take madame out to Bermuda. It was known as a rich man's station and Hatchett had no private means. However, madame had every intention of going and he supposed they would find some way round the problem—as they usually did.

He crossed over Queen's Bridge and was soon rattling along the tram tracks between the huge gaunt buildings of the shipyard. Even in plain clothes there was no mistaking Hatchett's profession. He was a square built man in an old, square built car—the two were oddly complementary—and he seemed always to be on the point of bursting out of one situation into another. He was short in stature and at times had a somewhat satanic appearance.

Throughout his service career he had been known as 'Stubby' Hatchett and the nickname suited him well. He had curly black hair, a wide mouth, and eyes set far apart. He had broken his nose boxing as a cadet at Osborne, and his flat features and red weatherbeaten face, combined with a short neck and thick shoulders, gave him a look of initial ferocity which had stood him in good stead on many a quarterdeck.

Over the next three years the ship's company of *Antigone* were to come to know that squat figure, with the telescope fiercely rammed under the left arm, as part of the landscape of their daily lives. He had a suggestion of the bulldog about him which his habitual stance unconsciously stressed.

In his own opinion Hatchett was strict and reasonable and very far from hidebound. He worked to the spirit rather than the letter of the Naval Discipline Act, and this view was generally shared by those who served with him for any length of time. To midshipmen and young seamen, however, he seemed at first sight to be the embodiment of naval wrath and discipline, a Grand Inquisitor and Martinet.

Yeoman of Signals Joseph Mellish, Official Number

P/J182976 was peering out of the office window as the Morris-Cowley barged round the corner of the dockyard building and came explosively to a halt.

'Here he comes,' he called out to the Chief Bosun's Mate who was squaring off the ruler and pencils on the desk. During the building of one of HM ships, whether in a Royal Dockyard or under private contract, a certain complement is appointed to stand by the ship. It is a curious hybrid life, a blend of sea and shore routines, a period when individual responsibilities increase and opportunities to take advantage abound.

Thus key officers and ratings are chosen with particular care. Mellish had fourteen years unblemished service to his credit and was on the roster for advancement to Chief Yeoman of Signals.

Chief Petty Officer Penniwick with seventeen years of service had already reached the top of his tree. The Chief Bosun's Mate in a cruiser is the Commander's right hand man and, as Penniwick was very sadly aware, this was likely to be his last sea-going commission. He had served with Hatchett before when the latter was a divisional officer in a battleship, and even in those days had tipped him for his brass hat.

Now they were together again. Indeed, Hatchett had specially asked for Penniwick to be drafted to the ship and although Penniwick was not supposed to have heard of this, his personal loyalty was intense. Whatever else happened in *Antigone* the Executive Officer was going to be properly interpreted to the ship's company so far as Penniwick was concerned.

' 'Morning, Penniwick. 'Morning, Mellish.'

Hatchett gave them a friendly nod and sat down at the desk.

'Good morning, sir.'

'You shouldn't be here, either of you. There won't be many more chances for local week-end leave. You should grab the opportunity while you can.'

They were both ready for this remark. Each Saturday morning was the same. There were those who took every moment of leave they could get, and those who would always be there. Mellish and Penniwick fell into the latter category. Work might not actually stop if either was on leave, but both knew it would slow down. Neither could

3

quite tear himself away from the bare unpainted ship that would soon be their home, nor from the office which they both regarded as the brain-box of the whole affair.

'Only get into trouble, sir,' said Penniwick with a wink at the Yeoman, 'and I've strict instructions from Mrs Mellish to keep her husband away from the Belfast ladies.'

'Well,' said the Commander, 'I came down here to work on the Watch Bill. Is there anything in the mail? If not you'd better both shove off.'

There was a small pile of letters on the desk. In the early days it had been a mere trickle, but, now that the ship's commissioning date was drawing steadily nearer, Job No. 86352 was receiving more and more mail, some of it addressed to HMS *Antigone* by name. Hatchett had already asked for the appointment of a captain's secretary to be hastened. To this their Lordships had returned one of their evasive replies. 'This matter must remain in abeyance,' the answer had read, 'pending the appointment of a commanding officer prior to commissioning.' It was a reminder that *Antigone* was not the first cruiser to be built and that Hatchett, though for the moment king of the castle, was still only temporarily in command, keeping the seat warm so to speak, until such time as a four-ringed post-captain should be appointed to the ship.

'Able-Seaman Pellatt's third badge has come through,' said the Chief Bosun's Mate, 'and Stoker Petty Officer Lazenby was taken queer in the night. He's gone to see the Surgeon and Agent.'

'What's wrong with him?' asked the Commander.

'Dunno, sir. He *says* it's a grumbling appendix.'

There was a wealth of implication in Penniwick's voice but the Commander said nothing. Lazenby and Penniwick had never seen eye to eye. He made a mental note to talk to the Commander (E) about it, but that would have to wait until Monday.

'Any signals?' he inquired. The Yeoman tendered his log. There were only two signals and both were routine ones about armament stores. The Commander initialled against his name and handed back the green file still unspotted and new.

'Copy for the Gunnery Officer,' he said, 'first thing on Monday.'

4

'Aye, aye, sir.'

The two ratings withdrew to a corner of the office while Hatchett glanced through the mail. The usual pile of 'S' forms were there, copies of store notes and demands made on the dockyard, a letter from the Drafting Officer about Engine Room Artificer Waterman, a letter from a wine merchant asking for the wardroom custom and at the bottom a note addressed to him personally. It came from a friend of his on the staff of the Captain Superintendent of Contract-Built Ships. 'Dear Bill,' it read: 'I thought you might like advance news of an appointment due to appear in Monday's CW list. It is for Captain Colin Trevesham to "Job No. 86352 and for HMS *Antigone* in command on commissioning". Do you know him at all? I did a commission with him in *Hawkins* a few years ago. A bit huntin', shootin', fishin', and, I think, rather well off, but certainly no playboy. In fact he's a very good one indeed. You should get on very well and, of course, he's just the chap for the America and West Indies Station.'

Hatchett folded the letter and slipped it in his pocket. So that's that, he said to himself. He'd never met Trevesham and knew nothing about him. He looked out through the window at the familiar dockyard scene. There away to the left lay the cruiser, her one streamlined funnel blotched with red lead, her decks a tangle of wires and pipes. They were welding at the base of the aircraft catapult and, as he watched the blue flame flicker and spit, he thought how greatly the ship had changed even in the four months he'd been with her.

In a few more weeks the riveting and welding would stop. The advance party of her complement of six hundred odd would arrive. The Acceptance Trials would be held and then the ship would be steamed to Portsmouth for commissioning. In his mind's eye he already saw her teak decks, white and holystoned, her brightwork gleaming, and her fresh grey paint spick and span. 'A bit huntin', shootin', fishin' . . . but a very good one indeed.' Well, that remained to be seen. So long as Trevesham left him to work the ship's company as he wanted then all would be well. He decided to take a walk round the ship. He wanted to be quite sure of what they were doing to the catapult, and he intended to have another look at the dough-mixer in the bakery which the Paymaster Commander was complaining about. This walk round the vessel was a daily routine and already Penniwick was holding open the door.

Well, well, well, he said to himself, so *Antigone* has a Captain at last . . .

Captain Trevesham received the news of his appointment whilst digging in his Hampshire garden. There was no need for him to be doing this since three gardeners were kept at Drakeshott. He did it for exercise and pleasure. He maintained that no one could prepare a celery bed as well as he could and neither the gardeners nor his wife saw any reason to disagree.

The Admiralty letter in its OHMS envelope arrived by the afternoon post. Timothy, his youngest son, came tearing out of the house with it as though his nine years depended upon it.

'Your appointment's come, Daddy. Open it quick and see if it's a battleship.'

Timothy had a fetish about battleships. To him they were the finest ships afloat with the sole exception of HMS *Hood* the world's biggest battle-cruiser and possibly —but not certainly—the other two battle-cruisers *Repulse* and *Renown*.

'I told you it won't be a battleship,' said Trevesham. 'I'm not senior enough, and anyway, how do you know it's my appointment?'

He wiped his hands and took the buff envelope from his son.

'It's got CW on the corner,' said Timothy, bursting with importance at the knowledge, 'and that's short for Commissions and Warrants. Daddy, if this is a commission, what's a warrant?'

'We'll go into that some other time,' said Trevesham. His hand shook very slightly as he slit open the envelope but he put that down to the digging. He took out the single sheet which would decree his immediate life for the next two-and-a-half years and might possibly alter the rest of his career. He skipped the preliminary wording and in an instant his eye fastened on the word *Antigone*. A great wave of pleasure swept over him. So they had given him a cruiser after all, and a brand-new one at that.

He picked his son up under the arms and swung him in the air.

'It's a cruiser, Timmy,' he said. 'The Lords Commissioners in their infinite wisdom have given me command of a cruiser. A cruiser with one funnel and four turrets of six-inch guns. Now we must go and tell Mummy.'

'Six-inch?' said Timothy, far less impressed. 'That's nothing—the *Nelson* has *sixteen*-inch guns! Nine of them in three turrets! I've seen them.'

'Never mind,' said Trevesham as they walked hand-in-hand back to the house, 'our cruiser will be a whole ten knots faster. She could make rings round your waddling old battlewagon.'

But Timothy was not to be shaken.

'She won't be as fast as a destroyer, will she?' he asked, and then broke away from his father to imitate a destroyer turning at speed.

'No, Timothy—destroyers can do about thirty-five knots. We shall only be able to manage a mere thirty-two or -three—however, we shall be four or five times the size, and we'll have a lot of things a destroyer doesn't have.'

'What things?'

By this time they had reached the house and had gone inside.

'Oh! I don't know,' said Trevesham with a little smile to himself, 'a detachment of Royal Marines for a start.'

'Why?' said Timothy.

'Never mind why. Then there'll be a seaplane.' He tried to think of other fittings and attributes which might appeal to a boy of nine. 'I expect we'll have a skimming dish, too,' he ended a bit lamely, and before Timothy could pose the inevitable question he went on, 'that's slang for a little flat-bottomed speedboat for getting about quickly in harbours.'

'Battleships still have steam picketboats,' said Timothy grandly, 'with brass funnels and canopies.'

But by this time they were in the drawing-room. Timothy ran over to his mother, who was writing a letter by the fire.

'Daddy's got a cruiser: Daddy's got a cruiser,' he chanted.

'Yes, dear,' said his mother. 'Now go and wash your hands for tea.' Then she looked up at her husband and for

7

a moment or so they said nothing but smiled into each other's eyes.

'I *am* glad, darling,' she said, 'how very exciting it is.'

Trevesham walked over to the fire and stood warming his back. The anxiety of waiting was over. It was a moment of enormous relief for both of them. His wife thought how handsome he looked with his grey hair and his tall, spare figure. She knew very well how keyed-up he had been these last few months. She did not understand the intricacies of naval appointments and promotions but she was aware that her husband was at a crucial point in his career. To get a seagoing appointment now meant that he was still in the running for his Flag, and she understood more deeply than he suspected how important it was. They had talked very little about it. His last job had been on the Staff in Malta. It was a pleasant position and Trevesham was a good Staff Officer. He had a flexible brain, tact and a background—all qualities of value on the Staff of a Commander-in-Chief. But you could be too good a Staff Officer. You had to be careful not to find yourself in a dead end almost without knowing it. It was very, very important that Colin should get his own seagoing command at this particular point in his career. He had five years seniority as a four-ringed Captain, and next month he would be forty-five years old.

'I *am* glad,' she repeated when Timothy had left the room. 'Is it one of the possibilities you mentioned?'

'It's *Antigone*,' said Trevesham. 'A seven-thousand-ton cruiser. Perhaps the best of the lot I could possibly be given . . .'

As he spoke he saw the ship as she would be in a few months' time, lying peaceably at anchor in a West Indies harbour, her quarterdeck awning spread white and gleaming against the green tropical foliage, her light grey paint reflecting the dappled sunlight dancing across the sea. He saw her as she would look from the bridge, driving ahead into an Atlantic gale. He saw her with her decks cleared away for action, the six-inch turrets following the director bearing, with the enemy in sight and the range closing rapidly. The enemy! he thought and grunted to himself. It was a sobering thought.

'When will you go, Colin, and will she be Home Fleet?'

'She's building in Harland and Wolff's in Belfast—I'll join her next Tuesday.'

'Belfast?' said Lady Diana. 'How dreary! I suppose you'll stay with Henry and Maud at Stormont.' Maud was a cousin of hers. Colin had once said she seemed to have a cousin in every Government House in the world.

'If they ask me,' he said absently. It was supremely unimportant to him where he stayed until they could live aboard the ship. He would have preferred a hotel or a club, but he knew it would give his wife pleasure if he stayed at Government House.

'Of course they'll ask you,' she said. 'I shall write off tonight. I suppose that means you'll be taking the car.'

'I'll take the Austin if you like.' Again the question of which car he took did not seem of any importance.

'You'll do no such thing,' his wife retorted. 'You must take the Bentley and your Cox'n will drive it.' His Coxswain! He would have a Coxswain of his own. The captain of a cruiser messed by himself and lived in considerable style, especially on detached service abroad, as *Antigone* would be for a large portion of her commission.

'I wonder if I could get Petty Officer Vincent as my Cox'n,' he said almost to himself. 'I might go and see the Drafting Officer at Portsmouth tomorrow.' Vincent had been his Divisional Petty Officer on a previous commission.

'That's a very good idea,' said his wife. 'I'll come with you. I want to do some shopping and Timothy has to go to the dentist.'

'*Antigone* is intended for the South American squadron,' Trevesham went on. 'At least she was last time I checked up on it. That means Bermuda and the West Indies as well.'

'Wonderful!' said his wife. 'Madge is in Hamilton. I shall go and stay with her.'

'Who's Madge? A cousin I haven't heard of?'

'No, darling, she's Hugh Eynsham's wife. Hugh is Garrison Major in Bermuda. You remember Hugh Eynsham. You used to play polo with him in Malta.'

'Oh, yes!' said Trevesham vaguely, his train of thought already on other things. To hell with Hugh Eynsham and polo, he thought. South America meant a lot of protocol, and protocol, moreover, conducted in Spanish. He'd ask

9

for a Secretary who could speak a few words of the language. Or if not he'd better start learning it himself. He could get along tolerably well in French, so perhaps the question of language was not so very important.

'I think I'll also look in on the Second Sea Lord's office,' he said, 'and find out whom they're giving me for this famous commission. I don't want a boatload of duds.'

But as he said it he knew perfectly well that both officers and men of HMS *Antigone* would be specially picked for him by the Admiralty and the Drafting Officers at Portsmouth. *Antigone* was the latest of a successful line of cruisers. On the America and West Indies station one of her more important duties would be that of 'showing the flag'. The local impression left by one of HM cruisers on a remote South American port could have repercussions far beyond the time and the place, the parties attended and the courtesies paid. There were German communities dotted about all over the South of Chile, for instance, and if war should come their continued neutrality might well be important. There was more to showing the flag than pleasure cruising or pure advertisement, and as Trevesham turned it over in his mind he knew he would be commanding a highly specialized team. Their selection was of great importance. He knew he must take what he was given, but there would be no harm in making his preferences known before the whole matter was crystalized and fixed. He decided to visit the Admiralty the day after the next.

The Admiralty, or to be more accurate the Paymaster Director-General's Department, had already selected a Captain's Secretary for the *Antigone*, and his name was Paymaster Sub-Lieutenant Derek Lysander Marsh, Royal Navy. They had done this from a short list of five or six Paymaster Sub-Lieutenants who were then available, not because Marsh was the brightest boy on the list but because he had taken the trouble to become an interpreter in the Spanish language. In addition to a rather pleasing sense of intellectual superiority, this brought him an additional one shilling and sixpence a day when appointed as such. And one and sixpence a day was of considerable importance to Derek Marsh. Only three months before he had been a Midshipman at five bob per diem, and even now, with a single gold stripe on his arm, he was only drawing at the rate of nine shillings and sixpence a day.

Money, or the lack of it, had always loomed large in the Marsh household. How different things might have been, he reflected, as he packed his tin trunk, with even a little more money. If his father had had more drive or 'push' as his mother called it, then perhaps they wouldn't be living in this detestable semi-detached villa in a Birmingham suburb. Perhaps he might even have gone to Dartmouth instead of to that dreary so-called public school in the Midlands to which he had scraped up a scholarship and the fees for which had in any case nearly bled his father dry.

But then if he had gone to Dartmouth he would have become an Executive Officer or joined the engineering branch and that would have been a pity. Despite all the 'sitting-on'—the 'branch inferiority complex' as he had heard it called—to which paymasters were prone—Derek Lysander Marsh was privately glad to wear the white distinction lace below his single gold stripe. At his tender age he already knew secrets and was in a position of trust not available to his brother officers in the gunroom.

If this had been so as a Paymaster Midshipman in a battleship, it would be doubly so now that he would virtually have his own little department in a cruiser. Not only would he be decyphering the most secret messages which arrived in the ship, messages in some cases shown to no one else but the Captain, but he would also prepare and type out the confidential reports on his brother officers and would, in fact, be privy to the inmost secrets of the ship, secrets of which even the Commander and other Heads of Departments might well be in ignorance. At the age of twenty he felt that was quite a position to be in, and he saw himself proceeding through the next two years as a sort of naval *Eminence Grise*.

He was catching the afternoon train to Liverpool and the taxi was ordered for a quarter to four, or fifteen forty-five as he insisted on calling it. Now his mother came fussing into the room torn between distress at his going and pique at not being allowed to pack for him as she always had done before.

'Aren't you wearing your uniform to travel in?' she asked. To Mrs Marsh the sight of her trim little son in his

11

uniform gave unending delight. She could never be made to understand why Naval officers grab the first opportunity of changing into plain clothes.

'No, of course not, Mother,' her son answered scornfully. 'The ship isn't even commissioned as yet. I expect I'll be living in digs to begin with, and in any case, the more I don't wear it the longer it will last.'

He secretly despised himself for making that sort of joke, but it seemed to please his mother and make her laugh. He knew that she was very near tears at his going, and he was certain he wouldn't escape without some sort of scene. He tried to see it from her point of view—it must be hard to watch your only son going off so blithely into the blue and to know that he would be away, thousands of miles away, half across the world for over two years.

But though he could see it with his mind and sympathize with his parents' loneliness, he could not control how he felt, and to sail in HMS *Antigone* to the South American continent seemed to him to be not only an enormous personal adventure, but also to be going as far away as it was possible to get, both in spirit and in fact, from 23 Colebrook Avenue, Birmingham. To others, a steady job, a modest security and a little stucco villa in the suburbs might represent Valhalla: to Derek Lysander Marsh it was hell on earth.

'Don't bother to come to the station,' he said, knowing full well how pointless it was to make such a suggestion. 'I can manage quite well by myself.'

'But *of course* I'm coming to see you off,' said his mother. 'And your Father's meeting us there.'

'It isn't as though we're sailing straight away. I expect I'll get a week-end leave from Portsmouth once we're commissioned. Or you and father could come down and see me there,' he added reluctantly.

'And you could show us the ship,' his mother said. 'I'd love to see your cabin and where you're going to be living.'

'Yes,' he said, doing his best to appear enthusiastic, 'you must come and see over the ship. That is if it's allowed.'

'You showed us over the *Nelson* when you were on her.'

'*In* her, Mother, you live *in* a ship not on it. Anyway, *Nelson* was different. She's not an absolutely brand new ship stuffed full of secret devices.'

He was letting his imagination run riot and this always led to disaster. But the pressure of emotion in the air was almost more than he could stand. Any moment now his mother would give way and then there would be the inevitable cataract of tears.

'Of course if you don't want us to come . . .' his mother began, a catch in her voice.

'Oh! Mother, it isn't that and you know it. Why do you always pick on a detail and try to build it up into something it isn't?' With a great effort he controlled his indignation and went over to his mother. He put his arm round her shoulder and gave her a hug. This was just like going off to school again, only worse.

'Cheer up!' he said. 'You'll soon get used to it once I've gone. And I'll write as often as I possibly can.'

But his mother's distress had, as usual, got beyond her control. The tears poured down her cheeks and her balcony of a bosom heaved in great sobs.

'I can't help it,' she said. 'I just hate you growing up and going away. I hate it. I hate it.'

'Well . . .' he said, hanging his head, 'there it is. There's nothing I can do to help.'

'It seems only yesterday I was nursing you in my arms. You were such a pretty little baby!'

'Oh! Mother, please . . .' This was going to be worse than he thought. 'Look! Go and knit a sock or make a cup of tea or *something* while I finish packing, will you?'

She nodded, hurt at his reaction, as she always was, and then went out of the room. He stood staring at the oblong tin trunk with his name and rank painted in sloping white letters on the top. He looked at his frock coat which had taken so many fittings to get right, and his sword in its black leather sheath. His eyes took in the piles of tropical uniforms, as yet new and unworn, his shirts and his collars and his socks.

'God!' he said to himself. 'What a business it is!' But already time was pressing on and so without further ado he threw himself into packing and put everything else out of his mind.

The Belfast Mail Packet sails overnight from Liverpool. Marsh could not afford a cabin but sat up in the first-class saloon dozing uneasily. To travel first class on the boat

13

was something of an extravagance, but Marsh felt that even in plain clothes the dignity of his rank demanded it. Moreover, he was not at all sure how he would fare with the Irish Sea. Almost any weather had made him sick in *Nelson,* and she was a 33,000-ton battleship that waded through most seas with a slow, ponderous stride. How the Mail Packet would treat him he had no idea, but he took the precaution of buying two packets of dry biscuits before they left harbour, and these he munched unhappily at intervals every time he detected an increase in the motion of the ship.

Down in the third-class saloon, unknown to Marsh, were three other passengers for *Antigone.* These were Petty Officer Cook Jenkins, Leading-Seaman Battersby and Able-Seaman Clarke. Jenkins, holding the substantive rating of Petty Officer, was nominally in charge of the draft.

The three men were very different, both in temperament and in physique. Jenkins was a pink-skinned, hairless, slightly rotund-looking Welshman, whose impeccable uniform belied the fact that he spent much of his life in an apron maintaining strict discipline in a steaming, heaving ship's company galley.

Except for the uniform there was nothing fancy about Jenkins. Years ago he had had the option of becoming an Officers' Cook, a branch that calls for more variety of talent and, in many respects, more inventiveness than is normally required for the ship's company, but Jenkins had turned down the chance. He was from the Welsh valleys and instinctively he preferred to deal with ratings rather than officers.

Barring a single lapse in his first year, when he had been absent over leave seven days and had been marked upon Ledger and Service Certificate as a possible deserter, Jenkins' conduct had been 'very good' and his efficiency for the last eight years had been 'superior'. But his divisional officers knew him as a tricky customer. 'A magnificent worker,' one had written, 'except when his temper gets the better of him. Good power of command, but apt to be harsh and merciless when ruffled or confronted with carelessness or stupidity in junior ratings.'

Leading-Seaman Battersby, too, had a temper. But whereas Jenkins was quick and irascible, Battersby was grave and his humour lay deeper in his veins. He was also a much younger man, tall, thin and good-looking in a plain, straight-haired way.

Ratings normally engage to serve in the Navy for twelve years from the age of eighteen and during the last two years of this engagement have the right to re-engage if they wish for another ten years 'in order to complete time for pension'. Petty Officer Cook Jenkins was twenty-nine, and he had just reengaged. Battersby, on the other hand, was only twenty-one, although at first sight he looked a good five years older.

Battersby was a Torpedoman. He held the non-substantive rank of LTO (Leading-Torpedoman) for which he drew an extra sixpence a day and wore on his right arm a badge of crossed torpedoes surmounted by a star. His duties in *Antigone* would be mainly concerned with the electrical installation. But Battersby was ambitious. As a Boy First Class he had received Accelerated Advancement to Ordinary-Seaman, six months ahead of the normal, at seventeen and a half. Then, when a few months over the age of eighteen with 'six months' practical experience in part of ship' behind him, he had been rated Able-Seaman.

To gain each of these steps had required study, extra effort, and the passing of an examination in addition to the normal seagoing experience which was his lot. Then after a year at sea as an able-bodied sailor he had got his 'hook' and with it leadership of his mess and the half-jeering, half-envious position of someone who is levering himself inch by inch out of the common herd and who was already well ahead of his entry.

Now he had his eyes on a commission. It was possible. He was eligible by the regulations so far as they went. Others had persevered and won through. It could be done, Battersby thought, provided he could really master the course of Pelmanism he was secretly taking. But only Battersby knew how discouraging and difficult it seemed, except at rare intervals. However he had one great asset, denied to his more easy going messmates. He had no ties of any kind, for Battersby was an orphan.

The third member of the Draft, Able-Seaman Clarke, inevitably nicknamed 'Nobby', wore three good conduct badges on his left arm and had the proportions of a barrel of beer, which also happened to be his favourite drink and spare time occupation. The possession of three Good Conduct badges meant at least thirteen years of uninterrupted blameless conduct, and Nobby Clarke had, in fact, some nineteen years' service to his credit.

He was a contented man who viewed the world without worry or any shred of personal ambition. Various assaults on this peace of mind had been made from time to time by divisional officers and others who had wanted to make him a leading-seaman, and even in one case to offload on his ample shoulders the responsibilities of a petty officer's rate.

But Clarke would have none of it. He was happy as he was. He asked little of life except frequent access to good beer. He perferred to be told what to do and in his long service had learned to carry out his duties efficiently, but with the minimum of effort. In his good-natured, unintellectual way he was a tower of strength, a twentieth century replica of one type of British seaman stretching back unchanged and unchanging for eight hundred years.

The three of them now sat in a corner of the third-class saloon as the mailboat pitched and rolled in the Irish Sea. It was shortly after midnight and Clarke, who had expended all his current resources on beer without its affecting him in any observable way, was now preparing to get his head down on a wooden bench. Battersby was diligently reading Volume One of the Manual of Seamanship and Jenkins was sitting up stiffly, staring into space and occasionally, when the spirit moved him, expertly rolling a cigarette.

From time to time one or other made a remark. But they had little common ground. Chance had thrown them together on this journey, and once aboard *Antigone* their duties and different parts of ship would scarcely ever bring them into contact with one another again.

Battersby came to the end of an old familiar chapter and shut the blue covered book with a snap. He knew parts of the Manual of Seamanship off by heart, but it gave him pleasure to read it again much as a music-lover will follow the performance of a symphony with the score.

'Sea's kicking up a bit,' he said. None of the three was seasick, but there had been casualties already in the third-class saloon.

'Yes. Squally it is,' said Jenkins as if that finished the conversation. He was suspicious of Battersby, and was on the alert in case any advantage should be taken of him. Jenkins might be a cook, but he was still a petty officer. He was not to be patronized in any shape or form by a member of the seaman branch. In the buffet at Liverpool Clarke had nudged him over a bottle of beer and called him Taffy. Jenkins had soon put stop to that. 'Petty Officer Jenkins to you,' he had observed curtly, 'and I'll thank you to remember it.' But Clarke had been quite unmoved. 'Sorry, Chief,' he'd replied, blandly promoting him, 'I didn't see the quarterdeck behind you,' and with that he'd winked at the barmaid and stood them all another round of beer. He'd found out just how far he could go with the PO Cook and that was all that mattered.

'I wonder what kind of seaboat she'll be,' Battersby remarked. 'The *Antigone*, I mean.'

None of them could manage to see *Antigone* as a four syllable word in which the second alone should be stressed. To Jenkins the ship was Ann*tigun*, Battersby came down on the last syllable calling it Anti*goan*, and Clarke favoured what would undoubtedly be the general mess-deck pronunciation. He split the word up into two, and called her HMS *Aunty Gone*. The naming of HM ships was literally all Greek to Able-Seaman Clarke and he was happy it should stay that way.

'I know someone who had a basinful of *Ajax* her last commission,' said Nobby Clarke, 'and he says she was a treat. Not too much top weight and dry as a pin. We're the same as *Ajax*, aren't we?'

'Yes,' said Battersby, 'I think so.'

'Once I did a commission in a "County" class cruiser,' Jenkins remarked in his sing-song Welsh accent, 'and they roll in a ripple. Couldn't cook in any sea at all, we couldn't.'

Don't suppose you can cook anyway, thought Clarke to himself, and quietly belched. However, one dud petty officer cook in a complement of nearly six hundred souls wasn't going to make a great deal of difference.

'You've been drafted as the Commander's Writer, haven't you?' Battersby was asking him.

'That's right,' said Clarke, 'typing out the flipping daily orders on the old Empire Number One.'

17

In his mind's eye he already saw the Commander's office as he would have it, all neat and tidy, his own particular domain. He would be seeing a good deal of the Chief Bos'n's Mate and the Master-at-Arms: he would have to find the ins and outs of the Captain's office where correspondence was dealt with, and the ship's office where the ledger and pay was kept: he would need to be on good terms with his opposite number—no doubt a three badge Stoker—in the engineer's office: he must learn his way round the Colour-Sergeant, Royal Marines, know most of what mattered in the three seaman divisions of the ship —the Foc'sle, the Top and the Quarterdeck: keep in with the Paymaster-Commander so that demands on the Commander for working parties did not get out of control: and so that on the other hand he could get what was wanted from the Victualling and Supply Departments: he must be tactful with the Gunnery and Torpedo Departments and the other specialists, such as the Communications and Air officers who naturally thought their own jobs the most important in the ship: he must be polite to the Chaplain, the Surgeon-Commander, and the Instructor-Officer on the comparatively few occasions when they would need hands or assistance of some kind or another from the Executive Officer.

All these things he would have to do and, at the same time, keep his mouth shut when he inevitably overheard secrets or opinions which could so easily turn into juicy rumours for the lower deck.

On top of it all if his Commander was difficult, and he knew nothing of Hatchett except that he was a 'pressure merchant', then he would be the one who bore the brunt of his spleen. However good the basic organization of HM ships—and the main outline had been arrived at after the experience of centuries—the day-to-day working of a seven-thousand-ton cruiser was no sinecure, though that was not a word which Clarke would have used.

Clarke knew very well that it called for big and small adjustments almost every hour of the day. He would need to do what he was told without getting in the way. He must be a sympathetic listener and spare with his opinions. He must save his Commander from as many petty pin-pricks as he could and yet, at the same time, see that he was

18

properly informed both in fact and opinion of everything that concerned the lower deck, the welfare and the fighting efficiency of the ship's company.

He was not entitled to an opinion of his own (a Commissioned Gunner had once said to him 'You *think?* You're not entitled to think, you're an Able-Seaman') and yet it was to a great extent through his eyes and his ears that the Commander would focus on the daily problems of the lower deck. He would have an unwritten licence to say things to the Commander which would not have been proper from a petty officer or anyone else. To Able-Seaman Clarke, who shunned the responsibility even of leading-rate, it all seemed quite natural and in order that he should have been drafted to fill this position in the ship after nineteen years' experience of the service and centuries of the sea in his bloodstream.

He cushioned his cheek with his hand on the hard wooden bench as he turned over on his side for a bit of shut-eye, midway across the Irish Sea. It all lay ahead, he said to himself with a smile of anticipation, and no doubt it would call for the internal application of a great deal of beer.

The mail boat continued to pitch and toss on her way. Two decks overhead Paymaster Sub-Lieutenant Marsh opened his second packet of biscuits, and munched them moodily, one by one.

At twenty-past eight the next morning Lieutenant (E) John Sebastian Meldrum, the Senior Engineer of HMS *Antigone* stopped his car at the corner of Rostrevor Lane and waited for the Navigator to get in. This was a daily arrangement. It saved time and petrol since Meldrum and his wife had rooms in the next street to the Navigating Officer, and although none of them had previously met before joining *Antigone* they were now good friends. Meldrum and Spratt often played squash or golf in the dog watches. They discovered they had much the same outlook on life, for all went to parties and the cinema together and Spratt, who had been docketed by the Commander's wife as one of the ship's more eligible bachelors, soon found himself pleasantly in love with Susan Meldrum —a state of affairs that none of them took very seriously.

'Morning, Aggie,' said Meldrum as the navigator climbed in, 'how's your head?'

They had been to a cocktail party the night before at the Paymaster-Commander's, where the drinks had been lavish but exotic.

'Oh! all right,' said Spratt, 'I dreamt about Susan.'

'Here we go again,' said Meldrum as they trundled off down to the ship. 'You should try living with her. You wouldn't dream about her then, I can assure you.'

'It must be that pine-essence the Pay puts in his drinks,' the Navigating Officer went on. 'I've never tasted such a concoction. Still it seemed to work. For a whole five minutes Guns didn't talk shop. I can certify that. I timed him.'

'I think Pay wants to be voted wine-caterer for the ward-room,' said Meldrum. 'I was talking to Hale last night. Apparently he loves ordering things.' Hale was the Central Storekeeping Officer, a Paymaster-Lieutenant and second-in-command of the Accountant Branch.

'He's welcome to it. I've been lurked for the Canteen Committee,' Spratt said morosely, 'and if there's one thing I detest it's sitting on my backside listening to a lot of hot cackle from "elected lower deck representatives".'

'Now, Aggie, that isn't a nice attitude at all,' said Meldrum. 'This is the lurking season. I saw a list of "voluntary" jobs on the Commander's desk yesterday. To be filled in on commissioning, of course, but you know our Hatchett—always one jump ahead of the gun.'

Every morning it was the same. They compared notes and pleasurably vented their daily 'moans'.

'That's what comes of having a bloke who's a driver. He can never let up for a moment,' the Navigating Officer complained.

'It's size,' said Meldrum, who was a good six foot three. 'That's the trouble with you shorties. You're all full of wind and aggression. Sometimes when I look at you and Hatchett, I think I've got in among a shipload of midgets.'

Aggie Spratt smiled and said nothing. For as long as he could remember, his name and his size—he was five foot five inches—had attracted adverse attention and ridicule. Spratt had long ago given up worrying about it. He came of an old military family and his father, for reasons which were still obscure, had had him christened Augustus.

20

As a result his life at prep school and Dartmouth had seemed to consist entirely of replusing attacks on his dignity.

'There's a meeting of all officers in the wardroom at eleven, isn't there?' he said, going over the day's work in his mind.

'Yes. I hear the Captain's arriving the day after tomorrow. I expect Hatchett wants us all running around.'

There was a slightly tetchy note in his voice. The Navigator looked across at him and smiled.

'It strikes me you don't think so very much of our gallant Commander,' said Aggie. 'What's he done now to get under your hide?'

'He pinches my stokers for his blasted working parties,' said Meldrum, 'I wouldn't mind that so much—only he goes and fixes it up with the Chief over my head and then I'm left to work out the details.'

The Chief was the large and amiable Commander (E) who was Meldrum's immediate superior and had charge of the ship's Engineering Department.

'Well,' said Aggie without much sympathy, 'that's how the good book says it should be done. The Chief would gripe like hell if he went to you direct.'

Every morning they took the long way round to the dockyard office by way of the jetty where *Antigone* was lying. They did this on the outward excuse of seeing whether she was still there, but privately because both of them took pleasure in this first daily sight of the ship.

To their trained eyes she was different every day. Detail by detail she was subtly growing—sometimes the changes in the ship's outline were radical, as for instance when the turrets, each with their two six-inch guns, were lowered on to their mountings. At other times they were less obvious, such as the rigging of aerials on the mainmast or the fixing of davits for the ship's seaboats.

The most noticeable change had been the fitting of the single streamlined funnel casing, unique to that class of cruiser and giving the ship, as they thought, a most modern and cleancut look. Indeed, they were always telling each other, the ship had looked and felt 'right' from the moment she was launched.

'I see you've got your glass screens on the compass platform fitted at last,' said Meldrum dryly. 'Try not to put a spanner through them before the Acceptance Trials.'

'That'll be all right,' Aggie retorted. 'Just keep your greasy mechanics where they belong, down below and out of sight.'

They drove on to the ship's office ashore.

'Won't be long now before we're living aboard,' Meldrum opined. 'I must get Susan to beat the moth out of my uniform.'

'The sooner we get to sea the better,' said the Navigator. 'I've had more than enough of Belfast.'

The only riveting being done was on a bulkhead up forward in the foc'sle mess-deck. So, apart from the intermittent clanging and shouting which seemed always to form a background to work on the ship, apart from the sudden hooting of a tug passing the open scuttles of the wardroom and the smell of hot grease, red lead and fresh enamel which were always around, the Commander had comparative peace and quiet for his first conference in the wardroom.

The collection of key officers who had been standing by and 'building' the ship were waiting in the still uncarpeted ante-room. They ranged from Heads of Departments, such as the Commander (E) and the Paymaster-Commander to technical officers such as the Warrant Electrician and the Warrant Shipwright. The wearing of uniform was still optional. Rigs varied from the Senior's well-washed overalls to the threadbare monkey jacket of the Gunner, by way of the business-like 'gent's natty suiting' of the Central Storekeeping Officer.

The Commander swept in with a sudden burst and threw his bowler hat on a nearby settee. The chatter died down in anticipation. Marsh, the 'new boy' who had followed him in nervously, tried to merge unobserved with the others.

'Well,' the Commander began, 'there aren't enough chairs. So perch where you can and make yourselves comfortable.'

'Permission to smoke?' said a voice from the back.

'I'd rather you didn't, Torps, not as things are between decks at the moment. It's a wonder some of the mateys haven't blown up the ship before now. Oh! by the way,

22

this is Sub-Lieutenant Marsh, the Captain's Secretary and our latest arrival.' He looked round but Marsh was no longer with him.

'Where's he gone?' Hatchett said irritably. 'Scratch?'

'Here, sir,' said Marsh, stepping out reluctantly and blushing. He saw a sea of friendly, smiling faces, but it was still an ordeal to be stuck out there in front of them all like Exhibit A.

'So from now on there'll be a little more order and etiquette in correspondence leaving the ship,' the Commander went on, 'as soon as the Captain's Secretary has settled into his palatial office on the starboard side.'

Marsh had already inspected his office and judged it to be approximately eight feet by three, with just enough room to turn around without upsetting the ink bottles. However, it was against the ship's side and most important of all it had its own scuttle.

'Mr Marsh is also appointed as official Interpreter in Spanish to the ship,' the Commander continued, 'and one of his duties, whether he likes it or not, will be to instil a few words of the language into my head. Any other officers who want to learn to speaka da Spanish should get together with Marsh and make their own arrangements for dog-watch instruction.'

'That's jumping a few hurdles before we come to them,' the Torpedo Officer murmured to Spratt at his side. He badly wanted a cigarette and this conference had all the earmarks of turning into a lengthy session.

'I've got you all here,' said the Commander, 'to tell you three things. In the first place the Captain arrives the day after tomorrow. In the second—as from tomorrow officers will wear uniform during working hours, and thirdly, from Monday next we shall be living on board.' He looked sharply at the officers whose departments would be mainly concerned. The Paymaster Commander and the Commander (E) both nodded. 'It won't be luxurious to begin with—I need hardly tell you that—so don't expect it to be like the Ritz. I'll put detailed arrangements up on the board. Officers will have to use the gunroom bathroom for the first few days owing to a plumbing hitch in the wardroom bathroom.'

'A structural defect. Nothing to do with the Engineering

Department,' said the Commander (E) looking under his eyebrows at the Shipwright Officer. It raised a laugh.

'And that reminds me,' the Commander said, 'to warn you all once again that the ship is still in contractors' hands. We're living on board by courtesy of Messrs Harland and Wolff—so any belly-aching you want to vent must go through me first. Is that understood?'

There was a murmur of assent. The Commander looked round for a moment before going on. It's going to be all right, he thought. Already he was beginning to detect a team feeling in the officers around him. Whatever seed it is which produces a ship's individual style and spirit had already begun to germinate and would soon be poking its first tender shoots above ground.

'Before going on to detail,' he said, 'I'd like to thank you all for your efforts so far. I know it hasn't been easy for some of you.' The Gunnery Officer coughed and that, too, got a laugh. 'But so far we're still on schedule and it happens to be my opinion, based on what I've seen over the last three months, that HMS *Antigone* is the finest cruiser to join any fleet in the world. I'm not a chap for superlatives and you won't hear me talk often like this. However—I feel very privileged to be Executive Officer of this ship and I think she's going to be a happy one to serve in. Now then, let's cut the cackle and get on with the work . . .'

CHAPTER TWO

In March 1938, no one knew if there was going to be a war. Its likelihood ebbed and flowed. Theories abounded, theories of what would happen; theories of what to think and of what to do. Aggression, appeasement, the use of force, the practice of puzzled and somewhat rusty religious principles were all in turn urged and abandoned. The younger officers and ratings grew confused and depressed when they thought about it. The older ones knew in their hearts it was coming. In the meanwhile the event itself, propelled by its chief mechanic in Berlin, moved steadily nearer like an object coming out of the murky background of a film into clear and sharp focus.

The day their Captain arrived German troops marched into Austria, and two days later that unhappy country's union with the Reich was proclaimed. To those who could see, this was a heralding of war. It was another pressure in the physical and moral retreat imposed upon the so-called free nations, a process which was not to end even with Dunkirk. But on 7 March 1938 war had suddenly jumped very much nearer and in *Antigone* they felt that they and their ship would only just be ready in time.

While the news was much in the Commander's mind as he waited for the mail boat to come alongside the town jetty, he had no intention of letting it distract him from the business in hand. Although HMS *Antigone* was not yet in commission and normal honours, therefore, could not be paid, the Captain must be properly received. Commander Hatchett had worked out the arrangements, he had written the orders and with Able-Seaman Clarke's assistance had promulgated them to all concerned. Now it but remained to put them into effect.

It was cold and there were intermittent gusts of rain. At 0745 on a March morning with the wind battering along the cobbled jetty, Belfast was not at its best. Hatchett had decreed that he alone of the officers should meet the mail boat in which the Captain and his car were arriving, but he had with him Chief Bosun's Mate Penniwick and Petty Officer Vincent, the Captain's Coxswain, who had been rushed on ahead by depot at the Commander's express request. The rest of the officers and ship's company were to muster aboard *Antigone* in uniform at 0930 for the purpose of meeting their first Commanding Officer.

As soon as the gangway was in place Hatchett walked on board with the normal dock and harbour officials. He was in uniform and so naturally were Penniwick and Vincent, who remained behind on the jetty. Captain Trevesham would no doubt be in plain clothes for the journey but Hatchett had made arrangements for him to

25

change at the club, if he so wished, before first going aboard *Antigone*. Both Trevesham and Hatchett from their respective positions were aware of the great importance of this first meeting.

Hatchett imagined the Captain would be in his cabin or in the saloon, but in fact they met on the upper deck. The Captain of the Mail Packet was an RNR officer who had served with Trevesham in the war and who had invited him up on the bridge as they came into harbour. Trevesham had observed Hatchett and the two ratings down on the jetty. Seen from above Hatchett had looked even shorter and squatter than he was, yet even from that distance he gave an impression of energy and power. Trevesham wondered if this was a genuine characteristic or whether his Executive Officer was a bully with an outer dressing of strength. It was a question of some magnitude. Trevesham eyed him as he walked along the deck and concluded there was a bit of both in the man. He moved over to meet him and a moment later they were shaking hands.

'Very good of you to come and meet me, Commander,' said Trevesham with a smile. He liked the handshake. It was firm and controlled and oddly sensitive. It belied the slight strut in the walk.

'I've arranged to get your car out straight away, sir,' said Hatchett, 'and your Cox'n will take charge of it on the jetty. In the meantime, if you don't mind my old boneshaker, I've laid on a room and breakfast at the club in case you should want to change before going down to the ship.'

'That sounds admirable,' said Trevesham as they walked towards the gangway.

'I wasn't sure where you'd be staying, sir,' Hatchett went on, 'so I've provisionally got you in at the club. But if you prefer a hotel . . . there is accommodation available at the Midland. I'm afraid we can't live aboard until Monday next and, even then, I wouldn't recommend it for another ten days.'

'Well,' said Trevesham as they walked down the gangway, 'my wife has booked me in, so to speak, at Government House, but quite frankly the sooner I can live aboard the happier I'll be.'

He turned and smiled at Hatchett and in that brief

26

understanding exchange of looks the tone of their relationship was settled for the next two-and-a-half years.

'I'm very glad you've come, sir,' said Hatchett almost involuntarily. 'I think you'll be pleased with the ship.'

At 0930 as arranged, the officers were drawn up on the quarterdeck of *Antigone* facing the port side, which was alongside the jetty. Behind them were the key ratings who had stood by the ship. Next week the advance-party would arrive from depot. This party was calculated in numbers sufficient for the trials and for steaming the ship round to Portsmouth. Then late in April the ship would officially commission and the remainder of her full peacetime complement would join. At the moment, however, Captain Colin Trevesham, DSC, Royal Navy, was walking up the after brow on to the quarterdeck of *Antigone* to meet the nucleus of a cruiser ship's company, the core of specialist officers and men who formed the essential link between the building and the operating of a man-of-war.

'Ship's company—'Shun,' shouted the Commander, and then turned to salute the tall figure as it stepped on board for the very first time. The Captain was piped aboard by the Chief Bosun's Mate and the rest of the side party consisted of the Chief Quartermaster, Chief Petty Officer Bowling, and Able-Seaman Clarke as a somewhat portly, improvised sideboy. Later on when the ship was commissioned there would be Royal Marines and young seamen in abundance to furnish these ceremonies to their appropriate degree, but today Able-Seaman Clarke, as one of the few square-rigged seamen aboard, was proud and honoured to stand-in where later a boy of seventeen would be carrying out the duty.

Although it made no visible showing, a wave of emotion swept through the rigid figures standing there among the pipes, the wires and the cables which still littered the grimy deck. The Queen Bee was entering the hive. This was a moment they would all remember, because the status of the ship was subtly and invisibly changing. No longer were the officers and men a heterogeneous collection of experts with different qualifications and functions each intent on a distinct and specialized job, each with only a nominal connection with the others. Now they

27

were suddenly, almost magically, parts of a greater whole. They had a Commanding Officer aboard. And while Trevesham shook hands with each of them, inquiring their names and memorizing them in a deliberate and unhurried fashion, as his grave penetrating eyes recorded individual differences and marks, each member of *Antigone*'s crew knew that from now on the ship had being and her life cycle had really begun.

Commander Hatchett walked along the line just behind his Captain, introducing the officers. His orders had worked out well. There had been no hitch and no unexpected delay, the event was speeding along entirely as planned except for the appalling clang and splutter from an aircraft carrier next along the jetty. He had with difficulty managed to delay the riveting and welding in *Antigone* for an hour but other ships were, of course, beyond his control.

As the tall cranes swung with their loads and shunting engines hooted and puffed alongside the ship, Hatchett let his mind drift for a moment on how pleasant it would be when the ship was really theirs, completed and at sea away from this midden of wire and steel, this labour-ward where warships were born. The terms in which this thought presented itself were surprising. There was little poetry or whimsy in Hatchett. He was a roundly practical man. The truth of it, he told himself, was that he was rearing to get the ship cleaned up and hot on the job— whatever job it might first please Fate and the Lords Commissioners of the Admiralty to give her.

The Captain was now at the end of the line of officers talking to the Gunner (T). Warrant officers fascinated Trevesham. They were end products, a symbol of achievement distinct in their status and privilege, possessing experience and wisdom as great, in their own line of country, as a wardroom officer would need to achieve his brass hat or, in some instances, Flag rank. Trevesham showed nothing of this in his manner. He loathed snobs and hated patronage in any shape or form. For that reason and because warrant officers in the Navy are sometimes looked on by the arrogant as small fry, or as poor relations, he never admitted this fascination into the forefront of his mind in case he might unwittingly hurt somebody's feelings. But he always enjoyed talking to warrant officers and looking back over their long service lives, so empty of the frills and frivolities that were part of a wardroom background, so filled with that immense variety of quirkish experience which gave their personalities such a salty tang.

Talking now to the Gunner (T) about a previous commission in another cruiser, it was immediately apparent to Trevesham where the strength and resilience of the Torpedo Department would lie. He had not been at all impressed with Fossingham, the ship's Lieutenant-Commander (T). Fossingham was one of those people who know they have charm and he had put the full force of it into his handshake and the sincere look of dog-like devotion with which he had greeted his Captain. He was a weak man and he had married a wealthy American wife. His face bore the marks of a bitter, ill-controlled temper, and Trevesham had no doubt at all that when he came to inspect the wardroom wine bills Fossingham's would be standing way out on top.

Mr Partle, on the other hand, was the opposite in almost every respect. He was a modest, quiet little man in his neat uniform with its single thin gold stripe. He had an arthritic wife and a son of seventeen who had won a scholarship to a grammar school and who was taking his Higher Certificate that summer. He had a tidy little house in Waterlooville which he three-quarter owned and which would have filled the Lady Diana Trevesham with despair, but which to Trevesham and indeed to Mr Partle himself was a tangible measure of his success in the Service he had joined as a seaman boy. And Trevesham knew instinctively that it was on Partle's knowledge and ability that the Torpedo Department would largely lean.

As soon as he had finished talking to Mr Partle, Trevesham told the Commander to fall out the officers, only Heads of Departments remaining behind to introduce their own key ratings. The construction of a warship grows more and more technical as time goes by, so that in this muster of experts there were comparatively few ratings of the seaman branch in evidence. They would come later. But there were representatives of every specialist branch in the ship from engine room artificers to supply assistants, from shipwrights to stokers, from ordnance artificers to sick berth attendants.

29

Trevesham shook hands with them all and studied them with the same care he had given to his officers except that, aware of his limitations, he made no effort to remember their names. That could be done at leisure.

These were all trusted ratings he would come to know individually as the ship settled down. He might see them at intervals at Captain's Requestman whenever they were due for good conduct badges or advancement in rating. He would almost certainly never see them at Defaulters. The Commander had told him that in the four months he had been building the ship he had not had a single major defaulter. This might, of course, imply slackness on the part of their officers, but Trevesham was not inclined to think so. From all experience and indeed from the look of the men he was now meeting these were clearly the pick of the bunch. And that was entirely as it should be, Trevesham added to himself.

After the ratings had fallen out the Captain, accompanied by the Commander, took his first walk round the ship. Although both would be doing this many countless times in the future, although the Commander had inspected the ship every working day since he joined, it still gave them the most extraordinary pleasure. To Trevesham this had an added taste. In 1905 he had gone to Osborne as a cadet at the age of twelve and he had thus been in uniform for thirty-three years. This ship was his first major command. All his life he had striven to this end and now he was walking along the waist past the torpedo tubes and forward between the galley and the beef screen to the foc's'le messdeck for the very first time in a man-of-war which was all his, his to command, and his, within limits, to possess and use in a feudal manner and with feudal powers not accorded the other services. It was a moment of intense and private satisfaction. However many times they did rounds in the future it would never be quite as vivid as this.

'That's a new type of kit locker, isn't it?' Trevesham asked.

'Yes, sir, it's a new Admiralty pattern. The doors look as though they'll rattle a bit as they wear but Penniwick thinks they'll be popular with the ship's company.'

The stowing of kit and the fair apportionment of living space was always a crucial matter on the messdeck.

Men were going to have to live with only about two foot of deal table they could call their own, slinging their hammocks overhead at night and generally enduring a most cramped and communal life in tropical heat or northern chill.

Nearly six hundred of them would be cooped up like this for over two years. Where they stowed their belongings, where they washed themselves and their clothes, how far they had to walk to the heads, as shipboard lavatories are called, how long the cook of the mess would have to wait in the galley to draw meals for his mess—these and a dozen other questions directly affecting the health and morale of the ship's company had been thought out from every possible angle by the designers and builders of the ship.

Every man-of-war is a compromise. Speed, weight of armour, size of guns and living accommodation all vie with each other, for available space. In 1938 HMS *Antigone* represented the best compromise in a cruiser which had yet been devised.

'And this is the seamen's drying-room,' said Hatchett, 'the plumbers are very proud of the way they've fitted it up.'

Hatchett was proud of it, too. In a small space, the size of a dry heat room in a Turkish Bath, and having much the same temperature, it would be possible to dry the washing of half the ship's company in a matter of two to three hours. A laundry was also being fitted in the ship, but clothes had still to be dried. In the old days this had been done on the upper deck when opportunity offered. The new drying-room was obviously a great improvement.

They finished their tour of the messdecks and then climbed up to the bridge and compass platform. Here work was still going on fitting the repeaters, dials, telephones and speaking tubes, all of which would be necessary for effective control of the ship in battle. This was primarily the preserve of the Captain and Navigating Officer, since the Commander was not normally concerned with manoeuvring the ship at sea, and his action station would be in charge of the damage control section aft.

As they went up the ladder the Navigating Officer and the Chief Quartermaster came out of the charthouse to

31

be somewhat self-consciously on hand when their domain was inspected.

'Well,' said Trevesham, looking round critically. He was completely impervious to the petulant over-the-shoulder stares of the dockyard fitters who regarded this visit as just another unnecessary interruption of their work. 'There's not a lot of room, is there.'

Even allowing for the tools and other equipment encumbering the deck, it struck him that his bridge was more cramped than he had expected.

'The visibility's pretty good, sir,' Spratt said defensively. He felt the Captain was disappointed and that in some way he was responsible.

'Have you served in one of this class before?' Trevesham asked.

'No, sir,' said Spratt, 'but I did a commission as a watch-keeping officer in a "County" class cruiser.'

'Oh! yes,' said Trevesham, eyeing the layout of the bridge. 'Which one?'

'The *Berwick,* sir.'

'Good. She's to be our flagship, I believe, or at any rate in the same squadron. So you'll know your way around her.'

'Yes, sir,' said Aggie Spratt. 'I think we shall be much more comfortable at sea in *Antigone.*'

The 'Town' and 'County' class cruisers were around ten thousand tons, and their freeboard was considerably higher than the 'Leander' class. They were armed with eight-inch guns instead of the six-inch in *Antigone,* and although living quarters were more spacious in the bigger ships, they were known to roll their guts out in any sort of sea.

'And our silhouette's not so enormous,' Spratt added, thinking how the two types of cruiser would appear on the horizon. There was no doubt in Spratt's mind as to which was the more useful type of ship. However, opinion in the wardroom was far from unanimous on this point. He knew the Gunnery Officer did not agree and they were apt to burst into furious argument about it at the slightest provocation. But the Lieutenant-Commander (G) Tom Brasson, Royal Navy, was a typical product of Whale Island, the Navy's Gunnery School, and to be able to pitch a salvo of eight-inch shells at the enemy instead of six-inch ones was all that mattered. He and Brasson were two incompatibles and there was little love lost between them. Brasson considered him frivolous and he in turn thought Brasson a stupid and obstinate man.

Last of all on this initial tour the Captain inspected his own quarters, at the base of the superstructure aft on the upper deck. The day cabin ran along the starboard side. Aft of this, so that they looked out on 'Y' turret and the quarterdeck were his sleeping cabin and bathroom. For the size of ship these quarters were palatial but *Antigone* was fitted as a flagship and it was quite possible that Trevesham would have to surrender his accommodation to an Admiral at some stage or other. If *Antigone* was ever to function as a flagship then Trevesham would move into the Commander's cabin on the port side and a 'general post' in accommodation would take place to the disgruntlement of the ship's officers. It was an honour to be flagship, there were advantages such as better berths in harbours, but these honours were apt to be paid for in other ways.

The Captain's quarters had been fully furnished. The mahogany table and roll-top desk, the leather armchairs with their chintz covers, the heavy curtains and the thick carpets were all in place. Once finished off, the cabin had been kept sealed until Trevesham's arrival. The square ports were all closed. There was a smell of polish and fabric and newness about the room. The builders, the Admiralty Store Officials and the Commander had all got together on this with the result that the Captain's cabin was the showpiece of the ship. Trevesham realized this as he looked around, taking in the effect.

'It's like Buckingham Palace,' said Trevesham. 'I'm very grateful, Commander, for all the trouble you've taken.'

'Mr Blott, the Store Officer, and Harland and Wolff's deserve most of the credit,' said Hatchett. 'They've gone out of their way to be helpful. In fact, we've been showered with little extras,' he went on. 'The Board of Directors are presenting the wardroom with a radiogram. The Commander (E) has managed to win a mineral water machine for the ship's canteen. The dockyard sports club is giving the ship a football, a set of hockey sticks and some boxing gloves. The Ladies Guild is stocking up the ship's company library. One way and another we're doing pretty well out of Belfast.'

'My Secretary had better make a list of it all,' said Trevesham, 'so that we know where we are.'

'Yes,' said Hatchett dryly, 'the young gentleman should be in his office. Perhaps you'd like to try that second buzzer at the side of your desk.'

The Captain's office was on the main deck almost directly beneath the cuddy, as the Captain's quarters were already known. It was the most forward cabin on the starboard side of the wardroom flat and, had Marsh stopped to think about it, he might have derived a certain satisfaction from the watertight bulkhead which formed one of his four walls. But Marsh saw that bulkhead only as an infernal nuisance. The bulkhead ran right across the ship and was pierced by only two doors. The port one gave access solely to the wardroom pantry and the starboard door, which was immediately outside the Captain's office, thus took the whole fore and aft traffic of the ship below decks.

This did not especially worry him, but inside his diminutive office the bulkhead was riveted by means of four large anglepieces to the deck below and the deck above. These triangles of hardened steel jutting out from the deck made movement in the office even more constricted. Marsh had already nearly broken a shinbone over one of them and they had also caused him to make a monstrous fool of himself in front of the Commander.

This had happened through Marsh's technique of getting things done quietly and without causing a fuss. At least that was the view currently held of himself and his service abilities. He had been trained during his midshipman's time in a battleship by a Paymaster-Commander who believed that good administration should never be heard or seen. Marsh had studied his technique. From him he had learnt forethought. He had seen that any service event succeeded or failed in ratio to the preparation given it. From him, too, he had acquired a sharp eye for detail and a readiness to put things right the moment they showed signs of going off the rails. The angle pieces in his new Captain's office, therefore, became to Marsh a perfect case in point. They must go. They got in his way: they impeded his work and he decided that quietly and without causing any fuss he would have them removed. So he had sent for the foreman and had asked him to take the necessary steps.

The foreman, who had built many warships in his time, had thought it odd. He was used to the ways of constructors and knew those angle pieces were there for a reason. Before cutting them away, therefore, he had consulted with the Commander and Hatchett in turn had sent for Marsh.

'Did you give orders for this work to be done?' Hatchett asked sharply.

'Yes, sir.'

'Why?'

'They got in the way: they make it very difficult to get about in the office.'

'Holy suffering Moses!' said the Commander. 'Why didn't you come and ask me first?'

'I didn't want to worry you, sir.'

'Well, next time you have any bright ideas for cutting away bits of the structure, come and see me. I'd far rather bite your head off than have the whole ship collapse under me the first action we fight.'

'Yes, sir,' said Marsh, blushing furiously. He saluted and turned away. He felt like a small boy hauled up in front of a prefect. He suspected that the Commander and he would have a showdown before the commission was through and, after this experience, he knew pretty well who was going to come out of it worst.

When the buzzer from the Captain's day cabin rang it nearly made Marsh jump out of his skin. It was a loud angry buzzer and its note demanded an instant response. If he was going to live with that buzzer he would have to find some way of toning it down, but anticipation of his first private encounter with the Captain soon drove the thought from his head. He picked up the few papers he had for the Captain's attention, went out of his office into the main cabin flat, skirted the chests where the Confidential Books would be kept, crossed to the port side and ran up the ladder to the flat above which lay between the Commander's and the Captain's cabins and where, no doubt Requestmen and Defaulters would normally be held.

The Commander was leaving the cabin as he arrived. He smiled at Marsh as he walked over to his cabin.

'Captain's office caved in yet?' he inquired.

'No, sir,' said Marsh. 'We're strengthening up all round. I'm armour-plating the typewriter.'

It wasn't a very clever remark but he wanted to show Hatchett that he could rise above any ragging that might come his way. He knew that Captain's Secretary in a cruiser has a pivotal position. Like the flag-lieutenant to an Admiral he would, to a certain extent, control access to the Captain and a diplomatic personality was essential to success. It is through the Executive Officer that a Captain's will is effected in a cruiser, and the Commander and Captain would be conferring many times every day. But if the Commander was Prime Minister then Marsh was Clerk to the Privy Council. Although under the Commander for discipline and ship's duties, he would also have other and separate responsibilities on the side. He knocked at the door and waited. Nothing happened, so he knocked again.

'Come in,' said Trevesham. He watched his Secretary step into the cabin, drawing the curtain rather precisely across the door after him, 'always knock and come straight in, Secretary, unless you know I've got somebody with me.'

'Aye, aye, sir,' said Marsh standing tautly at ease. He was a little awed by Trevesham and this always stiffened him up.

'What have you got there?' asked the Captain, referring to the papers in Marsh's hand.

'Nothing important, sir,' said Marsh. 'We haven't got our proper stationery yet so it's a bit of a lash-up at present. I wanted to ask you what you want to see in the mail.'

It was a thoroughly professional remark but one more appropriate to a battleship where the Captain would normally be shown only a small proportion of the correspondence in and out of the ship. Marsh had never served in a cruiser before but he imagined that a somewhat scaled down capital-ship routine would be what was wanted. So Trevesham's next remark was surprising.

'I want to see everything in the mail as soon as you've opened it,' said the Captain, 'and I mean everything. Bring it all up as it is and then log it and attach the formers afterwards. Where were you trained?'

'In *Nelson*, sir,' Marsh answered, adding quite unnecessarily, 'Fleet Flagship of the Home Fleet.'

Trevesham allowed himself a smile.

'Thank you Secretary, I know.' The immediate blush with which this was greeted made Trevesham realize that his Secretary was younger and shyer than he thought. However, he was a sub-lieutenant and as such would be one of the three senior officers in the gunroom. He would soon learn to grow up.

'I know you chaps like to get letters logged properly and covered with rubber stamps before they get out of the office—but that's the routine I want you to work. I want to see everything as soon as it arrives—and you can bring it in whenever you like. I'll only keep it a few minutes and then you can deal with it in the normal way.'

'Aye, aye, sir,' said Marsh.

'I see you're an interpreter in Spanish,' the Captain went on. 'That's very enterprising, and I'm sure you'll have plenty to do when we get across the other side. In the meantime we have to get the ship completed and commissioned. So first of all you can bring me the Portsmouth Port Orders and any local orders there may be in force. Do they allow you a writer in the complement?'

'No, sir,' said Marsh brightly, 'not unless war breaks out. But the Paymaster-Commander says we shall be getting a Pay-Mid for training and I can have him for a time. Except for the typing, though, I'd much rather work on my own.'

'That's the spirit,' said Trevesham, and went on to question him about his home life and his previous experience. He had taken a liking to the youngster, except for his nervousness and stiff way of standing. As he probed further into his background he understood why the boy was so unsure of himself. Trevesham had been on the point of telling him he needed a haircut but, for the present, he decided to say nothing and ride him with an easy hand. There was a flow of spontaneous enthusiasm he had no wish to inhibit and when they touched on the ship's future in the West Indies and South America, he noticed that Marsh could scarcely keep his excitement under control.

'Well,' said Trevesham as he brought the interview to an end, 'so you think you can do the job, do you?'

'Oh! yes, sir. I hope so.'

Trevesham took a turn up and down the cabin and then walked over to one of the square ports. He stood looking out across the shipyard for a moment or so in silence.

'When we get abroad round South America,' he said, 'you'll have your hands pretty full. You'll find yourself a sort of unofficial flag-lieutenant in addition to your normal duties, the more so as you speak Spanish. When that happens I want you to remember that first things come first.' He turned and gave Marsh a thoughtful look. 'Whatever poodle-faking has to be done, this cruiser is still a warship and will be part of a Fleet. The news today is ominous, I've no doubt we're in for a fair number of other unpleasant shocks. Our prime job is to be ready to fight a war and, so far as the Captain's office of this ship is concerned, I don't want you to fall down on any detail of Fleet or Squadron work because of the more attractive business of showing the flag. Letters coming into the ship are to be dealt with promptly and meticulously. Our returns are to go in dead on time and it's your job, Secretary, to see that where other departments are concerned they have them lined up and ready. I want no excuses and I don't want to have to chase people so far as routine work is concerned. It sounds easy to say that here in Belfast before we're commissioned. You won't find it so simple later on. But your first job is to see that we don't fall foul of any of the rules and regulations, whether they're your direct concern or not. Is that understood?'

'Yes, sir,' said Derek Marsh, rather more impressed than he cared to admit.

'That said, I think we ought to get on together, you and I, and I look forward to my first lesson in Spanish at an early date. I gather you'll be instructing the Commander and the wardroom as well.'

'Yes, sir,' said Marsh, his face falling, 'that *is* the Commander's idea.'

Although they would all be living on board in a few days time, Chief Petty Officers Penniwick and Bowling, and Yeoman of Signals Mellish decided to ask the Captain's Coxswain, Petty Officer Vincent, to muck in with them in their digs. This was an honour. The digs in two adjoining houses in McCrumlin Terrace were not especially grand. Had he bothered to look around Vincent could, without doubt, have discovered more comfortable accommodation. But to be asked to join a small and exclusive club was another matter entirely. Vincent accepted with alacrity and both parties to the invitation felt they had made a wise move.

In point of fact the 'club' was more of a forum for lowerdeck ambassadors than a club for old friends. Before being drafted to *Antigone* none of them had previously met. But each in his separate way was the Head of a Department, and all thought it expedient to get together before life on board divided them into their several duties. Thus the team spirit in *Antigone* began to establish itself at the Petty Officer level.

Once aboard they would see each other—no doubt daily—but the conditions would be different and each would be absorbed in his own particular duties. Each was distinct, but an understanding between the four of them would benefit them all. Had the ship's Master-at-Arms been there he, too, would doubtless have been elected to the 'club' since the Master-at-Arms was, by King's Regulations and Admiralty Instructions, the senior rating on the lower deck. But HMS *Antigone*'s Master-At-Arms was not to join until the advance-party arrived.

While each of the four was headman of his own line of country, each was, so to speak, a 'winger' on the lower deck for particular officers. Penniwick was, of course, attached to the Commander as Vincent was to the Captain; Bowling, the Chief Quartermaster, owed his allegiance to the Navigating Officer and at sea would be mainly responsible for steering the ship; Mellish, who would soon be a Chief Yeoman of Signals, was in charge of the ship's visual communications in the same way that Chief Petty Officer Telegraphist Burton, a morose unsociable man who had refused membership of the 'club', was responsible for the radio link. Both would come under the aircraft observer officer in *Antigone*, who in 1938 was also responsible for communications. But whereas Burton spent his whole life below decks—in every sense of the word a backroom boy—Mellish would be on the flag deck or the bridge at sea and in charge of the signal distributing office in harbour. In consequence he would never be far away from his telescope and his fingers would always be stained purple from helping out with the Ormig duplicator, a hand-turned rotary machine whose idiosyncracies had to be studied and flattered if signals in spate were ever to be handled with any speed.

The 'club' was looked after by Mrs McKendrick and her sister, Mrs Derryman. Penniwick and Mellish shared a bedroom, thus securing a reduction. Bowling, and latterly Vincent had rooms to themselves.

All four were permitted the use of Mrs McKendrick's front parlour, a cheerless room with a piano, a number of lace mats and hideous striped wallpaper, but the club's normal meeting place was in the private bar of the Antrim Arms. Here every evening they would meet after supper and mull over the day's events, the current news and the morrow's work. Occasionally other shipmates would drop in, such as the Supply Chief Petty Officer in charge of the Central Stores, or a Chief Electrician or Engine Room Artificer.

But in general they stayed in their own cliques. In 1938 the Navy had had nearly twenty years of peacetime organization, and the caste system was visibly and invisibly the framework of it all. Chief and petty officers mingled freely among themselves but a leading-seaman or AB was unlikely to be found in the same bar and certainly not in the same 'club'. Seaman spoke to seaman and stoker to stoker. Different duties on board ship tended to draw the dividing lines as well as age or seniority in rating. There was no open hostility between stokers and seamen, for instance, as there had been in certain ships, but each branch worked in its different part of ship. Their duties rarely overlapped and, generally speaking, each little division kept naturally to itself.

The night of the Captain's arrival was a gala one for the club. Petty Officer Vincent, the Coxswain, had driven his Captain to Government House and had returned with the car. He was on his way to the garage, and the car was now on view outside Mrs Derryman's house. Vincent was to pick up the Captain at 0830 the following morning. Theoretically, the car was his for twelve hours. Had he chosen to ply for hire or given joy rides to the children of McCrumlin Terrace, the Captain would probably have been none the wiser. But such an action was quite unthinkable to Vincent. He had charge of the car and he had no intention whatever of abusing the trust. He could not resist the temptation, however, of displaying it to the inhabitants of McCrumlin Terrace and the regulars of the Antrim Arms. He drew up outside Number 17 with a silky flourish and got out with an air. Mrs Derryman's fifth child, a snotty-nosed boy of three-and-a-half, immediately began pawing the black mudguards.

'Leave that alone,' said Vincent, in magisterial tones, 'or I shall eat you alive for my supper.'

The child ran screaming into the house and after instructing Mrs McKendrick's twelve-year-old girl, who was lolling in the doorway, to keep an eye on things, Vincent went up to his room to get, as he announced, a clean handkerchief. The other three were already at supper and had seen the car and the Coxswain arrive. Although Vincent was the most junior of them all, and though none of them expressed it in words, everyone felt that he and the captain's Rolls-Bentley lent tone to the place.

'Well,' Bowling summed it up, 'I suppose that car won't do the ship's reputation any harm.'

They looked at the car through the net curtains without moving from the table. None of them interrupted his eating, but there was an air of pride and pleasure in the room, the more so when both Mrs McKendrick and Mrs Derryman were summoned by their respective children to come and marvel at the car. Vincent put his head round the door.

'Don't wait for me,' he said, 'I'm just going to put the state coach away and I'll join you down at the Arms.'

'We'll have your bit of pie put back in the oven,' said Bowling gravely. 'It can't get more shrivelled than it is.'

Bowling was a tall, cadaverous man whom one might have associated at first sight with the undertaking business. However, this impression dissolved after one or two

41

pints in the Antrim Arms where his quietly told and apparently innocent stories already had a reputation.

Vincent strode out into the street 'like a Ruritanian monarch' as Penniwick put it, got into the car with a dignified nod at the two landladies and their children and then drove off in great style.

'I know someone as loves himself in that motor car,' said Penniwick. 'Shoving himself off for a clean pocket handkerchief! That's going to cost him a couple of rounds.'

But it was said without malice.

'He'll find the gig altogether another cup of tea,' Bowling remarked, 'and I understand the old man likes his bit of sailing.'

The gig was a smooth-skinned or carvel-built boat a little longer than a whaler. It was reserved exclusively for the Captain's use. A survival from the days before power boats were commonly carried, it would now be used only for sailing and regattas and, of course, in an emergency.

Of the three of them, Bowling was the acknowledged expert on boats and he had already pronounced against the Captain's gig. She looked heavy, he said, and that would never do for *Antigone*. He had already planted the idea in the Commander's mind that a swap should be quietly arranged when the ship went round to Portsmouth, and Bowling had his eyes on a new gig which he knew to be carefully hidden away in the dockyard, awaiting completion of a rival cruiser.

Bowling was determined that *Antigone* should have that gig, but in order to prise it out of the dockyard, he and Vincent would have to do some neat under-the-counter manoeuvring with the tacit consent of the Commander and perhaps a word at the right moment from the Captain to the Admiral Superintendent of the dockyard. KR and AI frowned on such procedures. Bowling and Vincent were quite aware that both stood in danger of getting themselves and the ship an official rap over the knuckles. But Bowling thought it could be done and it was all in keeping with their motto: 'None but the best for *Antigone*.'

They had all been impressed by the Captain. In the private bar of the Antrim Arms the day was lived through again and the Captain's impact on themselves and the officers carefully gone over and analysed. The Chief Gunner's Mate and the Torpedo Gunner's Mate, who were Penniwick's equivalent in the Gunnery and Torpedo branches and who had another private 'club' of their own elsewhere in Belfast, had come across to compare notes. The general feeling was that the Captain had to prove himself to the Chief Petty Officers but showed signs of being all right.

'A bit of money of his own, a missus with a handle to her name, a billet at Government House and about twelve inches up on Stubby—that's good enough for me,' said the TGM.

'You think the Commander's got a down on the Torpedo Department,' Penniwick said, quickly coming to his Commander's defence.

'Certainly not,' said the TGM, who respected the Commander as much as Penniwick did but who could never resist taking a rise out of the Chief Buffer. 'The Bloke's all right, what there is of him.'

'Well,' said Penniwick, summoning up all the portly dignity he could manage. 'I'll lay you a bet the Torpedo Officer doesn't last six months in *Antigone*. And if he does it'll be because of you and Mr Partle and the rest of us.'

'If Lieutenant-Commander Fossingham leaves the ship,' the TGM retorted, 'it will only be because of his brass hat.'

'His what?'

'He's in the zone for promotion.'

Fossingham would not have been pleased to hear the ribaldry which greeted this piece of news. Fossingham was known as a great evader of issues and he had a comfortably high opinion of himself. Whoever else was fooled by this, the chief and petty officers of *Antigone* were not. Loyal as they were, they kept their opinions to themselves, except on occasions when equals were gathered together as they were that night, but they had an uncanny nose both for ability and humbug. They might poke Charley at the Gunnery Officer's Prussian efficiency but they respected him from top to toe. The TGM, however, was unhappily aware that the Head of his Department had already been nicknamed the SOD or, as Bowling gravely explained it, the Ship's Only Dud.

There were six of them there in the bar, a smart and imposing body of men, a good advertisement for their ship and the service. Long years of intelligent discipline, character, experience in dealing with other men and the sea; wives and families seen only for brief periods and often at long intervals; a reserve of speech and a power of command; humour, pride in their uniform and the Service to which they had devoted their lives since boyhood; a meagre rate of pay yet an acceptance of other intangible rewards and perquisites at least partially in lieu; health of body and an almost undue sharpness of mind; kind, emotional hearts which veered between sentimentality and complete self-sacrifice—all these qualities and facets showed their traces in the six blue-uniformed chief and petty officers who were so important to HMS *Antigone* the day German troops marched into Austria in the spring of 1938.

'I see,' said Yeoman of Signals Mellish, sucking a hollow tooth, 'that little old Hitler is sharpening up his knife. I wonder when it's going to come.'

'Won't be long now,' said Bowling, the corners of his mouth dropping in their accustomed way. The Chief Quartermaster was already known to his friends as the prophet of doom.

'If you ask me,' said Penniwick robustly, 'it's all part of a bluff. They won't fight. Why should they when barking and snarling fetches them all they want? You wait and see. One of these days we'll snap back, then you'll see.'

'Who will?' asked the Chief Gunner's Mate, a small replica of the Gunnery Officer's aggressiveness. 'That animated toothbrush we have for a Prime Minister? He couldn't say "Boo" to a goose.'

'I agree with Arthur,' said Mellish, jerking his thumb at Penniwick. 'One of these days the little old Corporal's going to have his bluff called. Wouldn't surprise me if we got tough and sent a cruiser to Berlin and that cruiser was the old *Aunty Gone*.'

'Hmm!' said Bowling, 'that'll be a rare navigational feat: but no doubt we could do it.'

And there for that evening the international situation was left in the Antrim Arms. The clouds were gathering, they all knew that, but each of them felt it wasn't to come quite yet. When it did then no doubt HMS *Antigone* would be ready.

By the time the advance-party arrived, key officers and ratings had been living aboard the ship for a couple of weeks. As the Commander had warned them, this had been something of a picnic. Work was still being carried out in various parts of the ship, amenities were few and the meals provided by the Paymaster-Commander were kept as spartan as possible. Facilities, too, were limited. Officers were still crowding into the gunroom bathroom and, as in dry dock, the shoreside heads had to be used. However, they were at last living in the ship. Any temporary inconvenience was greeted with the usual inital grousing, but in general life on Board HMS *Antigone* was considered far preferable to the scattered boardinghouse existence ashore.

This settled feeling was naturally stronger on the lower deck than it was among the officers, most of whom had established some sort of home with their wives in Belfast. However, married officers and ratings were still permitted to sleep ashore if they so wished, and on certain evenings the ship was so sparsely filled that it looked as though a plague had decimated the messdecks. But the pioneer days were coming to an end and no one was sorry to see the advance-party and its stores arrive.

The empty living quarters were now partially filled. The noisy disrespectful business of sailors settling into a new home had begun. Life was ringing through the ship. A skeleton harbour routine was being worked and most of the officers had now joined *Antigone* with the exception of the midshipmen, the chaplain and the schoolmaster. Neither the warrant officers' mess nor the gunroom was yet in use and all officers were messed in the wardroom. By the time the Acceptance Trials began, the wardroom had a variegated, overcrowded appearance, since in addition to ship's officers, various dockyard and Admiralty officials were always coming and going.

But the ship was becoming a ship. She was beginning to sound and smell and feel a ship. No longer was she a hulk, dark and deserted at night, in which hordes of workmen would begin another day's labour in the morning. HMS *Antigone* was now referred to less and less by her

45

job number and more and more by her name. By this time there were well over a hundred officers and men aboard. The ship was humming with activity, the auxiliary machinery was being run so that dynamos and ventilating fans now provided the background noise. Cooking smells from the officers' and ship's company galleys added their flavour to the usual dockyard odour of oil and dirt, and anywhere near the engine room there was now to be savoured that peculiar and unique blend of steam, oil and as Marsh put it to himself, 'burnt electricity', similar to the smell in the London Underground, which at once identifies maritime machinery to the nose.

They even had a small detachment of Royal Marines 'embarked', and both the ship's company brow forward and the officers' gangway aft sported armed sentries who guarded access to the ship. The Master-at-Arms had joined so that the ship now had a policeman and a regulating office aboard. The canteen had opened in a modest way. The ship's scran bag, into which all property found sculling was put to be redeemed after payment of a small fine, was now in operation. A deck log was kept and the ship's keyboard, controlling the opening and closing of storerooms, compartments and magazines was now under a sentry's control. A bugler sounded off 'Colours' in the morning and 'Sunset' at night. Evening Rounds were made at 2100 and the first Captain's Requestmen and Defaulters had been held. Though not yet the small seagoing township it was her destiny to become, *Antigone* was alive. The chrysalis had become a rather uncertain little butterfly. The status and condition of the ship had undoubtedly changed.

Now that he had a few more hands at his disposal Hatchett had started to clean up where he could. Decks were hosed down and scrubbed in the morning, though they were scarcely dry before a new day's shipyard litter began to arrive. At least once a day Hatchett went down on the jetty to look at *Antigone* from the outside. He was tempted to try and paint the ship before leaving Belfast, but the trials programme, the swiftly changing Northern Irish weather and insufficient hands for the job made him put the idea reluctantly out of his mind.

It was not that Hatchett was looking for a job. Every

moment of the day was bespoke. Madame in the rented house in Cushendall Avenue saw less and less of her husband as the ship's departure from Belfast drew steadily nearer. Madame accepted this state of affairs with a sigh. She was used to it by now, though she still did not like it. But she had long ago given up the fight.

The last four months had been a most welcome break. She and Stubby—even she had fallen into the habit of calling him that—had lived together as man and wife. They had woken up in the same bed in the morning, and he had come back to eat the dinners she ordered at night. For a time he might have been any businessman going off to the office in the morning and returning exhausted in the evening.

But the wheel turned as it always did. Another of HM ships had claimed him and was quietly removing him step by step from her power and out of her orbit. She knew every variation of the process. Now once more she was in for a further long period of being alone.

Madame poured herself a double pink gin and thought enviously of other men's wives. Even Lady Diana Trevesham (and madame sniffed to herself as she thought of her) had a house and a family to go back to and to fill her attention. Lack of finance did not compel the Treveshams to let their home as it did the Hatchetts. And the Treveshams had a family of three, madame had none and was now unlikely to surprise her husband, as for many years she had been hoping to do. Perhaps, after all, they should have adopted. They had discussed it often enough. But even as the thought formed in her mind, she acknowledged with a sigh that nothing would come of it.

She sipped her lonely gin, curled a strand of her hair round a finger and gazed into the sitting-room fire. Then she got up and looked in the mirror. That new tinted rinse she was using was quite a success. In her opinion she certainly looked the Commander's wife. She swallowed the rest of her drink and went upstairs for her coat. The Brassons were having a few people round at their place for drinks and she and Stubby had agreed to meet there.

Madame liked the Brassons. She got on with them as well as with any of the other officers and their wives, and in some ways a good deal better. Of course, the Brassons were typical. She knew that but considered it a quality in this decadent day and age. They were service to the marrow, but at least you knew where you were with them. Tom Brasson himself was a bit hearty and his jokes were lamentably weak, but he and Noreen were always most scrupulously correct. They made her feel she really was the Commander's wife. It was true that Brasson had a loud voice and a red face, that his handshake made her wince and that he was something of a snob, but they made a great fuss of madame and the other wardroom wives at their functions were always kept properly in thir place.

This evening the party had a two-fold purpose—to return hospitality received from other officers and to entertain two Admiralty officials concerned with armament supply. In madame's long Naval experience these cocktail parties never varied very much, and this made her feel at home. In Malta, or Hong Kong, Portsmouth or Belfast there were always the same people from the same ship drinking the same martinis and exchanging the same coinage of conversation. Aggie Spratt and the Meldrums might look on these affairs as a rather tedious but inescapable duty: to madame they were the breath of life.

Stubby had not yet arrived so she felt it incumbent upon her to maintain the dignity of their position by herself. To begin with she found herself talking to the Captain, Royal Marines, an officer identifiable in any clothing or circumstance by his wooden expression and his fine, sandy coloured moustache. But Captain Taw-Street, RM, who ranked as a Lieutenant-Commander afloat but only as a Lieutenant ashore, had one ruling passion in life—to possess a fine horse and to ride it all day long. As a topic of conversation this had its natural limits and in any case madame detested horses. So when Fossingham and his American wife came over madame graciously disentangled herself and allowed them to lead her away into a corner to discuss a 'private plot' they were hatching. John Fossingham was a great chap for parties and he threw himself into social affairs with a zeal unknown to the Torpedo Department of the ship.

'Now, what it is,' said Annabel Fossingham in her Boston drawl, 'is a point-to-point down across the border.'

'Thank you very much,' said madame. 'I've had my fill of horsiness for one night.'

48

'Ah! but that's not all,' Fossingham put in quickly, 'this affair's on Lord Ballymeath's estate.'

'And I was at school with his wife,' Annabel continued. 'They're just loaded with money—well, she was a Vanderhast—so we thought we'd get them to throw open the castle to the officers for a fancy dress ball.'

'Charter a charabanc or something,' Fossingham said. 'What do you think? How do you think the Commander will view it?'

This was a delicate question to fire at madame in her husband's absence, and she knew it was designed on purpose to get her involved. She resented this manoeuvring but did not want to be the one to throw cold water on the scheme.

'Well,' she answered carefully, 'it sounds a wonderful idea, but isn't it rather a long way to go?'

As luck had it the Commander came into the room at that moment. She nodded pleasantly at the Fossinghams and quickly went over to meet him. That had been a narrow escape. Madame quite liked the Fossinghams. They were good value at a party. They had that indefinable fascination of the extravagant for the threadbare. When first an idea presented itself they would grapple on to it with a fierce possessive enthusiasm as though their whole lives and happiness depended upon it. But at the first breath of delay, should there be any opposition or lack of support, then the idea and its attendant scheme were banished never to return. The Fossinghams were wealthy, madame told herself as she greeted her husband, and the rich so often have grasshopper minds. She did not imagine the fancy dress ball at Ballymeath Castle would be mentioned again. At the next party there would be a new and more lavish proposal.

'Hallo, old thing,' Stubby said to her affectionately, 'you've had another hair-do. Where are the drinks?'

He took her arm, squeezed it, and then together they went over to pay their respects to the Brassons. This was his invariable greeting whenever they met at a party. They had been married fifteen years and Stubby had nearly always remarked on her 'hair-do', though almost never on any new dress she might be wearing. Madame had come to accept this state of affairs, but it always surprised her that a man as sharp-eyed as Stubby, who could spot a piece of cotton waste jammed behind a locker at twenty yards without batting an eyelid, should be so completely inert to feminine dress and appearance.

'Sorry I'm late, Mrs Guns,' said Stubby, shaking hands, 'only we've got the Admiral Superintendent coming the day after tomorrow and I had a lot of homework to do.'

'Homework' was the process by which Stubby, seated bubbling in the Commander's office, produced the daily orders and the organization for any special event. Even at this moment Able-Seaman Clarke would be wrestling with the sprawling forceful writing and beating it letter by letter through the heavy old Empire typewriter.

'Very kind of you to grace our humble home,' said Brasson, giving him an extra strong martini. The Brassons kept two jugs going at their cocktail parties. One contained a double strength mixture for 'firsts' and important people, the second was for follow-on drinks and the 'field'. The Commander and his lady fell, of course, into the first category. Across the other side of the room Augustus Spratt nudged the Senior Engineer.

'Watch old Honest Tom selling himself,' he remarked, 'with all the subtlety of an auctioneer.'

'Now, Aggie,' said Susan Meldrum, 'you made a resolution not to be nasty to Gunnery Officers. Remember? Anyway, I like Noreen. I think she has a lot to put up with.'

'Ha!' said Spratt. 'You're dead right there. Can you imagine anyone climbing into bed with Brasson? And for life! It must be like sleeping out on a parade-ground.'

'Charity, charity, charity!' said Meldrum. 'What a horrid little fellow you are!'

'I'll bet he has her doubling round the bedroom like a Whale Island GI,' Spratt said morosely and added darkly, 'I know for a fact that their youngest child sleeps with a rifle in its cot.'

When *Antigone* commissioned there would be some twenty officers in the wardroom and about fifteen of them were now in the Gunnery Officer's house. The Warrant Officers' mess would cater for another nine or ten and the gunroom about a dozen. Though in this early period both Warrant Officers and Sub-Lieutenants were messing in the wardroom, none had been invited to this party. This was not because of snobbery, as Spratt had at once assumed, but because in 1938 the shadings of naval etiquette were very real and important to someone of Brasson's make-up. Like spoke to like and this was a party for the prime officers of the ship.

The Commander (E) and the Senior, the Paymaster-Commander and the Central Storekeeping Officer, the Surgeon-Commander, the First Lieutenant, the Navigating Officer, the pilot of the ship's floatplane and the observer, the three Lieutenants of the Foc'sle, Top and Quarterdeck Divisions (each of them in charge of one of the six-inch gun turrets), the Torpedo Officer and the Captain RM—those were the officers then in the room and they, capped by the Commander and the Captain, made up the hierarchy of the ship.

All those officers—or the appointments they filled—were indispensable to the ship. After them stood their number two's and number three's—the Gunner and the Gunner (T), the Warrant Engineers, Electrician and Shipwright, the Sub-Lieutenants and the Midshipmen, the Instructor-Lieutenant and the Chaplain. They, too, had essential jobs to fulfil—jobs that had been analysed and defined through the slow pressure of experience, but it was upon the prime officers of the ship that the weight of responsibility lay.

HMS *Antigone* was a cruiser—a ship in size between a battleship and a destroyer, having some of the characteristics of both, a 'big' ship as the Navy classified its vessels, a highly organized compact of power and speed, armour and cruising range of a quality which made her invaluable in war. It has been said that there are never enough cruisers in wartime, and indeed a ship such as *Antigone* might well be looked on as the best 'general purpose' warship which had yet been devised.

If war should come then Brasson knew well that of all jobs in the ship at that moment represented in his drawing-room, his own—that of Gunnery Officer—would be the most vital of them all. It was his ability and his efficiency which could make or mar the sum total of all their efforts. To his brother officers, Tom Brasson might often appear an aggressive, dominant man with an eye fixed firmly on his own promotion. To Brasson, himself,

51

he appeared as the one officer through whom the whole purpose of the ship would mainly be expressed should *Antigone* find herself in action with the enemy in war.

'Have the other half, sir,' he said to the Commander. 'We've got a long way to go as yet.'

CHAPTER THREE

On a fine mid-April morning HMS *Antigone* completed her Full Power Trials out of Belfast Lough. The exact performance figures would be kept a secret, but everyone in the ship knew her speed to be well over thirty knots. She was an impressive sight seen from other ships and to be on board was an exhilarating experience.

The Commander (E) and the Senior Engineer in their white boiler suits might have their attention anxiously divided between a dozen different things as they stood on their gratings in the quivering engine room, but to the Captain's Secretary in his cabin over the port screw it was pure excitement. He had never been so fast at sea. At thirty knots the stern of the ship settled down in the water so that the scuttle of his cabin seemed to be only a few inches above sea level and the thick glass was continuously sprayed and caked with drying salt.

The vibration and din were enormous. Marsh supposed he would get used to it in time, but at present the thought of sleeping in his bunk while the ship did anything like this speed was unbearable. However, this was unlikely to happen very often on peacetime cruises. *Antigone*'s economical speed was a much quieter fourteen knots, and with an eye to the cost of oil-fuel and the Naval Estimates, the Admiralty required very good reasons from a Commander-in-Chief whenever greater despatch was demanded of one of HM ships.

The timed part of the trial lasted an hour. During this hour the ship was 'flat out', but once accustomed to the speed, very little seemed to be happening. Marsh had plenty to do in the Captain's office, but it was all work which could be finished off later. Now it was a sunny day and the ship was at sea. Rather nervously he made his way along the upper deck and then up two more ladders to the flag deck.

He did not want to be in the way. When a warship is at sea its character changes. King's Regulations and Admirality Instructions, the intricacies of naval administration, fleet and port orders all lose their importance. The ship is at sea. Certain jobs—apparently simple—have to be done, and done all the time.

The ship is in three watches. These—except for the Dogs—are of four hours each, and all personnel not on watch are understood to be resting, or may do what they please. So far as the ship is concerned, the daymen—that is, those officers and ratings not organized in watches and not actively concerned in keeping the ship at sea—fade much further into the background. Although on this occasion *Antigone* was only at sea for a few hours, these factors combined to make Derek Lysander Marsh feel he was nothing but a passenger. And so in a sense he was.

He stood now on the flag deck with the wind and occasionally a gust of spray beating into his face. Away from Belfast the air was clean, the sun shone and sparkled on the water and seagulls raced round the ship, on watch for scraps from the galley and apparently in no way put out by the speed of *Antigone*.

Marsh stood with his hands stiffly behind him in the training ship way which was now second nature to him. His heart sang and the clear, fresh air seemed to dance in his lungs. He did not venture up on the bridge itself in case someone told him he was in the way and thus dented his dignity, but down where he was, and from the compass platform where the Chief Quartermaster was conning the ship, he could see all he wanted to see.

By this time they had turned and were heading back for Belfast, the Antrim coast to starbroad and the blue hills of County Down to port. The trial was over and they were easing down, a sudden plume of black smoke pouring out of the funnel. Marsh wondered if this was being done on purpose since no oil-fired warship makes smoke except by intent. But in this instance the stokers, new to *Antigone*'s boilers, had not been quite quick enough to achieve complete combustion and, at that very moment, had Marsh but known, the Officer of the Watch was curtly pointing this out to the engine room 'with the Captain's compliments'.

Except for this peccadillo, however, the ship and the builders had come out of it well. *Antigone* could produce the speed she was designed to produce, and both Trevesham and Spratt saw that she handled beautifully.

It was just as well that Marsh had not climbed up on the bridge. In the Navigating Officer's view you couldn't move for the passengers. There were official passengers —the dockyard and Admiralty officials concerned with timing the trial and observing the ship's behaviour, and there were other 'passengers', such as the Gunnery Officer who came up on to the bridge to have a good vantage point and because he had nothing better to do.

'Lot of spare dinners about,' Spratt murmured, frowning sideways at the Gunnery Officer, so that both the Officer of the Watch and the Captain could hear. 'Can't move for the feet.'

The Captain said nothing. The ship was not yet his, and although he felt just as strongly about it as the Navigating Officer, he decided to bide his time. He would talk to the Commander before they next went to sea. The Commander would bruit it around in the wardroom that no one was to be on the bridge whose duty did not take him there, and that would be that.

Trevesham was not fond of written orders. He knew that certain commanding-officers produced a sheaf of standing orders and temporary instructions covering almost any eventuality in the ship. Technically they had cleared their own yardarm to some extent and several commanders-in-chief would have endorsed this bureaucratic point of view. Signals drawing attention to articles in the Station Order Book were a daily feature in certain fleets, a feature matched and copied on a lower level by indecisive or over-zealous commanding-officers.

To Trevesham this was a mark of insecurity and 'old womanhood'. Standing orders, of course, there had to be, but in his view they should be commandments in their simplest, shortest and most understandable form. Trevesham preferred to leave as much as he could to the individual wisdom and experience of his officers. He believed strongly in the steadying influence of plain common sense to be applied at all levels with the minimum of official guidance. Any officer or man who could not latch-on to this idea was not likely to last very long with Trevesham.

'Well,' said Spratt, summing up the trial as they came alongside in Belfast, 'she's certainly no sluggard.'

Although they had a civilian pilot aboard the Captain had in effect been handling the ship. He had brought her alongside, if anything, too cautiously, but it pleased him to realize that she was far more flexible than he had thought. She was indeed a pleasure to handle. Never again, Trevesham mused, would he be likely to have command of so lively and balanced a ship. If things went well and his service career proceeded as it should, the next step for him would probably be command of a capital ship. But there was no fun in urging a great ponderous battleship out of harbour and in some conditions the risks were entirely out of key. *Nelson* and *Rodney* for instance, whose sterns had been chopped down by the Washington Naval Treaty of 1926 so that they had a lopsided look were, in fact, extremely difficult to manoeuvre under certain conditions of wind and tide.

Trevesham had been in *Nelson* when she had gone aground on leaving Portsmouth Harbour, and that had not been her captain's fault, but simply the reluctance of thirty-three thousand sluggish tons to answer to the helm at slow speed. Compared with such a ship *Antigone* was a joy to manoeuvre and, although under a quarter the size, she had her own proportioned majesty. She was no glorified picket boat, no jumped-up destroyer. She was 555 feet long and her arrival alongside a jetty was an impressive affair.

As soon as the bridge had rung down 'Finished with engines' and the Commander (E) had ordered steam to be shut down, the various post mortems on the trial began. There had still been a surge in the emergency lubricating system when they had switched over at speed, a slight leak on one of the condensers had come to light and, of course, there had been the matter of the involuntary smoke-making which Stoker Petty Officer Lazenby was busy explaining—or rather failing to explain—to the Senior Engineer.

The engine room was hot—the thermometer had gone up to the hundred mark—and there had been more vibration than the experts had expected but, by and large, the Full Power Trial had been a success. HMS *Antigone*'s seventy-two thousand horse-power had been tested and had been passed. Ship's complement and builder's personnel had again worked harmoniously together, and so far as the Engine Room Department was concerned, HMS *Antigone* could be signed for as suitable for service with the Fleet.

The main Gunnery and Torpedo Trials would come later. Here the equipment was largely standard and provided from Admiralty sources. Calibration and testing was not a matter affecting the departure of the ship from Belfast, and since in any case *Antigone* was not the first of her class, no special difficulties or departures from standard practice were visualized. Other equipment such as the catapult for the float-plane, and the various W/T installations were now also in place and in a few days' time HMS *Antigone* would be ready for steaming round to Portsmouth for commissioning.

There was already a crowd round the ship's company notice-board when Able-Seaman Clarke put up details of the Farewell Dance.

'Here, look at this lot,' Able-Seaman Kavanagh sang out, 'the flipping Lord Mayor in his Parlour! Who's told *him* about the *Aunty Gone?*'

Although the lower deck realized that a great honour was being paid to the ship, naval irreverence won the day. If the Lord Mayor of Belfast and the City Fathers could have heard their high offices described outside the regulating office of *Antigone* they might well have cancelled the arrangements.

'Buffet refreshments,' Nobby Clarke murmured, standing aside so that others could read his handiwork, 'and I have it on good authority that still lemonade will be available for the thirsty sailors.'

'What—no beer?' a rather naïve young seaman called out.

'Not for those as hasn't yet been weaned,' Abel-Seaman

Clarke retorted with dignity, 'the beer is reserved for the Commander's Writer—and friends,' he added quietly as the Master-at-Arms put his head out of the regulating office. He was not quite sure he had the measure of the Master-at-Arms, a ferocious, piratical looking man in the best tradition of the Regulating Branch, a man of commanding presence whose awful authority blazed out of black eyes, and whose thick bushy eyebrows seemed to meet in one continuous line across the bridge of his nose. It was an unfortunate moment for him to manifest. Able-Seaman Kavanagh, who was a good seventeen stone, and his friend, Able-Seaman Rillington, of similar girth, were at that moment executing a tango. Kavanagh, Rillington and Clarke were the ship's prize beer drinkers, and together they weighed well over fifty stone. A stoker had whipped out a mouth-organ and was playing an impromptu tune.

'Look,' said Rillington, 'I'm Greta Garbo,' and he tapped Kavanagh on the chest in a mock effeminate fashion. 'And I'm going to dance with this lovely, lovely Lord Mayor and his beautiful corporation, if I die in the task.' Face to face the two men were kept apart by their stomachs, so that each had to dance with arms stretched out in front on to the other's shoulders. The two already had a reputation as ship's clowns.

'You'll be having a lovely, lovely dance on the quarterdeck if you don't watch out,' said the Master-at-Arms. 'You can keep that for the Concert Party. Now stop larking about in the flat.'

Having delivered himself of this stricture and seen it duly observed, he withdrew into the regulating office again to commune with the Regulating Petty Officer, a dry and rather bitter little man. Rillington, Kavanagh and Clarke made faces at each other and went their several ways. They were used to being jumped on and yet it did nothing to repress their high spirits. The stoker, however, pocketed his mouth-organ and said, in tones of the deepest scorn which penetrated the office door: 'Flipping Crusher!' Then like a flash he was through into the messdeck and away before he could be identified or suffer retribution.

The ship's company dance at the City Hall was part of a 'double feature' to speed *Antigone* on her way. The

57

other half was to be a cocktail party given by the Captain and officers on board to return hospitality and take their official leave of Belfast.

'We look like having to do it on the quarterdeck,' said Hatchett as he and the First Lieutenant went over the list of guests together. 'We'll never squeeze them in down below.'

The First Lieutenant, who in a cruiser is usually not a Lieutenant but a Lieutenant-Commander, stood in relation to the Commander much as the latter did to the Captain. Lieutenant-Commander James Collard, Royal Navy, was what was known as a salt horse; that is, he was an executive officer who had never specialized in any one branch of the service, such as Gunnery or Torpedo.

Collard was a large, good-natured officer of thirty-four whose seniority as a Lieutenat-Commander dated from 1933, and who was thus some way through the zone for promotion to Commander. It was quite possible he would never get his brass hat, and time pressed on his ample shoulders even more urgently than it did on Fossingham, the Torpedo Officer.

But Collard showed far fewer signs of strain. He was a placid, contented man who refused to allow his peace of mind to be ruffled by 'promotionitis'. He was married and had two children, he had an unhurried sense of humour and he was immensely liked. In addition to his other duties Trevesham had selected him as 'Snotties' Nurse', the officer in each ship who is appointed to supervise the midshipmen, and who is broadly responsible for their instruction and discipline. He had no trace of the Gunnery Officer's aggressiveness, indeed at first sight he might seem a little heavy and dull, but once his mind was made up he could not be shaken from his purpose, and those who worked with him looked on their First Lieutenant as a tower of strength. At the moment he and the Commander stood on the quarterdeck working out details for the party.

'It means spreading the awning and putting up side curtains,' said the Commander, thinking as always of how much better he could use the hands. 'However, it's good practice for later on.'

'I suggest we put the bar aft round the capstan grating,' said Collard, 'and perhaps Torps could rig up some coloured lights. In view of the shortage of hands and one thing and another, I'd rather the suggestion came from you.'

'If only we had the Band,' said Hatchett, thinking how effective the Royal Marine Band would look puffing and blowing round 'Y' turret. 'However, we haven't, so we shall have to make do with selections from *Floradora* on the radiogram. Torps had better rig that up, too.'

'He won't touch the radiogram,' Collard ventured. 'He reckons that comes under the Communications Department: not his pigeon at all.'

'What?' said Hatchett. 'I never heard such nonsense. Quartermaster!' he called over his shoulder.

'Yes, sir.'

'Ask the Torpedo Officer to come and see me when he's free.'

'Aye, aye, sir.'

'In the meantime,' said Hatchett, 'see if the Pay's got some French chalk available for the deck and find out what kind of eats we can lay on for the guests. Oh! and Number One—better see the police know what's going on: just in case we may be infringing some local bye-law. We should be all right as the Governor and the Prime Minister and the Lord Mayor have all accepted— but you never know. There may be a Sinn Feiner lurking around with a bomb.'

The First Lieutenant saluted and went down the ladder from the quarterdeck to the tiller flat. Hatchett rammed his telescope under his left arm and took a turn up and down the deck. He knew Collard was no teller of tales. He would never have mentioned his troubles with Fossingham if he could have put them right by himself. This 'passing of the buck' was something which had to be nipped firmly in the bud.

'You sent for me, sir?' said Fossingham from behind him.

'Ah! yes, Torps,' said Hatchett, 'it's about this party of ours. We'll be enclosing the quarterdeck with side curtains and screens. Can you manage some coloured lights and radiators?'

'Certainly,' said Fossingham. 'I'll get the Warrant Electrician on to it right away.'

'And we'll need another yardarm group for floodlighting the sentry's beat on the jetty. We don't want the Governor to surprise us out of the dark.'

'Well,' said Fossingham reluctantly, 'we *can* do that, of course, but I've only got Battersby and one other LTO.'

'That's the spirit,' said Hatchett, quite unmoved, 'and we need the radiogram moved up on deck or a spare loud-speaker wired up.'

'Yes, sir. I'll tell Peter Osborne to get on with the job.' Lieutenant Osborne was the ship's Communications Officer and Observer.

'No, Torps, I'd rather you did it yourself.'

'Well, sir,' Fossingham hesitated. He had been out-manoeuvred and was seething inside, 'it's not really my pigeon, but if that's what you want, then of course I'll look after the thing.'

'You're not doing me a favour, Fossingham,' the Com-mander said eyeing him levelly.

'No, of course not, sir.'

'Then don't try to make out that you are. I don't want this matter to crop up again. Is that understood?'

'Yes, sir.'

The Torpedo Officer saluted and walked angrily away. Now why? mused Hatchett, why should he behave like a petulant child? He could understand it over something that mattered but these little storms always blew up on the flimsiest details, over points of difference where emo-tion should never have entered. He walked over to the side of the quarterdeck. Fossingham was the only officer in the ship who sported a large American car—a Cad-illac—and there it was parked on the jetty next to his own ancient Morris-Cowley, as near to the gangway as he dared to put it, a sort of vulgar, unspoken challenge. Fos-singham had been pulled up already for dangerous driv-ing. That was a feat in itself in Northern Ireland where there is no speed limit away from Belfast. The police had not gone on to prosecute, but only because they had given the uniform and the ship the benefit of the doubt. This had been a humiliation to Fossingham, a blow to his pride, and he had bitterly resented being told of these facts by the Superintendent of Police sitting there in the Commander's cabin, trying to tidy up the matter and still do his duty. The Torpedo Officer is going to be something of a problem, thought Hatchett, as he turned away and gave his attention to other things.

In the event both the cocktail party and the ship's company dance were memorable successes. The cocktail party, although loaded down with high officialdom, turned out to be a far more relaxed and gayer affair than the officers of *Antigone* had dared to hope. No doubt the Northern Irish temperament had a lot to do with this loosening-up process. Belfast was proud of the ship and this feeling was continuously expressed by civic and Government officials, and by those who had anything to do with her building or fitting out.

'She's not the first cruiser to be built at Harland and Wolff's,' said one of the shipyard managers, 'and we certainly hope she won't be the last. I speak only for my part of the show, but I say without hesitation she's the best one we've ever done. We'll all follow your career with great interest—that I can assure you. So when you're basking in the Pacific spare a thought for us all back here. It'll probably be raining.'

One of the chief foremen in the engineering shop, a short, bowler-hatted Scot who had at first bluntly opposed every single request, suggestion or change proposed by the Commander (E) or the Senior, and then later on had gone out of his way to meet their wishes, said much the same thing. 'There'll be a dirty great gap in the yard when you've gone and Ah don't mean just another free berth. Ye've caused us all so much extra trouble, we'll be missing you till we go to our graves. Ah'm a Scot, Mr Meldrum, as ye may have guessed, and we're no very sentimental north of the border, but Ah'm telling you there'll be many a sad heart at seeing you lot go. We expect great things of this ship, so don't you go letting us down.'

As the party wore on and a hundred and fifty guests drifted about the quarterdeck, or were shown round the ship by individual officers, Captain Trevesham, too, found himself relaxing. He had been touched by the warm-heartedness of the Ulster folk he had met. Under pretext of getting himself another drink he drew to one side and looked round the scene.

His wife was over by 'Y' turret talking to the Lord Mayor and Mr Kennedy, one of the warrant engineers.

He thought how pretty she still managed to look, now that she had come to accept her grey hair. It had been a wise move to get her over for the last few days of the ship's stay in Belfast. She was a catalyst with new people and strange places. He remembered her father, the old Earl of Kilmoragh, saying to him when they had first got married: 'Diana won't change. She blends other people without them knowing—as her mother did before her—but she'll stay herself completely unaltered. You watch and you'll see.'

That had been a long time ago—it was over seventeen years since they were married, but the old man had been right. She had a way with people. She got them to talk, opening up their reserve without seeming to lose any of her own essence. She was elegant and mature without being in the slightest degree patronizing, and he was grateful for her presence now in the ship.

This was not exactly the way Mrs Hatchett looked on the Captain's wife. But then madame was jealous, and did not always realize how deep-rooted the feeling went. It didn't seem fair somehow to her. She had nothing against the Treveshams—indeed that was part of the trouble—but they seemed to have so much and she and Stubby so very little. When she thought about it at all, she had to admit that what she really meant was that the Treveshams had private means—a settled home and a family, whereas they had none of these things. In moments of tranquillity madame knew she did herself an injustice to let such thoughts possess her. She resolved to put them out of her mind, to accept her life as it was and indeed to be grateful for the success and position which had come her way. But these inner resolutions were too weak to last very long. She was driven by life and another day brought another mood.

It seemed to madame that she had always been the poor relation at the feast—the waif in the snow gazing in through the window at someone else's brightly lit room. Madame's father had been an impoverished quartermaster in the Indian Army. Without private means in an age when this could determine one's status in life, the threadbare struggle to keep up appearances, to grab a rich husband, merely, indeed, to survive, had stamped out the main features of her personality beyond hope of change. How different her own girlhood had been, she felt, from that of the elegant Lady Diana.

Over on the other side of the quarterdeck stood the Meldrums, attended as usual by Augustus Spratt. In the early stages of a party they wrestled with strangers, guests and other shipmates, but in the end they always gravitated to each other.

'Ye Gods,' said Spratt, running a finger round the inside of his collar. 'I've just had half an hour of the Bullock Major. I need an extra strong drink. I had to send him away to water his horses.'

There are various nicknames for the Royal Marines, such as boot-necks, leather-necks, and Jollies, but Captain Taw-Street, RM, was already known by the most common of them all. Meldrum went off in search of more drinks, and Susan smiled at her honorary lover.

'Cheer up!' she said, 'it's only for two-and-a-half years.'

'I know—and the worst of it is I won't have you to come home to at the end of it all. You're looking especially luscious tonight.'

'Thank you, Aggie, you're looking beautiful, too.'

'If I were to push Meldrum overboard one night into a shark-infested sea would you consider an offer?'

'Oh! no,' said Susan, 'I don't think I could ever live with a dwarf.'

The trouble was that behind the banter she knew he was in love with her, and while it flattered her it also disturbed her. She was very fond of her husband, but at times he was terribly stodgy and dull. They had been married five years and had a daughter of two.

'Besides,' she went on, 'I don't see you supporting a family—and that's what I want.'

'It isn't all you want, and you know it.'

'Now, stop it, you two,' said Meldrum, coming up from behind. 'I turn my back for five minutes and there's a cuckoo in the nest. Why don't you get a wife of your own, you horrid little man?'

It never got much further than that. Perhaps it was a pity, and perhaps it was just as well, thought Susan. She knew that the moment *Antigone* sailed she would think of no one else but her husband—that was the extraordinary, infuriating paradox. She was never more loyal than

63

when John was miles away on the other side of the world. It was when she had him to herself all the time, when they were like any normally married civilian couple, that her thoughts began to stray and someone amusing and attractive like the Navigating Officer would trouble her peace of mind.

Derek Lysander Marsh stood further aft talking to the First Lieutenant's wife. He felt lonely and bored. Mrs Collard, like her husband, was large and placid. She struggled hard to shine at these affairs, but she did not enjoy them very much. If her conversation produced a glow, it was a dull one. She was a good wife and a good mother. Indeed, Marsh could not help but notice as she sat on the capstan cover that she would shortly be a mother again. But she reminded him of a comfortable cottage wife, fresh from her oven, and as they had nothing in common at all their joint effort to communicate soon ran down into a kind of ineffective muteness. This was the more painful to Marsh since he sensed that behind it all Mrs Collard understood exactly how he felt and was trying to help him.

'When you're round at Portsmouth,' she was saying, 'you must come out and spend a day with us at Liphook.'

'Thank you very much. I'd love to.'

'Jimmy could bring you out after Divisions on a Sunday,' she went on. 'I expect we shall be having the midshipmen, too.'

Almost unconsciously Marsh looked down at the single resplendent stripe on his sleeve. Mrs Collard caught the look and the expression. She realized too late that he was still unsure of being a Sub-Lieutenant and that by lumping him in with the midshipmen she had hurt his feelings.

'If it isn't infra-dig, that is,' she floundered on, 'to ask you along at the same time.'

'Of course not,' Marsh said, a little too quickly. 'After all, we're all messing together.'

'I expect you'll be glad when they join. It'll be cosier, won't it?'

'Cosier? Yes, that's certainly one description of gunroom life.' Then, thinking that that sounded sarcastic he hastened to add: 'I mean—we'll be living so much on top of one another, we'll probably be biting our heads

64

off in a few months' time. Of course, it's worse for the mids. They haven't even got cabins.'

Marsh was prouder of his cabin than of anything else. It was only a few months, since he, too, had been slinging a hammock. Now, even though he had to share the cabin with another Sub-Lieutenant, the luxury of a bed, a wash-basin and a desk of his own was still a giddy pleasure, and one which would take a long time to pall.

'Would you like to see the gunroom?' he asked suddenly, 'and I could show you our cabin as well.'

'I'd love to,' said Mrs Collard, getting heavily to her feet and setting off for the ladder. He was quite a nice boy underneath, she decided, in spite of his shyness. She had the sudden absurd feeling that he was far too young to be up for a party like this. Someone should have bathed him, tucked him up in bed, read him a story and then drawn the nursery curtains. As she clambered laboriously step by step down the ladder she smiled to herself and thought about her own two boys now at home and asleep. Perhaps one day they, too, would be showing their First Lieutenant's wife over a gunroom in some other brand new ship.

Back on the quarterdeck near to the bar a Cad's Corner had been established. This consisted of two young watch-keeping lieutenants who each had charge of a seaman division of the ship, the Observer Officer and the pilot of *Antigone*'s aircraft. None of these officers was married and their average age ran out at twenty-five.

They were a rorty lot, brought up in the Dartmouth tradition of working hard and playing harder. No inferiority complexes showed upon their unfurrowed foreheads. They were bursting with life. Quick-witted, possessing great drive and somewhat inclined to arrogance—it was from their ranks that the future Admirals of the Fleet would be drawn. Lusty, apt to drink more than they should, and to break up the mess on guest nights in a juvenile fashion, yet never missing a watch or a duty however desperate the hang-over might be—these four and the other young bachelors of the ship would give *Antigone*'s wardroom its active character.

They were the positive energy in the ship, and whether commanding a six-inch gun turret, a seaman's landing party, a boat's crew or a watch on the bridge at sea, they could be completely relied on. They had been trained to be alert and on their toes. If sometimes they seemed aggressive, their thrust was essential to the ship. The Surgeon-Commander might occasionally be found snoozing in the anteroom after lunch, but Lieutenants Cravenby and Crawford, Osborne and Grey-Bennett would be up and about—subject to the hierarchy of command, but running their own part of the ship in their own highly individual fashions.

'Have you seen the little number with the fringe?' Cravenby asked the others as they got themselves drinks. 'Watch out for her. Father's a parson and life at the vicarage is very, very dull. She wants to be written to, when we're abroad.'

'We saw you slipping away with her, "unnoticed",' said Osborne. 'Bad luck!'

'I was showing her the ship, what there is of it up my end.'

Cravenby was in charge of the Foc'sle Division. Apart from the chains and anchors and his turret he was somewhat at a disadvantage when it came to displaying his part of the ship to visitors. It was a windy business taking a girl up on the foc'sle, and there were none of those nooks and crannies round the bridge to which Crawford, who was in charge of the Top Division had access. The foc'sle and the upper deck for'ard were ship's company preserves. They were not to have their privacy invaded. Moreover, you never knew when a half-clad, hairy stoker mightn't poke his head up through a hatch and express a highly flavoured remark.

'I was chased by a widow from Londonderry with a feathered hat and a moustache,' said Crawford morosely. 'Roll on, South America, I say. I can't wait to get in among the señoritas—and all that.'

'Well,' said Grey-Bennett, 'while you children were desporting yourselves *I* was making up to the Torpedo Officer's wife.'

'You're welcome.'

'She's a very attractive woman.'

'I dare say, but she married Fossingham. There must be something wrong with any girl who does that.'

'Oh! Annabel's all right,' said Grey-Bennet in the

manner of a connoisseur pronouncing on a wine. 'She just needs understanding, that's all.'

There was a sudden horse laugh from the others which made them all look round guiltily to see if they had been overheard or observed. Grey-Bennett, who upheld the traditions of the Fleet Air Army by wearing his hair rather long and the top right button of his monkey jacket undone, felt called on to explain a little further.

'Of course I had all that build-up about Boston,' he went on, 'but you chaps never look ahead. Now—as a result of tonight—*I* am all set for Bermuda. Annabel used to winter there year after year.'

'Fancy that!' said Cravenby.

'Got all the names and addresses,' Grey-Bennett went on, patting his pocket book. '*You* want the best popsies, *I* have them. And don't forget I shall usually be flying ahead of the ship to pick up the mail and—er—make local arrangements.'

'Why is the Fleet Air Arm always so fond of itself?' Crawford said sourly. 'I think *Antigone*'s going to get pretty tired of you and your arrangements.'

'Well,' said Grey-Bennett with a smile at Osborne, 'it's rather like asking why a Rolls-Royce is better than a hansom-cab. Just keep on the right side of the Flying Department and you'll find out the reason.'

By this time the guests had almost all gone ashore, and the marines were dismantling the bar. The Commander once more had his telescope in his hand 'like a conductor with an outsize baton' as Spratt had observed. Now he came briskly across the quarterdeck to where they were standing.

'Which of you bright boys is coming to the ship's company dance?' said Hatchett, 'and who wants a lift in my car?'

Down at the City Hall the ship's company dance was a somewhat more noisy success. After the initial formalities had been disposed of, the bar was thrown open and *Antigone*'s sailors, their wives and their girl friends began limbering up. Sailors are by nature good mixers. This, combined with a Northern Irish readiness to enjoy the passing moment without inhibitions, resulted in a warmth, a spontaneity and a friendliness they were long to remember.

Though the officers and their wives had been invited, this was primarily a bluejacket's party. The British seaman is adept at creating his own entertainment whatever the conditions. The resources of the City Hall were at their disposal. A generous flow of refreshment had been laid on and the ship's company of *Antigone* soon took charge of the proceedings.

With the full consent and support of their hosts, they invaded the band's rostrum and put on an impromptu show of their own. Able-Seaman Elcock crooned 'like Bing Crosby but sadder' as the Chief Quartermaster put it; Stoker Kelly provided a mouth-organ solo and Able-Seaman Rillington, an old concert party hand, turned in a humorous monologue from his repertoire. But the star turn of all was only discovered after the officers had arrived.

The Chief and Petty Officers had one corner of the bar to themselves and there was considerable competition in enticing the officers over to drink with them. During one of these forays the Chief Gunner's Mate found out that Mr Legg, the Gunner, was an expert at cutlass swinging and that he had a set of cutlasses to hand on board *Antigone*. Without further ado the Gunnery Officer was prevailed on to drive Mr Legg back to the ship for his equipment. An hour later under a spotlight quickly rigged up in the hall, a display of this ancient and spectacular art was put on to vast applause.

'And if nothing else comes out of tonight,' said Hatchett to the First Lieutenant, 'we do at least know we've got the makings of a first-class concert play in *Antigone*. Now who's going to get that organized for me?'

'We want a volunteer,' said Collard, 'and preferably one with experience. I think the CSKO is our man. I overheard him saying the other day he'd actually met Gracie Fields.'

The Central Storekeeping Officer, Paymaster-Lieutenant Hale, was already editing the ship's magazine. He was to date HMS *Antigone*'s only connection with the arts.

'Right,' said Hatchett decisively. 'Tell Hale he'd better volunteer to organize the Concert Party or I'll have his reasons in writing through the Paymaster-Commander.'

'That shall be done,' said Collard, and so in due course the Concert Party came into being.

Before the party ended farewell speeches were made, both by the Lord Mayor and by the Captain of *Antigone*. To Trevesham these were always unnecessary frills on the top of a full evening, but tonight there was a nostalgia in the air. The next day HMS *Antigone* would sail. Her active service life would have begun. It was unlikely she would visit Belfast again since even a major refit would probably be carried out in one of the Royal Dockyards. Or so it seemed at the end of April 1938.

'I don't want to get sentimental,' the Lord Mayor said, 'but on behalf of the City—and indeed I'm sure I can say the six loyal counties as well—I want to wish you all Godspeed and a happy commission. Soon, perhaps, you'll have forgotten us here in Belfast. You'll be about the world and the King's business and we shall be at work on your sister ships of the Fleet.' He paused and looked round at his blue-uniformed audience. He had intended to make one of his usual formal speeches, appropriate to such an occasion but now he suddenly said what was in his mind. 'I don't know whether it's the stars or what it is that make some ships more popular than others—but at all events when HMS *Antigone* sails tomorrow we shall all of us feel as though a favourite daughter is leaving her home to get married. We shall be glad and yet sad. However, these things happen, so good luck to you all and may your first commission be served in a peaceful world.'

He stood down to terrific applause, though in some quarters of the hall the response was ironic.

'They'll have me crying me eyes out yet,' said Able-Seaman Kavanagh. 'Poetic—that's what it is!'

Able-Seaman Kavanagh, Rillington and Clarke were strategically placed for the buffet in general and tactically placed for the beer supply in particular. They had hardly budged the whole evening except when Rillington was doing his monologue.

'Any tears out of you,' said Nobby Clarke, 'are likely to consist of Irish wallop at this stage of the evening. However, I get your intent.'

'No,' said Kavanagh, 'it's poetic—that's what it is. The poor old *Aunty Gone* getting married at last. And who's the bridegroom? Who's the lucky boy?' He leant forward conspiratorially: 'US'—he hissed, 'that's who it is—US!'

'If the Three Fat Men of the Sea will let me get a word in . . .' Captain Trevesham began from the platform with a look toward Kavanagh, Rillington and Clarke. A shout of approval from the ship's company greeted this opening remark, and Trevesham had to pause while their messmates took advantage of the confusion.

'. . . I'd like to assure the Lord Mayor that we're not likely to forget Belfast nor the great kindness and generosity of her people. And I can further assure him that these feelings are very far from being mere sentimentality. I don't know when or where one of HM ships has ever had such a send-off as Belfast has given *Antigone*, but we shall do our best to live up to it. On behalf of us all—thank you, sir, thank you, Belfast, and thank you— Ulster. I think we can best express our feelings at this time by giving three rousing cheers to the Lord Mayor and Corporation.'

He nodded to the Commander, who stepped forward and called out:

'Three cheers for the Lord Mayor, Belfast and Ulster. Hip, hip, hip . . .'

The hoorays which followed nearly raised the roof, and thus HMS *Antigone* took her official farewell of the great ugly city in which she had been built. The next day at 1130 on a dark squally morning the Navy's newest cruiser sailed for Portsmouth to commission and begin her service with the Fleet.

It took her about thirty hours to steam round to Portsmouth through the Irish Sea, past Anglesea and the Isle of Man, Fishguard, and Land's End, Plymouth, the Isle of Wight and Spithead. She made the journey at her economical speed and Marsh found his cabin habitable though noisy. For most of the voyage the sea was choppy and there was a beam wind from the west. This caused *Antigone* to roll, and once in the Atlantic beyond the shelter of Ireland she took on quite a considerable movement. This meant that he had keep his scuttle closed.

It was a matter of private despair to Marsh that even in the battleship *Nelson* he had been seasick for the first

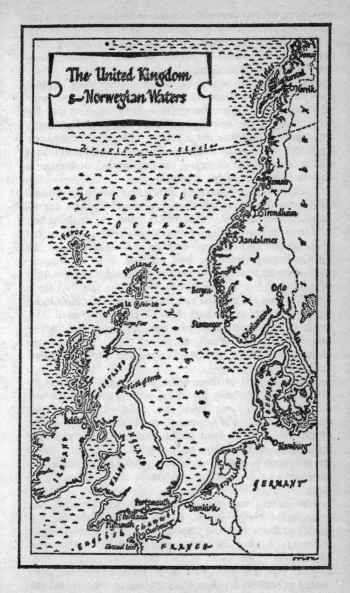

The United Kingdom
& Norwegian Waters

Arctic circle

Tromsö
Lofoten Isles
Narvik

Atlantic Ocean

Faroe I.

Namsos

Trondheim

Aandalsnes

Shetland Is.

Orkney Is.   Fair Isle
Scapa Flow   Bergen   Oslo

Hebrides   Stavanger   Kristiansand

SCOTLAND

Firth of Forth

NORTH SEA

Belfast

IRELAND   ENGLAND

WALES

DENMARK

Hamburg

Portsmouth   Dunkirk

Portland   Zuyder Zee   GERMANY

Plymouth   CHANNEL   Cherbourg

ENGLISH   Channel Isles   FRANCE

orion

71

two days of any voyage. *Antigone* looked like causing him the same anxiety and trouble. Most annoying of all it was not an immediate collapse, quickly started and quickly over: instead it played on him a whole repertoire of tricks and illusions.

He was usually all right on the upper deck within easy reach of the leeward guardrail. But a passage even of thirty hours cannot be made entirely on deck. So he went down to the heaving anteroom and played at reading a paper. This was not a success. The print dizzied his eyes and the regular straining noises as fittings and furniture took up the changing stresses seemed to foment a nausea in the pit of his stomach.

Then followed a macabre little game which he played with himself and usually lost. He would pretend not to notice. Feverishly he would cast around in his mind for problems to solve, things to work out, even poems to repeat. On one occasion in *Nelson* he had fallen back on the Lord's Prayer which he had gabbled away to himself with ever increasing momentum until on the twentieth repetition of 'Lead us not into temptation' he had been forced to make a hurried exit for the heads. Once sick, he would feel an astonishing health. His brain would be keen, and his eye clear. He was, for some five to ten minutes, once more master of his fate. Then, to his chagrin and fury, the whole damned process started again.

After the third of these bouts Marsh gave up, went to his cabin and morosely lay down, cursing his fate. He was never sick when lying down and, when all was said and done, he supposed *Antigone* to be a great improvement on *Nelson*. Here at least he had his own bunk and half his own cabin. In *Nelson* he had been forced to lie about the gunroom in a state of misery until his hammock had been slung in the evening and escape could be sought in sleep.

Sea sickness was not looked on as any form of disgrace in the Navy—indeed it had been of slight comfort to him to know that the Captain of *Nelson* himself was a martyr to it—but in every mess there is at least one hearty extroverted joker, a 'jolly lump' as Marsh put it to himself, who got some kind of perverse amusement from talking of onions fried in thick grease or who would ostentatiously consume helping after helping of fat, dripping bacon. At least he could now hide in his cabin and get away from that kind of thing.

But the tiller flat in *Antigone* on to which his cabin gave was a noisy place at sea. Outside his cabin was a ventilating fan which ran with a high pitched whine. Then just forward of the watertight door was the main servo-steering motor which faithfully started up and stopped as each tiny correction to the ship's course was made in the conning tower and which was rarely still for more than a few seconds at a time as the ship yawed in a beam sea. Moreover, below his cabin was a storeroom and in it was something that sounded like a tin can or metal marble which clattered and rolled in accordance with the motion of the ship.

The ship herself, to those whose business it was to judge, behaved well at sea. She was comparatively stable and to Trevesham and Spratt she had a comfortable, easy feel. These two were perpetual inhabitants of the bridge superstructure while the ship was at sea. The Navigating Officer's permanent cabin was there and next to it was the Captain's sea cabin. The bridge block itself was some way for'ard from the rest of the officers' accommodation and in harbour Spratt felt occasionally like an outpost of Empire. Indeed, in the early days a wardroom wag had once asked if he wanted an escort to see him home after leaving the mess. At sea, however, the bridge block became a kind of Piccadilly Circus, and those officers whose cabins were in the wardroom flat felt as though they were suddenly living in the suburbs.

The passage round to Portsmouth was not used as an opportunity for any other practices or manoeuvres. The ship was still only partially manned, and although the Gunnery Officer was itching to exercise his gun's crews and the director control, even he was forced to admit that the procedure was pointless if the various instruments could not be manned.

'Though I wouldn't put it past him,' Spratt muttered darkly to Crawford, who was Officer of the Watch, 'to press gang a crew of cooks, writers and sick berth attendants so that he can have his little game.'

Instead, Brasson fell into the habit of coming up to the

bridge to smoke a pipe and 'find out whether the ship was lost'. The Captain's wishes about passengers on the bridge having been put about, he was careful only to do this either when Trevesham was resting in his sea cabin or when he had some specific question to ask of the Captain and thus had an excuse to be up on the bridge. The Navigating Officer, however, was convinced he only did so in order to annoy the watchkeeping personnel and because of the 'exasperating Whale Island habit of minding other people's business for them'.

But these minor irritations did little to mar the private satisfaction which Spratt always enjoyed of taking a ship from A to B, exactly as planned and almost at the minute. Except for the sub-lieutenant who was joining at Portsmouth all the watchkeeping officers had a chance of getting the feel of the ship. Below in the conning tower the Chief Quartermaster, too, had an opportunity of testing the ability of his helmsmen in keeping the ship on her course.

The Commander spent the time at sea in putting the finishing touches to his Watch and Station Bill. This intricate document is the key to a warship's organization, and by this time Hatchett could have drawn it up in his sleep. Three days from now they would be commissioning. Hundreds of ratings, together with their bags and hammocks, would be marched down from the Royal Naval Barracks to join the ship. Each of these ratings would have a basic job to do and several variants depending on whether the ship was at sea or in harbour, at peace or at war. Each rating would be given a commissioning card on joining the ship. This card would show his number on the Watch Bill, his mess, his part of the ship, the number of his kit locker and other details, such as any special duty for which he was being drafted. In conjunction with this the Quarter Bill had been worked out by the Gunnery and Torpedo Officers to cover the employment of the ship's company at 'Action Stations'.

The test of efficiency in this manoeuvre was not to be rigid but flexible. Whatever the ship might be required to do, the situation had, where possible, to be thought out beforehand so that the right number and quality of trained men would be available where they should be at the time they were required. But if the situation could not be foreseen, the men had to be there just the same. The skeleton must be capable of bearing the weight. To dispose of some six hundred fighting men so that guns and torpedoes could be fired, anchors weighed, boats hoisted out and manned, meals cooked and eaten, ship kept clean and ship's company healthy day in and day out in any part of the world was no small matter.

This blending of skills and duties, this balance of work and play, had been arrived at step by step over the years. It was as integrated and interdependent as a watch. Yet it had to allow for all sorts of extraneous and sudden requirements. One day they might be painting the ship, the next landing a detachment of men to guard an oil refinery; one day they might be striking down stores and provisions, the next cleaning up the mess in the wake of a hurricane—there had to be men for all sorts of jobs, often at no notice at all. A cruiser was the most versatile ship the Navy possessed. *Antigone* had a lot to live up to and Hatchett appreciated this keenly now that their commissioning lay only a few hours ahead.

This feeling of an approaching First Night was shared to the full by the Master-at-Arms. He and the Regulating Petty Officer had been fully occupied for the last few days in making out the Commissioning Cards under the supervision of the Commander. But for the Jaunty there was a refinement. He knew by name and repute a number of the ratings who would be joining the ship. He had not been fourteen years in the Regulating Branch for nothing. Looking down the lists he knew who was good and who was a skate.

Even before the main draft notes had arrived—which are the nominal lists of the ratings drafted to a ship by the depot—even before the Master-at-Arms had joined *Antigone* himself he knew a number of the men who would make up the character of her ship's company.

He knew the Three Fat Men of the Sea, for instance, and he knew that Leading-Seaman Battersby was a candidate for commissioned rank. He knew that Stoker First Class Danny Evans, P/KX.812356, would be likely to celebrate his draft by going on the beer for a week in Tonypandy and then spending the next three months in the Second Class for Leave. He knew that Blacksmith First Class Rogers would try and smuggle service provisions ashore for his mother and that Telegraphist Jacobs was a sea lawyer who kept a copy of Karl Marx in his kit-bag. Master-at-Arms Kirby might not be omniscient but as things went in *Antigone* he came pretty near to it.

Of everyone then aboard the keenest anticipation was probably to be found among the chief and petty officers. Unlike the officers, the majority had not brought their wives across to Belfast. They had homes established in Portsmouth and growing children who went to day schools. Certainly they were paid about double to three times the pay of an able-seaman, but they had a higher standard of life to keep up, more costly uniform to maintain and greater standing expenses all round.

An able-seaman has little option over his life. He must take it much as it comes—the rough with the smooth—and he must like it or lump it according to his temperament. A chief petty officer could save a little money for other things—to buy his own house or to send his son to a grammar school, or even to save up for a business of his own when his Naval time should have expired. He could do those and other little things, or he could live a good deal better himself. The frugal existence of most chief and petty officers in *Antigone* showed clearly where their money went and their eagerness to get home to wives and children was intense.

The Captain and the Commander were both aware of this feeling. They appreciated how important the petty officers were to the life of the ship. They knew that if that body of men felt contented *Antigone* could scarcely fail. They had learnt out of long experience that back in a Home Port life must be made as easy and reasonable for them as ingenuity could devise. Hatchett was delighted, therefore, when the Captain sent for him some two hours before reaching Spithead and after consulting him said he would address the Chief and Petty Officers. Hatchett had it piped round the ship and a few minutes later the Captain came down from the bridge and aft to the quarterdeck.

'I've got you together before we reach Portsmouth,' said Trevesham, 'because I want you to know my ideas and the policy over the next few weeks. Commissioning a new ship is a tricky business. We have all the hard work of storing, trials and the working-up period ahead.

76

A severe strain is bound to fall on the chief and petty officers during these first critical months. Both the Commander and I appreciate that fact. He and I have a great admiration for the way you behaved in Belfast. We've come so far, but we've still a long way to go. You're all experienced men and I needn't go over the snags we'll come up against. Some concern the ship as a whole: some only your own departments—but there they are waiting for us in the future. When they appear we must tackle them with energy and be confident of success.' He looked round the cluster of lined, understanding faces. 'We *can* do, all of us, and we shall.' He smiled briefly at the murmur of support they gave him. 'We get into Pompey in two hours time, and when next we set off in approximately a month we shall be a fully-manned warship, with all that that means. During this time it is my wish and intention that the maximum leave consistent with the regulations be given. As soon as the work is done, I want no unnecessary hanging around on board. Our wives and children see little enough of us as it is. With the possibility of trouble ahead, they're likely to have even less of us than before. So take this opportunity —all of you—and make the most of it you can.'

The Home Fleet had sailed for its summer cruise and Portsmouth was comparatively empty when HMS *Antigone* sailed up-harbour. The Commander-in-Chief had allocated them the flagship berth at South Railway Jetty and she slipped alongside with the deft assurance of a ship long in commission. It was a satisfactory arrival. Critical eyes watched the manoeuvre and critical, autocratic eyes would from now on be fixed on everything *Antigone* did until she left the Portsmouth Command for her foreign station.

Portsmouth was not Belfast. This obvious fact concealed other meanings behind it. *Antigone* was out of the cradle, and if her nursery days were not yet at an end, the ship was now within an exclusively naval domain. From now on the atmosphere would be a service one. There would be more doubling around, the pace would be brisker, details such as the dress and bearing of libertymen going ashore would be under intensive scrutiny. The free-and-easy discipline of a ship in the builders' hands, plain clothes and office hours—all these lay behind them in the past.

'Any tendency to lounge about on the upper deck when not actually working,' the Commander wrote as a footnote to the Daily Orders, 'will cease forthwith. Attention is drawn to the regulations in force about smoking. This is to be confined exclusively to standeasies and the dog watches, when spitkids will be placed *and used*. Men will not appear on the upper deck out of the rig of the day whatever the excuse or convenience.'

'*Antigone* did not appear to respect my flag when passing yesterday,' signalled the Commander-in-Chief a few days later. 'I noticed men continuing to move about after the "Still" had been sounded.'

These and other pinpricks were a necessary part of the shaping process. 'Flipping merry hell,' said the sailors, and 'Here we go again,' said the officers as, day by day, new lapses or failures were picked up and acidly remarked on. Excuses were neither called for nor accepted. The regulations laid down clearly what was to be done. They had to suit themselves to the regulations and, where these left off, service custom began. It was for *Antigone* to conform as quickly as possible. Any petulance, any slightest questioning of authority and a 'can' or 'bottle' of enormous proportions would be handed out by the sharp-eyed, sharp-tongued Staff or by the Commander-in-Chief himself.

If this seemed, at first, a sorry process, it behoved them to remember that one of the Commander-in-Chief's duties was to ensure that new ships were not brought into service before they were in all and every respect ready for the tasks they would have to complete and the responsibilities they would have to bear.

Thus the day of commissioning came and went. This was a day of grace. HMS *Antigone* was left entirely to herself. No one made rude signals to the ship and no one expected her to be other than she was—completely absorbed in the domestic business of receiving her ship's company aboard and coping with the headaches and trouble of a sort of human furniture removal.

Draft after draft marched down from the Depot and were disposed about the ship. Those who had stood by the ship were now 'old hands' and found themselves in

78

the position of London policemen during the tourist season. 'Which is the way to the heads, mate?' 'Where's the regulating office?' 'Call *this* a mess?—Cor!' 'What's the name of the First Lieutenant?' 'How do you spell *Aunty Gone?*' 'When's the canteen open?' 'Ere! 'ow can I get a draft away from this lot?' The same round of questions and comments could be heard time and time again, all over the ship. The sailors had arrived. HMS *Antigone* was alive.

CHAPTER FOUR

Once commissioned, *Antigone* worked the normal daily routine of a cruiser. Details would vary with climate and station, but the framework of a naval day remained essentially the same. Hands fell in at 0600 and the first immediate task was to clean the ship. Barefooted sailors hosed down the deck and other sailors followed on with squeegees and mops. This took about fifty minutes to an hour, by which time libertymen who had been granted all night leave—the 'watch ashore'—had mostly returned to the ship.

Then 'Quarters Clean Guns' was piped. Out came the tins of metal polish and the cotton waste. In another half-hour the paintwork of the superstructure and all the separate bits of brightwork which catch the light and contribute, like individual diamonds in a bracelet, to the general sparkle of a ship were cleaned and polished. In peacetime when in harbour the mouths of the six-inch guns were covered with brass tampions on which were embossed the ship's crest. The Gunnery Officer was for having these chromium plated—even if need be at his own expense—in order that *Antigone* should be the last word in up-to-date smartness. But this did not appeal to Hatchett. He preferred the traditionally richer look of polished brass, just as he preferred the warmth of gold to the coldness of platinum.

'There's a tinny look about chromium,' he said, 'which may just be all right for the fittings of a picket boat, but definitely isn't good enough for *Antigone*.'

This was one of the first questions Hatchett asked when dealing with almost any problem nowadays. 'Is it good enough for *Antigone?*' It was a point of view he wished all officers to acquire, and they were not slow in following his lead. Things might be all right for the flagship of the Home Fleet, it did not necessarily follow that they were good enough for *Antigone*. This attitude might smack of arrogance, but it helped to build up the fighting spirit of the ship.

The hands went to breakfast at 0730, and from then until 'Divisions' at 0900 were occupied in scrubbing out and cleaning themselves and their own messes. *Antigone* was fitted as a general mess ship: that is to say the catering for the entire ship's company was done by the Paymaster-Commander. In the old days each mess had chosen its own menu, drawn its own provisions and the cooks of the mess—two men told-off daily by the leading hand in charge—would prepare the food and take it along to the galley for cooking.

Nowadays this was all done by the galley staff and a general mess party of six seamen under a captain of the hold. The system was more efficient but impersonal. The standard of catering was higher but individual choice had disappeared. Both old and new systems had their protagonists but in 1938 general messing had come to stay and the system was even being extended to the three officers' messes, where it was accorded a much more hostile reception.

At 0800 Colours were hoisted. For this ceremony the Royal Marine Band paraded on the quarterdeck, and ten minutes before the White Ensign was hoisted the air was sweetened or made hideous according to individual opinion by *Heart of Oak* and other specialities of the Royal Marine Band as they marched and countermarched to the crashing of cymbals and the thunder of boots. As the White Ensign was slowly run up its staff on the stern everyone on the upper deck stood to attention, officers turning aft and saluting.

The gunroom and Marsh's cabin, which he now shared

with the Sub-Lieutenant, were both immediately below the quarterdeck.

'It's like living underneath a tribal compound,' the Sub remarked one day as they were shaving and good solid Marine boots stumped about overhead. The Sub was a dapper young man called Darbigh, who put up with Marsh—a mere 'pusser'—with slight executive disdain. He was a taut, sharp-tongued disciplinarian, very much king of his little castle. Now that the midshipmen, too, had joined he made it abundantly clear that he was standing no nonsense from them.

Although Marsh was paymaster sub-lieutenant and there was also a sub-lieutenant (E) in the gunroom, Darbigh's outlook was brief and to the point. 'There's only one Sub of the mess,' he said, 'and that's me.' Whatever this lacked in finesse it made up in force. The young gentlemen of the gunroom were not going to 'sit around on their backsides doing sweet Fanny Adams'—not with Sub-Lieutenant Darbigh up and about.

If the Master-at-Arms was the terror of the lower deck, Sub-Lieutenant Darbigh was the scourge of the gunroom. Watching his manner and his methods, the First Lieutenant wondered if perhaps he was going to be too much of a good thing. From Hatchett's point of view, however, he was ideal. He did not anticipate any trouble from the midshipmen at all.

Divisions held on the upper deck at 0900 was the one big parade of the day. No one except watchkeepers and daymen—and not all of them—were excused Divisions. For one reason or another 'Evening Quarters'—its equivalent at 1600—was not such an impressive affair. At nine o'clock in the morning, however, every warship in harbour could be seen emptying itself of its human content on to upper deck and foc'sle. Then the long serried lines of bluejackets would be inspected. Divisions would be reported to the Commander and Captain. They would close aft for Prayers on the quarterdeck, and then afterwards the particular day's work would be got under way.

Special parties would be told off, divisional drills and training classes, storing ship, or whatever was to be *Antigone*'s main concern for the day would be started. Sometimes the ship would appear to be wholly concentrated on one job of work—such as painting the ship's side. At other times half a dozen different drills and occupations would be going on at once. Work on the ship's aircraft and catapult, the searchlights, the ship's boats, the four-inch high-angle and pom-pom guns, the torpedo tubes which in *Antigone* were on the upper deck in the waist, and upon anchors and cables on the foc'sle might all be in progress while, at the same time, important visitors were being received with the appropriate respect and ceremony on the quarterdeck.

All these different activities might seem to be receiving attention and to be proceeding independently of each other—yet behind them all there was a connecting skeleton. To the able-seaman holystoning the teak decks in the grey morning light, naval routine may well have seemed ant-like and soulless. To the Commander stuck at his desk like an angry bull and doing his best to produce some sort of rabbit for everyone out of a very small hat —to him and to his faithful Nobby Clarke, manipulation of the daily routine was a test of intelligence.

Hands went to dinner—the main meal of the day—at noon. At about this time, too, wardroom officers would be collecting in the anteroom in twos and threes. Pink Plymouth Gin, Gimlets or glasses of beer would be signed for on buff chits and served by the wine steward or one of the white-coated Marine mess attendants. The day's successes and failures would be kicked around in a reasonably lighthearted fashion. Visitors from other ships in harbour or dockyard officials might be there, together with some of the warrant officers or sub-lieutenants.

'Forenoon drinking', which has a notorious ring about it in certain ships, in most cases served an invaluable purpose. Problems were hashed out and knotty points settled amicably and without endless paper work. Requests were made of the Commander for hands and working-parties and already a bazaar technique was being arrived at by those officers such as the Central Storekeeping Officer who had to handle large quantities of stores without undue delay.

On most mornings the CSKO would come scowling into the Mess and demand a large gin 'to stave off imminent collapse'. He usually timed his entry to follow that of the Commander who would be sitting on the leather-padded fire-guard, his back belligerently to the fire, his telescope for no reason at all still stuck under his left arm. The CSKO would be brought his drink and would then look at Hatchett, sizing up his approach. But Hatchett always got his word in first.

'Sorry, CSKO, it can't be done.'

'Oh! very well, sir, we'll just leave the perishables on the jetty,' the CSKO would retort. 'I haven't signed for them yet. They can weather off in the rain. Who cares about a few thousand pounds?'

'How many extra hands do you want this time?'

'I could make do with a dozen or fourteen.'

'You can have a leading-hand and two from the Foc'sle Division—and that's the lot.'

'Look—at a pinch ten able-bodied sailors would do. Or stokers?' he added, turning to the Senior Engineer. But Meldrum never let himself be caught that way.

'Sorry, old man,' he said, 'all my gash hands have been swiped by the Commander.'

'You can have Able-Seaman Pottlesham as well,' Hatchett grudgingly conceded.

'Is that the King's Hard Bargain with lumbago? I'd rather manage without. He's the one who dropped a jar of rum the other day on a steel deck. A rather well-meaning accident, I thought, which didn't come off.'

'I don't know how we're ever going to get this ship to sea,' the Commander complained. 'All the ship's company have been trained to do so far is strike down stores.'

'A little bird tells me,' Hale said softly, 'that two hands from each of the three seamen divisions would never be missed, and the Captain, Royal Marines'—as he said this he leapt to his feet with a tremendous clatter in imitation of Taw-Street—'has promised me two of his best Joeys. I can just get by with eight hands tomorrow if the crane doesn't let us down.'

'Very well,' said Hatchett, 'put a chit into the office. One of these days I'll shoot my writer for his little birdsongs behind my back.'

Once Hatchett said 'Put a chit into the office' the matter was agreed and closed. Hale knew he would get his hands and Hatchett knew that they would not be wasted. Behind this could always be seen the bland spherical features of Able-Seaman Clarke whose 'little birdsong' would have been carefully worked out on available resources with an eye to the sick list, the short leave list and daily defaulters, and the news of which would have reached the CSKO and the Paymaster-Commander by way of the supply chief petty officers and occasionally through the ship's office. If the game seemed needlessly complicated, there was in fact no compulsion about it. A warship is very sensitive to 'buzzes' and this rumour-mongering can be used to serve positive as well as negative purposes. It is one way of balancing up two apparent impossibilities. It is a way of finding out the form and of sizing up the values of a given situation. In addition, both Hale and the Commander rather enjoyed bartering away ten minutes before lunch over a couple of drinks.

When the hands turned to at 1315 the forenoon's work was usually taken up where it had been left off. Later on the ship's company might be agreeably surprised by an unexpected 'Make and Mend' when pressure on the ship was less intense. At present, however, no one could see a way out of the wood. The hands were driven as hard as their petty officers knew how and still the jobs which needed to be done mounted up on the Commander's 'Waiting' list.

The 'Secure' was sounded at 1540. This marked the end of the full working day and at 1600 one watch and a part was given leave. Despite the Commander's and the Captain's intention, a great deal of dog watch work had to be done, but this was usually of the non-manual kind. The ship's office writers, the supply assistants in charge of stores and provisions, the gunnery and torpedo writers and, of course, the Captain's office saw very little respite over these weeks, although Marsh often took an hour off to play squash with one of the midshipmen. This last period at Portsmouth was still a 'married officers' time'. The bachelors, some willingly and some not, were lured or bribed or otherwise requested to look out for their married shipmates so that the latter could shove off ashore and see something of their wives before their two-year stretch abroad.

So, as at Belfast, by the time 'Sunset' had come and gone and the Colours had been lowered for the night, by the time Evening Rounds had taken place at 2100, the ship was as deserted as it was ever likely to be again.

After the Duty Commanding Officer and his cortège had gone rounds the ship's day was almost at an end. 'Pipe Down' would not be sounded for another hour, but only personal activities such as reading or letter writing or listening to the radio would now be in progress.

A last stroll up and down the deck might be taken: perhaps a last glass of port would be consumed in the wardroom over *The Illustrated London News*, but the ship, lying silently alongside the ancient jetty, would be all but asleep. On a moonlit night the masts and rigging of the *Victory*—Nelson's flagship—could just be seen over the dockyard buildings. Occasionally the ferry to Gosport could be heard clanking on its chains across the harbour, or a passing boat would make the still water lap against the ship's side. A train at the harbour station would emit that strange electric croak unique to the Southern Railway, the rattle of a rifle butt on the concrete would reassure the Quartermaster that the marine sentry was still guarding the gangways to the ship, and below decks the hum of the ventilating fans provided a soft bank of noise in which all other extraneous sounds seemed to be absorbed. Then 'Pipe Down' would be sounded and the hammocks slung along the darkened messdecks would bulge out with their accustomed shapes. The wardroom pantry was locked up and a cockroach or two would quiz each other on the tiled galley floor. *Antigone* was asleep, safely watched and guarded, until 'Reveille' should sound off some seven hours later and yet another day of her life began.

They did their gun trials in the Channel off the Isle of Wight and then went round to Portland for the remaining technical trials.

'Here we go gathering nuts and may,' said the Navigating Officer when the Commander-in-Chief's signal arrived. 'Have a drink, Guns, before we stop speaking to each other over the exercise period.'

'Thanks, I will,' said Brasson, pocketing his copy of the signal. 'Well, it looks as though we'll soon be out of nappies at last and doing some real work for a change.'

Brasson was delighted at the prospect. 'To *Antigone* repeated Captain-in-Charge, Portland and RN Air Station, Lee', the signal had read, 'from Commander-in-Chief, Portsmouth. Carry out full calibre six-inch shoot in Area X as detailed in my letter 023/5618 of 10th May.

Battle practice target will be towed by HM Tug *Resolve*. On completion carry out four-inch high-angle shoot at drogue towed by aircraft from RNAS Lee callsign Beer Queenie 3. Proceed on completion to Portland for Torpedo, A/S and Aircraft trials as ordered by the Captain-in-Charge, Portland.'

So off they went on a fine, fresh morning half-way through May. As soon as they passed Spithead the ship went to Action Stations and the fun began. Although *Antigone* was a new ship, the guns' crews, the director personnel and indeed all ratings concerned with loading, aiming and firing the armament were fully trained men. They would need to get used to *Antigone*'s humours, to her special little ways, but everyone knew what he was doing and was long practised in his own particular duties.

Moreover they had 'gone through the motions' plenty of times already in harbour. They had the feel of their instruments. Now it only remained to work together as a team. The long service tradition of the Navy justified itself again and again. These were all trained men and no one wasted any time.

Once the ship was properly worked up and attached to her squadron then ordinary-seamen and other young ratings would be duly instructed to take over these duties, so that after a further round of experience they, too, could be drafted to other ships as Trained Men. Thus the deep-grained 'know-how', the constantly widening knowledge and technique fed all the time into an invisible bank of naval wisdom. It was upon this bank that the sudden vast expansion of war was to make such overwhelming demands.

Out in the channel there was a lop on the surface of the sea. This would make spotting the fall of shot a little more difficult, but the conditions were almost exactly what the Gunnery Officer wanted in order to test out his minions. As *Antigone* drew out away from land the masthead lookout reported 'Enemy in sight' and the four turrets, each with their two guns, began silently swinging round and following the director bearing. The enemy consisted of a wood and canvas screen towed at some distance astern of the tug *Resolve*. They were used to this game in the squat little tug. To them it was merely another day's perambulation at sea mingled with mild curiosity, since *Antigone* was a new ship, to observe just how bad her gunnery would be.

They were to make three practice shoots at the target. As *Antigone* turned on to course to make her first run, the Navigating Officer stuffed two bits of cotton wool into his ears. They would get the full aural benefit of the broadside up there on the bridge and he was already slightly deaf from an earlier commission in HMS *Royal Sovereign*. In that battleship the main armament consisted of fifteen-inch guns and the secondary of six-inch guns similar to those in *Antigone*. It was Spratt's opinion that the solid roar of a fifteen inch broadside was more bearable than the sharp ear-splitting crack of the six-inch guns. In any event, he told himself, it was a noisy business and not his cup of tea at all. Then he thought of Honest Tom's round shining face up in the director control-tower and he smiled at the vision. Brasson would be enjoying every minute of the day.

Brasson, in fact, was keeping unusually quiet. He gave the minimum orders needed and then made himself all eyes and ears. He sat now in the middle of the director control-tower watching and assessing the officers and ratings on whose alertness and ability the ship must rely.

In front of him sat Chief Petty Officer Rigby, the Chief Gunner's Mate, whose job it was to keep the director trained on the target. In front of Rigby were the two range-takers. From their eyes was obtained the prime information on which the transmitting station, that most complex calculating machine down in the bowels of the ship, began to work. The result of this work was passed out to the turrets, individually corrected and aligned to suit their position in the ship and their relation to the target. This constantly altering range was modified by other factors such as rate of change, deflection and inclinometer readings.

To Brasson's right sat Sub-Lieutenant Darbigh, his Spotting Officer, and down in the transmitting station, Mr Legg, the Gunner, kept an anxious eye on his rather surprising team of Royal Marine Bandsmen, their trumpets and bassoons forgotten and their whole attention strained towards keeping one set of pointers lined up with another.

By this time all guns were loaded and the 'gun-ready' lamps had come on. The actual order to 'Shoot' was given

87

by the Gunnery Officer. This supremely satisfying moment to Brasson stood on a pinnacle of involved calculation—allowance for the roll of the ship in a moderate beam sea, the temperature and barometric pressure which affected the flight of the shells—these and a dozen other details were worked out for him by machines. But the machines could not see and they could only partially judge. They relied on human eyes and human nerves. The object of this practice was to test both men and machines. Both were interlocked. A bad alignment could throw off a turret and so could a headache in a rangetaker's head. Brasson's experience tended to stress the importance of his equipment: his instinct made him subordinate this to the standard of training which his officers and men had achieved. To blend the two and work them both up to their top efficiency was his only recipe for success. It was easy to say this glibly in the mess: to put it into practice called for a nice judgement, plenty of drive and patience.

The shoot, as it turned out, was not very good. Trevesham watched the fall of each salvo through his glasses and wondered what Brasson was doing to pin down the trouble. He made no comment himself, but was privately glad they and the tug had the sea to themselves. The first run was the best of the lot. *Antigone*'s second salvo straddled the target but from then on a disintegration set in. Salvoes fell consistently short and then consistently over: a stray shell from 'A' turret wandered over towards the tug and drew forth an indignant protest, the rate of fire dropped down second by second and one of the guns in 'Y' turret had a jam.

'I'm afraid there's nothing to be proud of at all, sir,' said Brasson, when he reported afterwards to the Captain. 'I'd like to get the results analysed straight away and then start tightening up all round.'

'I got the impression that "A" turret was having a little private war of its own,' said Trevesham, but Brasson would not be drawn out at that stage.

'Yes, sir,' said Brasson, 'a lot of things came to light. I'm sorry we didn't do very well—but Mr Legg and I will get down to it straight away. We won't be caught napping again.'

He saluted and walked off the bridge. There's one thing about Honest Tom, thought Spratt, and that is that he doesn't try to dodge out of the blame. He rejoined the Captain, who was leaning on the coping watching the guns being cleaned.

'Well,' said Trevesham to his Navigating Officer, so that no one else could overhear, 'I wouldn't care to be in the Gunnery Department for the next two or three days.'

They had Portland almost to themselves. However, there were no berths alongside for a ship of *Antigone*'s size. This meant anchoring out in the harbour. It meant that the ship could only be reached by water, and thus *Antigone*'s first Boat Routine came into force for the transport of officers and libertymen to the shore.

It is said in the Navy that a ship is judged by her boats. In *Antigone* the Boat Officer was the First Lieutenant, and this was a happy choice. Apart from the work and responsibility entailed, Collard had a natural interest in boats. He had spent a good deal of his boyhood at Falmouth. From then on every spare moment he could manage had gone on sailing or in going to sea in a fishing boat. In *Antigone* he and Bowling, the Chief Quartermaster, could spend hours discussing the merits of different types and classes.

Boats of every kind had a fascination for Collard. Pulling, sailing—even motor-boats had something to say to him. He was a big, slow and somewhat inarticulate man but the sight of a boat would bring him alive. He could tell in a flash whether a boat was right or wrong and usually what was right or wrong with her crew. Like some people are with motor cars, he was a bit of a gadgeteer. He liked things to be 'tiddly'. The curtains of the motor-boat were piped with blue and some of the ornamental woodwork of the canopy was picked out in gold leaf. He felt that expenditure on white manila rope was no extravagance although sisal would have done the job just as well and much more cheaply. But manila felt good and looked good. He made it clear to the Commander that only manila was good enough for *Antigone*, and so Hatchett authorized the issue with a good grace.

Now that they were away from Portsmouth the ship's life took on yet another colour. Round at Portland neither officers nor men had any domestic connection with the shore. The ship had her full complement aboard and she was out there alone in the harbour, a small floating fortress surrounded by a moat of water. Although attached to the Portsmouth command for administration, although she had to comply with local orders and routine, *Antigone* was now an independent and sovereign warship, riding calmly and majestically at her moorings.

Commanded by a four-ringed Captain, her size compelled respect, in the order of things, from lesser warships entering and leaving harbour. Surrounded by battleships and aircraft-carriers she would have seemed comparatively insignificant. But the Home Fleet was away in Scottish waters and *Antigone* was the only cruiser at Portland, and thus the biggest ship then in port. She was impressive in her light grey paint—itself a presage of foreign voyages to come since ships of the Home Fleet were painted a darker shade. The destroyers, sloops, minesweepers and submarines based at Portland—all smaller in size and junior in status—sounded off to her first in the simple way the Navy has of paying respect to its own hierarchy.

A sloop leaving harbour would call its hands on the upper deck to attention and the commanding officer would salute as his ship passed the cruiser. This honour was acknowledged in *Antigone* by the Officer of the Watch causing the 'Still' to be sounded and all activity visible from foc'sle to quarterdeck would cease. Then, after a moment or two, *Antigone* would sound the 'Carry-on' and normal work began once more. Then and not till then might the sloop stand her own men at ease, although by that time she might be nearly out of the harbour mouth.

'Makes us feel pretty important, doesn't it?' said Midshipman Mottram as he and Lieutenant Crawford, the Officer of the Watch, took a turn up and down the quarterdeck. Mottram's father was an Admiral and he had been brought up in a highly Naval tradition, but *Antigone* was still his first ship. At just eighteen he was neither blasé nor shy.

'We *are* important,' said Crawford, a little pompously, 'and don't you forget it. We're an independent command. We could go half-way across the world at a moment's notice without refuelling or reprovisioning. Those chaps,' he jerked his thumb at the sloop which had just saluted them, and which was now passing the breakwater, 'have to work in flotillas and come back to mother at night. Small ships are all right if you happen to like that sort of higgledy-piggledy life.'

He was glad Cravenby, Osborne and Grey-Bennett were not around to overhear him shooting that line. He suddenly remembered how he had once been a midshipman himself, nearly six long years ago, and how he had led on his own Officers of the Watch to make fools of themselves to the subsequent relish and delight of the gunroom. He shot a glance at Mottram to see if he were merely 'acting innocent'. These opinions and gems of instruction, dug out of their elders and betters by cherubic young midshipmen, were apt to be served up with keen imitative malice on gunroom guest nights. Midshipmen have a certain licence and usually an embarrassing ability to mimic their worthier senior officers. The Commander's strut, 'the Stubby walk' and the First Lieutenant's slow gait were both outrageously parodied in the gunroom—usually in the Sub-Lieutenant's absence. None of the young gentlemen took off Darbigh, however. That was a little too near home.

A leading-seaman walked smartly up to the Officer of the Watch, a painted board in his hand, and saluted.

'Permission to go aloft, sir, and reeve a new main aerial?'

Crawford gave his assent and took possession of the board on which was painted 'Safe to Transmit'. Mottram watched curiously, his round jacket blowing open in the wind. He must have been told the reason for this procedure before but, for the moment, he had forgotten.

'Why does he have to ask permission, sir?' Mottram piped up, and received another penetrating look from the Officer of the Watch, 'and what's the board for?'

'You ought to know that by now,' Crawford replied. 'No one's allowed aloft while any W/T transmission is on. We don't want the poor chap electrocuted, do we? As long as that board's not hanging in its right place in the W/T office, no wireless message can leave the ship. Quartermaster!' he called out suddenly, his eye on the launch secured to the port boom.

'Sir?'

'My compliments to the Cox'n of the launch and he's left a fender over the side.'

The Quartermaster sped away to convey this message

to its proper recipient. The Officer of the Watch in harbour is charged primarily with the safety of the ship, then with the employment of the hands and the running of the ship's routine, and finally with the manning and use of the ship's boats. He has to keep constantly alert to everything going on, both in his own ship and in other ships in the vicinity. If this were to call for action or response from *Antigone*, then the Captain and Commander would need to be informed.

On this particular forenoon, however, the Captain was ashore conferring with the Captain of the Anti-Submarine School, and the Commander was exercising his damage-control parties somewhere between decks. It was a sunny morning and nothing much was happening in the harbour. Except for the Commander and his party the hands were mainly employed by their Divisional Officers in their different parts of ship.

The previous day had been given over to trials of Asdic equipment which had entailed endlessly hunting one of the submarines of the Sixth Flotilla. This had left everyone on board with the impression of total frustration and failure. Today, therefore, was devoted to the doing of those small practical jobs about the ship which were always accumulating. It was only to be a short hiatus. That afternoon they would move across to Bincleaves to run torpedoes in conjunction with the Whitehead torpedo factory.

Lieutenant Crawford and Midshipman Mottram paced up and down the deck. Although, in fact, they were running the entire ship, they appeared to be doing nothing at all. Indeed, Mottram kept wishing to himself that the Officer of the Watch would shove off below for a stand-easy and leave him in charge. Now, if it had been Grey-Bennett, Midshipman Mottram would have been on deck almost the whole forenoon by himself.

Grey-Bennett regarded himself as a superior being whose main job in life was to fly an aircraft. He resented having to undertake any ship duties. He obliged with reluctance. 'If only *Antigone* were an aircraft carrier . . .', he was fond of saying, but not very surprisingly he and Osborne, the observer, were in a minority of two. However, to be on watch with either of them gave the midshipmen a chance. Had the ship suddenly started to sink

Midshipman Mottram would himself have had to take the first emergency steps. As it was, with Crawford, he was nothing but the usual appendage—another wart on the fair skin of the quarterdeck as Sub-Lieutenant Darbigh was apt to point out in moments of candour.

'Submarine *H*.34 leaving the *Titania*,' the Yeoman of Signals reported from the flag deck. HMS *Titania*, an ancient liner, was the depot ship of the Sixth Submarine Flotilla, but as *Antigone* had swung in the tide bows on to the dockyard she was difficult to observe from the quarterdeck.

'Warn the Officer of the Day *H*.34 will be passing us in approximately three minutes,' Crawford said to one of the sideboys. He and the midshipman watched the submarine silently manoeuvring away from the trot and preparing to leave harbour. Three or four sailors in white submarine sweaters stood in line on the casing a few inches from the sea as the boat slipped past *Antigone*. The Commanding Officer on the conning tower, a lieutenant in an old monkey jacket, called them to attention and saluted. They looked like toy sailors on a toy boat, dwarfed by the cruiser. The bugler sounded off the 'Still' on the quarterdeck of *Antigone* and Crawford returned the salute to the submarine for some three or four seconds. Then the 'Carry-on' was sounded. Shortly afterwards the sailors on the submarine doubled along the casing and up on to the conning-tower. As soon as they were out of the harbour *H*.34 would be submerging to periscope depth.

'A bit wet for them if she suddenly started to dive,' said Mottram, wondering whether he would enjoy specializing in the submarine service.

'Not my cup of tea,' said Crawford, 'not my cup of tea at all.' There was a pause as they watched the submarine slip past the breakwater.

'Do you think there's going to be a war, sir?' asked Mottram. The question seemed almost grotesque on such a fine dappled morning with the sunlight dancing along the sea.

'Yes,' said Crawford, 'I'm afraid I do.'

'Soon?'

'Whenever the Führer is ready for it. He hasn't gone to see Musso for nothing.'

Hitler had just visited Rome on another of the Axis meetings, and the papers were full of speculation.

'Besides,' Crawford added, looking at the jetty through his telescope, 'Chamberlain must be doing something about it. He's put the Income Tax up to five and six in the pound. It's war or ruination—or both. Quartermaster!' he ended sharply.

'Sir?'

'Tell the Commander and Officer of the Day the Captain's motor-boat is just leaving the jetty.'

The air of peace and tranquillity vanished. Two side-boys sped away on the Quartermaster's orders and the Bosun's Mate and Corporal of the Guard edged over to the starboard quarterdeck ladder. The Captain of HMS *Antigone* was returning to the ship and must be properly piped aboard.

'Well, there's going to be a war,' said Midshipman Mottram importantly as he went into the gunroom. 'I have it on the personal authority of Lieutenant Crawford of the Top Division.' Crawford was possessed of rather a glassy smile and a tendency to draw his head back so that his chin disappeared into his neck. Whatever other qualities he had, these two facets of his personality were now immortalized in the gunroom by Mottram's mimicry. He stood up straight and still, leaning slightly back on his heels as Crawford did when saluting the Captain. At the same time he managed to prod Midshipman Watling some distance below the belt—a double feat which delighted his audience. 'And don't forget we *are* important,' he went on exaggerating Crawford's drawl. 'I mean—with Income Tax five and sixpence and Hitler and Musso together again, well—I mean to say—where would the Navy be without *Antigone* and the Divisional Officer of the Top Division? I can tell you—a damn sight less chocker than I am. I've had my whack of Crawford's little lectures. The fellow's a pompous ass.' He began imitating Crawford again: 'Small ships are all right if you happen to like that sort of higgledy-piggledy life.'

This time for no reason at all he took hold of Watling's arm and twisted it up. Watling, who was the butt for most gunroom humour, let out a yell of agony.

'What sort of higgledy-piggledy life do *you* happen to

like, you scab?' Mottram began, but Watling had been goaded to fight and one of the interminable gunroom feuds got under way. Marsh, in an armchair and secure in his rank (except on guest nights when he found himself de-bagged with the rest of them) looked up over the top of his paper.

'For heaven's sake, children——' he started, and then at that moment Sub-Lieutenant Darbigh came into the mess. The scrum abruptly broke up.

'Mottram,' said Darbigh severely, 'the Snottie's Nurse wants to see you in his cabin.'

'Oh!' said Mottram, his face falling and his manner back to the innocent diffidence of the forenoon watch. 'What have I done?'

'It's your Journal. He says it's the worst one he's ever seen.'

'Oh, Lord!'

'I fancy you'll be stopping on board till it shows an improvement.'

'Oh, but Darbigh——'

'Oh, but nothing. Go and see him now—and bring the other Journals back with you.'

It was part of the training of young officers that they should write up a daily narrative of everything that happened to the ship and to themselves. This they did in great tomes known as Midshipmen's Journals . . . and these were inspected by the snottie's nurse and the Captain once a week. Some found this literary chore fairly easy, to others—and Mottram was one of them—it was a daily nightmare.

The First Lieutenant was in his usual position in his cabin, his back to the door, when Mottram knocked and entered. He had a habit of working on books and papers laid out on his bunk so that although it meant standing he could smoke a pipe and gaze reflectively out of his scuttle. This enabled him to keep an eye on the port lower boom and on the boats secured to it. It also enabled him to deliberate somewhere in his mind, while indulging in long, slow seadreams.

'Come in,' he said, taking his pipe out of his mouth and looking round. 'Oh! it's you, Mottram.'

'Yes, sir. The Sub-Lieutenant said you wanted to see me, sir.'

Mottram stood tensed and uneasy. He knew he was in trouble and experience of many a similar summons from his Term Officer at Dartmouth gave him to realize that the worst could and probably would happen. The intellectual superiority he had enjoyed over Lieutenant Crawford had long ago vanished. The snottie's nurse was another proposition entirely.

'I can't let this Journal of yours go in to the Captain,' Collard said slowly. He seemed to look at and then through the midshipman so that Mottram felt a twitching in his shoulder blades. The colour mounted in his cheeks. The sweet smell of the First Lieutenant's tobacco filled the air and gave a spurious feeling of peace to the cabin. At least what was peace to Collard was certainly not so to Mottram as he stood with his hands stiffly behind his back waiting for the axe to fall.

'I don't know what's wrong with you, Johnny,' Collard said. The use of his first name like that was disconcerting. He didn't resent it because there was nothing about Collard you could resent. But the sudden non-Service intimacy was a little unfair. He felt he had been taken unawares, almost by stealth. He still said nothing. Long experience had taught him that this was the wisest procedure.

'You're the brightest one of the lot,' Collard went on, 'but you seem to think you can skate round any real effort. How long did it take you to write up that Journal?'

'Oh! I don't know, sir,' Mottram said unhappily. 'I couldn't seem to get into the mood.'

'It's not a question of moods. It's purely and simply a job of work. It has to be done and you know it. You might as well do it properly. You can do so. But not if you leave it till the last half hour.'

'Yes, sir.'

'I don't believe in punishment.' Mottram brightened visibly. 'I can't force you to give whatever there is in you to give. That's up to you.'

'Yes, sir.' There was a note of eagerness in Mottram's voice. Perhaps he was going to get away with it after all. The First Lieutenant relit his pipe and, through the puffs of sweet scented smoke, looked at his problem charge standing in its round jacket rather like an indignant duck.

'What were you going to do in the dog watches today?' asked Collard.

'I was going to land and play squash with the Captain's Secretary. That is if we could get a court.'

'Well,' said Collard, as though he had arrived at a decision, 'you don't want me to stop your leave, do you?'

'Oh! no, sir.' The note of eagerness was now desperate.

'So I'll leave it to you and you can work it out for yourself. It's very good for you to take exercise. On the other hand, that Journal has to be re-written and here in my cabin by Divisions tomorrow. *How* you do it I don't care. If you think you can land and play squash and still get this Journal presentable—then I shan't restrict you. On the other hand, you know—as well as I do—exactly what will happen if you fall down on this chance. So there you are. You'd better paste those last three pages together and start again.'

'Thank you, sir,' said Mottram. He wished like hell he could stop blushing. It was so embarrassing at a moment like this. 'Can I take the other Journals? The Sub told me to bring them back.'

Collard nodded and the interview was at an end. The second motor-boat was just securing to the boom. There seemed to be some fuel oil or tar on her rubbing strake which would have to be got off the hard way. He watched the crew climb up the rope ladder and go inboard to their dinner. He rather envied them. They had a simple and pleasant job to do. They did not—and would never have to—bring pressure to bear on a thorny young midshipman whose father had once been your Commanding Officer in a Dreadnought of the Channel Fleet.

The rest of the trials at Portland passed off successfully. By this time the equipment and machinery had all been tested and accepted. The ship was complete. She had her right officers and men, her guns and torpedoes had been fired, her aircraft had been catapulted off and duly recovered, her engines were in perfect condition, she had most of her stores and provisions aboard, and all that now remained was to return to Portsmouth, say farewell to wives and families, suffer a brief inspection by the Commander-in-Chief, and then sail abroad.

The next stage would be to 'work up' either at Gibraltar or Malta where full facilities were available. Then at long last and after all this preparation HMS *Antigone* could be passed as a fully fledged and efficient warship, ready in all respects for service with the Fleet.

By this time it was the third week in May. They would sail at the beginning of June. All things being equal they would then arrive in Bermuda and become part of the Eighth Cruiser Squadron in early July. This prospect sparkled and danced in everybody's mind. From wardroom to stokers' mess there was a continual foretaste of adventures to come. Whatever the job in hand, everyone aboard had his own idea, his own private picture of white coral sand, of palm trees studded with scarlet birds, of languid dusky women in even duskier 'joints', of their fine ship riding at anchor in some South American port, of blue days in the Pacific and of dark nights in the Straits of Magellan. Even Able-Seaman Clarke occasionally saw himself surrounded by crates of beer in some Peruvian waterfront dive, the daily orders brought out ahead of time, the Commander's office closed temporarily while its staff attended to other urgent business ashore.

In the meantime they had to comfort their wives and families, soft-pedal the joys to come and generally tidy up their personal affairs. Lieutenants Grey-Bennett and Osborne had also to buy some new uniform owing to an involuntary diving display they conducted on the return passage to Portsmouth, when their aircraft was being hoisted inboard at sea. This incident, recorded by the CSKO in *Antigone*'s newspaper, and later in verse by Leading-Seamen Battersby, immediately took its place in the ship's mythology. Like all such incidents it had its funny as well as its sombre aspect. Those not on deck at the time were up there in a matter of seconds, as the rumour whipped round the ship. 'Hey! Marcel's fallen in the drink!' echoed through the messdecks, and seamen, artificers, cooks and marines raced up the foc'sle and along to the waist to be in on the fun.

Lieutenant Grey-Bennett was known as a fancy fellow. He had fair wavy hair (hence his nickname Marcel), and rather obvious good looks. As a naval aviator he was paid for the additional risks he undertook much on the same scale as a submarine officer and, being a bachelor, he was thus able to indulge his whims to a greater degree

98

than his brother officers. His reputation had been early established—or ruined according to the point of view—by his claim that he had to run up to Town for a haircut since no provincial barber could be trusted to trim his locks.

There was, of course, no doubt that flying the Osprey floatplane was a chancy business. A pilot had to be quick-witted and forceful in personality. Aware that there was something slightly ludicrous in the whole business of keeping an aircraft aboard and of catapulting it off, aware that he was not really of the herd and by thus standing apart had incurred a kind of half-conscious hostility from his shipmates, aware that in addition to the natural hazards of flying from and landing upon the sea, he would be quickly expendable in war, Lieutenant Alan Grey-Bennett was rather a cocky, self-willed young man, apt to lay down the law in the wardroom and to resent the vagaries of Fate.

As head of a minor department, with direct access to the Captain, he had quickly fallen out with Hatchett. Although Osborne, his observer, was an older, more stable officer, and thus redressed the balance, he felt himself all the time ploughing a lonely furrow through the faint mockery of the wardroom and the ship.

Getting Marcel airborne was quite an affair. Since there is no space in a cruiser for a flight deck or runway, initial flying speed was provided by the catapult. This in turn was powered by explosive. The impression of a circus turn thus rested on solid fact. Marcel and his observer were literally fired off into the blue. In addition, unless they pressed back hard against their seats, they stood the risk of breaking their necks before the aircraft had moved a couple of yards along the catapult and, even then, the take off momentum was so critical that the aircraft dropped dangerously near the sea as it built up its speed. Spectators of this feat tended to cheer, much as they would applaud an antique steam roller or a veteran car. There was something remarkable in its happening at all.

Once in the air the next anxiety was to land the contraption safely in the sea, hook it on to the crane and hoist it back aboard. This was no problem on a flat calm day. Usually, though, there was some sort of sea and on their return passage to Portsmouth conditions got rapidly worse during the half hour in which the aircraft was flying around. Speed was therefore increased in *Antigone* and an abrupt turn across sea and wind was made, thus smoothing out the surface of the Channel in the lee of the ship sufficiently to allow the aircraft to land. This it safely did. However, time was now of paramount importance. The smoothing out of the sea was being lost moment by moment. The aircraft taxied to the ship's side but was now bobbing up and down like a cork while attempts to grapple on to the hook of the crane were made by Osborne, from the back seat of the aircraft. Until they were safely hooked on, *Antigone* steamed slowly ahead and the aircraft engine was kept going so that way was maintained both on aircraft and ship. It was a little like a game of nautical hoop-la, the prize being an elusive hook sometimes ten sometimes thirty feet above the level of the sea.

At the fourth attempt they got hooked on but the aircraft had swung in the wind so that a tripwire was caught up round the tail. As the crane hoisted, therefore, the floatplane up-ended itself in a neat hingeing movement and ejected both Grey-Bennett and Osborne into the sea.

'Holy suffering Moses!' shouted the Commander, who was watching from the flag deck. 'Mr Partle, get a line over the side!' Mr Partle, the Gunner (T), happened to be beside the starboard torpedo tubes in the ship's waist. With commendable haste he and an able-seaman threw out a lifeline to the two swimming figures already dropping astern, where they would be in danger from the screws.

The Torpedo Officer was in charge of the crane. When the accident happened the operator had hoisted the crane instead of veering it and Fossingham was raging at him. This had the inevitable effect of paralysing the man. Then the Commander arrived on the scene and took charge. Grey-Bennett had hold of a line, but Osborne was drifting astern. He could stay afloat in his flying suit but he could only swim with difficulty. By this time *Antigone*'s main engines had been stopped in case Osborne might be endangered by them and one of the seaboats was manned and lowered. There was a moderate swell and *Antigone* lay almost beam on to it so that she was rolling about twenty degrees. In the meantime the tripwire had taken a couple of turns round the aircraft, so that it was now hopelessly entangled. Each time the ship rolled it dunked the whole 'bunch of knitting' in the sea and the crane could not be raised for fear of tearing off part of the tail.

It took them five minutes to cut the tripwire and let the aircraft swing clear. Then, at that precise moment, the crane motor jammed. It was the *coup de grâce* for Fossingham.

'This seems to be an afternoon for the Torpedo Department,' said the Commander in a state of icy, controlled fury. 'Let me know when the crane can be worked.' And with that he walked aft to survey the scene from the quarterdeck and to allow the Warrant Electrician to find out and remedy the trouble. By this time the seaboat had rescued Osborne and Grey-Bennett. It had pulled alongside again and had hooked on to the falls. Seaboats in the Navy are always hoisted by hand in the old reliable non-mechanical way. The First Lieutenant had this well under control. Hatchett watched the seamen running the boat up to the davits in a series of simple clear-cut movements. It made a welcome contrast with the crane, its aircraft dangling helplessly on the end.

He walked forward as the two dripping airmen climbed down out of the boat.

'Well,' said Hatchett, a trace of a smile on his face, 'what's the meaning of this? I've got enough on my plate as it is without fishing a bathing party out of trouble.'

Osborne laughed as the water poured off him on to the deck, but Grey-Bennett scowled.

'Whose head do I have for that little spree?' he asked sourly. It was a wonderfully pompous remark for a young man with two stripes on his arm who had just fallen into the sea.

'You don't have anyone's head except your own,' the Commander said tersely. 'Go and get dry. Come and see me as soon as you're presentable.'

As he continued for'ard to report to the Captain the crane motor was freed and the floatplane was hoisted aboard back into its usual position on the catapult. He climbed up the ladder to the bridge as the engine room telegraphs rang down revolutions for 'Half Speed Ahead'. It was becoming more and more obvious, he reflected, that the Captain would have to have a talk with both Fossingham and Grey-Bennett. They were the only two officers who seemed still to be out of line.

But in Portsmouth for their last few days in England everyone thought first of their wives and families. All the important jobs connected with commissioning a warship had now been done. Only a few odds and ends remained to be tidied up: miscellaneous stores continued to dribble in and the ship was cleaned spick and span for the Commander-in-Chief to walk round and inspect. But by and large the ship's life had gone into hiding. As soon as leave was piped people hurried off ashore, a preoccupied look in their eyes. Often they carried little presents for the wives and children they would so soon be leaving behind. Everyone seemed to be withdrawn into his own private world. Habit, discipline and training took them through their duties on board. The routine purred on as usual, but their hearts were elsewhere.

Even the bachelors got caught up in the pre-departure fever. Duty week-ends at home alternated with lurid nights-out in London. Fiancées, popsies and crumpets were wined and dined, danced and pursued with a kind of emotional furore. The pace and the pressure were heightened and individual resistance seemed to melt in the urgency of it all.

'It reminds me of the eve of Waterloo,' Cravenby observed as he sliced the top off his breakfast egg, a glazed look in his eyes, 'and, of course, we all remember that little lark.'

'Personally,' said Crawford, who had been in the same party in London, 'the sooner we sail the happier I'll be. Milly had a look of orange blossom in the eyes last night. Another few weeks of this and I'll be anchored for life.'

If the full-blooded bachelors aboard behaved with that brash irresponsibility towards the other sex which distinguishes the young naval officer, and for which later on they can pay so dearly, then married officers were in a more nostalgic mood and those, like the midshipmen and sub-lieutenants who were too young to be properly classified as bachelors, complied with their duties to home and parents as loyally as they could.

Some regarded this period as the last few days of the

holidays before returning to school. Others saw their imminent departure as a happy release. But the entire ship's company felt and expressed in some way the uncertainty, the mounting emotion and the tingling expectancy which entered into every activity on board during thost last few days in England.

This emotional state was not, of course, confined to the officers. The pebble had been thrown into the pool, and everyone connected with *Antigone* responded in some way or other to the ripples. So there were farewell dinners, last parties and a general tidying up of six hundred separate family affairs. The ship's company of HMS *Antigone* snatched at their last few nights of home life. In return wives and children were shown endlessly round the ship so that during the next two years they could carry a picture in their minds of the messdeck and the ship in which their menfolk would be living.

Young Mr Marsh put off going home as long as he decently could. He was ashamed to admit it even to himself but he was very much happier on board. Number 23 Colebrook Avenue, Birmingham, now stood in his mind as a sort of prison without bars, a dungeon from which it had taken him eighteen years to escape, but in which a small vital part of himself would always remain imprisoned. He hated feeling as he did. It made him feel an arrogant little snob. Never once did he accuse or reproach his parents, even in thought, yet all the time he felt ashamed of his home. It was not only a question of middle-class poverty—most naval officers nowadays had a background of threadbare gentility—it was more difficult than that. Colebrook Avenue was in a different order of worlds. A labourer's cottage in the country would have been easier to pass off than that semi-detached villa in its neat, soulless, suburban street. Derek Marsh had no delusions of grandeur. He did not regard himself as a prince born in a hovel. But when he thought about that stucco house with its neat bow windows and its coloured-glass fanlight he could have wept.

However, the pattern of his life was stronger than his feelings abut it. Marsh knew that as long as his parents were alive he would be enmeshed in their web of circumstance. He was learning patience. He sensed that to accept was one step towards eventual release. He knew, too, that he would only hurt his parents if he left England without a final visit home. So, on the last week-end in May, he steeled himself against the ordeal and put in forty-eight hours at Number 23 being cosseted, questioned and stuffed into liverish rebellion with every favourite dish his mother could remember. He returned to the ship drained of nervous energy through trying to interpret his life on board *Antigone* in terms which his parents could visualize and understand.

'And we're coming down on Wednesday in the Austin Seven,' his mother said as she kissed him good-bye. 'Daddy's got two days off from the office. So you can show us the ship and we'll watch you sail away to foreign climes.'

So, there it is, thought Marsh, there never was a complete escape. He had felt awkward and alien at home, and now he was in for another session of embarrassment before they finally sailed. Yet even as this thought entered his mind, he reflected that but for the self-sacrifice of his parents he would never have arrived at being the Captain's Secretary of HMS *Antigone*. The least he could do would be to put a cheerful face on it all in token of a debt he could never fully repay.

Other officers, all in their separate ways, made the most of their last few hours at home. Mr Partle, the Gunner (T) distempered the main bedroom of his bungalow at Waterlooville—the room in which his arthritic wife would spend so much of her time. He had had a long talk with the local doctor so that in his absence Mrs Partle would have adequate attention, and he had interviewed the headmaster of the grammar school, leaving instructions for his son's success in the Higher Certificate.

Susan Meldrum had returned with her child to the old stone house in Wiltshire where her parents lived. Mrs Collard at Liphook was placidly—and it seemed to Collard for ever—awaiting the arrival of her third baby. Madame, at Hatchett's insistence, had booked herself in for a fortnight's spree at the Strand Palace Hotel the day after the ship sailed. Noreen Brasson and the children had settled in to their spartan apartment near Eastney Barracks. Lieutenant (N) Augustus Spratt had returned to Cheltenham for an austere week-end with the General. Captain Taw-Street, RM, had enjoyed his last few days hacking in the New Forest, and Annabel Fossingham had departed in the *Queen Mary* for New York and Boston, where she intended to stay until *Antigone* arrived at Bermuda.

Perhaps Captain Trevesham felt their imminent departure as keenly as anyone on board. He had few business arrangements to make. His wife was fully competent in the running of Drakeshott during his absence. She had done it before and no doubt she would do it again. Yet each time he went away on another commission it seemed as if he were forfeiting a part of his personal life. It was as though in some mysterious way it was being lived for him without his knowing. Strange as it was his condition and estate in HMS *Antigone* seemed to be reflected in his leisure at home.

As Commanding Officer of a seven-thousand-ton cruiser he was but little concerned with the practical business of doing. He was the receiver of reports and the maker of decisions. Like a reigning monarch he was never worried by detail except when he chose to interest himself in some particular project. Everything awaited his word. A nod set hundreds of men to work, his signature could put a man in prison for ninety miserable days. He carried the supreme responsibility for a ship costing well over a million pounds and for the lives and welfare of some six hundred men.

He could expect to be excellently served. Each function for which he bore responsibility would be the domain of one principal officer and beneath him a highly organized department. In peacetime the Navigating Officer would make it difficult for him to run the ship on the rocks, but should some such disaster occur then, of course, Trevesham would be held primarily to account. This state of affairs was not exactly repeated at Drakeshott, but there was a similarity. The running of the ancient house and its home farm depended upon a hierarchy too, and once again Trevesham stood alone at the apex of the triangle.

He and his wife had considered it their duty to dine every officer at Drakeshott before they sailed on their commission. This they had done in batches of four or six at a time—usually a mixed bag consisting of a Senior and a Junior Wardroom Officer, a Midshipman and a Warrant

Officer. The first pioneers of this social encounter with one accord dreaded the evening, but Trevesham and his wife were excellent hosts. Awkwardness and shyness melted before the interest they took in their guests and after the first batch had been out to Drakeshott, there was no more feverish casting around for plausible excuses.

The Captain's Secretary, acting in his unofficial capacity as Flag-Lieutenant, took some private credit for the success of these parties. He briefed Lady Diana on the background and interests, so far as he knew them, of the officers invited, and he was so young and small and eager to please that she took him to her heart. He was asked to three of these parties and felt immensely flattered. To begin with he was unsure of the etiquette and a little over-awed by the majesty of Drakeshott, but soon he felt the ground solid beneath his feet. The Captain would always be somewhat grave and remote even to Marsh, who saw him more frequently than any other officer, but Lady Diana instantly won his devotion.

The climax to this social loosening-up process consisted of a garden party at Drakeshott for the chief and petty officers and their wives. To this were also invited the heads of departments and divisional officers. It thus took on the characteristics of a family party. Already a change could be seen from those early days in Belfast. Then everything was new. People were reserved and suspicious of each other, each jealous of his own particular position and careful to see that others were aware of his especial importance. Now it was already in large measure a gathering of old friends. The 'club' which had formed itself in the two McCrumlin Terrace houses still tended to come together on these occasions—the wives more choosy than their husbands, but since all were much of the same seniority and status there was little danger of a loss of face.

Other groups with similar interests also came together —the Supply Branch and the writers, the cooks and officers' stewards, the artificers of each grade, whether engine room, electrical or ordnance, the chippy chaps as the shipwrights were called, the painters and the plumbers, the stoker chief and petty officers, and the sick berth attendants.

All of them came to the Captain's house for a garden party their wives would never forget, each contributing an individual colour to the scene, from the ferocious-looking Master-at-Arms, whose weakness was chocolate ice-cream, to the Colour-Sergeant Royal Marines in his special uniform with the scarlet sash.

The Lord Lieutenant of the County was there, Lady Diana had roped in a Dowager Duchess and a rather seedy-looking Irish peer. It was something of a show, and it went with a swing. It was all done on a grand scale and in honour of *Antigone*. Not a drop of rain fell the whole afternoon, and however wrongly the snobs might misunderstand the purpose of the party, it gave a cohesion, a feeling of pleasure and a glow of pride to the hundred odd chief and petty officers whose spirit could make or mar the commission.

'My wife tells me we owe this mostly to you two,' Trevesham said to his Secretary and the wardroom messman who were looking down on the throng from the terrace. 'I don't believe her, of course, but I congratulate you both. You must be getting your hands in for South America.'

He nodded at them with a smile and went on down the steps. Marsh looked round at the beautifully kept hedges, at the rolling lawn filled with uniforms, and then at the old weathered facing of the house. It seemed a long, long way from Number 3 Colebrook Avenue, Birmingham.

At last the day came for them to sail. Now everything and everybody was aboard, the ship was stored, provisioned, oiled and ammunitioned. Mails had been diverted to Malta. Her trials were complete, the ship had been fully accepted and now it only remained for her to 'work up' before joining her proper station. The Commander-in-Chief, Portsmouth, had walked round the ship and had sent them a farewell signal. 'I congratulate *Antigone* on her cleanliness and appearance and on the smart bearing of her ship's company. The Service has reason to be proud of its newest cruiser and your Home Port expects great things of Miss Oedipus. Good luck to you all.'

'Good Lord,' said Hatchett, 'so that's who we are. Schooly!' he called out to the Instructor-Lieutenant.

'Yes, sir?'

'What did Antigone do apart from being the daughter of a rather curious Greek gentleman? Did she slay the

Gorgon or clean out any stables, or what? This calls for some kind of erudite answer.'

The Instructor-Lieutenant, a solemn officer, looked even graver than usual.

'No, sir. King Creon had her bricked up alive for disobedience.'

'What kind of disobedience?'

'She buried her brother, Polynices, against his orders.'

The Commander's face fell.

'A fat lot of help that is,' he said.

However, Trevesham did not call on his Commander for assistance.

'Yeoman of Signals,' he said, 'make to the Commander-in-Chief: "Your 0925/3 greatly appreciated. No one is going to wall up this little girl. *Antigone* will do her best not to let Pompey down".'

They sailed at a quarter-past ten on the third of June. It was a mild sunny day and a large crowd of relatives and friends had been given special permission to enter the dockyard and wave the ship farewell from the jetty. The last wire was slipped, and a tug towed her stern away from the jetty. Then, out in the stream, *Antigone* slowly turned towards the harbour mouth. A blaze of white handkerchiefs appeared on the jetty as the band on the quarterdeck struck up appropriate tunes. With slow elegance *Antigone* moved down harbour as the figures on shore blurred together into one solid mass. Slowly and quietly she slipped out to sea, leaving Fort Blockhouse to starboard and the *Vernon* to port, past the piers of Southsea, past Spit Fort, out into the short chop of the Channel and away into a fresh westerly breeze.

Soon the familiar outline of Portsmouth was hardening into a thin grey line as each revolution of the screws carried them further and further to sea. On board no one spoke very much. No one was proof against the sudden poignancy of saying farewell, of knowing that they would not see their Home Port again for another two years. The long lines of motionless sailors, the Captain on the bridge, the Commander on the flag deck, the cooks in the galley and the Chief Quartermaster in the conning-tower had all of them a lump in the throat by the time Spit Fort was dropping astern and HMS *Antigone* had at long last sailed abroad on her first commission.

CHAPTER FIVE

Marsh thoroughly enjoyed the passage to Malta. They had good weather and he was only queasy for a day. South through the Bay of Biscay the ship settled into an easy regular motion as the Atlantic swell came in from her starboard quarter. Every moment he could snatch away from his little office, he spent on deck. The sun shone. The wind was no more than a zephyr. It grew steadily warmer and his skin began to go brown.

'Are you sure you don't want to swap?' he asked Darbigh. Marsh had the outboard bunk under the cabin scuttles. Their leisurely cruising speed allowed them to keep the scuttles open all night. It was the next best thing to sleeping on deck.

'No, thanks,' said Darbigh, 'I'm a practical man. I'd rather your bunk got flooded out first. I get all the fresh air I need on the bridge.'

So Marsh kept his bunk along the ship's side and each night he went to sleep to the regular churning of the screws, the slight motion as the ship gave to the swell, and the kiss and fizzle of little waves striking against the side before settling back into the sea as spray.

'This is the sort of life a rich man pays hundreds of pounds to enjoy,' he used to say in the gunroom. But the midshipmen paid little attention. They took it all for granted. They were absorbed in the daily round, the watches they had to keep, the instruction they had to take in and the Journals they had to write up. Marsh seemed to be the only one in the gunroom alive to the simple poetry of wind and sea, the only one who could stand aside for a while and reflect. With the possible exception of Midshipman Watling, a pale-faced boy whom everyone sat on, there was no one to whom Marsh could express these feelings of adventure and excitement. 'The simple poetry of wind and sea' was an idea likely to have a very rough passage in *Antigone*'s gunroom.

The ship was developing its inner invisible muscles. They were learning to work together as a single unit. The various co-ordinated functions necessary to fight the ship, indeed even to keep her satisfactorily at sea were practised and practised again.

'It's like learning to drive a car,' the First Lieutenant explained. He and Marsh were going through the Divisional sheets for the Quarterdeck Division when 'Action Stations' had sounded off. He reached for his tin hat and gas mask as watertight doors began clanging shut. 'First you do it consciously, slowly and awkwardly. Then one day, suddenly you don't have to think about it any more. You change gear and drive automatically. That's exactly what we shall be learning to do this month during our working-up period.'

'But why Malta?' asked Marsh. 'It's such a long way out of our way.'

'It should have been Gib,' said Collard, 'but the Spanish Civil War's a little too close for working-up purposes. We might find ourselves in the thick of somebody else's argument.'

During the dog watches he sunbathed or played deck hockey on the quarterdeck. This was a ferocious game played with walking sticks and chocks of wood, or sometimes with little grummets of rope like small thick quoits. Marsh was a keen player. He liked to take his exercise in short bursts and deck hockey was more vigorous even than squash. Considering the violence with which the gunroom took on all comers, the casualties were remarkably few. The quarterdeck gave them just the right amount of space and a sufficiency of natural hazards, such as capstans and bollards, to make the play interesting. Then afterwards there were long tankards of shandy in the gunroom or wardroom, a luxurious bath and a seagoing dinner for which nobody dressed.

Marsh and Darbigh shared with the Sub-Lieutenant (E) an enormous Marine servant. This stalwart, who went by the name of Parker, was literally almost double Marsh's size and sported a beautifully waxed moustache in the style of a Guards Sergeant-Major. Marsh had once complimented him on it.

'Well, sir,' Parker had replied, ponderously scratching the back of his head. 'Mrs Parker isn't a one for moustaches, as you might say, but seeing as we'll be away showing the flag for two years, I thought I should do honour to the detachment by—er—growing.'

After that it was never referred to again. Parker was not a very good wardroom attendant. He was slow and heavy, but once trained to a certain routine he was quite unshakeable. He took pleasure in laying out clothes and he liked his officers to be smart.

'This seagoing routine's all very well,' he said to Marsh one night as he turned down the beds, 'but I do like to see a nice line of boiled shirts sitting down to dinner in the mess. It's got a bit of formation in it.'

'Formation' was one of Parker's general purpose words covering a large variety of meaning. Anything smart and well done had 'formation' in it, anything expedient or sloppy lacked that quality. Parker was a child of ceremony. Without knowing why, he was convinced to his marrow that the right observance of ceremony was the bastion upon which the Royal Navy's efficiency depended. In harbour officers dressed for dinner every night in mess undress, which is the Navy's equivalent of a dinner jacket ashore. This was right and proper. But at sea, watch-keepers had to be served a running dinner in their monkey jackets, since most of them were either coming off or going on watch, and Parker would shake his head and give his moustache a little twirl. The ship might be plunging through the heart of a gale, but to Marine Parker something was missing. There was no formation in it at all.

During this first passage abroad Marsh was torn between pleasure in being at sea and eagerness to sample Gibraltar and Malta.

'Of course we did Gib in the Home Fleet,' he told Darbigh one night, 'but I've never been to Malta. What's it like?'

'Dghaissas—goats—smells—I don't know which strikes you first. Malta's all right if you don't have too much of it. It's very "service", of course, but the bathing's good. We'll be a good catch if there's anything left of the Fishing Fleet. I gather the Med Fleet's away on its summer cruise.'

'What's the Fishing Fleet?' asked Marsh. It had peeped into conversations before but he had never been quite sure of its definition.

'Popsies,' Darbigh said briefly with pursed lips and a faraway look in his eyes. 'Unmarried popsies—some with money and some without, some as God made them and others improved—but all of them without exception on watch for a husband. And some of them keep a damn sharp lookout at that. However, we're there to work-up. We'll be a stranger in their midst. As we're not joining the Med station they'll probably leave us alone.'

'But—do they just go out to Malta on spec?' Marsh asked. He was intrigued by this idea.

'Not exactly. Most of them go to stay with relatives or friends. For instance, the C-in-C has a perfectly hideous niece who lives at Admiralty House and haunts the Snake Pit and the Club at Sliema. It's all terribly proper, of course. Very snobby and social but for chaps like us it can be a lot of fun. Of course if it's tarts you're after then you'll have to visit Auntie—but that's another story entirely.'

'But what sort of people are they?' asked Marsh. The background of Colebrook Avenue did not allow for this sort of thing.

'Well,' said Darbigh, 'my sister came out last year.'

'Good heavens,' said Marsh. That really struck him as extraordinary.

'I've an uncle who's an Engineer-Commander and he has a dockyard appointment. But it didn't do her much good,' Darbigh added, shaking his head. 'Hockey has been her downfall.'

They called in at Gibraltar with stores, mail and two puppies for the Admiral. Marsh stood next to Hale, the CSKO, on the after-superstructure as they entered harbour, the vast Rock dominating the scene. The after-superstructure above the Commander's and Captain's cabins housed the officers' galley and had been decreed as the most suitable place for 'passengers' entering or leaving harbour. Marsh thought it ideal. He was out of the way and he had an excellent view.

'Gib's pretty full,' said Hale as he surveyed the harbour. 'I'm glad to see there's no berth for us at the detached mole. We'll be able to walk ashore.'

112

The detached mole, as its name implied, was the middle section between the two encircling arms of the harbour. Any ships allocated this berth, although technically alongside, still had to run their ship's boats in order to communicate with the shore.

The Surgeon-Commander stood on the other side of Marsh.

'This makes my eighteenth visit to Gib,' he said, 'and every time that great lump of a rock gets more and more impressive. I suppose the little man causing all the trouble over there'—he nodded towards Spain—'is going to want Gibraltar as soon as he gets into the saddle.'

'Who says he's going to win?' Hale asked sourly. 'Franco can bomb Barcelona. He'll never get a Catalan to surrender—or to co-operate if he does win in the end.'

Almost to a man *Antigone* favoured the Republican side.

'I don't think they can hold out very much longer,' the Surgeon remarked. 'Barcelona's been cut off for nearly two months. Look! There's a Republican destroyer over by the coaling jetty. I suppose she took refuge and we had to intern her.'

Over on the other side of the harbour there was indeed a badly damaged ship flying the red, yellow and purple flag of Republican Spain. Her upperworks had been smashed into scrap iron and one gun pointed drunkenly down at the sea. It was the first time Marsh had seen a warship, or a ship of any kind which had been through an action at sea.

'Gosh!' he said, 'she took a pasting.'

They examined her in silence as *Antigone* drew alongside the south mole.

'Well,' said Hale in the end, 'that could be us in a few months' time—if we run into one of Hitler's pocket battleships.'

Marsh said nothing. He had thought about war many times, but this first impact of another war, a war which the Royal Navy had to stand by and watch, seemed to force the issues at stake into a new and personal light. Marsh had a vivid imagination, but even a dolt could have pictured the chaos and the bloodshed aboard that Spanish destroyer. It could, indeed, be *Antigone* lying there crippled in some foreign harbour across the sea.

But this was June 1938. Who could be sure at that time whether war would break out or not?

'Personally, I wish we could get it over and done with quickly,' said the Surgeon-Commander, 'if the war's going to come.'

'It's coming all right,' said Hale tersely, 'a gipsy told me.'

Gibraltar was crowded. Refugees from Southern Spain, now entirely in Franco's hands, continued to seek asylum day by day. Though not yet in a state of siege the condition was so familiar to Gibraltar, its buildings and its inhabitants, that Marsh could not but feel it was only just around the corner. Yet cramped and crowded though life might be, there was something exhilarating about the garrison. There they stood, in and about and under their Rock, lodged at the tip of Spain, defiant and British.

Antigone was only to stay in Gibraltar a night. Later that afternoon Marsh and Hale landed for a walk and climbed halfway up the Rock towards Europa Point.

'I suppose if they start bombing this place from the air,' said Marsh, 'it won't be the fortress they think it is, but it still looks pretty solid to me.'

'Like the Maginot Line?' Hale said.

'Yes, in a way.'

They stood resting on their walking sticks, tired and hot. They had climbed up steeply past the Rock Hotel to a turn in the road from which the dockyard could be seen lying below as if from an aeroplane. It was an impressive sight.

'Is that the *Barham*?' asked Marsh, pointing to a battleship in one corner of the harbour.

'No, it's *Ramillies*,' Hale answered as they studied the scene, 'then come the two "County" class cruisers— the *Sussex* and the *Devonshire*—and then us. Old *Antigone* shows up pretty well, doesn't she in such distinguished company?'

Even from that distance *Antigone* did seem to have a special gleam about her fresh paintwork and her new white awning. She was noticeably smaller and neater than the three-funnelled 'County' class cruisers next to her, which appeared oddly antiquated to Marsh. *Antigone* was the only one of her class in Gibraltar and every inch of her looked smart and new.

114

'Are we going to be a "happy ship", do you think?' Marsh asked after a pause. He had a considerable respect for Hale who was about six years senior to him and his immediate superior in the Paymaster branch. Hale had been through most of the professional experience which still lay ahead for Marsh, yet he was of Marsh's generation. The Paymaster-Commander, on the other hand, seemed to Marsh to belong to another age with a style and an experience all its own. The Paymaster-Commander had been at sea in the Great War. Marsh bracketed him with his own father. Whereas between him and Hale there was scarcely a gap.

'I think we are already,' Hale answered, his eyes still on the ship in its complicated dockyard setting. 'I think it's something which either happens or it doesn't. *Antigone*'s got the right feel about her already.'

'Have you ever done a commission in an unhappy ship?'

'Yes,' Hale answered soberly, 'I most certainly have. I was in *Rodney* during the mutiny at Invergordon.' He paused for a moment, lost in thought. 'Things have altered a lot since then.'

They walked slowly back, making their way to the Bristol bar. This was packed out with naval officers in blue blazers and grey flannel trousers, knocking back gin and sherry at almost duty-free prices. It was a great meeting place for old shipmates, a mart for Fleet gossip and a forum where news and views were exchanged. 'If you're going to Villefranche, there's a little number in the rue Blanchard . . .' 'Algiers did us proud, but Oran . . .' 'If you're going home to pay off, old man, could you take a small parcel for me . . .' These and other snatches fell on their ears as Hale and Marsh forced their way to the bar.

Meldrum was over in one corner of the room talking to the Senior Engineer of the *Sussex*, Cravenby and Crawford had been playing tennis with two 'oppos' in *Ramillies*, and Spratt was swapping drinks with an old termmate who had command of a destroyer. There was a buzz of friendliness in the air but a friendliness entirely unsentimental. This was a meeting of friends who were also rivals, and in the Mediterranean Fleet, the crack fleet of them all, competition and rivalry between individual

115

ships was intense. Reputations, promotions and careers depended upon this rivalry in a personal sense.

Command of the Mediterranean Sea was not a British achievement which had come about by accident. They might be a team—and a Fleet was a team in the broadest sense of the word—but it was one made up of star performers. Star performers in any profession have temperaments which fire them along, and in the Bristol bar that evening there was enough explosive personality to blow up the Rock itself. That they were for the moment relaxed and unaggressive only served to veil the real nature of things. These were all disciplined officers who knew the rules of the game inside out. Within the compass of those rules they competed with each other as fiercely and toughly as they could—for the benefit of the Service and of themselves.

'If the Germans and Italians could see this den and understand it,' said Hale when eventually they got their drinks, 'they might get a line on what makes us tick.' He waved vaguely at the mob. 'After all, we invented the idea of the pub, but I wonder if the Master Race ever stops and thinks why.'

This was a little above Marsh's head, but it gave him a line of thought. In a setting like this he was constantly visited by a sense of wonder at being a Naval officer at all. The stucco frontage of Number 23 Colebrook Avenue suddenly rose up in his memory—and here he was at Gibraltar, a small member of a large and powerful community, a self-gathering and self-dispersing community which tomorrow would be individually and separately on the high seas and the day after might be at war. He breathed in the hot, smoke-filled atmosphere and thought to himself how odd it all was.

'Well, anyway,' Hale continued, 'thank heaven we're not joining the Med Fleet with every day a Brasson Benefit and the C-in-C kicking our backsides every stroke of the bell.'

Any gunnery activity was now known on board as a Brasson Benefit. No one in the ship had been allowed to forget that early and lamentable full-calibre shoot. Ever since then the fire control system and the guns' crews had been ceaselessly drilled and exercised. At the slightest chink in the daily routine Brasson would ask for Action

Stations to be sounded off. Each time he found something new to tighten up, someone else to chase. Brasson had a remorseless will-power. He was cordially feared and disliked. The ship's company called him names and his fellow officers tended to jeer in the Mess. He bullied, he threatened, he punished. A second's lapse and a rating found himself on the quarterdeck as a defaulter, an officer explaining himself to the Commander. He was highly unpopular but he was getting results. Thus inevitably he gained in respect. Honest Tom might not have a friend on board, but *Antigone*'s gunnery was going to be the best in her squadron.

Contact with the Mediterranean Fleet had put Brasson even more on his mettle. They had scarcely sailed the next morning when 'Exercise Action Stations' sounded off and *Antigone* was given another gruelling forenoon. To Brasson the blue waters of the Mediterranean were far more attractive than the Pacific or Caribbean. In the Mediterranean a warship was a warship, not a perambulating cocktail shaker. Moreover, in another three days they would arrive at the Mecca of naval power—the flat little island of Malta. He conceded in theory that the Torpedo and other Departments in the ship must also be worked-up at the same time, but under the surface Brasson claimed this last golden month as exclusively his own. In July they would be sailing half-way across the world for the dubious purpose of showing the flag. The month of June, though, spent as it would be at Malta was his—his to use and develop in a truly service atmosphere where the finer points of ballistics were fully appreciated and where, indeed, in Brasson's view first things came first, however grim this outlook might appear to some of his shipmates.

Commander Hatchett supported the Gunnery Officer in every possible way. He liked his drive. He admired his tireless energy. He knew that Brasson had the recipe for success, he knew he was getting results and that the ship's reputation would benefit. But the Gunnery Department was still only one part of the picture. The Executive Officer in a cruiser must hold a balance. The torpedo and the aircraft might not be quite as important weapons in war as the four six-inch turrets, but they were fitted in

117

the ship for a purpose and it was Hatchett's duty to see they were efficient. Moreover, *Antigone* must go where she was sent through gale, hurricane or other adverse conditions. The basic seamanship of the crew must never be allowed to slip into the background.

'I don't want to discourage Brasson or Fossingham,' Hatchett said to the Captain when they discussed the working-up programme over a glass of sherry one night. 'I know Torps thinks he's had the thin end of the wedge already. But two weeks is all they can have between them. I must take a clear week for Executive drills and at least four days to clean up the ship—I'd like longer if it can possibly be managed.'

'I can ask the C-in-C for another couple of days,' said Trevesham, working it out on the little calendar he always carried in his pocket with the cruise programme written on the back. 'But it means giving up the rifle range at Gib on our way back. You know what a battle it was to get it in the first place.'

Hatchet snorted and rammed his telescope deeper under his left arm.

'After those damned puppies had been sick all over the quarterdeck I should have thought the Admiral would have given us the Rock.'

Trevesham smiled.

'You must remember we're nothing but a flea in the Med Fleet's ear. A nuisance wished on them by the Admiralty. At least that's what R-A Gib told me.'

'Well, sir,' said Hatchett morosely, *'somebody's* got to want us. I only hope when we get to Bermuda they don't tell us to turn round and go back again. Mind you, Guns wouldn't mind. He wants to have us attached to the Med.'

'That could come about, too,' Trevesham said, looking out at the sea. 'I saw that happen during my last job out here.'

'Oh! yes, of course,' said Hatchett. 'I was forgetting.'

'When Mussolini invaded Abyssinia we had over fifty warships assembled in Alexandria alone. We had *Ajax* and *Exeter* from South America, *Sussex* from Australia—in fact, a whole foreign legion of cruisers from other stations all over the world. That could very easily happen again.'

'Then it won't hurt R-A Gib and Vice-Admiral Malta

to be nice to *Antigone*,' said Hatchett. 'They might need us later on.'

'I don't think you need worry. They're giving us the flagship berth for a start. I think we shall be well looked after in Malta.'

As Gibraltar had been full, so Malta was virtually empty. Hatchett stood up on the bridge as *Antigone* entered Grand Harbour. It was a hot June day and Malta was very familiar. While the Captain and the Navigating Officer brought the ship slowly to her buoy, Hatchett allowed himself to think back on the past. As a rule he never indulged in day-dreams. He was a square-headed practical man whose habit it was to be active. Soon the ship's routine would claim him again, but for a moment or so he stared up at Castille and over to Valletta remembering his many previous visits to Malta. Unlike Trevesham, he had never served on a Staff. He had never held an appointment on shore in Malta. He had always been afloat, landing in the dog watches and returning in a dghaissa at midnight. He had approached his Malta, as most sailors do, from a seagoing ship.

How differently Trevesham must view it, he thought, as he watched him, grave and motionless, over on the starboard side of the bridge. They had almost nothing in common except a mutual respect. Physique, experience, outlook, wives and background—everything that makes a man what he is—differed in them both. Hatchett bore no malice in this and, strangely enough, no envy. Had he been six-foot tall, and had he enjoyed a considerable private income, he would no longer have been Stubby Hatchett, and that was all there was to it. He would have had the problems of a man of six foot, and in all likelihood he would not have married madame.

They had met in Malta. Alice's father had been a Garrison Quartermaster after a lifetime in India. He remembered how desperately pretty she had been, and how consistently she and her father had been snubbed by the haughty service society of the island. The nineteen-twenties were not a good time for genteel poverty. Alice had her looks and her eager young body, but very little else. In his mind's eye Hatchett could still see the mean little house—just on the fringe of respectable Sliema—where she and her father were billeted. They went almost

119

aggressively to the club, to naval and army cocktail parties, to dances and on picnics. She could not afford to turn down invitations, to be choosy or temperamental. Hatchett was not supposed to have noticed but she only seemed to have one evening dress, an orange velvet affair which was later dyed black.

Poor Alice, he thought, for her there could never have been any other escape than marriage. Not that he had married out of pity. She had this wild, animal attractiveness so often the chief feature of the European girl born in a tropical climate. It was her one great asset and she used it sparingly and well. But in 1923 it was not strong enough to counter-balance the lack of any sort of dowry and the background of a father with one of the more menial of army appointments.

By this time *Antigone* had secured to the buoy and Hatchett, acting almost automatically, went down on deck followed by the Chief Bosun's Mate. He watched the ladders being shipped outboard, the main booms swung out from the ship's side, the hoisting out of the Captain's motor-boat and the spreading of the quarterdeck awning. But all the time he was remembering back fifteen years.

He had been a Lieutenant, and in those days young naval officers were not encouraged to marry. Those were the days of the Geddes axe and of Emile Coué. By some lucky fluke Hatchett had avoided the one and Alice, as she later confessed, had secretly embraced the precepts of the other. In handbag or reticule, discreetly hidden in a handkerchief, was that little secular rosary so much a fad of the age. 'Every day and in every way I'm getting better and better.' She told her beads each night before going to bed, and whenever opportunity offered in the day. She never defined what 'better' might be, preferring to leave that to the Almighty, but as her second and then her third season in the island wore on, she began to know in her bones that any escape from Malta would do.

And then Stubby had come along. He had not been much of a catch as the Fishing Fleet judged these things, but he had fallen for her, hook, line and sinker. He spent all his pay and a good deal of credit in taking her out and buying her presents. He was no Rupert Brooke, he kept telling her, but he loved her with every atom of his five-foot seven inches, and what was more he was prepared to fly in the face of naval disapproval and marry her at once.

'Permission for dghaissamen to come aboard, sir?' asked the Officer of the Watch. Hatchett walked aft to the quarterdeck to examine the scene. About a dozen of the little phoenician harbour boats propelled by oars from the bow, each with its tiddley white canopy and its brown-skinned boatman, were hanging round the stern of *Antigone* waiting to ply for hire. In Malta ship's boats were used to the minimum amount and most wardrooms and gunrooms took on their own dghaissas.

'Not yet,' said Hatchett. 'Tell them to lay off until the Captain's gone to Castille.'

Castille was the headquarters of the Vice-Admiral, Malta, and Trevesham's first duty would be to wait on the Admiral. Then no doubt the call would be returned aboard *Antigone*. These formalities completed, the ship would be temporarily under Vice-Admiral Malta's command and could then get ahead with her working-up programme.

Hatchett stumped along to his cabin. Malta was unbearably hot and in 1938 tropical rig was never worn in harbour. Shorts and shirt might be all very well at sea, but Number 10's with the white drill uniform buttoned up to the neck was the rig of the day in Malta. Hatchett threw his cap and his telescope down on a chair and glanced through the signal log which the Yeoman of Signals was proffering. But still, as he went through the motions, his mind was on that other Malta he had known so many years ago.

To begin with Alice had had to go on living at home. In 1923 officers of the Royal Navy were not paid marriage allowance. Money, money, money had been the key-note of those early difficult years. In those days a large number of serving officers had an income of their own to bolster up their totally inadequate pay. Hatchett had no private means. Their social life became more and more restricted. Alice 'made do' and never once complained. At the end of certain months Lieutenant Hatchett could scarcely settle his mess bill and his tailor's account was long in arrears. But both he and madame refused to give in. They recognized it as a test of endurance. Had not Nelson been a penniless parson's boy? All things were possible to those with the will, and though Coué was now out of fashion, Alice still kept up with her beads. And now here he was, second-in-command of a cruiser, back in Malta in a position of power. It was odd how things worked out in the end, thought Hatchett, as he finished leafing through the signals and handed the log back to the Yeoman.

'Well, Mellish, glad to be in Malta?' he asked.

'Yes, sir,' the Yeoman agreed, 'glad to come and glad to go. I've had a basin of Malta in my time, sir.'

'We all have,' Hatchett remarked, 'and I don't suppose it's the last time we shall see Dockyard Creek.'

'No, sir. I don't suppose it is.'

Mellish tucked the log under his arm and was just leaving the cabin when Hatchett was struck by a thought.

'It's about time they made you a Chief Yeoman, isn't it?' he asked. 'When is your Rate due to come through?'

'In about six months, sir, I think. If I don't fall down, that is,' he added with a grin. The thought of a Yeoman of Signals falling down on any job was incongruous and funny to Mellish.

'Do we have to do anything about it with depot?'

'No, sir, it won't make any difference to the roster.'

The 'rooster' as Mellish pronounced it, was the means by which a petty officer was advanced to chief petty officer. This was run by the manning depot—in *Antigone*'s case Portsmouth—and although it was supposed to be a closely guarded secret almost everyone concerned knew exactly where he stood on it.

There was a knock at the door and a sideboy appeared.

'Captain's going ashore in five minutes, sir—from the Officer of the Watch.'

'Very good,' said Hatchett. He reached for his telescope and his cap as the Yeoman and the sideboy disappeared from the cabin. All around him the routine—his routine —hummed on. Dinners would be cooking in the galley: the Captain's motorboat was just coming alongside the starboard ladder: the Master-at-Arms would be watching the daily issue of rum to the ship's company: the engineers would be starting in on that auxiliary feed pump which was troubling the Chief: the Paymaster-Commander would be down in No. 2 store mustering bedding—all around him in every part of the ship, the bees and the ants—who were neither bees nor ants—would each be about his particular duty, each of them contributing something vital to the life of the ship and all of them set in motion by him. As he rammed his cap on his head he caught sight of the calendar and stopped dead. 'My God!' he said aloud, 'I must send her a cable.' Fifteen years ago to the day he and madame had become engaged.

They spent the rest of June in and around Malta. It got steadily hotter. Hatchett worked the ship's company as they had never been worked before, and towards the end of the period he began to think he had pressed them too far. No one likes being roasted up in a crucible. A mild form of dysentery, known as Malta Dog, ravaged the ship. There was a steep rise in the number of defaulters and tempers frayed out all round. Hatchett brooded over this. He did not like the slave driving reputation he was getting with the ship's company. It came back to him in dozens of different ways, but the best barometer he had was the quiet opposition of Able-Seaman Clarke. Each had considerable respect for the other. Hatchett trusted his three-badge Able-Seaman writer as he trusted the First Lieutenant. But he refused to give way to the sulky toothsucking and occasional dumb insolence with which the lower deck reacted and which Clarke tried to convey to his master without giving offence.

'If you suggest a Make and Mend once more when I'm making out the orders,' growled Hatchett, during their last lap at Malta, 'I'll put you in the Captain's Report.'

'Aye, aye, sir,' Clarke answered cheerfully, 'that would mean cells, sir, wouldn't it?'

'Yes,' said Hatchett, 'or worse.'

'Very restful—in cells I understand, sir,' Clarke went on blandly. 'Some of the ship's company prefer it to Executive Drills. At least, that's what I heard down on the messdeck, sir."

'Did you?' said Hatchett. 'Well, for your private information, there won't be another Make and Mend till we leave Malta for our proper station—whether the messdeck likes it or not.'

'Aye, aye, sir.' Clarke said with robust indifference. He had done what he could. Now that the Commander had proved unshakeable again the ship's company would just have to lump it.

Hatchett gave them a break when the ship went round to Ghain Tuffeha to scrub out boats and take in sand. Then everyone who could swim had the chance of a bathe. There was a different feeling in *Antigone* that evening and the next day they beat all their previous times for the various 'Evolutions' they had been practising.

'It certainly paid off,' the First Lieutenant remarked. He and Hatchett were watching the laying out of a second anchor from the foc'sle. 'I think we're in danger of getting a bit stale.'

'If someone would tell me how to do my job without driving the ship's company, I'd be grateful to know,' growled Hatchett. 'I could do with a break myself.'

'We all of us could.'

They watched the evolution in silence for a moment or so. Hatchett had been a little doubtful about Cravenby of the Foc'sle Division. However, now that England was far, far behind them he seemed to be settling down much better than expected. Thinking this over Hatchett was inclined to put it down to the steadying influence of the First Lieutenant. He was like a sturdy old father confessor to the younger officers of the ship.

'The gunroom want a whaler for a sailing picnic on Saturday afternoon. Have you any objection?' Collard inquired.

'No,' said Hatchett, 'as a matter of fact we might organize a wardroom boat as well. An afternoon's sailing would freshen us up. I'll ask the Captain.'

'Good. I'll lay on the boats and the messman can pick us up a bumper tea.'

'I suppose there's more to the gunroom boat than just a sailing picnic,' Hatchett remarked, struck by a sudden thought. He knew that the snottie's nurse would have the gunroom's confidence and that there were certain things better unknown by the Executive Officer. If Collard showed no disposition to enlighten him, then he would be ill-advised to press the point further. Collard gave the Commander a rather slow, sleepy look out of the corner of his eyes.

'Well,' he said, 'Midshipman Mottram knows some people with a house out beyond Sliema. I think the idea

is to sail round there and—er—hope that the girls will
have come by car. But I have a feeling you aren't supposed to know about this.'

Hatchett laughed.

'They don't change very much, do they?' he said. 'I
don't care what they get up to provided they don't damage the boat—or the ship's blessed reputation.'

'I gather Malta thinks we're all right,' the First Lieutenant observed. 'We have some sort of glamour because
we don't belong here: people get all misty-eyed when
they hear we're going to Bermuda and South America.'

'I get pretty misty-eyed myself when I think about it,'
Hatchett said tersely, and then shouted down to the boat:
'Watch out for that strop as you pay out the wire.'

Soon this particular period of stress and strain would
be over. Throughout Hatchett's experience events had
presented themselves in definite cycles. The working-up
period was no exception. There was the initial thrust and
effort. Then a gradual slackening off calling for a shock
of some kind to be applied to the machine. After this second wind the process rolled on unimpeded until all its requirements and conditions had been fulfilled. In another
ten days they would have finished with Malta. They
would be inspected. Their skill would be tested and the
Admiral would write his report. Then heigh-ho for the
West Indies and the Eighth Cruiser Squadron.

All this time the ship's life was broadening out.
Hatchett had made Lieutenant Crawford of the Top Division the sports officer. Despite the heat the sailors' passion
for football in any weather came out and inter-divisional
matches were arranged—and enthusiastically played. There
was more to this than pure recreation. A ship's team had
to be selected.

'Let's have no nonsense abut it,' Hatchett told Crawford when briefing him. 'Everything *Antigone* enters she's
to go in and win. The chippies are making a posh, glass-
fronted showcase for the cups and trophies. It's your job
to see that it's filled.'

'Aye, aye, sir.'

'Moreover, once round South America, we'll have to
take on all sorts of local teams—playing fair and foul. A
lot will be expected of us. If you need anything we
haven't got—let me know and I'll get it for you—but I

want to see a proper sports programme drawn up and put into operation.'

Hale had also been fired into starting up the Concert Party. He had brought a pile of sketches and songs from a previous ship and, together with the Bandmaster, was concocting a ship's ballad called the *Agony Anthem*. Here again the hard work lay in the first few weeks.

'They won't come to rehearsals, sir,' Hale complained one day to Hatchett in the mess, 'and I can't force them as it's voluntary. They gripe about being overworked and all that. The talent's there all right if only I can prise it out of them.'

Hatchett turned this over in his mind for a while. He saw the problem clearly and fully understood the ship's company's reluctance to be goaded on in the dog watches after a tiring day's work.

'I think the way out of that one is to put on a show of some kind straight away—to act as a magnet. Have we got enough solo turns to do that?'

'Yes, sir,' said Hale, 'if you'll build me a little stage on the quarterdeck. I've got some hessian in the store for a curtain and Torps is rigging me up some lights, but the chippies are a bit brassed off. They say they've a waiting list of jobs to be done and the ship might be built of wood, the way it's being used up.'

'Hm!' said Hatchett, 'I wonder if the dockyard could help us. Chief, have you any ideas on that?'

The Commander (E) had had more to do with Malta Dockyard than any one else. This was in no sense an engineering problem, but he knew who was and who was not co-operative in the dockyard.

'Yes,' he said, 'I'll have a word with Jevons if you like. I'm seeing him tomorrow forenoon anyway: jot down what you want and if it isn't too fancy, we'll put in a demand.'

And so it continued. Hatchett burnt up his energy, day by day, in a blaze of pressure. He drove himself harder than any of the others. He never gave in. He was up with the hands at six in the morning, and when he turned in at night he went out like a light. He whispered, he shouted, he coaxed and he ordered. Like a good impresario with a team of highly strung artistes, he came to know each of his players, learning their qualities and their weaknesses. He never seemed to relax. There is a differing time for every person and every event. Hatchett knew that this period of time was crucial for him and for the ship. Later on, when things were running smoothly, he might allow himself a break, but now he understood full well the call for his maximum effort.

Remote on his pinnacle, alone in command, Trevesham watched his Commander and was grateful for all he was doing. Hatchett put him fully in the picture whenever this was needed. He consulted with the Captain several times every day, but never once did he try to shrug off a responsiblility that was his and his alone. When one of the midshipmen ran the second motor-boat into the jetty and holed it, Hatchett took all of the blame. He had never yet run any of his officers into the Captain and any 'can' handed down by higher authority he accepted without question. Trevesham would make a suggestion where it seemed his advice was needed and Hatchett took it all in good part. They had nothing in common and yet between them there was almost an ideal working arrangement. To outward eyes Trevesham might appear like the constitutional monarch of a minor realm. To Trevesham himself he appeared especially favoured by Fate. His Commander was forging the ship into the best instrument of his will that could be devised. It was with pleasure and gratitude that Trevesham wrote on his Commander's half-yearly report for Promotion, 'An exceptional Executive Officer with marked organizing ability and strong power of command. Recommended for immediate promotion to Captain.'

If the Commander was immersed in the day-to-day practical work of the ship, the Captain of *Antigone* seemed to do nothing but sit in his cabin writing reports, letters and returns. All correspondence and all signals entering or leaving the ship had to be seen and approved by the Captain. There were only very minor exceptions to this rule which applied throughout the service. It was a good rule. Responsibility for mistakes could never be ducked. If *Antigone* said something she meant it. In 1938 'your reasons in writing' for any lapse or incident held overtones of authority stretching up stage by stage to the Lords Commissioners of the Admiralty themselves.

Trevesham was good at paper work, though this was

127

not a quality which any post-Captain cared to claim in those days. His years on the Staff had taught him to be quick and terse. He had seen how lazy thinking could slow up the work of the Fleet all round. He had observed its effect on a ship's reputation. He realized it as possibly the least of the virtues but one which, if absent, could mar an otherwise excellent record. Above all his Staff experience had taught him never to 'waffle', never to leap into print unless it was vital to the ship. Trevesham would never be called 'an old woman of the sea' as certain verbose officers were dubbed when their letters and reports circulated round the C-in-C's Staff.

It was a lonely life. Unlike the Commander, who messed in the wardroom, Trevesham had no communal role to play. He lived quite by himself. Occasionally he visited the mess but only when asked. Once the wardroom had dined him on a guest night but it had been a stiff, rather formal affair. Everyone had been on his best behaviour. They laughed politely at his jokes and Cravenby, who was to the wardroom what Mottram was to the gunroom, had rather nervously launched out into mimicry of a celebrated dockyard figure well known to the ship. This had loosened things up a little. But he was still the Captain. The gap could only occasionally be bridged and never for long.

'Looking back on these first few weeks abroad,' he wrote home to his wife, 'gives me the most extraordinary feeling. I seem to be different in myself. Before, I was always immersed, always identified to the full with whatever was going on in the mess or the ship. Now I'm remote and I seem to be remote in myself as well. There seems to be two "me's" and one of them watches the other receiving reports, going rounds, reading out prayers and judging defaulters. Occasionally I take the gig away sailing in the dog watches with my silent Petty Officer Vincent, and then my two selves seem almost to be one—but as soon as I'm back on board there's that tall fellow you've been married to all these years playing his part (not overplaying I hope) while another Trevesham watches him do it.

'Of course with it all I enjoy myself enormously. You would, too. Perhaps, when you come out to Bermuda, you'll see what I mean. All my service life I've taken the business of command as part of the nature of things. The Captain, the Commander-in-Chief and the Lords Commissioners of the Admiralty are parts of an ordered universe I've taken for granted since I first joined *Osborne*. But when it befalls you to play yourself the role of a colonial monarch, the thing suddenly takes on a different aspect. When everything revolves round *you,* when you are suddenly the centre of it all, you have to experience the extraordinary poised lightness which responsibility brings. Everything happens through and because of you. From one point of view I'm fettered by the rules and regulations. Instead of doing anything myself I have to see things done. There are days when I look back and conclude that I've achieved nothing whatever except to sign a few letters drafted by the Commander (E) or the Paymaster-Commander, walk round the messdecks and honour certain daily ceremonies with my presence. I suppose the King must feel like that from time to time after dealing with state papers and laying yet another dreary foundation stone. Yet you have to *be* a Captain or a King to realize that the figurehead side is the least part of the job.

'*Antigone* looks her best at present. We have just painted ship and now the Commander is enamelling selected parts of the upperworks. We have to keep within a strict Admiralty allowance, but Hatchett makes the most of every drop of paint he uses. She's the smartest vessel in Malta—just as she was at Gib. I gather we're envied by other ships and establishments in port—the proof being a nickname we've been given in the Fleet Canteen (or so my steward tells me). We're known hereabouts as "Flash Annie".

'I dined with the Governor on Thursday and gave Margaret your message. I've also managed to get in two afternoons' polo with the Army. Young Grey-Bennett, our pilot, rides quite well and of course Taw-Street, our Captain of Marines spends his every free moment in a saddle. He's something of a wardroom joke, I understand from Hatchett, but he takes it with great good nature and has even organized riding lessons for the midshipmen.

'Malta continues to be Malta. No one talks about a war although, if anything, the storm clouds are gathered out here more ominously than they were at home. I think

129

the long anticlimax (from our point of view) of Spain and the Nyon patrol following hard as it did on Mussolini's private war in Abyssinia, had dazed people into a state of perpetual semi-crisis. Coming into it again as a visitor—instead of living with it as we did before—I see the snags and dangers only too sharply. I think we're in the kind of lull which Hitler wants us to have and which exactly suits his purposes. But I mustn't talk politics. It's a bore, I'm told, and anyway perhaps it will all blow over in the end.

'Your letters are a great joy. One forgets at home how much more they mean abroad. The whole ship waits on the mail. Marine Camberwell, our ship's postman, lands every morning with the messman and his return to the ship is as eagerly awaited as the dinner hour. The more I see of my sailors the more akin to them I feel. I never had these feelings when I was Executive Officer of a cruiser. I don't know what goes on inside Hatchett, but I don't think he has time for such notions either. For him one day tears helter-skelter into another but for me there's time to look at people and wonder what makes them go on.

'You find things out about yourself as well. Snatches of opinion float in from the quarterdeck as the hands scrub it down in the morning. Of course, I'm not supposed to overhear anything at all. Like Timmy in the nursery— nothing he said could ever be heard outside! I gather there's one body of ship's company opinion which thinks I don't sit on Hatchett enough, and a nameless Able-Seaman referred to me blasphemously as "God's Brother —the Honourable Colin". I strike some of the lads as "snooty" but others opine that what a ship needs is "a bit of style" and "the Captain of Flash Annie's got a load of that all right".

'So you can picture your husband in his immaculate Number 10's inspecting Sunday Divisions, striding his quarterdeck, being piped over the side and sailing his gig "loaded down with style" and having an altogether surprising kinship with the Deity. However—I expect we shall all survive.'

When he read through the letter it struck him that somehow or other he had missed the mark. It did not really convey what he felt. He had a certain facility with words: indeed his letters painted a deeper picture to his

130

wife than he suspected and, compared with someone like Brasson, whose letters home were little more than a bald list of facts and statistics, his writing was full and rich. But somehow the inner purpose behind everything dodged out of sight. His insight into the ship's life could not be stencilled out in a letter.

Sometimes when he took a breath of fresh air on the quarterdeck before turning in he glimpsed a part of the pattern. The bells of Malta rang out softly over the water, mingling in the warm Mediterranean night with an occasional splash and drip of an oar and the sing-song querulous voice of a dghaissaman. It was a quiet time.

Across the harbour the medieval houses rose indistinctly out of the sea itself. Life would be teeming inside them, as it only does in Malta, but at this distance seen across the still water, they were merely a part of the décor, a background outlined by the moon and picked out in little lights. Above his head the canvas awning gave an occasional twitch. Below, and throughout the ship, people were climbing into their bunks and their hammocks. The day had spent its energy and now all was peaceful and calm. Then it was that Trevesham seemed to fathom himself and the ship in a way not possible during the day.

Occasionally on nights like this he *knew*. But what he knew he could never define. The Quartermaster and the corporal murmuring together beside 'Y' turret saw only the tall familiar figure of their Captain pacing up and down the deck. There was nothing unusual in that. Soon he would make a remark to the Officer of the Watch and then, walking forward on the starboard side, would have disappeared for the night. The bosun's mate would continue to relate endlessly the story of how he nearly backed the winner of the Derby in 1931, the corporal, whose feet hurt, would shift from one foot to another and the Officer of the Watch would walk over to the port side and look forward at the boats secured to the boom as though he suddenly expected to find them sunk. It was all a part of the routine. It happened. But to Captain Colin Trevesham, DSC, RN, as he slowly undressed and got into bed, there was always some other factor looming just out of sight behind it all. He could never lay hold of it and bring it forcibly into the forefront of his mind. But all the time he felt it to be there . . . Or was it?

The day before *Antigone* left for Bermuda, the Admiral sent for Trevesham and showed him the report he had written on the ship's working-up. It was addressed to the Secretary of the Admiralty, copy to the Commander-in-Chief America and West Indies Station. 'Be pleased to lay before Their Lordships' the submission began in the phraseology which carried straight back through the years to Pepys, 'the following report on HMS *Antigone* . . .' Then in much more terse and pointed terms it went on to survey *Antigone*'s work department by department and to give the Admiral's views on the success they had achieved.

'You're not as good as you think you are,' the Admiral said when Trevesham handed it back, 'but you'll do.'

'Thank you very much, sir,' said Trevesham. By any objective standards it was a good report.

'You'd have to smarten up before we could accept you in the Med,' the Admiral continued with the trace of a smile, 'but you'll do for the America and West Indies Station. I understand that over there almost anything goes.'

'That remains to be seen, sir.'

'The Fleet Torpedo Officer isn't too happy about Fossingham,' the Admiral observed, after a pause. 'What's your feeling about him?'

'He's a good officer,' said Trevesham loyally, 'he'll come into line.'

'He's in the zone, isn't he?' the Admiral asked.

'Yes,' Trevesham answered, 'he's in the zone for promotion all right.'

The Admiral kept silent for a while.

'Well,' he said eventually, 'I'll leave that to your new Commander-in-Chief. We've done enough for him as it is. Hm!' he snorted indignantly. 'They're wishing an Australian cruiser on us next month. I don't know what the Admiralty think we normally do out here—sit on our backsides twiddling our thumbs, I suppose. Anyway, good luck to you, Trevesham. I hope you've time for your pleasure cruise before the balloon goes up.'

'I hope so too,' said Trevesham, 'and thank you, sir, for the facilities and help you've given us.' He could not help adding, 'I'm sure if we do come back *Antigone* will astonish the Mediterranean Fleet with her efficiency.'

132

They shook hands and then Trevesham returned to the ship. It was the end of one period and the beginning of another. HMS *Antigone* was now fully fledged. She had been passed as efficient and was now a sovereign and independent unit of the Fleet. The stresses and strains of the nursery now lay behind them forever. They had come of age. The next day they sailed from Malta and headed west.

CHAPTER SIX

Leading-Seaman Battersby had settled down well. His job in *Antigone* was not too difficult. But ambition still gnawed at his thoughts. During the passage to Bermuda he put on a spurt and finished his course of Pelmanism. That was all to the good but he had no real idea where he stood over becoming an officer. The Torpedo Officer had interviewed him and told him to carry on the good work. 'You must gain more experience,' he said. It struck Battersby that this was easy enough to say. It meant very little, but it was the sort of friendly, vague encouragement he had received from his officers ever since first beginning the climb. They seemed to want to help him and yet all the time it was left more and more to Battersby to think out for himself what to do. He decided he must develop his initiative; and initiative, as the Manual of Seamanship pointed out, is a prime naval quality.

He was lucky with his messmates. They accepted him cheerfully and, after the first few weeks, without question. They were absorbed, as he was, in their own private lives within the smaller compass of their mess and the greater one of the ship. They left him alone. When they thought about him at all, they put him down as 'a bit highbrow and what have you'. No one would have been surprised if he had signed the Pledge and given up smoking. They shrugged him off and left him to his own devices. Battersby could have asked for no more. In the closest living part of the whole beehive—a seamen's broadside mess—he was still able to keep himself a little distinct.

It was a wonderful voyage. Three days to Gibralter and nine across the Atlantic. Peerless weather, a steady, restful routine and the daily approach of new, unexplored events—what more could he wish? His messmates might bellyache because pea soup only appeared on the menu three times in one week, but Battersby's mind was at another level. To him HMS *Antigone* was a twentieth-century replica of the *Golden Hind* and, if the Captain bore little physical resemblance to Sir Francis Drake, he was nevertheless a splendid symbol to Leading-Seaman Battersby of the spirit of adventure.

Out in mid-Atlantic the ship would be stopped for half an hour in the dog watches and 'Hands to bathe' would be piped. This had a mixed reception with the ship's company but Battersby was one of the first up on deck and over the side.

'What about all them lovely sharks?' Able-Seaman Rillington said. 'I hear there's droves of them following the ship.'

'A nip and a crunch,' said another AB, 'and you've nothing left worth having. You don't get me in for love nor money.'

Battersby grinned and dived in from the ship's waist a little flat. It took courage anyway to go in from that height but Battersby believed firmly that the only way to learn was to do it, so in he went with a tremendous splash and a bruised chest. Once in the blue, clean ocean he felt a singing exhilaration. The sweat and toil they had all endured at Malta seemed to be washed out of the memory by the gentle Atlantic swell and the salt on their skins as they dried off afterwards on the upper deck.

'Not for me,' said Able-Seaman Kavanagh watching from the foc'sle, 'it's too deep—even for the Three Fat Men of the Sea. I *do* like to be able to touch bottom with my little pink toes. No—you don't get me in till I see our lovely Master-at-Arms floundering for his life.'

The next day the Master-at-Arms did have a bathe, so Able-Seaman Clarke, Kavanagh, and Rillington, stung by ship's company opinion, lowered themselves ponderously over the side and into the sea. None of them enjoyed it

134

very much, but as Rillington remarked: 'We owe it to the public.'

The Three Fat Men of the Sea were, in fact, acquiring a public through the Concert Party. During their last days in Malta, Hale had managed to get a stage rigged up on the quarterdeck and 'The Antigoneers' Concert Party had given its first performance. This was little more than a string of solo acts. They went on too long, and some of them were embarrassing, but the Commander's hunch had been right. They stimulated interest in the Concert Party and for the next few days the ship's company comics came out of hiding and volunteered to join up. Now Hale was rehearsing an opening and a closing number. The Royal Marine Bandmaster was writing a special score, and Stoker Kelly was at work on his mouth-organ band.

Battersby had come into it on the electrical side. Of all the LTOs in the ship Battersby was looked on by the Torpedo Gunner's Mate as the easiest to 'lurk'. He never complained and he never answered back. Cox, the senior of them, always had a ready and plausible excuse; Cooper could think one up the moment he was detailed for a job; Stevens was too slow, but Battersby always replied: 'Yes, I'll have a go at it,' when a gash job came up. The result was that the TGM trusted Battersby far more than the others. He could be relied on to get the work done without being chased up. So he was left to himself and, as a reward, was immediately lurked for the next voluntary job.

'You'll have to run a line from No. 14 Junction Box in the gunroom flat,' the TGM said, 'and don't let them keep adding to the load. Lieutenant Hale asked for some footlights and a couple of spots—so don't go illuminating the whole quarterdeck for him. We still have a few fans to keep running as well, you know, on the ship's electrical supply.'

That was typical of the service, Battersby felt, to give with one hand and take away with the other. Rig up some footlights, they said, but go easy with the cable and don't use any current. Even the basic materials he needed were begrudged him. In 1938 twenty years of cheeseparing by successive Governments, naval disarmament and the long years of the slump manifested at Battersby's level in a kind of instinctive reluctance to issue electrical stores of

135

any description. However, Lieutenant Hale was the Store-keeping Officer for the whole ship.

'And if *he* can't let you have a few extra sockets and switches off of his allowance,' the TGM said craftily, 'then the poor old Navy must be in a bad way indeed.'

The stage-manager of the 'Antigoneers' and the hardest working of the lot was the Colour-Sergeant, Royal Marines. Battersby took an early liking to this brisk and businesslike non-commissioned officer who had willingly accepted the extra effort and work which the Concert Party involved.

Colour-Sergeant 'Forky' Forrester was the senior Royal Marine rank on the lower deck. He combined in the RM detachment the duties of Chief Bosun's Mate and Master-at-Arms. In appearance and by tradition he was more of a soldier than a sailor. He wore a short bristling moustache. He had a chest like a Guards Sergeant-Major and from it issued a voice which could be heard all over the ship. Lower-deck wags had even claimed that when he whispered in Malta a detachment of the Garrison started doubling about in Gibraltar, but this rumour had never been proved.

To Battersby the most extraordinary thing was that behind all this, Forrester was a draughtsman and an artist. He took pleasure in painting, in drawing maps and in lettering. More ferocious even than the Master-at-Arms on parade, he could come straight down from bawling out a bandsman at Divisions and devote himself to the most delicate and intricate map he was preparing of the ship's cruise.

'The problem with any concert party in any ship,' Forrester said to Battersby as they rigged up the stage, 'is to impose order on chaos.' He broke off to shout at one of the working party: 'Not on the bollard, you dolt, we don't want the whole boiling issue in the drink!'

'You can count me in as a permanent stagehand if you like,' said Battersby.

'Done!' said Colour-Sergeant Forrester as though he had just auctioned off a particularly difficult article. 'You're in for the duration.' He shot Battersby a penetrating look: 'Got a sunny, happy disposition, have you?' he asked.

'Well,' said Battersby, 'I think I have to myself.'

136

'You'll need it! We haven't hardly started yet. If our show's going to be worth anything at all—it means work —hard work and plenty of it. Watch 'em try and skittle out of it when this begins to dawn on them all. You have to catch 'em while they're hot. Get them into the habit. Make 'em feel rotten if they miss a rehearsal.'

It was Forrester's attitude which attracted Battersby. He had attack and he got things done. When any problem showed up, he went after it straight away.

'Sometimes you have to stalk them Indian fashion,' Forrester told him when Battersby commented on it one day, 'at other times you can go bald out with an axe. Things don't get done of their own accord, you know. If you don't put effort into a thing you don't get nothing out.'

Forrester certainly put effort both into the Concert Party and into his proper job of running the RM detachment. Taw-Street might pace the quarterdeck looking, according to the lower deck, as though he had just lost his horse. But Forrester kept the detachment on its toes. In any ship the marines are in a special position and very often they become the butt of the ship's company.

'No one's going to laugh at this detachment,' Forrester had told them, 'or I'll have the reason. Remember you're all *Royal* Marines. We have a tradition—an *esprit de corps.*' He looked them up and down sharply and then bawled: '*Royal* Marine Dobson—front rank—two paces forward and explain the joke.'

'N-no joke, Colour Sergeant.'

'Then take that stupid grin off your face and see me afterwards in the office.'

In general the ship's company of *Antigone* thought well of their Royal Marines. They began, as sailors normally do, by scoffing, but the jeers gradually became good-natured and even by the time they reached Bermuda had changed into a kind of grudging respect. They never let the ship down. This, Battersby felt, was due almost entirely to Forrester. If the Royal Marine detachment was considered funny in itself there was nothing he could do about that: what he could ensure was efficiency.

'In this detachment,' he told them, 'no one falls down on the job. Anyone who does once, will never do so again. Anyone who does so again goes straight home to England via the Detention Barracks and I'll personally see he doesn't enjoy himself on the way.' He looked along the wall of wooden faces. 'I don't love you,' he went on with heavy scorn, 'I don't love you not at all. However—I've got you and if you work and behave yourselves as Royal Marines should, then you might win a little bit of my great big heart. Royal Marines—Dismiss!'

Petty Officer Cook Jenkins, too, had settled down into a satisfactory routine. He was the senior Petty Officer Cook, under the Chief Cook, in the ship's company galley. After some early doubts he found *Antigone* to his liking. The oil-fired range embodied a couple of improvements he had himself suggested in an earlier ship. He found it easy to handle, and his staff was a good one. And to Petty Officer Cook Jenkins they were all 'his' staff.

Like the Colour-Sergeant, Royal Marines, Jenkins was the one in the galley who got things done. But unlike Forrester, he had no power of arousing devotion in those beneath him. He was respected, but feared. So, initially, had Forrester been, but as time went by, the Marines had come to regard his parade ground ferocity and his eccentricities with affection. Jenkins, however, remained unaccepted and vaguely disliked. He was free with his temper. No one ever quite knew when he would fly off the handle next. To his staff and the ship's company Taffy Jenkins was Welsh and unpredictable.

His immediate superior, Chief Cook Otterby, was more in keeping with the generally held picture of a cook. He was large and fat and rather slow. He had reached his position without exceptional effort but mainly by the principle of 'Buggin's turn next'. He liked to be on good terms with everyone. He hated a fuss. Being a lazy and rather lethargic man he was trapped by his own weakness. He agreed too readily with the Paymaster-Commander when the menus were being prepared. Then when the work had actually to be done, Jenkins could put him in a dither of distress by merely mentioning some practical objections. The meals were always prepared and cooked as the Paymaster-Commander had intended, but Jenkins made it quite clear that it was thanks solely to his own cooperation.

Petty Officer Jenkins' big moment was when 'Cooks to

138

the Galley' was sounded off and the daily dinners for the ship's company were served out by messes.

'Why is it Cooks to the Galley, PO?' asked one of his novices, 'when us cooks are all here?'

'Because in the bad old days,' Jenkins growled in reply, 'you had a lot of amateur cooks told off from each mess who actually prepared and cooked the meals for their particular parts of ship. Now, of course, they get lushed up with some proper cooking by experts. That is by *some* experts,' he finished off, fixing the assistant cook with a piercing stare.

To Jenkins, with his chip on the shoulder, it was always 'the bad old days'. There was a lot of hatred in Jenkins. Hatred of the Tories, of the coal owners in the Welsh valleys where he had spent his formative years, of privilege in any shape or form which had not been earned by one's own effort. To say that he hated his officers and the service was somewhat wide of the mark. He respected the Paymaster-Commander because he had daily, tangible proof that he knew his job inside out and was on top of it (and of Jenkins himself). But Lieutenant Grey-Bennett, RN, with his haircuts and his mannered voice was anathema to the Petty Officer Cook and it was lucky that professionally neither came into contact with the other.

Oddly enough an enthusiasm and a sport threw them together. Both were keen water polo players—on the face of it an unlikely interest for either of them. But in the inter-part matches which had been held at Malta, it soon became evident that *Antigone* had the elements of a strong ship's team and the sports committee under Lieutenant Crawford's chairmanship had unanimously suggested Grey-Bennett as its captain.

'Hell!' said Grey-Bennett, when Crawford told him about it. 'I *knew* this would happen. Why can't I be just a boffin in the team?'

'Because you're the only officer considered good enough to play for the ship—and anyway they've elected you as captain. Your number two on the lower deck is PO Cook Jenkins.'

'That bolshie!' Grey-Bennett remarked. 'Can't we do better than that?'

'No,' said Crawford, 'you've been told off—so get on

with it and win us a cup. That's what Stubby wants—and the ship's company for that matter.'

So there it was. Jenkins loathed being sent for by Grey-Bennett to discuss and decide on the team. Nor was it any pleasure to Grey-Bennett. There was always a smell of pomade in the pilot's cabin, and Jenkins' first action when he knocked and came in, his cap under his left arm, was to sniff.

'Good evening, Jenkins,' said the pilot, 'got a cold?'

'No, sir, I thought I smelt something, sir, as I came along the flat.'

'Hm!' said Grey-Bennett. They could declare one-all on that one. 'Well, now,' he went on, 'I don't think we need waste a lot of time on this. There's no doubt about it you're the best forward in the ship and next to you I'd put Leading-Stoker Sidgwick. Agreed?'

'Thank you, sir.'

Jenkins glowered with a mixture of pride and hatred. He had not expected to be flattered so curtly and abruptly but, being as objective as he could, he had to acknowledge the accuracy of Grey-Bennett's judgement.

'How about you for goal, sir?' he countered, and then added reluctantly: 'You've got the longest reach of us all.'

'Yes,' said Grey-Bennett, 'that's what I thought as well. I'll try it if you like.' He paused and then looked at Jenkins with the trace of a smile. 'I expect you and I will get along somehow or other.'

'Just as you say, sir,' said Jenkins, his smooth pink face a degree or two deeper in shade.

As he walked for'ard after this meeting he quickly explained things away to himself. It was all a trick, of course. That fancy young officer merely wanted to catch him off his guard. Well! flattery wouldn't do it. And yet—Grey-Bennett sounded quite genuine. Jenkins *was* the best water polo forward in the ship. For that matter Grey-Bennett was certainly worth his place in the team. There was no sentimentality in that. Jenkins clucked his tongue to himself. The less he had to do with the officers the better.

By the time HMS *Antigone* sailed up the Narrows and steamed proudly into Bermuda Dockyard, Able-Seaman

Clarke in the Commander's office was ready to take on the Old and the New Worlds combined. The nine days at sea had given him the break he needed. The office was up-to-date, no returns outstanding, the routine perfectly under control and his Commander in a much sweeter temper than he had ever been since leaving England.

Things were much as Nobby Clarke wanted them. He had the measure of everyone on board who mattered to the Commander's office. He knew who could be relied on and who would need chasing, who was easy and who difficult, the trouble makers and those who did the jobs they were given without any sort of fuss. He was on good, friendly terms with the Captain's Secretary: he had a working arrangement with the Master-at-Arms and a free and easy understanding with the ship's office and the Victualling Chief Petty Officer.

Although as an Able-Seaman he had to draw his spirit ration each day officially weakened down to grog by the addition of three parts of water—(whereas Chief and Petty Officers could draw theirs neat)—a medicine bottle would appear from time to time in his bottom right-hand drawer filled with brown cough mixture, bearing an extraordinary resemblance to rum.

Whenever this bottle appeared the most remarkable concord appeared to obtain between the Executive and Engineering Departments. Demands for stoker working parties were somehow deferred or shelved, advance information of value to the Senior Engineer found its way miraculously to his ears and the ancient rivalry and dislike between the two branches might never have existed.

If anyone had known about that little bottle and if anyone had called it a bribe Able-Seaman Clarke would have been genuinely horrified. He never saw it in that light at all. To Nobby it was one of the few modest 'perks' of his modest station in life. In all probability he would have treated the Engineering Department in exactly the same way if no one had slipped him a drink. The fact that somebody did was a token to him of a little personal success and esteem—and one which gave him much private pleasure.

'Hands to stations for entering harbour,' the pipe sounded out on the ship's loudspeakers and Nobby trundled up on deck with the Quarterdeck Division.

The Caribbean
& Bermuda

Munich Dash

Bermuda

H·M·S "Malabar" was
on Ireland Island

Ireland I.

Hamilton

Castle
Harbour

Frith
Sound

Atlantic

STO.
DOMINGO

PUERTO RICO

Antigua

Martinique

St. Vincent

Barbados

Port of Spain

Trinidad

La Guaira

Caracas

VENEZUELA

BRITISH GUIANA

SURINAM

FR. GUIANA

BRAZIL

orion

'Honouring us with your presence, Mr Clarke?' said the Divisional PO, who by this time knew the gamut of excuses which Nobby could summon up for avoiding any particular function. There was always something to be done in the Commander's office. But Nobby never rose to that kind of taunt.

'Don't it smell lovely,' said Nobby, 'after Malta?'

The fresh green grass, the dark rain-soaked trees, and the coral sand all gave Bermuda a look and a sweetness of smell highly impressive to the ship's company.

'It's much wetter than they told us at Cooks,' another seaman complained. 'I'll have my money back on this cruise.'

They fell in properly and watched in silence as *Antigone* sailed past the giant hotels of Hamilton; past Government House; past Spanish Point with its sweep of the Great Sound and its almost enclosed lagoon to Ireland Island where the little Naval Dockyard known as HMS *Malabar* nestled by itself on a spit of coral rock. Nobby could see two other cruisers in harbour—the *Berwick* and the *Ajax*. *Berwick* was a 'County' class cruiser of ten thousand tons flying the C-in-C's flag; *Ajax* was a sister-ship to *Antigone*. As they berthed slowly alongside, everyone on board *Antigone* was aware of being critically examined by the other two cruisers.

'We're 'ere!' the seaman next to Nobby whispered out of the corner of his mouth, 'now watch 'em get us running around.'

'No talking in the ranks,' the First Lieutenant snapped. There was an air of tenseness in everyone on the upper deck. Nobby, who was proof against most of the stresses of Naval life, nevertheless recognized how critical this first impact of *Antigone* was upon their Commander-in-Chief and the other ships of the squadron. He drew in a deep, slow breath. It seemed to symbolize the state of everyone else on board. They stood rigidly on show and hoped that all would be well. The ship slipped nearer and nearer to the jetty where a berthing party of negroes under the command of a Lieutenant-Commander with a bicycle was waiting for the first lines to snake ashore from the foc'sle and the quarterdeck.

'Bicycles!' murmured the seaman next to Nobby. 'Look at all those flipping bicycles!'

In 1938 there were no cars in Bermuda. Transport was by means of the horse, the bicycle or the odd little railway which connected Sandy's with Hamilton, running along the backbone of the 360 islands which comprise Bermuda.

As soon as *Antigone* had secured and the brows were out, her induction into the Eighth Cruiser Squadron began. Calls were made and returned on the Commander-in-Chief, the dockyard authorities and on the other two ships of the squadron. Then other connections at other levels were made. Surgeon met surgeon, engineer met his opposite number in other ships and *Antigone* was made to feel at home and part of the family. Nobby saw this welcome reflected at second-hand in his officers and especially the Commander. He also saw it directly with his own eyes when he met an 'old ship' of his at the Fleet Canteen on Boaz Island.

'Strike a light!' said Nobby, 'what are you doing out here, Ginger? I see you haven't lost your gazelle-like figure.'

Ginger Lewis, like Nobby, was a well-covered three-badge Able-Seaman. Both were Portsmouth ratings.

'I'm in *Berwick*,' said Ginger Lewis, setting up a supply of beer beside them. 'I'm Commander's writer for my sins and misdemeanours.'

'Go on!' said Nobby, exhibiting one of his rare moments of surprise. 'That's what I'm on over in *Aunty Gone*.'

'Cor!' said Ginger, then after a moment's pause: 'What a name for a ship! Still, she looked a bit of all right coming into harbour today. Got things nice and comfy, have you?'

'Things is all right,' said Nobby non-committally. 'Of course, we can get 'em better.' He jerked his head in the direction of South America: 'You been down south, Ginger?'

'I been through the Canal. I got one or two things I could pass on to you. How do you go on for coming across in the dog watches tomorrow?' He shot Nobby an appraising look. 'How do you go on for boats in general—easy is it?'

'I shall have to have a word with my First Lieutenant,' Nobby said cautiously and importantly as he and his old ship steadily lowered their glasses. 'Of course,' he went on, 'I shouldn't wonder if the Executive Officer of *Aunty Gone* didn't have to send over his slave for some local information of a confidential and verbal nature.'

Then they looked at each other and smiled.

'Fancy you being over in *Berwick*!' said Nobby, 'and up to the same old tricks—makes it feel quite like home, don't it?'

'Home!' said Ginger, 'that's where we're going as soon as the Regatta's over. To pay off! No one thinks about nothing else over in *Berwick*. Not now!'

'When is the Regatta?'

'Third week in July—as soon as *Exeter*'s cruise is over. Got anything good for it?'

The Fleet Pulling Regatta in which ships' reputations were made or lost was also a great opportunity for lower-deck gambling. On the day itself ships would run totalisators on board but beforehand there was usually a fair amount of private money at stake.

'We got a good Stokers' Cutter,' said Nobby carefully, 'and I could fancy our Young Seamen's Whaler. If you're laying out money,' he added, 'you want to keep clear of our Chief and POs' Gig. But there's no horrid gambling going on, is there—not in this posh fleet?'

'Well,' said Ginger confidentially. 'I do make a little book over in *Berwick*. You should do the same, Nobby —a bit of inside information comes in handy with the odds.' He leant over and whispered as though passing a state secret. 'You want to watch out for the *Ajax* Marines' Whaler—never give better than evens on it. How say we get together, Nobby? We could lay off some money with each other.'

'I'll have to think it over.'

'How do you stand with your Crusher? All right is he?'

'Well,' said Nobby with a wink, 'what the eye don't see, the regulating office don't hear about, now does it?'

'That's how it is with me, too.'

The canteen was very full and Nobby remarked on it as the pile of empty bottles beside them steadily grew.

'Ah! well,' said Ginger, 'that's Bermuda, that is. There's a bit of bathing and you can see a film twice a week in the old sail loft, but otherwise it's the canteen or nothing.'

'Don't they have no pubs around here?'

146

'Pubs!' said Ginger scornfully, 'you should do a run over to Hamilton. Take a couple of thousand quid—you'll need it. It's an officers' port, Hamilton is—nothing over there for poor three-badge Able-Seamen. We do better just as we are.' He looked round the splendid array of bottles and was struck by another idea.

'Want to come in with me on some bicycles, Nobby? Or have you brought your own?'

'No.'

'*Ajax* did. Upset the market, she did. However, it's steadied up again. Now—when we go home to pay off —we shall have a lot of wheelers to sell. All your officers will need 'em. Can't get along in Bermuda without them.'

'How many can you let me have now?'

'Well,' said Ginger, with the crafty look of a street trader, 'I could do you five—good light ones with new number plates—suitable for Lieutenants and below. Then I got a couple more what would fit a Lieutenant-Commander or above—a bit heavier and safer like.'

'I'll see what I can do,' said Nobby. 'Quite like old times, Ginger, ain't it?'

All around them the canteen buzzed with life. Nobby looked about him, his hands folded benevolently across his ample belly. He was content and at ease. When it came to the point one pub or canteen was much the same as another. He had surveyed countless similar scenes in his nineteen years of service. He felt at home. Over in one corner he could see the other two Fat Men of the Sea. Had he not bumped into Ginger he would probably have been sitting with them. Outside the sub-tropical night was unexpectedly cool and damp. Bermuda was not quite what he had expected and he remarked on it to Ginger.

'We had it explained to us once,' Ginger answered, his brow furrowed with intellectual effort. 'It's on account of the Gulf Stream or something. Very temperate it is—like me. It rains a lot here—drizzle mostly. Of course they don't put that on the posters. Don't want to frighten the money away, do we?'

It was a curious staccato language they spoke. They swapped the most trivial, half-finished jargon, yet a look or an inflection made it convey exactly the meaning they wanted. Nobby had had little to do with the Army or the Air Force but he thought the Navy could beat both the other services at picking up 'know-how' and passing on its essentials by means of this verbal tick-tack. What was going on all round him then was something essentially Naval. It was the giving and taking of facts and experience gleaned all over the Americas, digested by life at sea and applicable only to the lower deck. Nobby supposed the officers went on in much the same way at their level, but for the sailors of *Antigone* the canteen at Bermuda was an invaluable mart of 'buzzes', short practical advice and the immediate reactions of their sister ships to people and places which *Antigone* would soon be meeting. If wardroom officers put each other in the picture over a glass of gin, the lower deck did it most noisily over beer in the Fleet Canteen. But the result was the same. *Antigone* as a whole was finding her way around with remarkable speed.

The ships of the America and West Indies Station were to be in company for the month of July. Ten days after *Antigone* arrived the fourth cruiser, HMS *Exeter*, reached Bermuda and a day later the fifth, HMS *York*, sailed into port. The Eighth Cruiser Squadron was thus complete. The modest dockyard facilities of Bermuda were now fully extended. With over three thousand officers and men in port the Navy seemed to be all over the island. Liberty boats were run across the Great Sound to Hamilton: sailors festooned the little train, they rode bicycles everywhere and they walked.

But Bermuda, as a general rule, left the Navy to its own individual devices. An occasional picnic or a dance might be semi-officially arranged, officers were welcome at the Mid-Ocean Yacht Club and visits were fixed up to the perfume manufactory with its fields of heavy-scented Easter lilies stretching all around—but in general the Bermudans took the Navy much for granted. Sailors came, they spent a little—a very little money—and then they went away again. The Bermudans, with a strong piratical strain in their history, were in 1938 almost indifferent to the Navy. Their interest was far more basically centred in the two great Furness-Withy liners, the *Monarch* and the *Queen of Bermuda*, which ran to New York and brought them the island's life blood of dollar-spending American tourists.

Bermuda is shaped very slightly like a sea horse with

Ireland Island forming its snout, Hamilton its belly and Castle Harbour its tail. Thus the Navy were tucked away on one tip of the island and were able to work together as a squadron unfettered and unobserved. Since berths alongside were at a premium *Antigone*, as a junior ship, was soon moved out to the anchorage.

'And personally I prefer it,' the Chief Bos'n's Mate observed to the Coxswain as they watched a cutter and whaler's crew practising for the Regatta, 'keeps us more to ourselves, like, if you see what I mean.'

'Yes,' said Vincent. 'When people have to catch a boat they think twice about going ashore. And *Aunty*'s got to win that Regatta.'

The ship's chances of doing so were slight. The art of working up a successful pulling boat's crew takes time and much practice. *Antigone* had been commissioned only for two months, the rest of the squadron for anything up to two years. Moreover, most of the other ships had had the advantage of competing against each other in the previous year's Regatta.

'Although,' said CPO Bowling, who had joined the other two on the upper deck, 'their cruise programmes can't have done their boat work a lot of good. If we can stay out of sight out here, and get in some really hard practice, we might surprise them all yet.'

The last cruise programme of the squadron had in fact been glamorous but of little Service benefit to the ships themselves. *York* and *Berwick* had been up either side of North America, one to Alaska and the other to Newfoundland, *Exeter* had been down to the Falkland Islands and *Ajax* to Buenos Aires and Rio de Janeiro. They had steamed vast distances, they had exercised independently in accordance with the orders and they had shown the flag. But they had very, very rarely gone away pulling in boats.

'We should do all right with the cutters,' said Bowling, looking down on the heavy double-banked boats with their twelve oars, 'and the whalers are coming along nicely, too. But if we get anywhere but a bad fifth with that bastorial gig, I shall be more than surprised.'

Despite much diplomatic manoeuvring *Antigone* had not been able to exchange her gig before leaving Portsmouth and it was still a thorn in Bowling's flesh.

'She's not all that bad,' said the Coxswain, 'the Captain likes the way she sails.'

'Oh! well,' said Bowling grudgingly, 'I suppose she's water-tight. She won't actually sink during the race—but if I could find a way of staving her in while no one was looking—accidentally, mind you . . . ,' he tailed off and the others laughed. It was the Chief Quartermaster's favourite hobby horse. One of these days perhaps something would happen to the gig.

The little group of chief and petty officers on the upper deck was joined by the Yeoman of Signals. These four—the Chief Bos'n's Mate, the Chief Quartermaster, the Captain's Coxswain and the Yeoman of Signals—comprised one of the best-informed and critical groups on the lower deck. From each of them the ship's company would glean a point of view based upon fact. Just as a newspaper both creates and reflects public opinion, so these four acted in much the same way towards the ship's company of *Antigone*. They did this almost unconsciously and without awareness of the full effects. They simply knew their own minds and their judgment was respected throughout the ship.

CPO Bowling looked at the others and smiled. This was unusual for him but for some reason in their company a feeling of friendship and affection animated his heart. He did not know why this should be. Bowling took things much as they came and his gaunt figure suggested a grave and somewhat gloomy dignity rather than an openhearted joy.

But as he looked at Penniwick, Vincent and Mellish he was conscious of the rich and all powerful team-feeling which had begun to grow in the ship. It lay deep. It was still tender and young. It might not yet be strong enough to win them regattas and cups, but the spirit was there. It seemed to be especially so among his three other companions. He could almost see it in the way they stood by the guardrail. Penniwick with his hands behind his back like a portly Mr Pickwick, a symbol of solid power; Vincent, leathery and lithe; Mellish with his humorous intelligent face and his signal-pad.

In front of them and below lay the pulling boats at the port main boom. The crews were climbing up the rope ladder and along the boom, while other crews ready for practice stood waiting impatiently on the upper deck. Bowling remembered how frightened he had been as a seaman boy to climb up a rope ladder or monkey about in the rigging of the training ship. It was a kind of gnawing terror in the pit of the stomach. He had been all right with other people around him, but alone it was a dizzy, sickening ordeal. He had only conquered it—one of the earliest victories over himself he could remember—by going back afterwards and making himself climb up alone. He had nearly died of fear but he had won and from then on it had never been as bad.

'Get a move on down there on the boom,' Penniwick shouted, 'we haven't got all day.'

Bowling and Vincent left the others and went down below to change. Both were in the Chief and POs' Gig and it was time for their practice. Nobby Clarke might not fancy them as a bet and Bowling had no belief in the boat, but there was nothing lackadaisical in the way they went at their practice. This was one crew which needed no driving. Almost literally they had forged themselves into a team. The Stokers' Cutter and the Young Seamen's Whaler might do much as they pleased, but the eyes of the ship were on them, the chief and petty officers. Anything less than their maximum effort would damage the ship's reputation and their own authority.

As Bowling changed into his practice clothes—'like a long animated corpse' he had once heard himself described—he reflected once more upon the strangeness of being a chief petty officer. It was a very private thought. The ship's company would not have associated a sense of wonder with their Chief Quartermaster. In his singlet, his shorts and his gym shoes he looked rather like a tall cadaverous schoolboy with greying hair. Bowling himself was always surprised by the length of his frame. The proportion of girth seemed to be missing. He was very tall, and his thin legs and body were covered with jet-black hair. It was not a body intended for shorts. It provoked immediate mirth, but this was a good corrective to any oversize ideas he might acquire from time to time. Moreover, Bowling's dignity had long since deepened and retreated from the surface of things. You might feel an impulse to laugh if you caught sight of him from the back, striding along the deck in shorts, but when you studied his face there was nothing of the buffoon to jeer at. It was a grave, lined and experienced face, and the eyes were cool and steady.

The Chief and POs' Gig was being trained by the First Lieutenant. This had been Bowling's idea and at first the others had resented it. They felt, as chief and petty officers, that they could manage quite well by themselves. But Bowling had watched Lieutenant-Commander Collard at work on the gunroom whaler. He had seen that their placid, unhurried First Lieutenant, whatever he lacked in fire and dash, was a natural teacher. He might be slow in speech and reserved in manner, but he had a sharp eye and a knack of seeing instantly what was wrong and of putting it right. So Bowling had persevered with his crew. He secured their grudging agreement and then asked Collard if he would take the boat in hand. It had needed but a single dog watch to convince the other chief and petty officers that Bowling had got them an asset.

That afternoon there was a stiff lop in the Sound and conditions were far from perfect.

'I suggest we change numbers one and two around,' said Collard. 'I think Burton will be better off as bowman. What do you think, Briggs?' Briggs invariably agreed. The First Lieutenant was never tired of experimenting, but there was always a purpose behind it. Any momentary disappointment or irritation disappeared in the underlying pleasure of building something up.

It was very rarely that Collard coxed the boat. He would not be coxing it in the Regatta and every time he usurped the position of CPO Briggs, who with the Navigating Officer was one of the two smallest men in the ship, he knew he was making things more difficult instead of easier. Often he would sit in the stern sheets as a passenger letting Briggs work up his crew and only occasionally commenting or offering advice: at other times he would watch from a motor-boat and reserve his comments until later. That afternoon he gave them a good half-hour and then made them pull briskly back to the ship.

'Well,' he said, as they got back on board, 'I don't know what we're up against but we should give them a run for their money.'

'Thank you very much, sir. Same time tomorrow?'

'Same time tomorrow.'

'Any good news from home yet, sir?' Bowling ventured as the First Lieutenant turned to go aft. Collard had told him about the third baby and its lateness.

'Yes,' said Collard, a wide smile on his face, 'I had a cable this morning. It's a girl.'

'Congratulations, sir.'

'Thank you, Bowling. It's wonderful news. We always wanted a girl.'

'Missus all right, sir?'

'Yes—they're both fine.'

'Well,' said Bowling, 'that ought to bring us luck if nothing else does.'

A Fleet Regatta is a sort of maritime Derby Day. There is the same careful preparation behind the scenes, the same mounting excitement, the same exact rules, starters, stewards and judges. If there were no charabancs on Epsom Downs there were instead five cruiser-loads of hotly enthusiastic sailors, each with his own favourite for the day.

Each of the cruisers now anchored in a double line out in the Sound, provided a separate contribution to the day. HMS *York* and HMS *Antigone* had supplied the power boats which towed competitors to the starting line and away from the finish. HMS *Ajax* had laid down the buoys marking the course, HMS *Exeter* fired the starting gun and the finish took place under the control of the Commander-in-Chief in HMS *Berwick*. The orders—'the drill'—had been carefully worked out weeks beforehand and now on a fine, breezy day in July the Regatta began.

To Mellish, whose years of examining seascapes from the signal bridge had given him a sharp and at times poetic outlook, the scene had the flavour of a medieval tournament. He saw the little cutters and whalers in the guise of chivalrous knights jousting at each other, the results of the races as a flourish of trumpets instead of a string of pendants from the flagship's bridge, and if the reward of victory was scarcely a kiss from a wimpled lady, it was at least a public honour in the form of a cup awarded by the Commander-in-Chief and followed by traditional celebrations. Mellish had the romantic approach. Long hours of interpreting coloured bunting at sea had given him an instinctive understanding of heraldry and its purpose. To his eye the flags and pendants were always dancing to a gay little tune of their own. A medieval tune heard by no one but himself.

'Here we go,' he said to Petty Officer Vincent as they stood watching the first race from the signal deck. 'It's too late now to give up smoking or cut down on the beer. *Aunty*'s in the ring and she's got to fight her way out of it as best she can. What are the odds on the Artificers' Whaler?'

'Pretty poor,' said the Coxswain, 'the *Exeter* has an edge on them all.'

The *Exeter* and the *Ajax* were joint favourites for the whole Regatta. So far as the betting on the ship's totalisator was concerned *Antigone* came a good last. Her ship's company would loyally shout and encourage their own boats at full voice, but you put a bet on to make money. The poor support for *Antigone* showed up in the little canvas booth in which the Paymaster-Commander and his staff worked out the odds. They all wanted their boats to win but thought it highly unlikely they would.

The first surprise came in the third race. This was for the Marines' Whalers. *Ajax* had been heavily backed to win, as Nobby's friend in the Fleet Canteen had forecast, and almost at once the *Ajax* boat drew ahead. Mellish, watching through his telescope, realized what an advantage this gave. They set the pace—and it was their rhythm which dictated the race or was likely to do so nine times out of ten.

'It looks like they were right,' he said to Vincent, '*Ajax* got a length ahead at the start and now she's holding it easily.'

Yet even as he said it another boat began creeping up. Mellish watched it in silence for a moment or so.

'Who's in Number Four berth?' said the Yeoman over his shoulder, his eye clamped to his telescope. It was the signal department's job to keep the ship's scoreboard up-to-date.

'That's us,' the Leading Signalman answered, 'how's *Aunty* doing? Last again is she?'

'No,' Mellish said, a note of excitement in his voice. 'I think we've crept up on the *Ajax*.'

He was about eight seconds ahead of anyone else on board in this assessment. Then suddenly a shiver seemed to go through the ship. The crowds of sailors on the upper deck in their white drill shorts, the officers with their binoculars, the cooks peering out of the galley door—everyone who was watching the race seemed to catch on to what was happening at the same time. A great roar went up from the ship.

'Come on, *Aunty*!' they yelled. 'Let 'em have it. Come on the Joeys!'

Mellish had been right in his hunch. *Antigone*'s whaler was steadily gaining. The ship was berthed opposite the *Berwick* on the other side of the course and the finishing line lay between the two ships. Right until the end, therefore, they had to watch the pulling at a fairly acute angle. By the three-quarter buoy, however, it was obvious that *Antigone*'s Marines were nearly half a length in the lead and pulling superbly. Down on the upper deck Mellish could see Captain Taw-Street nervously stroking his moustache and moving his head in a curious little circular way which meant he was wholly absorbed. At his side Colour-Sergeant Forrester stood stiff as the proverbial ramrod, not saying a word. Mellish leant over and spoke to Vincent so that the junior ratings on the bridge could not hear.

'Take a look at old Forky,' he said, 'he's willing them to win.'

With only a cable to go the *Ajax* boat put on a spurt and drew level. The *Ajax* Marines had not acquired their reputation for nothing. But a spurt is a spurt and *Antigone*'s boat kept steadily on. They held their neck-and-neck positions for a while well ahead of the other three boats. By this time they were nearly opposite *Antigone* and everyone on board could see the young bandsman who was coxing the boat almost breaking the veins in his neck with the effort. The cheering now rose to a vast crescendo. From the bridge it looked as though the entire ship's company was up on deck.

'Come on, *Aunty*! *Aunty*! *Aunty*!' they yelled, and '*Tiggony*! *Tiggony*! *Tiggony*!'

Then about fifty yards from the finish *Antigone*'s boat put on their one and only spurt and inch by inch drew ahead. By the time they crossed the finishing line they had *Ajax* beaten by nearly a length. It was *Antigone*'s first win of the day.

This unexpected favour by Fate seemed to put new

155

heart into the ship. The odds on the Seamen's Cutter and the Daymen's Whaler both shortened, and although neither boat won, they got a second and a third. Then came another surprise. The Stoker's Cutter pulled off an easy first and the Commander (E) and Meldrum were observed dancing a little jig together on the quarterdeck. Although they had only won two races out of six, they lay equal second for the Regatta Cup, which was awarded on points.

Mellish put down his telescope and lit a cigarette. Normally this was an indulgence he never allowed either to himself or to the ratings under him. Even during stand-easies and in the dog watches the Yeoman of Signals liked his flag deck to be spick and span and immaculate. Those who wanted to smoke could do so on the upper deck. To Mellish the signal bridge and the signal distributing office was the real heart of the ship, to be treated with proper respect. You couldn't jump to a hoist if you were bleary with cigarette smoke, as he himself had been so forcibly told when a signal boy. But today was Regatta Day. Like Christmas it was a time for special dispensations and Mellish enjoyed his cigarette the more for realizing the great concession it was.

By now, Petty Officer Vincent had left the bridge, since the race for the Chief and POs' Gig was next but one on the programme. This would be the last race before lunch and then the day would be half gone. Mellish looked down on the ship and beyond her decks to the squadron so peacefully anchored in the Great Sound. He felt relaxed and content. It was a fine sight to look at on a sunny July day. The coral rock gave the sea a richness and a clarity unique, it seemed, to Bermuda. The colours ranged from deepest blue to emerald green and the whole setting was rimmed by beaches of white coral sand with the junipers, the palms and the pines reaching up behind them.

In the foreground the five cruisers looked majestic and calm. It was remarkable, Mellish reflected, how peaceful a fleet of warships can appear—their main armament trained fore and aft, their awnings spread and their attendant boats fussing about them like chickens round a hen.

He thought of other Regattas in other fleets, of Malta, Singapore and Hong Kong, of windswept northern Scapa and of tropical Ceylon. He had served in each of those places and each picture as it arose in his mind had its own associations, its own special flavour. So would this little Regatta today, this small gathering of cruisers scarcely numerous enough to be called a fleet.

Yet, as Mellish looked down the line, in many ways this little Regatta was the prettiest of the lot. It had the air of a village celebration instead of the smart, rather pompous efficiency of one of the major fleets. But only someone who had been a Leading-Signalman in the fleet flagship of the Mediterranean Fleet could appreciate such differing tastes and values. He thought back a little wistfully to those days. He had come a long way since then.

As he finished his cigarette the Warrant Officers' Skiff race had just begun. This was looked on as light relief. It carried fewer points towards the cup than the whaler or cutter races but to the delight and astonishment of everyone on board, *Antigone*'s boat stroked by Mr Partle came in first. This put the ship an undisputed second to the *Ajax*.

Then just before the dinner break came the race for the Chief and Petty Officers' Gig. Mellish had watched the First Lieutenant restlessly pacing up and down in the waist just before the race had begun. He talked to no one and seemed wholly bound up in his state of nerves. This was so unusual for the calm, placid Collard that on an impulse Mellish went down from the bridge and spoke to him.

'First Lieutenant, sir, would you care to come up on the flag deck?' he asked. 'There's a much better view from there.'

Collard looked at him both sharply and in a preoccupied way.

'Thank you, Mellish, I think I will.'

They went up together and stood watching the race. Collard or any of the officers would have been perfectly at liberty to go up on to the flag deck anyway, had they wanted to do so, yet to be invited up by the Yeoman of Signals was a subtle compliment. The First Lieutenant felt, as Mellish had wanted him to feel, that he was one of them, that this race was his race and that it was appropriate for him to be among them at that time.

As if in answer to the same unformulated summons the Chief Bosun's Mate, Chief Petty Officer Penniwick, the

157

Chief Gunner's Mate and the Torpedo Gunner's Mate had also appeared and stood a little apart until Collard spoke to them all. The final rating to join the group had been the Master-at-Arms who, though not a founder member of the 'club', was now one of its staunchest pillars.

'Well,' said Collard as the starting gun was fired, 'I think they'll do wonders even to finish in that boat.'

'It's anybody's race so far,' said Millish, cheerfully when the boats had gone about fifty yeards. He was squinting through his telescope. 'I can see Briggs swearing at them already.'

When they had pulled about a third of the race *Antigone*'s boat lay a close second.

'I just don't believe it,' said Collard, looking through his glasses, 'they're pulling magnificently. But this is too good to be true.'

The wind was freshening and this was a slight advantage to *Antigone*'s heavier boat. The little group on the flag deck fell silent as they stood and watched. Below them the crowd was spasmodically cheering, but as the position of the boats could not be properly gauged by the naked eye, interest in the race was still unfocused. Once again no one expected *Antigone* to win. The gig's reputation was known throughout the ship and the boat had been badly supported on the Tote.

By the half-way mark the *Ajax* boat had gained nearly two lengths and *Exeter*'s gig was moving up into second place. The group on the bridge fell silent. They all knew how the drag and the heaviness of the boat would seem to increase as the race neared its end. At some time or other they had all pulled in races like that.

'They must have shot their bolt too soon,' Mellish murmured. 'They're slipping back.'

Then with about a third of the race to go a tiny accident occurred. No. 2 in the *Ajax* boat caught a crab and this was such a surprise that almost before the boat recovered its rhythm he caught another.

'Now, Briggs—now's your chance,' Collard said in a hoarse whisper. He could not even be sure that Briggs would have noticed this mishap in the hurly-burly of the race, but in fact both he and the Coxswain of *Exeter*'s boat had caught the incident out of the corner of their eyes, and both had passed on the news to their own crews.

To Bowling who was stroking the boat and who had almost reached that point of exhaustion beyond which any race is irretrievably lost, the news came like a flash of lightning. He nodded at Briggs and the little Coxswain ordered a spurt.

'We can do it,' he yelled. '*In*-out, *In*-out, *In*-out: come on the lot of you—*Aunty*'s got to win: we can do it: we can do it . . . ,' and then a few moments later: 'We're catching up—we're going ahead.'

This was not strictly true when Briggs said it but it had the effect he wanted. It put new heart into the crew. A few moments later *Antigone*'s boat had indeed begun to forge ahead. Somewhere inside that gaunt exhausted frame Bowling had tapped another source of energy and to Collard and the others watching on boat it was the Marines' Whaler all over again. Inch by inch *Antigone*'s gig drew level with the *Ajax* boat. The shouting on the upper deck now reached a frenzy. The three Fat Men of the Sea were jumping up and down like ponderous rubber balls, Hatchett was up on a bollard leading the cheers and six hundred yelling sailors roared with a Cup Final intensity which carried across the water to the little boat and fired them on to one last, desperate, heart-splitting effort.

They crossed the finishing line neck and neck. From both *Ajax* and *Antigone* identical roars claimed a victory but Collard and the group on the signal bridge were not so sure. They kept quiet and waited, watching each other sideways, hardly daring to breathe. Only Mellish had his eyes glued to his telescope and his telescope trained on the flagship. The seconds passed with no result declared. Collard turned to the others, looked at them for a moment or so, and then smiled with his eyes.

'I shouldn't think so,' he said with practised Service pessimism.

'No,' said Penniwick, shaking his head, 'not a hope.'

'Besides,' added the TGM. '*Ajax* is the favourite. She's *supposed* to be winning the Regatta.'

Then they heard Mellish draw his breath in sharply. There was a slight pause as he straightened up and looked at the others.

'*Aunty*'s got it after all,' he said, and grinned like a Cheshire Cat.

CHAPTER SEVEN

On 19 July 1938, King George the Sixth and his Queen paid a State Visit to Paris. Two months later Mr Chamberlain flew to Munich to plead with Hitler for another year's uneasy peace. Between those two pegs on the line of history lay the decline and fall of the 'thirties. From then on it was but a matter of time.

Daladier was the Radical Premier of France. Italy still had a King. Income Tax stood at five-and-six in the pound and Germany was at work promoting trade agreements and non-aggression pacts with Russia and Japan.

The gathering storm, as Mr Churchill described it, was unmistakably there, but those who by habit were immersed in the market place felt no especial call to study the dark horizon. An LNER express train touched a speed of 125 miles an hour. Susan Lenglen had died, the hundredth air raid on Barcelona took place in the long-drawn-out Spanish struggle and President Roosevelt was importuning Hitler by telegram to give up all idea of war.

Meanwhile the Royal Navy's newest cruiser began the Caribbean tour so carefully thought out and organized for her. At home the Plans and Operations Divisions of the Admiralty might be burning the midnight oil. The Departments responsible for mobilizing the Fleet might be dusting off their skeleton orders. The Lords Commissioners of the Admiralty might be, and, indeed, were, numbering the resources of the Navy with the utmost care, but at the level of HMS *Antigone* life was a matter of proceeding in execution of previous orders, and the orders concerned themselves with courtesy visits and with showing the Flag.

On board only Trevesham and Hatchett had served in Admiralty appointments. Both knew and visualized what must be going on in Whitehall as the summer wore on. All Heads of Departments on board *Antigone* had read and understood the secret orders kept in a safe in the Captain's day cabin which outlined the likely course of events if the Fleet should be mobilized. The Commander (E), the Paymaster-Commander, the Surgeon-Commander, the Gunnery, Torpedo and Communications Officers, the Navigator, the pilot of the ship's aircraft and the Captain, Royal Marines, all knew what their departments must do should the emergency come. In the meantime *Antigone* sailed south to Barbados and began her first routine duties of the commission.

In the late summer of 1938 the Royal Navy was still weakened by the various disarmament treaties of the 'twenties and the 'thirties, but it was nevertheless a formidable weapon. The two main fleets—the Home and the Mediterranean—had fourteen battleships and aircraft carriers on active service between them. Five cruisers of seven to ten thousand tons each were in Home waters, seven were stationed on Malta, four covered the East Indies, from Ceylon and Singapore, six operated out of Hong Kong, five formed the America and West Indies Squadron, and one was at the Cape. The Royal Australian Navy had four cruisers and New Zealand two. Other capital ships and cruisers of varying size and antiquity were in reserve refitting for further service with the Fleet. By the time war broke out there were some sixty-three cruisers on active service, or ready in reserve. The British Empire might sprawl its communications across the world but they were far from defenceless.

From the Admiralty point of view, therefore, *Antigone* was but a tiny twig on a distant bough. She had blossomed: she had been favourably observed and now she could be left to herself. She had taken her place in the Fleet. She was a set of numbers in the most secret codes and cyphers: she was a call sign in the communications network: the General Post Office sacked up her mail every day: tailors, wine merchants, stationers and foreign agents all noted her movements for their different purposes: friends, relatives and lovers wrote letters and pined against the day of her return: dockyards recorded the state of her bottom and oil companies the quantities of fuel she used: victualling yards and local ships' chandlers ministered to her needs: Armament Supply Officers watched by means of her regular reports the age of the

161

cordite in her magazines and the number of hours her torpedoes had been run: the Surgeon-Commander requisitioned the drugs he needed and the Chaplain mustered his prayer books from time to time in accordance with the King's Regulations and Admiralty Instructions.

By now her teak decks had been scrubbed smooth and white, her light grey paintwork gleamed, her quarterdeck awning was a splash of white canvas against the emerald sea, every piece of brightwork that could be seen sparkled in the tropical sunlight, her White Ensign fluttered proudly in the breeze and to six hundred full-blooded officers and men of the Royal Navy she was something more than just another man-of-war, she was HMS *Antigone*, their ship, the finest of them all.

July slipped away and soon August had nearly gone. They had visited Barbados, the most 'British' of the West Indian islands: they had called in at Antigua, the hot, beautiful, steamy little island where Nelson had built and maintained a dockyard: they had painted ship at St Vincent, they had paid a courtesy visit to French Martinique, and they had spent a week at Port of Spain, the capital of Trinidad. Next on the programme was their first South American port—La Guaira in Venezuela—and then after that they were to visit Colon for five days as guests of the US Navy before traversing the Panama Canal and continuing their cruise down the West coast of South America in the calm blue waters of the Pacific.

Already these visits had a rhythm and a technique. Already a pattern was establishing itself. Already the prospect before them had the appearance of variations on a single theme. The ship would arrive about breakfast time: the Governor, the Mayor, or the Consul would call. Later in the morning the Captain, often accompanied by his Secretary, would return the calls and it was then considered that official courtesy had been adequately served.

Late in the forenoon the Consul or an ADC from Government House would return to the ship. Over pink gin in the wardroom he and Stubby put their heads together on the programme of events. Invitations to receptions, parties, expeditions and picnics were received and returned. While this stage manager's meeting wore on the Consul or the ADC would usually mellow on unaccustomed Plymouth gin. Then the real 'form' was found out. Crawford, the Sports Officer, Hale in charge of the Concert Party and Collard were usually at hand and joined in as necessary. Sometimes Marsh, as Captain's Secretary and interpreter, Darbigh as sub of the gunroom and Mr Partle as president of the warrant officers' mess would be invited to these informal conferences at which the Consul or the ADC got the feel of the ship and *Antigone* the measure of the port she was visiting.

In the evening there would usually be an official reception for the officers at Government House. This meeting up of locals and ship could key the whole visit. Private dinner parties and dances were arranged, promises to show the ship to hot little numbers in white organdie were made by midshipmen and junior officers, games of tennis, golf and bridge were mooted, bathing and sailing parties organized—whatever the island or the ship had to offer was discussed and exchanged. Down in the town a ship's company dance would act as the same crucible for the lower deck. Friends would be made and dated up. A good deal of beer would be drunk. The red light district would brighten up its lights. The Navy was in port and a lot of lusty sailors with strong brown bodies would be lose in the town.

As the week wore on football and cricket matches were played off, the local cane sugar factory with its attendant rum distillery would be visited, the Concert Party and the Harmonica Band put on a show in the local hall, the Royal Marine detachment might Beat the Retreat in the main square. Perhaps there would be an expedition to climb the local volcano and then one afternoon towards the end of their stay the ship would be open to visitors, and as a climax to the week an At Home or possibly a dance would be given by the officers on the quarterdeck. The next morning the ship would sail.

That was the pattern of events. The mechanics of each visit varied in detail: the size of the port, the enthusiasm of the local community, the efforts made and the amenities available all played their part in giving each new place a special flavour and a taste of its own. Moreover, *Antigone* herself was acquiring a distinctive style.

But what mattered—the whole point of the visit at all was the impression *Antigone* left behind her. As she sailed

163

out of harbour for her next port of call she would always leave one tally of herself more vivid than the rest. This was what mattered. This would be the typical picture of her which remained in the memory of Governor, Consul, merchant or cabaret girl. The appearance of the ship, the personalities of her Captain and officers, the bearing of her ship's company, the behaviour of the football team defeated by the locals, the look of the patrol landed on the jetty when leave was piped, the manners of the midshipmen and the energy young wardroom officers forced themselves to put into routine social affairs, all these single memories built up one composite picture of HMS *Antigone* so that after a passage of time whenever the ship's name was mentioned a single frame or a sequence in a motion picture came back into the consciousness and people said: 'Ah! yes, she was a wonderful ship and what a week that was!'

There was more to this process than the mutual exchange of entertainment. The Admiralty, and behind them the Government which found the money for these cruises, had other values in mind. In 1938 the Royal Navy enjoyed a matchless reputation all over the world. It could almost be said to have no enemies. It was held in quite extraordinary esteem even by those who had fought us, and who would soon be fighting us again. This was unique.

The Royal Navy represented to lonely communities at the ends of the earth a practical working model of decency, of restraint, of power held deep in reserve which for centuries has characterized the British seamen. The idea behind the British Empire was at base a projection of the family and a visit by one of HM ships was something of a reunion of brothers and of cousins. It is good that families which have grown up and gone out into the world should meet from time to time—letters, newspapers, films and the radio are not enough. They can never replace that extraordinary regeneration which takes place when members of a family meet again after a time away.

This link, this subtle replenishment of spirit has been one of the peculiar responsibilities of the Royal Navy for well over two centuries of the world's history. It has never been abused. Thus people trusted and respected one of HM ships in a foreign port much more than they would consciously admit. The British sailor is a far from perfect specimen of humanity, but he is of an unchanging type, and his broad shoulders and tolerant heart carry a burden of responsibility of which luckily he is but dimly aware.

The cruise had other and more practical aspects. Any ship needs food and fuel. In peacetime these necessities can be drawn from the most economical or convenient sources, but in war the whole course of the world's history can be changed by the lack of a few tons of oil fuel at the right place and the right time. Exact details of facilities available to warships legally or illegally are recorded in all the principal Admiralties of the world. But statistics on paper are one thing: practical experience of them another. Harbours silt up and cranes break down: old-established ships' chandlers go out of business and new ones take their place. Whatever information filtered back from Consuls, commercial firms and intelligent travellers, the severely practical reports demanded of HMS *Antigone* provided the Admiralty with an up-to-date picture exactly keyed to what a modern warship requires in peace or war.

Thus by the time *Antigone* set sail for La Guaira she already had character on several different levels. She was a major man-of-war. She looked smart: she behaved impeccably. To the jaded tropical palate she was an astringent, a sharp reminder that there is more to ceremonial than merely dressing up and strutting about: to the Commander-in-Chief and the Admiralty she was a newly trained and powerful addition to the fleet: to wives and relatives in England she was a picture on the mantelpiece and a name they wrote on envelopes: to her own ship's company she was home: her turbines hummed and her guns were ready: she was complete in herself and she wore her White Ensign with an air.

La Guaira, the port of Caracas, lies approximately ten degrees north of the equator. It is well named. 'Guaira' in Spanish means smelting furnace and that is exactly what the port seemed like to *Antigone*. The brown hills rising up from the harbour were oppressive: the place had an airless desperation and those whose duty kept them aboard felt sour and ill-tempered.

Certain officers and men, however, looked back on their

visit to Venezuela with pleasure. These were the few who were able to get up to Caracas for a couple of days. Caracas, the capital of the country, stands at three thousand feet above sea level and was a city of some quarter of a million souls. So, when an invitation was received from the President for a party of officers and men to go and stay at the Hotel Majestic, there was keen lobbying in the ship.

'I've had a private note from the Ambassador,' Trevesham told his Commander as they considered this problem in the cuddy over a glass of sherry. 'He says I would be expected myself since there's a wreath to be laid on Bolivar's tomb and the Germans were pointedly not asked when the *Emden* came here last year. So we'll have to land a guard of honour and it looks as though you'll have to mind the ship for a couple of days. I'm sorry about that.'

'It doesn't worry me, sir,' Hatchett replied, running his finger round the inside of his collar, 'it's only this damp heat which gets everyone down. I don't intend working the ship's company very hard for the present.'

'We might get you away for a few days when we're through the Canal,' Trevesham said pensively. 'I want everyone who can take some leave not to miss an opportunity.'

'Don't worry about me,' Hatchett said firmly, 'I've done a stretch in the Persian Gulf.'

'I'll take Marsh with me as interpreter and ten other officers are invited. I'll leave their selection to you. I think Taw-Street ought to be one of them, though. They want the Band to give a concert in the main square one evening. The Ambassador also suggests that officers who can ride will be very welcome. Who else knows one end of a horse from the other? There's our airman, of course.'

'Well, sir, there's Crawford. I think he ought to go and keep an eye on the football team. I'd like both Guns and Torps to get away from the ship—and possibly Collard. He needs a break but I'll have to force him out of the ship at the point of a bayonet. I honestly think he's happier on board. As you say, Grey-Bennett rides a horse,' he added, struck by a sudden thought, 'but I think it would do that young gentleman good to stay on board.'

He and Trevesham exchanged the glint of a smile. Al-

166

though they were so dissimilar in themselves their understanding of their officers and ship's company was almost
exactly matched. No tedious explanations were needed.
Neither Trevesham nor his Commander were tyrants but
if Hatchett thought it better for Grey-Bennett to stay
aboard, then Trevesham knew it would be for a good
service reason and not out of personal spite.

'I'd suggest two snotties and two warrant officers,'
Trevesham went on, 'but I'll leave it to you. Marsh and I
will be staying at the Embassy: the others will be at the
Majestic and the troops are being entertained by the police in their barracks.'

'The chit says seventy "marinos" are invited. That allows a few over after counting in the guard and band and
the football team. The Consul's laid on four coaches for
1315 at the jetty. When do you want to go ashore, sir?'

'The Ambassador's invited me to lunch. He's sending a
car down at eleven o'clock.'

'Then I'll have your boat alongside at 1045,' said
Hatchett, tucking his telescope under his arm and preparing to go. 'Venezuela seems to be doing us proud. I wonder if it's going to be like this all the way round.'

'It wouldn't surprise me,' Trevesham answered, 'that is
if ever we finish the cruise.'

Hatchett paused by the door. The thought of war was
in everyone's mind at that time.

'You think the Germans will start something up during
the summer holidays?' asked Hatchett. 'That's rather un-
sporting, isn't it?'

'It's the season,' Trevesham answered dryly, 'and
they're great psychologists—the Germans. They know all
about the British, their week-ends and their holidays.
They don't think we'll bother if it interferes with our leisure.'

'A few more days of La Guaira,' said Hatchett, 'and I
don't think *Antigone* will bother either. I wonder if the
Führer realizes that.'

To Derek Lysander Marsh the expedition to Caracas
was a fairy tale, an adventure quite out of the run of his
ordinary life. He felt enormously important. To be invited
to stay with his Captain at the British Embassy, to be privileged to translate the President's formal greeting from
Spanish into English and the Captain's equally careful re-

167

ply back again into Spanish, to be at the very centre of official receptions and private parties, to know that although he was only a Sub-Lieutenant with a single gold stripe on his shoulder pads, he was nevertheless in a position of power and influence—these were heady experiences which he relished and relived over and over again in the privacy of his daydreams.

But except for a letter home, he had to keep it all very much to himself. Had he allowed an inkling of the self-importance he felt to be seen in the gunroom, the Midshipmen—and even Sub-Lieutenant Darbigh himself—would have pounced on it with shouts of delight. Marsh had been a Midshipman too long himself, not to realize how wary he needed to be. Even as it was the innocent, irrepressible Mottram was always leading him on, dropping guileless looking tripwires in his path, asking his opinion and waiting like an anxious spaniel for some careless reply which he could distort and build up into a gunroom canard. And Midshipman Mottram was a dab hand at that.

But Marsh fell into none of these traps. Since joining *Antigone* he had lost a great deal of his diffidence. He was better inclined to laugh at himself, to take himself a little less seriously than he had done while still a very new Sub-Lieutenant. He was weathered to it now. Being one of the three head men of the mess had taught him a lot and he was gaining confidence in himself which he had once despaired of acquiring. He had begun to mature. No longer on the defensive, he even stood up to Darbigh from time to time. After all, he told himself bravely when his heart quailed at the prospect of a row, he *was* the Captain's Secretary. They might laugh at him personally for being a shy little beaver of a person but no one laughed at the job. He was someone in the know and Marsh was coming to realize what a real power it brought him.

So when the news got out in the gunroom that he was going up to Caracas with the Captain, he shrugged his shoulders and threw it away with a joke. He was madly excited inside but he pretended that three days of 'tarting about the Embassy' was likely to be far drearier than to be with Midshipmen Watling and Blackburn at the Majestic. It could just be 'a great big bore'.

This tended to be the gunroom point of view. The trip

168

to Caracas, said the midshipmen, might well be more of a lurk than a lark. It carried with it a top load of formality and etiquette. It meant swords, clean white gloves and stiff official parties which photographed well for the papers but which bored the pants off a Midshipman of nineteen.

To Marsh with his background of a Birmingham suburb there was a certain snobbish pleasure in mingling on equal terms with the great, but most of the Midshipmen took it entirely for granted. Their minds were far more intent on popping into bed with the prettiest girls they could find. Indeed, from talk in the mess, it might seem that they thought far more of sex than of the Service. This was quite true, they did. Marsh was beginning to find their endless, lusty bawdiness repetitive and adolescent. He longed for the more informed and wider life of the wardroom. The gunroom, to his changing eyes, had already become little more than a nursery. He was growing up. Already he resented the thought of another whole year held down in their company. Yet in the matter of sex Marsh was at something of a disadvantage: he had never yet slept with a woman.

He kept this one secret very much to himself. Now that he was twenty-one, it seemed to him a disgrace, an oddness to be ashamed of, a blight in his life. Whenever it came up in the gunroom he told a series of lurid lies. He put it about that he had a wild week of incessant debauch in London during his last leave. She was Hungarian and nothing could satisfy her passion. Indeed as he thought about this imaginary dark-haired girl with that faint suggestion of gipsy blood in her veins, his prowess as a lover tended to get out of hand.

One night in the gunroom after too many gins he had let himself go. There would never be another one like Magda, he said, not for Derek Lysander Marsh. Her bed had been a battlefield and each night had seen its own campaign of love. She had fought, she had kicked, she had bitten—he even had a cut on his ear to prove it. Midshipmen Watling and Staines-Bassett, absorbed in this saga, examined his left ear and there was indeed an old scar on the lobe, but only Marsh himself knew that he had received this token of passion from the family cat. However, it was enough for the gunroom. From then on Marsh was treated with more respect. He was an elder Romeo in this all important arena of love.

Apart from anything else it was wonderful to get away from the ship. Marsh sat up in the front of the large Embassy car trying to take in everything at once. He had slipped his sword belt round so that the sword was between his legs and surreptitiously he unbuttoned his white uniform jacket. It was an art to relax inside the starched coffin-case of white drill, buttoned up to the neck, and still finish the journey looking smart and fresh.

He glanced round at the Captain. He was apparently at ease talking to the Counsellor who had come down to meet him in the car. Once out of La Guaira and up on the road to Caracas he had taken off his cap and Marsh with relief followed suit. Although he had plastered down his hair, his cap seemed to be cutting into his head. Royalty must feel like this, he thought, and at the same time wondered if his bladder would hold out till they reached Caracas. That third cup of coffee at breakfast had been a grave mistake.

The Embassy driver was taciturn. He responded politely but briefly to Marsh's attempts at conversation. He made it clear he was there to drive and not to talk and so as the journey went on Marsh fell to thinking about the ship and his life. In his daydreams it was always the same. The ship was always there. Even when he was chasing the naked Magda along a vast empty beach, her hair streaming in the wind, the ship would be at anchor in the bay. I must have things a little out of proportion, he thought, I must practise detachment. Yet even as he said it he knew he was perfectly happy as he was. He had made his escape. His real home was no longer a semi-detached house in a suburb, it was HMS *Antigone*, and when that commission came to an end, it would be another of HM ships. He asked for no more.

But suppose one day he met up with Magda—well, at any rate an English Magda—suppose in the far, far distant future he had enough resources to marry, what then? Wasn't marriage in any shape or form a return to slavery? It looked like it to him. Far better remain a hard-drinking bachelor like the Surgeon-Commander than become a comfortable, dull turnip like Collard and his wife.

170

And yet he was fond of Collard. His slow placidity had inevitable pull for someone as volatile as Marsh. He wondered what if anything could disturb such deliberate calmness. Did nothing matter? Had Collard never lain tossing and turning in his bunk hopelessly caught in wild dreams of success, or heroism—of Magda? He could not imagine anyone—not even Collard—losing any sleep over that buxom, maternal wife. Then suddenly he sat up with a jerk. The Captain was speaking to him.

'You're an expert at these things, Secretary,' said Trevesham. 'How many guests did we invite to that cocktail party in Trinidad?'

'Two hundred and forty-four, sir,' he answered promptly and then added: 'Over four hundred came.'

'Yes,' said Trevesham with a smile, 'that's what we found at Barbados as well. About fifty per cent more come to these "At Homes" than are asked. I believe down the west coast it gets progressively worse.'

It was perfectly true. Marsh remembered those parties in detail. He had seen the Government House lists lopped down and down. He had even supervised the writing of the invitations (a lurk for the midshipmen). Then when the party took place it seemed as though the whole island was coming aboard. He remembered watching them swarm over the quarterdeck and up on the superstructure, and he remembered the Navigating Officer saying, 'There goes another quid on the mess bill.' Not one of the gatecrashers would imagine that the officers paid for these parties themselves. There was a tiny official allowance for entertaining, but like all allowances in 1938 it bore no relation to the expenses incurred. However, Marsh reflected, on the long haul it was a small price to pay for the pleasures of a West Indian cruise, and in any case both Trinidad and Barbados had royally welcomed the ship.

They reached the Embassy in good time for lunch. Despite a sudden attack of nervousness Marsh tagged along behind his Captain trying not unsuccessfully to convey the impression that he did this sort of thing every day of the week. Then after lunch they put on their cocked hats, epaulettes and swords and drove with the Ambassador to the Presidential Palace. It was but three years since President Gomez, the fabulous dictator of the country for a quarter of a century, had died and although there had been 'adjustments' since then, his influence still lay heavy over official Venezuela. His wealth, his vast family, his eccentricities—these were still discussed as they had been in his lifetime, half behind the back of one's hand and with a quick precautionary glance over the shoulder. But successive new regimes had liberalized the conduct of affairs and the President welcomed *'lallegada bienvenida del crucero Antigone de Su Majestad Britanica'* as though he meant it—or so it seemed to Marsh's excited mind.

As it turned out there was no need for Marsh to have interpreted at all. Trevesham had realized this when the invitations originally arrived in the ship. The Ambassador, of course, would take care of any formal encounter between the Commanding Officer of one of HM ships and the head of a foreign state. However, had Trevesham been an Admiral, he would have had his Flag-Lieutenant with him. As a post-Captain, he could only call upon his Secretary for similar services, and when cruising alone as *Antigone* was now doing, the diplomatic responsibilities to be shouldered by Captain or Admiral remained much the same.

So he had insisted on his Secretary coming along. It was excellent practice for what lay in store for them at other South American ports where a member of the British diplomatic service might not be so readily to hand. He had had a word with the Ambassador in private and after the latter had discreetly tested young Mr Marsh's facility in Spanish, Trevesham's intention was put into effect. Blushing furiously Marsh translated the flowery official speeches. He was not entirely accurate but he never once faltered. Then, blushing even more than before, he received the congratulations of the President and the Ambassador, looking as though he would like to have sunk into the floor.

The rest of the afternoon was spent visiting the tomb of Simon Bolivar, the liberator of South America, and in being photographed every few minutes with some new dignitary of the state. In the evening there was a reception for the British community and the Diplomatic Corps at the Embassy to which, of course, came the other *Antigone* officers staying at the Majestic Hotel.

It was a distinguished, pleasant, smartly dressed gathering, and as Trevesham shook hands and was introduced

172

by the Ambassador to men who had reached the top, as he had, in other fields, he felt a private glow of well-being and satisfaction. The visit was a success. HMS *Antigone* was keeping up the tradition in the way expected of her, and the Royal Navy was being as warmly welcomed as it had been in the past.

He looked round at his officers. He did not sentimentalize about being the Commanding Officer of one of HM ships. He was coming to know his ship's company's qualities and defects with much more accuracy now that they had been four months in commission. Instinctively he knew the range, the top and bottom limits of each of his officers and not a few of his men. There was plenty in the cupboard, he thought. If we have to fight a war I couldn't ask for better than these. And, as the Ambassador had told him that afternoon, the news from the Sudetenland was getting steadily worse.

'It does us all a power of good to see you chaps here,' said one of the guests to Trevesham, 'reminds us we still have a Navy after all. Besides,' he leant forward confidentially, 'it puts the Germans' nose out of joint. We do nothing but hear how Hitler's going to make the world one big Germany. Gets a bit boring after a time. You see, our propaganda's no good—no good at all—and theirs is, I'm sorry to say. At least, so far as this country's concerned.'

Luckily at that moment the Ambassador came to Trevesham's rescue and took him away to meet somebody else. He was always finding himself the butt at these affairs, a new person of importance at whom the pet local theories and grudges could be fired, a new pair of ears. Normally it was easy enough to be what people wanted him to be and to skirt round topics which might be inflammable. Trevesham would agree with whatever was being propounded, but always with certain undefined reservations. That was usually enough. Occasionally, though, they tried to get him involved, tried to make him take sides. Once that happened then Trevesham had a little gramophone record of his own about the Silent Service which he put on. It implied that he could say a good deal more than he did—which was true—but that if he did it would be bad for the ship, the Service and the country—which was open to opinion.

Only his wife knew all the gramophone records he kept for these difficult occasions. He thought about her now with tenderness as the party continued. The children would be home for the holidays, playing their games, planning their expeditions, their friends littering up the house. Over it all Diana would preside as she always had done, trying to be father as well as mother without its being obvious, trying to make up for his many absences at vital moments in the family life, writing him full accounts of what went on so that in Singapore or Scapa he would still feel he belonged and was missed. She was a wonderful woman. Suddenly in the middle of this Embassy party in Venezuela thousands of miles away from her across the sea, he had a longing for his wife which seemed to twist his inside.

He continued to shake hands and drink cocktails. He was familiar with the process. He could even smile at it now. He was getting too old, he told himself, to have these attacks. No one seeing him there with his greying hair and lined face, his long row of medals and the four gold stripes on either shoulder, could guess what was going on inside him then. He prided himself on that. No one ever had guessed at his feelings.

Yet there was little solace to be had from merely keeping it hidden. It was all very simple. He was a lonely, ageing man and he wanted his wife. In his younger days this yearning at sudden moments had an almost paralysing force. But then—as now—there was no way out. It had to be endured and then, after a time, it went away.

He walked over to where Crawford and Collard were talking with two Scottish businessmen. Crawford looked flushed and tetchy.

'How did the football match go this afternoon?' asked Trevesham.

'We gave them a trouncing, sir,' Crawford replied with a quick look at one of the civilians. 'But Mr MacDermot here has just suggested we should have let the local side win—more politic.'

'Nothing of the sort,' the Scotsman said indignantly. 'I'm just telling this young man that that's how *some* people think here,' he dropped his voice and looked over his shoulder, 'in some quarters, that is.'

Trevesham looked quickly at Collard. He seemed in a

174

way unfurnished without his pipe but he was very much on the alert and at once came to the rescue.

'It's a pity the local team wasn't stronger,' he said. 'It's high time our chaps had a defeat. They were much too cocky this afternoon.'

'Och! it's only a game,' the other Scotsman chipped in, 'we're getting altogether too serious about it. There'd be something very wrong with the Royal Navy if this officer didn't want his own team to win.'

'Aye,' MacDermot morosely agreed, 'it'll not do your ship's reputation any harm.'

'Well,' said Trevesham, 'we don't want a shipload of prima donnas. There's nothing like a drawn game to stop that sort of nonsense. See what you can do about it next time, Crawford.'

'Yes, sir,' said the Sports Officer. As his Captain turned away he was astonished to see him wink at the First Lieutenant.

'Hm!' said Collard, clearing his throat, 'I wish one could smoke a pipe at this sort of party. But I suppose I should have the whole Embassy round my neck if I lit up now.'

Trevesham got back to the ship the day before she was due to sail. The usual 'At Home' had been fixed up for *Antigone*'s last night at La Guaira and a cavalcade of guests arrived from Caracas. After the comparative coolness of the capital, La Guaira seemed unbearably hot. It struck Trevesham as he stepped aboard that something was wrong. He was properly received by the Commander and piped aboard in the ordinary way, but there was a sullen look, so he thought, on the faces of his boat's crew and the side party. The Commander followed him along the quarterdeck and into his day cabin.

'I'm afraid we've had a little trouble since you went away, sir,' Hatchett said with a frown, his telescope and cap as always rammed under his arm. Trevesham looked at him for a moment in silence.

'I'm sorry to hear that, Commander,' he said. 'What kind of trouble? Onboard or ashore?'

'On shore, sir. Leading-Seaman Callingham and Able-Seaman Johnson got into an argument in one of the waterfront dives. They started a free-for-all and of course

175

two of our best Irish stokers had to join in. They broke up the place, tried to set it alight and then made their escape in a stolen taxi.'

'Where was the patrol?'

'They were the other side of the town dealing with Marine Hutchinson who'd passed out on a home-made brew of wood alcohol and red wine. The police took our four bright boys into custody and refused to release them in spite of the personal efforts of the Consul. I had to go ashore yesterday morning myself and see the Intendente with the Consul. We've got them aboard now and I cancelled leave yesterday except for Chief and Petty Officers. They're all in your Report, sir, and the Consul is arguing the damages with the police and the dive owner.'

Hatchett looked so down-in-the-mouth about it that Trevesham was moved to remark:

'Well—there it is—no use crying over spilt milk. I'm sorry it had to happen while you were holding the fort, but I expect we'll survive. I'd better talk to the ship's company on the way to Colon. I suppose we can blame it on the climate, but they'll have to stand a good deal more of this before the commission ends.'

'It *has* been sticky hot,' said Hatchett, thrusting out his jaw, 'but, good heavens above, it's not all that bad.'

'A couple of days at sea and we'll have it out of our system.'

'The rest of the ship's company are pretty narked,' Hatchett went on. 'They reckon the ship's been let down —as indeed it has—there's been a lot of grumbling and dumb insolence and, of course, having their leave stopped hasn't helped anyone's temper.'

'As to the leave,' said Trevesham, 'you did exactly what I would have done. It's a pity this free-for-all had to happen in a foreign port. It won't look pretty on our Punishment Return.' He paused for a moment and lit a cigarette. He did this deliberately to try and lessen the tension. Hatchett was putting too much feeling into this 'incident', his values were in danger, he was too sharp and strung-up in himself. Trevesham looked at his short explosive Commander through the cigarette smoke. It was high time he had a break. 'However,' he went on, 'between these four walls I'm not at all sorry this has happened. If there was a row in a brothel I've no doubt

176

something provoked it. I don't suppose the cabaret owner is exactly an angel. I'm not sorry to know we have some sailors aboard with a bit of spirit and a good lashing of human temper. I'm a little afraid of a milk and water ship's company. Fighting men never have been eunuchs.'

For the first time since he came back he got a smile out of Hatchett.

'I believe what started the trouble,' the Commander said, 'was an especially repulsive stuffed parrot which Callingham tried to win from the top of the bar. I also hear by bush telegraph that the bird in question is now living aboard *Antigone*: I don't imagine he'll be visible for Rounds.'

The next morning *Antigone* sailed west the seven hundred miles to Colon. Once they were at sea Trevesham turned the ship over to the Officer of the Watch and came down below for Defaulters. Already with the fresh sea air blowing through the ship, the events at La Guaira showed up in a different light.

Both Hatchett and Trevesham knew the whole cycle of lower deck crime and punishment, the garish excess of bad drink and tawdry women, the hangovers and bouts of venereal disease, the poverty stricken words of contrition, 'We didn't intend no harm, sir . . . we told the bloke afterwards we was sorry, sir . . .', the blessed though painful absolution of scale punishment laid down in the King's Regulations and its human interpretation within the narrow margins allowed—this was an important mechanism of Naval life automatically brought into play by your own misdemeanour, not to be tampered with by those administering the regulations, a simple, well-understood payment, for wrongs committed. For coming back on board drunk—a day's pay: for absence over leave up to three hours, a day's pay and a day's leave stopped: for minor acts to the prejudice of good order and Naval discipline, Number 11 punishment which entailed, among other things, a harder routine, work in the dog watches and a stoppage of grog. These, their refinements and variants, were the experience of everyone on the lower deck. Men knew where they were. It was all part of the ancient stability of Naval life.

'Leading-Seaman Callingham, Able-Seaman Johnson, Stoker First Class Dawson, Stoker First Class O'Leary,' said the Master-at-Arms in rich ominous tones. 'Three paces forward—quick march! Off caps!'

Trevesham stood on the other side of the table with its green baize covering, his gold peaked cap slightly aslant, his hands stiffly behing his back. Calmly and unhurriedly he studied his four defaulters as the charge was read out. To his left stood the Captain's Secretary with the regulations, the men's Service Certificate and Conduct Sheets: to his right the Master-at-Arms, the epitome of police authority on board: slightly behind and to his right the Commander, the Officer of the Day and the Officer of the Watch concerned. The usual trappings of a simple maritime court of law were all assembled in the flat outside the Captain's day cabin as the ship gently rolled in the Caribbean at fourteen knots.

It was hot and the men facing him were sweating gently as they stood to attention proffering their clipped, pathetically poor excuses, their transparent inconsistencies matched only by their rough, toughened physique, and their dark, sullen eyes. It was possible to think of them as children facing their father, but they were bulky, piratical children and the father was more in the nature of a gold-laced Deity.

'You four,' said Trevesham, when he had heard what each of them had to say, 'have the dubious honour of being the first men on board to let the ship down. You all know why we visited Venezuela. You're well aware of the hospitality we received and the efforts we've all made to leave a good impression behind. I accept that none of you deliberately did what you did, but you're all grown men. It's high time you learnt self-control: next time it won't hurt you to think before getting yourselves in a jam like this.'

He looked at them again in silence as the ship creaked and swayed. Then he had their previous offences read out from the back of their Conduct Sheets: he called their Divisonal Officers—the two seamen were in the Foc'sle Division and Lieutenant Cravenby rallied loyally to their support: the Senior Engineer claiming in turn that Dawson and O'Leary were two of the best stokers he had—then he turned to the culprits again.

'Have you anything further you want to tell me?'

'No, sir,' they all murmured. Their doom was upon them and they knew it.

'Remanded,' snapped Trevesham, and the session was over.

'Remanded—on caps—'bout turn, dis-miss!' barked the Master-at-Arms. Remanded meant there would be four warrants to read out at evening Quarters. Callingham would lose his hook, being disrated to Able-Seaman —the other three would tenant the cells for, probably, five days or more. The Captain had not been lenient, and Trevesham knew that this would be remarked on throughout the ship. On the other hand there was nothing vicious in the punishment meted out, and Trevesham and Hatchett were both aware that the fate of these men would be the best deterrent, the best tonic to discipline which the ship could have.

Trevesham consulted for a moment with his Secretary: then stepped out on to the upper deck and walked forward to the bridge. It was a cloudless day and the sea sparkled with a million glittering lights. Away on the starboard beam a school of flying-fish leaped and sped along the water. Overhead the inevitable gulls wheeled round the mast and dived for occasional refuse from the ship. Land was still in sight on the port quarter, but soon they would have the whole ocean to themselves. It was a bland, matchless day and there was a feeling of exhilaration in simply being once more at sea. Not a day at all, thought Trevesham, for having to sentence four good men to cells on board.

He sighed to himself as he climbed up the ladder to the bridge. They were caught, as he was, but in different parts of the web. There was no real escape from the machinery of life. They were all of them involved—some a little more, some a little less. It was only outward appearances which differed. As he took over again on the bridge and looked round at the sea he felt very strongly that soon they would all be yet more involved. The unseen horizons were closing in. That afternoon a new bout of rioting broke out in the Sudetenland some three thousand miles away.

HMS *Antigone* reached Colon at the northern or Atlantic side of the Panama Canal, about mid-way through an early September forenoon. Shortly after Divisions that day Trevesham had cleared lower deck and when the ship's company had assembled on the quarterdeck, he climbed on to a grating to address them.

'In another couple of hours we shall be alongside in Colon,' he began. 'We stay there five days and then we pass through the Panama Canal. So Colon marks the end of the first leg of our cruise. It's a good time to take stock and I've one or two things I want to tell you. First of all I shall read you a signal I've just received from Caracas—"To the Commanding Officer, HMS *Antigone* at sea. Your visit an outstanding success. Please convey my congratulations to officers and men whom the British community in Venezuela now regard as old friends. We look forward to welcoming *Antigone* again before her commission is up." The telegram is signed "His Britannic Majesty's Ambassador, Caracas".'

There was a slight murmur of approval and some wooden grins from the sea of faces in front of Trevesham.

'It's a matter of great pride to me,' Trevesham continued, 'to receive a signal such as that. I congratulate you and thank you for the way you all pulled your weight. At the same time I want to couple with it a warning. The further we get from the rest of the squadron the higher our own personal standards have got to be. That applies to the ship as a whole and to each of us individually as men. Unfortunately the Commander and I have noticed, instead, a falling-off, a sloppiness both in your work on board and in your bearing as liberty men ashore. I know we're in the tropics. I'm as much subject to the climate as any of you. However, that's no excuse for laziness or bad work. There's too much shuffling about. More attention will be paid to the dress and behaviour of liberty men, and all slouching about the upper deck, either in or out of working hours will stop forthwith. Is that understood?'

This time there were no more grins but the same sea of wooden faces gazed up into his.

'Now, Colon is in the Panama Canal Zone and as such American territory. Our hosts will be the United States Navy. So there's an added reason—obvious to all of you —for smartening up and being on your best behaviour. We aren't exactly showing the flag to the Americans'—

180

there was a titter—'on the other hand the ship and everything about her will be studied and examined by highly critical eyes, however friendly they are. Now a word about liquor. Firstly, American ships are "dry". If any of you are invited aboard don't try and be clever and smuggle bottles of beer or spirits in with you. That only makes trouble both for you and your hosts—so if anyone makes the suggestion or it occurs to you as a bright idea—the answer is "Don't". Secondly, Colon has the reputation of being a pretty fierce city for drinking. The best advice I can give you is to stick to beer—and go easy on that. Americans drink more hard liquor than we do—they can afford to—and they're likely to be more hardened to its effect than you are. So however hospitable they are—go easy on the spirts and, above all, don't try and tell your hosts late in the evening how much better things are done in the Royal Navy. We all know there's never been a ship like *Antigone*, but Colon is one of the places where it's more polite and tactful to keep that kind of opinion to yourself. Most of you don't need to be told this sort of thing, but some of us forget more easily than others and those who do should try and make a special effort during the next five days. Apart from that simple advice I hope you'll all go ahead and enjoy yourselves as much as you can. I'm sure you will.'

The Captain stood down and walked off the quarterdeck. As he went one of the Fat Men of the Sea, Able-Seaman Rillington, observed out of the corner of his mouth, 'He'll have us all flipping teetotal before we're through. Cor! break your bleeding heart, *he* would.' Unfortunately, this remark carried further than Rillington had intended, and a few minutes later he came up against the towering figure of the Master-at-Arms, barring his passage to the messdeck.

'Able-Seaman Thomas Henry Rillington,' said the Master-at-Arms in cathedral tones, 'the Commanding Officer, Captain Colin Trevesham, DSC, Royal Navy, presents his compliments to you—'

'To *me*?' said Rillington, awestruck.

'—and begs to inform you that if you really want your heart broken he can arrange to do it for you cheaply and effectively any time by appointment on the quarterdeck.'

'Cor!' said Rillington. 'Am I in the rattle for that?'

'No,' said the Master-at-Arms with beetled eyebrows, 'but if I had *my* way you would be.'

At Colon, for the first time since leaving Bermuda, HMS *Antigone* lay alongside a jetty. This was a great convenience and something of a treat to her ship's company. There was no boat routine to be studied before a run ashore. Within the limits of the leave piped, officers and men were free to go and come as they pleased. That and the obvious, easy efficiency of their American hosts made a welcome contrast with other ports they had visited.

There was a sense of adventure, too, in their relations with the US Navy. In 1938 it was nearly twenty years since the Great War had forced a liaison upon the two greatest Navies of the world. Since then each had gone its own way, picking a delicate path through the pitfalls and restrictions imposed by Disarmament Treaties, each with a natural basic friendship for the other which was bedevilled by the politicians, the differences in training and outlook and the new distinct jobs which the two Navies expected to find themselves doing, should the cauldron boil over again. But contact between the two services speaking the same language showed up the protocol and the other man-made barriers as artificial and absurd. There was a warmth and a friendship—especially among the junior officers—which no intellectual objection could stifle.

The US Fleet Air Arm base at Coco Solo seemed to be the chief magnet for the younger wardroom officers and the gunroom. As soon as the official programme for the day had been complied with, their American counterparts would drive up alongside in their big convertibles and sweep away parties of young British officers to play tennis, bathe, go dancing or take in a 'movie'.

On some evenings the tide would flow back to *Antigone* and private dinner parties were fixed up, with the Commander's consent, in officers' cabins. If the British were a little envious that their young American hosts were nearly all married and had families, the Americans in turn seemed to be charmed by these candle-lit dinner parties, for which they were expected to put on their mess kit or tuxedoes, which were served by impassive white gloved Royal Marines and which normally included a good hock from the wardroom 'cellar'. As one of the Americans remarked a little ruefully, on board a US ship it was exceedingly difficult to entertain elegantly on a basis of ginger ale or coffee.

To Alan Grey-Bennett, as the ship's aeronautical expert, Colon came as an oasis in a long desert. Except for Peter Osborne, his observer, there was no one on board who knew or understood about aircraft. What was worse, no one cared. In the early days of the commission he and Osborne had talked shop in splendid superior disdain of their seabound brother officers.

But there are limits to the small talk two people can wring even out of aircraft technicalities. He and Osborne had long ago passed the point at which either of them had anything new or interesting to say about the ship's floatplane. Indeed, thanks to Augustus Spratt, they now found themselves scoffed at, their natural arrogance on the defensive, their moronic messmates actually daring to question the value of them and their contraption to the ship.

Spratt was the deadpan innocent in these wardroom inquisitions. He had a sharp mind and a photographic memory for jargon. His method was to involve Grey-Bennett in a long technical harangue so that he could then ask a question which for the moment sounded all right, but which was actually compounded of nonsense. At other times he would imitate Grey-Bennett launching out into one of his unfortunate but deeply cherished theories that the ship needed him more than he needed the ship. It all added up to the rueful fact that by the time *Antigone* reached Colon, Grey-Bennett was looked on as something of a joke.

The young American flyers, however, with their enthusiasm, their generosity and their lavish equipment took him at once to their hearts. They made him an honorary member of their squadron. They broke most of their own regulations so that he could fly with them. They adopted him as a kind of mascot with his long hair and fancy ways, his perfume and his drawl. They did not understand what fired him at all. In many respects he was as foreign to them as a Frenchman or a Spaniard. His affected habits raised plenty of eyebrows. Were all British aviators, they asked, on the lavender side? But when he proceeded to walk away with the best-looking, most unattainable girl on the Base, a red-headed five foot of dynamite called Thalia, who also happened to be an Admiral's daughter, they talked less about G-B's effeminacy and concentrated instead on furbishing up on their own technique.

It seemed a long, long way from Europe. The single sheet of radio news which the ship received each day continued to mention the worsening riots in Czechoslovakia. There were 'grave disorders' and 'serious undertones' in the events imminent in Europe, but the Panama Canal lay nearly five thousand miles away from it all.

News about political strife in the centre of Europe seemed unreal in the candent heat of Colon with its sudden tropical downpours and its oppressive, heavy-lying sunlight; its rich palm trees, its bananas; its cocoa; its negro labourers, its over-size American cars and the bright neon-lit bars of its port. In this setting, in the space of two days, Grey-Bennett began, built up and ended his courtship of the glamorous Admiral's daughter.

'Darling,' said Thalia casually to her British boy friend on the last night but one of the ship's stay, 'you have the cutest little ship in the whole wide world, but would she be any use in a war?' They had just finished dinner in Grey-Bennett's cabin and while it was being cleared away he had taken her up on the bridge. Around them lay the lights of Colon, but it was dark and intimate on the bridge, an almost routine setting for the romantic approach. He had no business to bring her up there but Grey-Bennett had never paid a lot of attention to the minor rules and ordinances to which he was subject.

'What an extraordinary question at a time like this,' he said, kissing the back of her neck. She had on a white brocade dress and her brown skin seemed to have a kind of furry glow in the darkness.

'Don't muss up my hair,' she said sharply, 'and what's so extraordinary about it?' She twitched her shoulders in an irritated businesslike fashion. 'You should take more interest in current affairs,' she went on. 'You British never keep up to date—*darling!*' She had turned and was looking up at him in the dimness of the night. There was a provocative, insulting tone in her voice which never fooled him for a second. She was simply a little out of her depth and afraid.

'That's right,' he answered easily, 'we're always caught

184

napping at the start. Always playing cricket when we should be marching about a dreary square. Always making love to pretty girls, instead of taking a serious interest in current affairs.'

Then without further ado he kissed her on the lips and thoroughly mussed up her long, reddish hair. It was a disappointing experience. She was taut and cold and her lips were hard. Suppressing his annoyance he realized too late, that with Thalia it was all in the looks. She had yet to awaken inside. There was nothing there underneath. She was a kind of three-dimensional colour photograph, strikingly sexy in appearance yet unfired by any passionate appetite, by any hot flow of blood in the veins.

'I told you not to muss up my hair,' she said. 'Can't you even think of anything new?' She walked across to the ladder. 'I'd like to get my things and go home.'

'I'm sorry,' he said, 'I thought American girls learned their way around when they were still at school. I've obviously made a mistake.'

He had followed her to the bridge ladder and was waiting for her to go down. Instead she turned and studied his face in the darkness.

'Yes, *darling*,' she said, a cutting edge of sarcasm in her voice, 'you have made a mistake. You've been here four days and the day after tomorrow you sail away. I'll never see you again. That's the mistake you made.'

Then, taking him completely by surprise, she put one arm round his waist and the other round his shoulder. She drew his face down to hers and she kissed him softly and clingingly and very full on the mouth. This time there was no doubt about it at all. The blood flowed hot in her veins and it was very obvious indeed that she was considerably more than an animated, three-dimensional photograph of a woman. It was a long, long kiss and as it went on it seemed to Grey-Bennett as though the fires of passion would never stop coursing. Then suddenly she broke it off without warning, tossed her head furiously and pushed him away.

'Damn you,' she said angrily, 'damn you for getting me involved like this. What's the *use* of falling in love when we'll never see each other again? I thought you goddam Europeans were supposed to be wise. There isn't any difference in you at all.'

He tried to kiss her again but she kept him away.

'It's no good,' she said, 'it only makes it worse. There's nothing we can do.'

'I'm sorry,' he answered, straightening his tie and smoothing his hair. She was becoming a bore. Why bring love into it at all? But all women were the same. They would romanticize. She gave him a long steady look in the darkness and then without another word went down the ladder to the upper deck. At the bottom, just aft of the torpedo tubes, stood the Midshipman of the Watch. He waited till Thalia had gone past and then saluted Grey-Bennett.

'What is it?' the latter said, frowning.

'The Commander's compliments, sir,' said the Midshipman in tones of sympathetic regret, 'and would you see him in his cabin when your guest has gone ashore, sir?'

'Very well,' said Grey-Bennett curtly, and swore long and low to himself. A can from the Commander was a perfect end to an evening such as this.

When they looked back on Colon, their five-day visit was indeed the climax of a period. But this was not apparent till later. On a diary or calendar five days looks to be a short enough space of time, but to everyone on board it seemed to stretch and to go on stretching. The days and the nights were packed out with events.

Parades, inspections and ceremonies, both British and American, took up the forenoons. Then lethargy and the midday sun stilled activity until around five o'clock when football, tennis and water-polo matches took place, followed in the evening by formal and informal parties which went on far into the night.

Trevesham had decreed that all-night leave was to be given to everyone who could avail themselves of the privilege. This was a wise and popular move. Another opportunity with similar facilities would probably not recur till they reached Lima in Peru. But the accent lay heavily on play rather than work.

'One of these days,' said Spratt as he and the Senior Engineer had a Horse's Neck in the wardroom, 'I suppose someone will tell us to do an honest day's work. When that happens, half the ship's company will drop down dead.'

186

'Speak for yourself,' said Meldrum, 'the Engine Room Department never relaxes.'

'That's right,' the Navigating Officer remarked, 'I did see the Commander (E) keeping a vigil at the Atlantic Bar last night. Rather a fluffy piece for a man of his bulk, I thought.'

Overwhelming them all, like an atmosphere or a climate, lay the hospitality they received from the Americans in the Canal Zone. They had been treated to nothing like this before. West Indian and Venezuelan receptions paled in the memory. The vigour, generosity, warmheartedness and scale of entertaining which their American hosts embarked upon astonished them all from Trevesham to the youngest ordinary-seaman aboard.

'They may have some peculiar ideas,' said Taw-Street, 'but, my God! they do really try. They've even found me a nag worth riding.'

'Gad!' said Spratt. 'Look who's rooting for them now!'

Towards the end of their stay the pace of this hospitality very nearly floored them all.

'They're quite extraordinary,' said Collard, 'they never let up. Don't Americans *ever* sit down quietly by themselves and read a book? I've never seen anything like it. The odd thing is I enjoy every moment of it. Couldn't keep it up for more than five days though.'

That was the general opinion. 'Thank heavens tomorrow we sail,' they all said, either aloud or to themselves. Yet all of them knew that as the cruise went on it would only repeat and grow worse. They might not strike that compressed intensity which the Americans put into their five days at Colon but they were all caught up in a circle of forced pleasure from which there was not nor could be any escape. It was as though they were all characters in a play. Individually or in groups they each had a small repertoire of roles they were expected to play. Their amateur days were at an end: now they had the prospect of a long tour with the same show in a lot of uncertain 'dates'.

The last night of their visit, the officers of *Antigone* returned hospitality with one of the biggest and liveliest parties they had ever given on board. The quarterdeck was a blaze of coloured light, the ship was illuminated all over —the equivalent of dressing her in the daytime with flags and bunting—the Royal Marine Band played for dancing

—a performance somewhat sedate and quaint to their American guests—the wardroom messman had gone overboard on flowers so that the whole after end of the ship looked like a tropical grotto at a horticultural show—good Scotch whisky flowed and there was a riot of noise.

'Talk about the eve of Waterloo,' said Meldrum as he and Collard collected drinks at the bar for their guests, 'there's a damned sight too much enjoyment going on, if you ask me. Even Schooly isn't sulking tonight.'

'I reckon everyone in the ship has made at least three friends for life since we've been at Colon. It's extraordinary. And the snotties all want to get married. I'm told Midshipman Mottram has proposed three times to a married woman. Of course, it doesn't affect staid old grass widowers like you and me.'

'Of course not,' Meldrum replied, looking sideways at the First Lieutenant, 'the thought never enters my head.'

'Look at Aggie Spratt,' said Collard, his hands full of glasses, 'working that charm of his to the bone.'

Meldrum looked over to where Spratt was standing underneath 'Y' turret.

'He's late on it, though,' the Senior retorted, remembering his friend's pursuit of Susan and delighted to have caught him out again. 'He always lets someone else pioneer the way. You know who's with him, don't you?'

'No.'

'Grey-Bennett's ex-girl-friend. The fabulous Thalia.'

This was indeed so. Grey-Bennett himself was Officer of the Watch. He had volunteered for this normally thankless duty after the short talk he had had with the Commander. He had rather hoped Thalia would boycott the party, but once again his knowledge of feminine nature was at fault. Thalia had no intention whatever of missing the best party of the lot, especially as her father was one of the principal guests. She had come aboard in his train, nodding a cold smile at Grey-Bennett as he saluted their arrival. Then to rub salt in the wound she had gone on to devote all her charm and attention to the Navigating Officer, as though there had never been anyone else in her life.

'And tomorrow,' she was saying, 'tomorrow you'll go through the Canal and south to Colombia and Ecuador.'

'If we can find the Canal and point the ship in the right direction.'

'How thrilling!' she said. 'I certainly do envy you all on a cruise like that.'

Yet even as she spoke the destiny of the ship was changing. Across the quarterdeck the Yeoman of Signals had just come up to the Captain's Secretary and given him a signal. This was the sort of thing which normally never happened at a cocktail party. But this was a signal in cypher and it was prefixed 'Immediate'.

In peacetime the Captain's Secretary of a cruiser is also the Cypher Officer. Marsh frowned and swore to himself. Then, swallowing the rest of his drink, he excused himself from his guests, went down below and began decyphering the message. Twenty minutes later Hatchett was summoned to the Captain's cabin and a few minutes after that the Commander (E) and the other Heads of Departments. The party came to its natural end without incident or fuss, but no officers were allowed ashore with their guests and two patrols went round the town recalling all libertymen to the ship. The Blue Peter was hoisted and the ship was prepared for sea.

That night *Antigone* sailed north to Bermuda at thirty knots. Across in London the British Prime Minister, the Right Honourable Neville Chamberlain, had that day flown to Munich for a personal meeting with Hitler.

It was the fifteenth of September, 1938.

CHAPTER EIGHT

The month that followed was a foretaste of graver things to come. Their lives suffered a complete and instant revolution. The cruise programme was first postponed and then cancelled. They had no means of knowing that the partial mobilization of the Fleet over the Munich period was a

189

false alert. Most of them felt that war was almost certain to come. Perhaps this was the moment.

They had just under sixty hours in which to get used to the idea. That was the time it took them to reach Bermuda at an average speed of 29.6 knots. The sea was calm. The sun continued to beat down. The ship was in the normal three sea-going watches and except for their speed this might at the outset have been any passage to any other port. In their minds, though, they were already putting away childish things and now each of them began making the plans and adjustments demanded by the coming of war.

They had been told nothing except to proceed to Bermuda with despatch. Warships are never encouraged to chatter on the air and although they could listen in to routine service broadcasts and the BBC no message of any kind was transmitted to or by *Antigone* during her passage. The German consul at Colon no doubt reported her departure: it would be known from Balboa that she had not traversed the Canal but her new destination, the object of her sudden change of plans and her future employment were all of them no longer in the international public domain. *Antigone* and every other major warship of the Royal Navy disappeared overnight. Their whereabouts might be guessed at but could not be known for certain until after this intelligence had ceased to be of any practical use to the enemy.

'The enemy'—they were already beginning to use this word. It would be one of the cardinal points of the new structure into which their lives were being forced. 'The sea', 'the weather', 'the enemy'—these were now the great realities affecting the ship. They had both a physical and an abstract meaning. They would soon be conditioning the ship's life and her movements. But the enemy, although known, had not yet been defined. We were still precariously at peace. It seemed to those on board that these were the days of transition, but no one could be sure.

As soon as he could on the first day out, Trevesham cleared lower deck and took the ship's company into his confidence. At thirty knots *Antigone* scarcely rolled, but the vibration and the noise made a formal address difficult. He mounted a grating beside 'Y' turret and told the men to close in round him.

'One or two of you will have gathered that we're not going through the Panama Canal,' he began, and was rewarded by a murmur of laughter. 'Instead we've been ordered to Bermuda and there we shall take on emergency stores, fuel and ammunition. We shall make ourselves ready in all respects for war.'

He paused and looked round.

'Now—that may mean a lot or it may simply be a precaution. You know as much of the international situation as I do. If Hitler intends to make war—then our duty is simple. If, on the other hand, he's bluffing then we, as a country, have to assess and counter that bluff and also try and predict where and how he's going to try it on next time. War has not yet been declared—and that's very important to all of us. It gives us time and time allows us another chance. I want to remind you that the less you speculate about these things, the better for all of us. If it comes, it comes.'

He paused again and then spoke with added emphasis.

'However, we must be prepared—as a Service and as a ship. That is our duty—and what we're paid for. You all know that. I'm talking to you like this because over the last couple of months the simple facts of life have become overlaid by this pleasure cruise we've all been enjoying. From now on things will be different. We have to adjust ourselves, and we must do it as quickly and quietly as we can. We have to forget all about picnic parties and football matches. We've a great deal of leeway to make up: we have to get into training for a much more rigorous life. That's why as soon as I've finished talking to you the ship will go to "Action Stations". So far as *Antigone* is concerned, war has begun. The ship will remain closed up at "cruising stations" until arrival at Bermuda, and if anyone wants to complain of the heat he can do so in person to the Commander or to me.' He turned and nodded to Hatchett. 'All right, Commander, carry on, please.'

This time he left a silent ship's company. There were few smiles and fewer jokes as the men went below, each working the thing out for himself. It was something of a shock even to three-badge able-seamen. But by the time

191

they reached the messdecks and 'Action Stations' began sounding urgently throughout the ship, they had recovered their traditional humour. They started grousing again.

'It's deliberate,' said Able-Seaman Kavanagh. 'Trevvy don't want me to enjoy myself on my birfday, that's what it is. And I had a dusky little number all laid on ready warmed-up for me at Bonaventura—in a grass skirt,' he added, fighting his seventeen stone into a gas mask sling and replacing his cap with a tin helmet.

'Roll on my flipping twelve,' Able-Seaman Elcock growled morosely. 'Who wants South America when he can be stuck up in a lovely, lovely little gun-turret all day long?'

'Who'd like my billet on the starboard pom-pom?' sang out another AB. 'It's ever so cool and airy up there—or it will be when they have us chasing the *Graf Spee* up into the Arctic.'

'Is that where we're headed for now?' a young ordinary-seaman piped up innocently. 'I mean, after Bermuda?'

'Come along there, on the messdeck, get a move on,' shouted a petty officer. 'Don't stand about yarning all day. Get a move on.'

Already they were tautening up. Routine orders were given with a new sharpness: routine drills were carried out with a new sense of urgency. The long, often tedious training which all seamen undergo now seemed suddenly to have acquired a deeper value. More corners were rubbed off: the standard of comfort went steadily down.

'Must we have all these watertight doors shut all the time?' the Senior Engineer griped to his Chief, 'the ship gets hotter and hotter and we've always compromised in the past.'

'I'll have another go at the Captain,' said the Commander (E), 'but I don't hold out much hope. He's got a bee in his bonnet about allowing bad habits to take root. He says there's enough carelessness in the ship as it is.'

Neither Trevesham nor Hatchett was popular. Minor offences multiplied and the punishment stiffened. It was like the working-up period all over again. This time, however, no attempt was made to cushion a hardening discipline: orders were given and no excuse whatever was accepted for delay or failure in carrying them out. As

192

time wore on, this tougher spirit worked its way down to able-seaman level. By then the impulse from the top had manifested in the form of an all-round quickening. The various 'muscles' in the ship were as flexible as they would ever be. Each new pressure was groused at and complained about but the ship became keyed up and efficient.

Bermuda Dockyard was ready for them. They berthed alongside at 0700 with the morning sunlight striking sideways across the jetty and up onto the limewashed buildings. It was pleasantly cool. Hardly were the brows in place before stores and equipment began pouring on board. Normally Bermuda is a sleepy little dockyard but now it seemed as though it, too, had suddenly awoken to the urgency of things. The horse-drawn carts were driven to the jetty at something approaching a trot.

'A rather different arrival from our last one,' Spratt observed to his Chief Quartermaster as he left the bridge. They had done nearly 1,700 miles in the previous fifty-seven hours. Now that at last the ship had come panting to a stop, the sudden peace on board was extraordinary.

'Yes, sir,' Bowling agreed. 'It's like a boxer being titivated in his corner between rounds. Where do you think it is next?'

'Oh! I don't know,' Spratt said wearily. 'The Falkland Islands, I shouldn't wonder.'

The ship breathed normally again. Deadlights and scuttles were opened and the stale air, which the ventilating fans could never dispose of, began seeping away. The racket and vibration of the last two days were forgotten in the dusty quiet of Ireland Island. The whitewashed stone building of HMS *Malabar* suggested a calmness and a lethargy unshakeable by crisis or war. Yet by the evening *Antigone* had been fuelled, stored, provisioned and 'bunged full of six-inch bricks' as the Gunnery Officer had it.

Marsh appreciated the break more than anyone else on board. The clatter, the surge and the ceaseless vibration of driving through the water at thirty knots had deadened and deafened him to the point of exhaustion. The greater the ship's speed, the more her stern settled down in the water. During the whole of the fifty-seven hour passage it had never been safe to open the scuttle, which was only a foot or two from the sea. At night the ship was darkened and, although an illusion, this seemed to make the airlessness worse.

Marsh had not been seasick but the inside of his mouth was coated, he felt constipated and his appetite had gone. Moreover there had been a string of cypher messages to decode which had kept him intermittently on the jump for the whole of the passage. The Paymaster-Commander and Hale, the Central Storekeeping Officer, had lent him a hand from time to time, but the brunt of the work fell on the Captain's Secretary. There had been no signals addressed directly to the ship but Marsh had been plagued by that form of refined torture known as an Admiralty General Message, which conveyed urgent administrative orders to every seagoing unit of the Fleet, and which in times of crisis automatically went out in cypher.

In the late afternoon the Commander-in-Chief came across from the Admiralty House in his green barge and was piped aboard a quarterdeck littered with drums of paint, protective mattresses and spare baulks of timber. During the short three day passage *Antigone* had lost her sleek polished look. The paint on her funnel had scorched and was flaking away. Salt spray, dried and gritty, seemed to have lodged over her exposed upper works wherever the eye could see. The Admiral gave it a quick look as he came on board.

'Don't hold anything up for me,' he said briefly and made his way into the Captain's day cabin, followed by Trevesham. As soon as they were off the quarterdeck the flow of stores and materials continued. The working party, stripped to the waist, guessed rudely at their fate as they trundled and heaved. The Midshipman of the Watch, redeyed from fatigue, yawned into his hand and thought about the ziz he would have that afternoon on the gunroom settee. Down in No. 2 store an exasperated supply petty officer re-stowed his blankets and bedding to make way for the additional quantities allowed to the ship in war. In the galley Petty Officer Cook Jenkins raged at his assistants. The Gunnery Officer fussed and fretted as his shells came aboard and were struck down into the magazines. Fossingham was examining a torpedo warhead with the calm Mr Partle. The Surgeon-Commander had sent a leading-stoker with suspected appendicitis to the hospital and was consulting with the Principal Medical Officer of *Malabar*. The canteen manager recounted his cases of cigarettes, and the wardroom wine-steward was mustering his wine store for the monthly audit. It was difficult to believe that only three days before they had been on the point of going through the Panama Canal.

'Well, Colin,' said the Admiral to Trevesham, 'this has interrupted your fun, I'm afraid. How did she behave at that sustained speed?'

'Very well indeed. A bit noisy and hot, but steady as a rock—and dry.'

'Good. You'll be off again this evening but at a somewhat more gentle pace. The Admiralty want you with a clean bottom. I can't dock you here as *Exeter* is in the middle of a refit. So you'll be sailed to Gibraltar to-night at 2200. However, you'll still remain part of the Eighth Cruiser Squadron and as far as I know you'll be back on the station in about sixteen days—unless of course the balloon goes up in the meantime.'

'Are we mobilizing?'

The Admiral shrugged his shoulders.

'The Cabinet won't make up their minds. It hinges on whether Hitler means what he told the Prime Minister at Munich. Personally I think the Führer is bent on war and I think we should mobilize. At all events I've been told to kit you all up on a war footing.'

'And if it blows over?'

'I'll get you back on the West Coast as soon as I can—perhaps cutting out the Northern ports. How has it gone up to now?'

'It's been something of a social marathon,' said Trevesham. 'We were just getting our second wind at Colon.'

'The Ambassador seemed to be very pleased with your visit to La Guaira and Caracas,' the Admiral went on, and then added as an afterthought, 'although I understand a certain stuffed parrot has taken up residence aboard, according to consular reports.'

'As soon as it makes an appearance,' Trevesham said, as though they were discussing high strategy, 'that bird will be *Antigone*'s first clay pigeon.'

Their sailing orders came aboard in the dog watches and at ten o'clock that night they sailed as the Admiral had forecast. Already a new secrecy had settled over the

195

ship. Except for Trevesham no one aboard knew their destination, nor until late in the day even when they would sail. During the afternoon Hatchett was told that no leave would be given and at six o'clock the Commander (E) was ordered to raise steam for twenty knots and keep it at half an hour's notice.

Just before nine o'clock rounds the Captain sent for his Navigating Officer and showed him the sailing orders so that he would have time to work out a course. He also put Hatchett in the picture. Immediately after rounds they darkened the ship. At nine-thirty a mail was closed on board and a few minutes later the sack had been landed at the Fleet Mail Office by the ship's postman. At five minutes to ten the last brow was out and exactly at 2200 they cast off, turned in the harbour and headed out to sea.

After that it was fairly obvious where they were going from their course. The buzz soon went round the ship to be greeted with groans and jeers as the watch below turned into their hammocks for yet another night at sea. Trinidad, La Guaira and Colon seemed to be as far away in time as they already were in space.

Two days out in the Atlantic they ran into a gale. They had had storms before but none as severe as this. There was a high following sea on her starboard quarter and *Antigone* rolled and pitched as she had never done before. Marsh, who was inevitably sick—to his chagrin and fury all over the code books and message he was decyphering—came up on deck and watched the black sea miserably from the waist just aft of the torpedo tubes.

It was early evening and the sky was like old lead, darkening off to the north into the colour of wet slate. The wind tore and whistled in the rigging. Each time the ship pitched the screws raced out of the water and there was a kind of shuddering groan as the structure creaked and gave to the strain. There was a buzzing in Marsh's head but once up in the fresh air he no longer felt sick.

He worked his way cautiously aft to the quarterdeck, clinging to the handrail which ran along the superstructure. It seemed as though the upper deck itself was nearly under water. He had never in his life seen such a sea. At times it looked as though a huge black wave some forty feet above and astern of them must surely smack down on the quarterdeck and founder the ship. The wave would race in towards the stern like a vast moving mountain of water. It gave Marsh a kind of tingle in his guts and as he watched it come near he wondered if perhaps it was the last one he would see. Then almost when it was on top of the ship its angry crest blowing, tearing, whipping away all the time, by some miracle the stern of the ship would lift and it would seem once more as though she were on top of the world.

Antigone was a staunchly built ship. She was solid and sturdy. She gave Marsh an almost defiant feeling of security, but the force of the storm was so immediate that he scarcely dared look into the sea. The thought of being swept overboard held him in a kind of sick paralysis. He was fascinated and at the same time very afraid. Drenched with spray and chilled by the wind he remained exposed to the storm almost an hour before forcing himself below to clear up the mess in the cypher office and make another attempt at the work.

By the time they reached Gibraltar, the British Prime Minister had flown off to his second historic meeting with Hitler, this time at Godesberg. It was now late in September. Gibraltar exhibited no outward signs of an increased tension. Two battleships, an aircraft-carrier and a destroyer flotilla of the Mediterranean Fleet gave the harbour a comfortably furnished look, as Spratt remarked to the Captain, the *Antigone*'s arrival created no sort of stir. She was given a temporary berth at the Detached Mole and within a couple of hours of arrival had entered the dry dock.

'I don't know,' said Meldrum, taking off his white overalls after the boilers had been shut down, 'perhaps we've got an inflated idea of our own importance, but to me there's a distinct feeling of anti-climax in the air. There's not that astonished delight at our arrival which we've come to expect.'

'It's those ugly great battlewagons that do it,' the Chief remarked, 'sitting over there monopolizing attention. What can a seven-thousand-ton cruiser put up against two thirty-thousand-ton battleships and a Vice-Admiral's flag?'

'Better them than us,' said Meldrum. 'What a dull life it must be! No sudden summons from the Panama Canal, no dirty dashes across the Atlantic Ocean, no glamour in their staid, stuffy existences.'

'Yes,' said the Commander (E) drily, 'and no port propeller-shaft casing to open up and repair.'

Antigone had a number of small defects resulting from the hard driving she had recently experienced. They kept her in dock a week. During this time they scraped the barnacles off her bottom, thus restoring the extra two knots to her full speed which a dirty hull had caused her to lose. Some invisible barnacles were also scraped painfully off her 'yachting-and-cruiser-on-detached-service' reputation. When the sixth signal from Flag Officer, Gibraltar, arrived drawing attention to minor infringements of the Station Order Book, Hatchett went and consulted Trevesham.

'I think we're being got at,' he said explosively. 'It looks as though we can't do anything right. After four thousand five hundred miles of almost continuous steaming, it breaks my heart that two seamen were observed improperly dressed in Main Street last night. We shall certainly "pay more attention to the dress regulations"—but I have the feeling there's a bit of jealousy somewhere in this.'

Trevesham gave his stubby Commander a gin and considered this outburst.

'I think you're right,' he said eventually, 'but there's nothing I can do about it except conform as gracefully as possible. I'm afraid it's a question once more of being just a flea in the Med Fleet's ear.'

'Well, sir,' said Hatchett, drinking his Captain's health, 'in the words of Able-Seaman Elcock—"roll on my flipping twelve". By the way, Torps and Guns have challenged us to tennis this afternoon. Can you manage a game?'

'I think that's the answer to the Station Order Book,' Trevesham answered. 'I'd like to very much.'

The Czechoslovak crisis worsened during the following week. *Antigone* came out of dock and was berthed on the detached mole 'like a leper' as Collard said, 'and just so that we have to run a boat routine'. They expected daily to be sailed back to their proper station. They did not belong to Gibraltar, and if jealousy was too strong a word for the attitude they came up against, then 'the residents' did appear to resent their presence. Gibraltar had the Mediterranean Fleet to compete with, and a cruiser from another station was something of a nuisance and a burden. It was made very clear that the First Battle Squadron and the aircraft-carrier were Gibraltar's first concern.

'The Admiral told me this morning,' Trevesham remarked to Hatchett, after a week of fretting, 'that no one in Gib knows our fate. "Keep out of the way and behave yourselves" was his only advice. The Admiralty have taken over the operation of all cruisers. No one here has authority to sail us back to Bermuda—much as I think the Staff would like to be rid of us. We must wait till the Admiralty remembers where we are and finds us a job.'

In the wardroom it was chewed over passionately every time a new buzz was received or a fresh slight put upon the ship. A condition of idle suspense was far more difficult to endure than the feverish activity of a crisis and a dash across the Atlantic Ocean.

'It's all very simple,' Augustus Spratt summed it up. 'Over there we were a big fish in a small pond, here we're the opposite. Hence our Cinderella complex—and if anyone wants the Pumpkin Coach for a private party— put a chit into the Commander's office and touch your cap to R-A Gib.'

On 28 September the fleet mobilized. The next day Chamberlain flew for the third time to Germany and on his return stepped down from the aircraft with a weak smile and an agreement in his hand. 'Peace in our time,' he maintained, was symbolized by the scrap of paper he had brought back from Hitler, but Germany's known outlook on scraps of paper induced a healthy scepticism in *Antigone*. They simply did not believe it. When the terms for dismembering Czechoslovakia came into the light, they felt ashamed and disgusted. We had bought time at the price of honour, and there was no surprise in the ship when the First Lord of the Admiralty resigned in protest on 2 October.

Mobilization, although it ceased after the Commons approved the Czech settlement on 6 October, meant a spate of administrative work for the Fleet. In Gibraltar this fell mostly on an overworked Staff and on their counterparts afloat. It seemed to Marsh that he was for ever *en route* to the Admiral's office to fetch 'By Hand of Officer' papers. Corrections had to be made to cypher books and other Most Secret documents—and these, of course, had to be laboriously done by Marsh himself. Orders and plans are a necessary prelude to action of any kind, and as the flood swept down on the Captain's office of *Antigone* Marsh sank lower and lower into a repetitive routine of filing, distributing and correcting from which there seemed to be no escape and which each red-eyed day found him further and further astern.

Their stay in Gibraltar dragged on well into October. By now they had been a month away from the America and West Indies station. Disgruntled tooth-sucking both in the wardroom and on the lower deck gradually died down into a day-to-day acceptance of the *status quo*. In general Gibraltar suited the sailors better than it did the officers. There were more facilities for them and they did not have to battle away in Spanish. A football league was set up, the beer was cheap and plentiful, the canteen had a well-run cinema with up-to-date films, and the garrison authorities kept the red light district under control without suppressing it entirely and thus creating an even less desirable situation.

The requirements of the British sailor on a 'run ashore' do not vary much from year to year. He wants to get away from the ship, he wants a bit of exercise or the vicarious pleasure of watching his shipmates triumph in one or other of the sports, he wants to drink more beer than is good for him and he enjoys a smoke-filled cabaret with the rough-and-tumble feminine company which this normally provides on a commercial basis. He relishes an argument and if this ends in a free-for-all then the run ashore can become a memorable event. He is an individual yet prefers to see his messmates somewhere round and about. The messdeck will have sharpened his wits and he likes to try them out against new opposition. He never thinks about consequences until it is much too late: he jumps into trouble with both feet and a joyful shout: he counts on the protection of the Deity and the Naval Patrol, and if the next day he has a sore head and a dose of clap then he accepts it as a kind of rough payment for pleasure received, and expects to be looked after in accordance with the regulations. This was a state of affairs well understood in Gibraltar and even for misfits such as

Leading-Seaman Battersby there was the Garrison Library and an occasional concert.

Gibraltar also had the great merit of being only four sea days away from London. After the first couple of weeks *Antigone*'s mail began to arrive 'nice and fresh and full of lovely disasters from home' as Able-Seaman Rillington put it on hearing from his wife that the roof of their house had fallen in. The arrival of mail was like water on a parching land. It is eagerly soaked up but there was never enough of it.

'Susan sends you her love from Wiltshire,' Meldrum said as he sat down next to Spratt one day late in October. 'She asks whether you've grown at all in the last six months. Our daughter apparently has a rate of increase of an inch every five weeks.'

'You and your prodigies,' said Spratt. 'Tell Susan that any time she wants to make a change, she has but to send me a wire.'

'You poor thing. Don't you have any girl to write you longing letters from home?'

'Yes,' said Spratt tartly, 'your wife does. But she still chooses to remain tied down to you. And when I look at that silly smirk on your face I think she must be a much less intelligent woman than I thought. However I've also had a coloured postcard from Thalia. It shows a ship going through the Gatun Lock. And guess what? It's the ship that was taking her back to San Francisco.'

Grey-Bennett had also received a letter from Thalia. Written in the childish Gothic hand taught in so many American schools, it unpicked almost every stitch of the carefully sewn front she had shown to the world at the Coco Solo Base and which for a moment or so Grey-Bennett had broken through on the bridge that night. Thalia, it seems, had had a bad attack of remorse. It turned out that she had a simple, unexplored heart very much the same as any other girl of nineteen and since it was Grey-Bennett who had first disturbed her emotions, it was he who now received the hopeless, tortured outpourings which his attraction for her provoked.

How odd and sad, he thought, as he read and reread the letter in the privacy of his cabin. Before he would only have laughed. He counted himself a better judge of human nature than anyone on board. Up to now he would have dismissed both his feelings for her and hers for him by saying it was a perfectly ordinary animal attraction. Sex was a far more simple affair than most people believed. You had to satisfy it lightly from time to time and then it left you alone.

But with Thalia it was all yearning and no satisfaction. It got them nowhere. He wanted her resolutely out of his mind but for some reason or another she would not go. If only he had the First Lieutenant's stolidity, he thought, as he combed his long wavy hair and looked in the mirror, then women would leave him alone.

Lieutenant-Commander Collard, it was true, did derive a considerable satisfaction from his wife's letters, but he had private miseries of his own. It was becoming more and more certain these days that he would never be promoted. He blamed no one for this but himself. He respected Trevesham and Hatchett in their different ways, but he could never quite see himself in their place. He plodded along doing his best not to make mistakes, and in general succeeding. He had as good a bunch of messmates as he was ever likely to come across in the Service and among them not one he disliked. At home he had a devoted wife, a new baby and two other children he longed to see—but underlying it all he felt himself a failure. I must be too smug and slow, he told himself; I enjoy what I have far too much instead of fretting away at my career as Torps and Guns both do.

Never once had his wife implied that he might have done better. She was a woman in a million and for hours he smoked his pipe, thinking about her, leaning against his bunk and gazing out of his scuttle at the warships and the Rock, his cabin filled with the sweet rum-scented tobacco he smoked, and somewhere in his guts a gnawing feeling of failure. His gross pay as a Lieutenant-Commander of over three years seniority amounted to thirty-two shillings a day. It was true that since the previous year a modest marriage allowance was paid in addition but even with that included, he did not see how he was ever to educate two boys and a girl.

Hatchett, whose married life had been as penurious as Collard's, wrote home briskly to madame once a week and got a Sunday letter back in exchange. He was pleased to receive these epistles but he took them very much for granted. In the old days he would have slipped a letter from Alice into his pocket and carried it about unopened for a while to mature its taste. Even long after they were married, the sight of her illiterate writing would always give him a thrill.

But now something seemed to have gone from their lives. He knew almost exactly what madame would say. There was a feeling of duty nowadays in their correspondence and nothing seemed to matter very much. When the mail arrived in the wardroom, it would be set upon eagerly by the others, carried away into corners and privately read. But although Stubby could see the familiar envelope in the rack, he would call for another gin before bothering to get it and even then, if there was a lot on his mind, he would often defer reading it till he turned out his pockets at night. Occasionally this worried him a little. He would pause, with the letter unopened in his hand, and think back to things as they once had been. What had gone wrong? Why were they now almost strangers to each other? Was it simply the fact that they had never had any children and that madame these days seemed almost unduly concerned about the tinting of her hair?

To Captain Colin Trevesham, DSC, Royal Navy, standing on his fawn carpet beside his well-polished mahogany desk, the arrival of a letter from his wife was far, far more relished than the half-bottle of champagne he occasionally allowed himself over the reading of it. There was nothing mechanical in the deep affection they had for each other, an affection bruised and tempered by the exigencies of the Service from which Trevesham had been free to retire, had he wished, so long ago, an affection which shone through all their writing to each other and which only seemed to deepen as the years went by. 'My dearest heart' he began his letters as he had done since first they had fallen in love and it was now more true than ever.

Sometimes as he sat at his desk with its ornate silver inkstand, he would stop in midstream and look at himself from the outside. There must be something a little ridiculous, he thought, in a man of his age and experience writing as he did to his wife. Possibly there was. He shrugged his shoulders and longed all the more to have her in his arms. But when his steward coughed gently and asked if

203

he could serve him lunch, the only trace of such feelings lay in the troubled look which he saw in his Captain's eyes, and the face that the sherry decanter had taken an undue punishing. That was as far as anyone ever got and indeed no one on board had yet seen him moved out of his inner calm by any of the ordinary events which touched their lives on board ship.

If it be true that man can exist without food and even for a short time without air but that once his flow of impressions is cut off he dies, then the mail from home represented to commanding officer and seaman boy a main current in that powerful and invisible stream of consciousness. It was a form of food. It nourished their being as the ordinary meals they ate fuelled their bodies. There was an appetite for the mail long before Marine Camberwell brought it aboard. Then when the letters and postcards had been read and reread, there was a pleasant period of digestion after which the goodness in them had largely gone. Certain correspondence, written in love or under other powerful emotion, can keep a life in itself for years after it has first been read, but to most of the six hundred odd souls aboard *Antigone*, the haphazard arrival of letters from home was in a way like dumping on deck of a case of oranges. They fell upon them, they sucked them dry and then they threw away the skins.

Towards the end of October when the furore of Munich had died into nothing, *Antigone* was ordered back to the America and West Indies Station. Once more they made the leisurely Atlantic crossing called for by 'economical speed'. The heat was off. The cypher books went back into their steel chest and 'Action Stations' was sounded-off only twice on the passage.

But once back at Bermuda they did not resume their cruise to the south. For one good reason after another the Admiral decided to exercise his squadron in company and till the end of the year they carried out a programme of sub- and full-calibre shoots, of HA-practices at drogues towed by aircraft, of the firing of torpedoes, of night-encounter exercises between darkened warships in a lonely part of the ocean, of landing armed parties of Royal Marines and seamen to storm and guard strong points on the island, all of which would have done credit to the Mediterranean Fleet.

It was a period of heady rapture to their round-headed Gunnery Officer, and Fossingham, in order not to seem lagging astern, 'blew the Torpedo Department's thin trumpet,' as Spratt put it, whenever there was a lull in the music. Even Grey-Bennett, with his sense of the dramatic, contrived to crash his floatplane magnificently alongside the ship after an engine failure. Indeed for three months they behaved like any other cruiser in any other fleet, and if the routine struck some of them as monotonous then at least it was familiar in its purpose, and in between times they had the limpid sub-tropical beauty of Bermuda to console them.

Christmas—their first Christmas abroad—came and went with that peculiar family warmth which generates when two or three of HM ships are together in port and hospitality can be exchanged. If this was to be the last peaceful Christmas for many a year, it was an idea which threw no shadow across their pleasure. *Antigone* put on a Concert Party in the little theatre on Boaz Island. The Mouth-Organ Band played in the Fleet Canteen, and on Christmas Day there was the traditional open house to the officers on the messdeck, when rum in mysterious quantities made its appearance and bottles of beer found their way forward from the wardroom pantry in a steady and illicit stream.

In the meantime the international scenery against which *Antigone* was projected continued to darken with a kind of metronomic motion of black and white. It was the great peak year of international hypocrisy, the last time that people inclined to believe the public statements of their politicians and diplomatists. On 6 December Ribbentrop was in Paris declaring that no territorial question existed between Germany and France. This Axis whopper was followed eleven days later by Italy's denouncement of the 1935 Franco-Italian agreement.

Nineteen thirty-nine opened with the British Prime Minister, by now pathetically overplaying his role as Mr Appeasement, setting off to Rome accompanied by Lord Halifax, the Foreign Secretary. The success of this visit could be gauged on 1 February when Italy called up another 60,000 men for military service. At much the same time Hitler demanded the return of the old German colonies and declared his intention of matching his submarine fleet with that of the Royal Navy.

'And so it goes on,' said the Admiral to a meeting of his captains in the flagship, early in February, 'and so possibly it may continue for months and for years. Therefore, since the Admiralty have given me an option, I have decided that the cruise programmes which were interrupted last autumn by the Munich crises should now be resumed. The little man in jackboots has wasted far too much of our time as it is. The reasons for showing the flag are now more firmly based and urgent than they have been before. My private view is that we may find ourselves at war before the spring is out but in the meantime I wish you all good hunting and an uninterrupted cruise.'

So in mid-February, 1939, HMS *Antigone* set off once more for the Panama Canal and the West Coast of South America. They were glad to be gone. They felt bilked of six months' 'yachting' by the Munich crisis. Now they intended making up for lost time. They were in no undue hurry. They could relax. Their pellmell dash to Bermuda and then on across the Atlantic now already lay some way back in the past.

This new cruise might not have that first intoxicating flush of excitement of the West Indian islands, Venezuela or Colon: it did have its own rhythm of leisure and movement and the peacetime values of ceremony, protocol, the right uniforms for the right occasion, a ship impeccably clean and a ship's company who took a natural pride in their ship, in themselves and in the smart appearance of both.

This time they did not stop at Colon. 'In any case,' Spratt announced to the wardroom for Grey-Bennett's discomfiture, 'Thalia has gone away so dash it, chaps, there's positively no reason for stopping at all is there?' But the US Navy turned out in force to cheer them as the electric mules hauled the ship through the Gatun Locks. They also received a signal from the Admiral: 'What's the hurry? Don't you have time for your old friends now you're grown up?' to which *Antigone* replied: 'Why don't you come along too? This is a party!' And a party they intended it to be, tempered as they had been by six months of abortive crisis.

Across the Gatun Lake, down through the Pedro Miguel and Miraflores Locks, past Balboa and out into the sparkling Pacific Ocean—'as calm and peaceful as the books all say it is,' said Spratt to his Chief Quartermaster, 'now if war breaks out we must play "hard-to-find" and see if we can't dodge it all by skulking away down by Peru.'

Peru, in fact, was to be their first destination. The old cruise programme had intended them to stop in Colombia and Ecuador, but now that they had lost so much time, their first visit was to be to Callao, the port of Lima, itself the capital city of Peru. This was at a distance of fifteen hundred miles from Panama, so between leaving Bermuda and dropping anchor at Callao they had steamed some 3,200 miles.

The morning of the second day out from the Panama Canal they crossed the equator. The previous night after rounds the ship had been stopped in answer to a hail emanating, it seemed, from the port hawsepipe. At a word from Trevesham a searchlight was illuminated and played upon the foc'sle. A dripping, emaciated figure dressed largely in seaweed and seashells declared himself Ambassador from King Neptune and required permission for his Oceanic Majesty to come aboard since the ship was entering his domain.

'My God!' said Spratt on the bridge, 'it's Bowling!' Spratt had not been put in the know. He was among the two-thirds of the ship's company who had never before crossed the line and who were to have their initiation the next day.

His Oceanic Majesty was then invited aboard. As the ship gently rolled in the warm Pacific night the ponderous figure of Able-Seaman Rillington was observed to be clambering inboard over the foc'sle, his gilt paper crown somewhat awry and his trident bent through the exertions of the climb. Then, recovering his breath and the dignity appropriate to a monarch clad solely in a collar of fishbones and a kind of spunyarn skirt, he bawled up the bridge an address of welcome in durable, intermittently scanning verse.

The next day King Neptune held his court aboard *Antigone*. The shipwrights had erected a platform over the torpedo tubes in the port waist. On top of this stood a rough and ready throne and in front a large canvas awning filled with sea water and serving as a bath. All the impedimenta of the traditional court was to hand—the lather and the wooden razor for shaving, the soap pills for resistant initiates, the scrolls of verse upon which the ceremony depended. Then, as soon as Divisions had been done with, the Court assembled and King Neptune's Growlers ranged through the messdecks rounding up stragglers and forcibly bringing to court reluctant and un-initiated members of the ship's company. One of the first victims was the Regulating Petty Officer, who as the Master-at-Arms' right hand man, had a not altogether en-viable reputation in the ship. Two well-muscled stokers, wearing only bathing slips, seized him firmly by either arm and hurried him up for the slaughter.

'Don't *want* to?' one stoker whispered hoarsely in his ear, 'well you've got to *have* it, see?'

'And *like* it!' added the other.

'Now what's this 'ere?' said Neptune bending a fero-cious look on the RPO. 'Skulking—eh? Doing a disrespect to my fishy court—eh? Read out the charge.'

'RPO Douglas—two paces forward, march!—off shirt!' roared one of the Dolphins. 'Regulating Petty Officer George Douglas did commit an act to the prejudice of Bad order and Oceanic discipline . . .'

'Enough! Enough!' said Neptune, 'I know an ullage when I see one. Off with his head!'

By this time the RPO had been stripped of his shirt, his shoes and his socks and was left standing on the equator in front of his Sharkskinned Majesty in nothing but tropi-cal shorts and a tattooed chest. The ship rolled very slightly and the water slopped in the canvas bath. RPO Douglas was the first unwilling victim of the day. His sour face showed only too clearly that he thought it all a child-ish game to be endured somehow or other but never to be approved. The Court was very much aware of this feeling and it added relish to the proceedings. Neptune leant forward and smacked his lips.

'Not going to plead for mercy—eh? Lost your voice, have you?' Then in a roar appreciated wholeheartedly by the ship's company crowding round. 'Well—shave off!'

A soap pill was administered forthwith, his face was lathered and he was thrown with yelling approval into the bath where three of Neptune's Police ducked him into a state of half-drowned submission. The Court then went on to consider the sad case of Augustus Spratt, accused of 'being a lieutenant in a rival Maritime Service with umpteen years of seniority and never having had the courtesy to visit his Majesty King Neptune's Realm before.'

'Adjudged Guilty before hearing the Defence,' said Neptune, wondering how the Navigating Officer would take it. Spratt, however, considered attack to be the best form of defence. Before Neptune could continue he whipped round and sprang a low rugby tackle on one of the Dolphins so that they both fell into the bath, and in so doing they tripped up another of the Growlers who tumbled in afterwards. This bold defiance of one small body against many large ones delighted the ship's company and Neptune, sensing the feeling, immediately stood up and commanded his men to hold off.

'Lootenant Spratt,' he declaimed with all the nearly naked majesty of seventeen stone, 'your surprise tactics have put the ship on a better course than we've had the whole commission. I hereby release you from the attentions of our Court and award you the Order of the Surprise Packet First Class.'

The traditional baptism of seasoned and seagreen marines continued. Some took it well, some had it rough. Trevesham, watching from the flag deck, saw most of his private opinions and impressions confirmed. He watched Grey-Bennett ducked and ducked again, but when the ordeal was over a cheer of sympathy went up as Neptune presented him with the Marcel Medal of the Order of the Permanent Wave (Water Polo Division). Midshipman Mottram was another one who was given the full treatment. But he tried to act clever and argue with Neptune's attendants, as Trevesham had seen him do often enough on the quarterdeck with the Officer of the Watch. This time, however, he was up against the tough solidity of Able-Seaman Rillington.

'Bring forward into our salty presence this squib, this quarter portion, this maritime louse, this snotty!' The ship's company cheered and Mottram, who had not expected such candour, blushed. 'Mid*ship*man Mottram,' Neptune continued. 'From the depths of our squally sphere we have observed you upon your watch. We have observed you snogging in the gunroom and we have observed you a-running of the motor-boat, a-bumping it upon the jetty. We hereby adjudge you guilty of being eighteen years of age. Nothing you say will be taken down in writing, all evidence will be used against you—and what's more'—he leant forward and glowered ferociously at the Midshipman—'you have nothing whatever to say in answer to the charge. Remove this small sardine!'

So saying he slapped his belly roundly and watched with obvious pleasure while Mottram endured his ordeal. Thus it continued for the rest of the forenoon, and then when Trevesham had invited him to inspect the ship, a parody of the normal rounds was undertaken by King Neptune and his Court, and the ceremony came to an end with the disappearance of his Majesty down the hawsehole whence he had arrived. The foc'sle was then cleared and a few minutes later Able-Seaman Rillington emerged in his normal rig and trundled off down to his dinner and a well-earned Make and Mend.

Two days later they arrived at Callao.

CHAPTER NINE

The ship was made very welcome. Callao itself is not an impressive port, but with Lima only a half-hour away and with the snow-capped Andes towering up behind, it fired Marsh's imagination. He read it all up in the ship's encyclopaedia. He wrote a little bulletin for the notice boards, and his enthusiasm for rich Peru with its three centuries of Spanish viceroyalty, its Inca background stretching away into history and its present material wealth began to inspire others in the ship.

The readiest of his friends to respond was Douglas Hale, the Central Storekeeping Officer. They saw a lot of each other these days. Their work brought them together and this association stretched over into leisure. By this time the Concert Party was fully evolved and practised. It needed an occasional rehearsal to freshen it up and there were always new numbers to be tried out. But the main creative effort was past, and Hale tended to leave its organization more and more in the hands of Colour-Sergeant Forrester.

Marsh had come to have a great liking for his immediate superior in the Paymaster Branch. He relished the sardonic outlook with which Hale reacted to life. He was a pricker of balloons and at the same time an encourager of fantasies. He had got into the habit of dropping into the Captain's office, perching himself among the Service Certificates and other papers Marsh might be at work on and then delivering himself of an agreeably malicious commentary on people and events. One of his two centre front teeth was broken, and that combined with thick eyebrows wich seemed to meet over his nose gave him a satanic appearance. Marsh often thought that he and the Master-at-Arms were a fine pair. They seemed always to be ferociously frowning, but with the Master-at-Arms this was his 'professional' personality. Hale, on the other hand, would ram his short pipe between his teeth and if something amused him he would begin to chuckle, usually in the act of lighting the pipe. Then his whole face was transformed. His blue eyes creased up into little slits and somehow or other he kept his pipe between his teeth while his mouth seemed to stretch half-way round his head.

They did a lot of walking together. They enjoyed each other's company. They rarely agreed about what they saw —Marsh was too romantic and Hale too practical—but they took pleasure in arriving at quite a wide area of common ground after some 'to-ing and fro-ing' by both of them. Hale was not married. He was as susceptible as Marsh but the thought of being anchored to one woman for life appalled him. 'I'm not a chap for the nappies and the Sunday afternoon pram,' he would say. 'For me it's the tiger-skin coat, the champagne, the Fernet Branca and much later in life the deep Club armchair by the fire in winter and by the window in summer.'

Lima, the ancient capital of Spanish South America, was good exploring territory for both of them. They landed in the 1315 Officers Boat and then caught the fast Italian-built tram to the capital. There they inspected the Cathedral, the vast Plaza de Amas, the baroque Foreign Office with its pictures and its atmosphere of Spanish magnificence, the houses of the Grandees with their delicate ironwork, their shallow staircases, their carvings and their clinging, ominous, indefinable atmosphere of the Inquisition which Marsh suspected still to be sitting behind their tall heavy doors.

Religion and especially Roman Catholicism always put Hale into a rage. He had been brought up a Catholic but now described himself as an atheist. He was sarcastically independent but much too violent in his views of tranquillity or contentment. Marsh, on the other hand, whose parents were Methodists, acknowledged no formal creed in himself. He wanted to believe in something, but when he came to think it all out, nothing added up. There was something socially inferior in Non-Conformism, he had discovered on joining the Navy. It was not quite respectable, just as to be a Roman Catholic in the Service gave you another kind of oddness. Since the Regulations laid down a strictly observed freedom to worship as your conscience dictated, 'RCs and Non-Conformist Church Parties' were always being fallen out early from Divisions or otherwise finding themselves in the limelight, and with Number 23 Colebrook Avenue in his personal background Marsh felt he had enough of a social inferiority complex as it was without getting himself involved in religion.

So quietly—when no one was looking—he altered the religion on his next-of-kin card to 'C of E' and, although he did not attend communion, he merged in with the others on board at the simple services on the quarterdeck or in bad weather on the messdeck. It was not a very brave line of conduct but it made life just a little bit easier for him.

Except for the overtones of religion, Marsh found himself continuously filled with wonder at the civilization which the Spaniards had imposed in the wake of their bloody invasions. To have built such lovely houses, to have created round themselves on the west coast of South America a replica of the extravagant, decorated and mannered life of Madrid at a distance of some nine thousand miles from Spain—when a journey out or home via Cape Horn and the Atlantic Ocean scarcely bore thinking about—to have exercised supreme power as the Viceroy of Spain among the Incas, in doublet and silken hose, perfumed, manicured and vicious—this was a picture which took hold of Derek Lysander Marsh when he was actually walking about Lima, in a way impossible for him to counterfeit by the use of imagination. As he strolled past the university of San Marcos or stopped to consider the huge eighteenth century bullring the four hundred years of the city's life seemed almost to be part of his own vivid experience. 'Pagans—bloody Pagans,' said Hale looking at the Archbishop's Palace, but Marsh was not so sure.

The spring of 1939 saw the ship further and further down the west coast of South America. Visits to the nitrate towns of Chile—to Arica, Iquique and Antofagasta (inevitably renamed 'Aunty Go Faster' by the lower deck) took up most of March.

'It seems a long way from Belfast,' Trevesham wrote to his wife on 14 March, 'and I can scarcely believe I joined the ship a whole year ago. Yet so much has happened that at times I feel I've never served in any other ship but *Antigone*. A whole year has passed since Austria fell and we are still at peace . . . I wonder if I shall be writing the same thing to you a year from now: we are so remote out here that the very idea of war seems somehow to belong to another world.'

Yet even as he wrote—on 14 March 1939—the air was hot with news. Czechoslovakia had been invaded, annexed and split up into Protectorates by Germany. Peace in our time, thought Trevesham as the news came through, peace in our time . . .

Most of them expected another Munich to boil up. Whenever the Yeoman of Signals brought the log into the wardroom as he often did in the late forenoon, it would touch off fresh salvoes of conjectures. 'Stand by for the North Pole at thirty knots,' Spratt said, leafing through Admiralty General Messages on the payment of Kit Upkeep Allowance and the correct maintenance of Hot Food Lockers Mark VIIC. They all knew that another real panic would begin with the arrival in the ship of a cypher message. Perhaps they kept a more wary eye than usual on Marsh, whose hurried departure from the party at Colon had marked the beginning of their dash to Bermuda and Gib. But nothing happened. The fans hummed, the loudspeakers repeated the pipes and orders of the bosun's mate on the quarterdeck, by noon the wardroom pantry was out of ice, and normal, everyday life continued to revolve in the ship as though no new and decisive step had been taken in world affairs.

By mid-April HMS *Antigone* had arrived in Valparaiso, the main port of Chile. It was getting appreciably cooler. They were now over three thousand miles south of the Panama Canal.

'Once again,' Trevesham told the ship's company, '*Antigone* is on show where it matters very much what we do and how we behave. The Royal Navy and the Chilean Navy have many bonds between them. Most of their ships are British, the Royal Navy lent them a hand during the struggle for independence a hundred years ago and the first President of the Republic was called O'Higgins. So we can expect a warm welcome. In return they will look to us for exceptional standards of smartness and efficiency. Valparaiso is the largest port we've visisted so far, there are several big British trading companies which operate in Chile and have their headquarters here, we shall be alongside the jetty and thus more than ever in the public eye. *Antigone* is the newest and most businesslike warship anyone will have seen around here for some time —so, with all that in mind, make sure your behaviour ashore lives up to the ship and her reputation.'

Their reception by the Chilean Navy and the local British community did indeed exceed anything they had expected. The old battleship *Almirante Brown*—immediately anglicized by the lower deck into *Admiralty Brown* —invited the officers to become honorary members of their wardroom mess; yacht and tennis clubs made them free of their facilities: the Casino at Viña del Mar threw open its doors and in addition put on a lavish ball in their honour: transportation on the local tramway system was offered gratis to '*los distinguidos marinos ingleses*' and the great terminal port of Valparaiso, as it had been before the cutting of the Panama Canal, took pleasure in HMS *Antigone* as it had rejoiced in Admiral Cochrane's arrival a century before.

One morning as their visit wore on, Hale sat in his usual perch in the Captain's office smoking his pipe and talking to Marsh as he worked interminably on his Service Certificates. He looked out of the scuttle at Valparaiso, watching the busy dockside life and thinking that if he were really energetic and active he would be down in No. 3 store stocktaking.

'It's pleasant to be back in a large port,' he said eventually. 'You feel part of the great big world again. Reminds you there *is* a great big world.'

'I like the little ones better,' Marsh answered. 'You know where you are.'

'You mean—so far as the Consul, the Mayor and the etiquette are concerned?'

'Oh! yes—that—and all the people you meet as well. The smaller the place the friendlier they are.'

'The more parochial they are,' Hale countered. 'I like to go ashore and forget I'm a Naval officer once in a while.'

'The whole ship knows what you like to go and do,' Marsh said tartly, but Hale only smiled and looked at his friend's rather earnest face. He'd be all right in another few years, he considered, when all the corners were rubbed off.

'It's about time we had a run ashore together, you and I,' he said, 'what's wrong with tonight?'

'All right. There's a cocktail party at the French Consul's to begin with, then we could look in at the Casino and work our way back from there.'

'Gomez says he can put us on to some good dives in the Calle Taraje. I'll see if I can catch him in the wardroom before lunch.'

Teniente de navio Gomez Alfredo Brauer was one of the three Naval Liaison Officers attached to the ship. His mixed German, English and Chilean parentage showed in his name and in a surprising aptitude to be all things to all men in quickly changing succession.

'He's got great charm, he knows everyone and everything that is to be known,' the British Consul-General had told Trevesham in Marsh's hearing. 'He's the ideal Liaison Officer—far and away the best of the bunch— and I wouldn't trust him an inch.'

'Luckily, we don't have to trust him much,' said Marsh, repeating this observation for Hale's benefit. 'We need this advice but we don't have to accept it.'

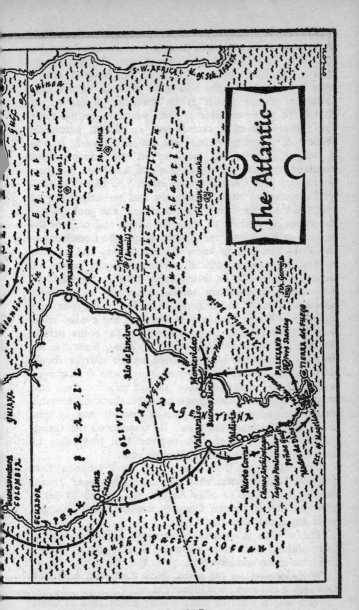

The Atlantic

GULF OF GUINEA

EQUATOR

S.W. AFRICA   S.W. of Sth. AFRICA

St. Helena

Ascension I.

Atlantic Basin

Pernambuco

Trinidad (Brazil)

TROPIC OF CAPRICORN

SOUTH ATLANTIC

Tristan da Cunha

Rio de Janeiro

Montevideo

GUIANA

BRAZIL

BOLIVIA

PARAGUAY

Buenos Aires

Punta Arenas

Sth. Georgia

FALKLAND Is.
Port Stanley

ARGENTINA

PERU

COLOMBIA

ECUADOR

Lima
Callao

Valparaiso

Valdivia

TIERRA DEL FUEGO

Puerto Corral
Chonos Archipelago
Taytao Peninsula   Peñas Gulf
Madre de Dios

STS. OF MAGELLAN

SOUTH PACIFIC OCEAN

This hot and somewhat muddled statement struck Hale as typical of the Captain's Secretary. He remembered his own days in a similar appointment some five years ago. It was a 'hot and bothered' type of job, however glazed over it might be by the additional glamour of the flag-lieutenant duties which HMS *Antigone* demanded of Marsh. In the immediate pre-war years, to be the Captain's Secretary of a cruiser was an almost automatic section of a young Accountant Officer's career. It was a restless, overworked job tied to the administrative regulations of the service on the one hand and the personality of your Captain on the other. You had to be lawyer, confidential clerk, diplomatist and messenger boy at one and the same time. You had to coax and goad officers far senior to yourself to write the letters and prepare the reports called for by the Admiraly and the Commander-in-Chief. You had to know the regulations and be able to find authority or official guidance for any course of action proposed by or thrust upon the ship. You had to keep six hundred ratings' service certificates and conduct sheets up to date and in order. You had to do your own typing and filing. You held the keys of the cypher chest and thus the security on your person of the entire British Empire. It was a sobering thought. These were the responsibilities which Marsh carried on his narrow shoulders at the age of twenty-one. Hale, who had moved over into the 'soap and baccy' side of paymastering, and was now a mature twenty-seven, looked back on Marsh's struggling and floundering with a tolerant and sympathetic eye. He knew the form. He understood the raging impotence to which the job reduced him from time to time and where possible he helped him out.

That evening in their alpaca suits, their 'chooch' hats and with walking sticks over their arms, they went ashore, as they had done so often before, determined to get a glow on at the French Consul's cocktail party and see what happened after that.

'The trouble is,' Marsh complained a little morosely, 'that nothing ever does seem to happen except that I drink too much and have a hangover the next day.'

'Well, go easy on the pisco,' Hale cautioned him, 'the Doc says it can make you literally blind.'

Pisco was a form of local brandy much used in Chile

as a basis for cocktails where its flavour could be disguised by vermouths and other drinks. But perhaps the French Consul would surprise them with something special that night. None of them looked forward to it very much. Twelve officers had been asked and only eight had volunteered. The others had been 'told-off' by the Commander and those who were attending out of duty included Meldrum, Cravenby, Grey-Bennett and Osborne.

They climbed into three taxis and set off to the French Consulate. Unlike Lima, Valparaiso was not a capital city. The Government and the Embassies were all set up in Santiago in the foothills of the Andes. So official life in the great seaport town gyrated round the Consulates and the Chilean Navy and Army messes.

'It may not have quite the glamour of the capital,' said Hale, as they rumbled through a dockside slum, 'but some solid business entertainment won't do us any harm for a change. They've laid it on lavishly enough so far.'

Valparaiso had, in fact, felt deep into its pocket. Parties which would have wrecked the finances of a smaller community were all in the day's work to the shipping and trading circles of Valparaiso and Viña del Mar. They put horses and yachts at the disposal of the officers: they gave a great 'beer fiesta' at the Stadium for the ship's company: they flocked to the vast old opera house in which the Concert Party performed—their largest theatre to date—and every evening there were two or three smaller parties, such as this present one at the French Consul's, to add variety to the round.

'Who's beating up the town tonight?' asked Meldrum as they went in to the party.

'We are,' said Hale nodding his head at Marsh. 'Want to join up?'

'All right. I must find out what my familiar is up to. He's been playing golf with the manager of a copper mine. Perhaps he'll come along too. If there's any strength left in his little legs.'

This suited both Hale and Marsh. They liked both Meldrum and the Navigating Officer. It added life to the party and there was a certain safety in numbers when it came to forays into cabarets and dives. They shook hands now with their host and hostess and then separated into the ordinary pools and eddies of yet another party. The

French Consul General was doing them well: there were champagne cocktails in ample supply and in the first quarter of an hour it was obvious that the party had a distinct style of its own. The house, the servants and the guests all seemed to have a gallic lightness, so that they all forgot for a while the earthy Latin-American background. Then suddenly, for Derek Lysander Marsh, it happened. In the space of not more than five seconds, out of the blue, unheralded and totally unprepared, he fell headlong into love.

'Gosh!' he said to himself with a kind of interior tremble, and then a moment or so later 'Gosh!' again.

And nothing material had happened at all. They had not even met. They were not even in the same group of people. She was standing by one of the arches of the patio, a cocktail in one hand and a cigarette in the other. She wore a dark-green dress of some kind of silk. It was certainly not an obvious colour for her black hair and her brown eyes, and indeed she was not possessed of a striking prettiness or an especially compelling figure. She had been listening to what an older woman was vivaciously saying to a grey-haired man, not speaking herself but looking at her cigarette and her drink held delicately in little gloved hands.

Then, as though a magnet was compelling her attention, she looked up and straight across into Marsh's eyes —a serene virginal, steady look as it seemed to him, a look that asked no questions yet received into it all the answers his being could convey—cool, unhurried, and with the suggestion of a smile.

'Gosh!' said Marsh once again to himself, and realized suddenly that he had not the faintest idea in the world of what his companions had been saying but that at this point he was expected to answer and couldn't. The colour flushed into his face and his hands shook at the wrists.

'I'm awfully sorry,' he blurted out. 'I missed what you said.'

'Quite so,' said Hale drily and then, following his gaze: 'And jolly good luck with it, *I* say.'

As soon as he could get away Marsh stumbled to the door and suffered himself to be shown the lavatory by a white-coated servant. There he leant his head against the cool tiles of the wall and felt as though he ached and yearned in every bone and fibre of his body. 'Don't think,' something inside him was saying, 'it's no good to think. This is just funny—that's all it is. But it's nothing to do with your brain. It won't answer. It won't move.' And then a little later as he clenched his fists and leant his forehead against his arms, he felt a wildness in his veins which defied expression. 'Hell and damnation,' he said, 'what's happening to me? I must be ill. This is fantastic—absurd.'

He tidied himself and went back to the party. She was still there by the patio arch. He caught his breath and looked desperately around for some means of getting nearer to her at once. Hale and the others had moved away, leaving him a more or less clear run. She had her back to him now and for a time he stood there staring at her and dreaming how she would be. Then on another impulse he walked over intending to introduce himself on some feeble excuse which he hoped would occur to him on the spur of the moment. But the two older people she was with continued to talk across her with the same damnable vivacity. He could not catch her eye. The palms of his hands grew stickier and stickier. He shifted from one foot to another and felt as gauche and awkward as a gangling schoolboy in a suit he had grown out of. Then, as though all along she had known he was there, she turned to him and explained:

'Ah! c'est vous: Antoine! Je vous ai vu à l'autre coté. Comment allez-vous?'

'Oh!' said Derek Lysander Marsh, a rare shade of beetroot. 'Er—how do you do?'

She drew him into her little circle with a gesture.

'Je vous presente à . . . Lieutenant de Vaisseau Antoine . . . tch! tch!' she clicked her teeth impatiently at the stupidity of the English in catching on so slowly.

'Er—Marsh,' he said, bowing at the others. 'How do you do?'

'Now,' said the girl in unexpected English, 'you take me over there'—pointing towards the fountain in the middle of the patio—'and you explain me some things. Why are you not sailing yesterday at the Club?'

'Oh yes, exactly—excuse me,' said Marsh, bowing again as she led the way over the tiled patio and out of their earshot. It seemed to him now that the situation was quite out of hand. Once again away from the others, she turned to look at him and smile. Her quick way of talking belied the serenity in her face.

'Parlez-pas français?' she asked. 'In English—better?'

'Much, much better,' Marsh agreed. 'I say—thanks awfully for getting us away like that. I couldn't think of an excuse to introduce myself.'

'Oh!' she exclaimed with that shrug of the shoulders and pouting of the lips which only a French woman can perfectly manage. 'Ils sont des amis à maman—for me a chaperone: you see, I live in Santiago and I am here for the sailing. Now tell me about yourself.'

She could not have been much over five foot but she seemed to Marsh to be perfectly composed. Most of the girls you met at these parties fussed and giggled. They tried, at all costs, to hold the centre of the stage and do most of the talking. They half-listened to you but only in order to cap everything you said with a funnier remark of their own. They were interested in no one but themselves. This girl, however, was different. She might talk with brisk animation but it was like a series of little mocking leaps out of a calm, contented sea of understanding.

'Well, of course, my name isn't Antoine.'

'Oh! What a pity! We once had a cat called Antoine. He was very much a man.'

'What's your name?' he asked.

'Lisette. Lisette Champlain. My father is at the Embassy in Santiago.'

'Is he the Ambassador?'

'No. He is the second—the chancelier, you say?'

'I don't know,' said Marsh, 'let's talk about us. Will you come and have some dinner tonight?'

'Oh! no. It's very kind of you—but you see I must stay with the Delbauts. They are responsible to my parents. Here in Chile girls do not go out alone.'

'I know,' said Marsh unhappily, 'it's the same in Peru and Venezuela. It's archaic.'

'Next year we got back to France.' Her face lit up with a wonderful smile. 'To Paris.'

'Next year, I suppose, we go back to England, but that doesn't help us very much now.' He looked into her eyes and he tingled all over. 'Isn't it odd? I feel I've known you a very long time.'

'Well,' she answered quietly, 'who knows? Possibly we have.' Then with a little toss of the head: 'I shall make the Delbauts take us to the casino tonight. They do not like it but it is good for them to make up a party.'

'Oh!' said Marsh thinking of Hale and the party they had embarked on themselves, 'must it be a party?'

She put her head slightly on one side and looked at him.

'We shall see,' she said and taking his hand led him back to her chaperones.

He never forgot that evening. It seemed almost to arrange itself. Hale did not want to change their plans and Marsh felt committed, and in turn did not like to upset his friends, but the pull of Lisette was too much. When it came to the point, there was no decision to make. Even though he would get nowhere physically with her—'to get a kiss out of one of these dames you have to risk marriage,' Hale commented—even though the ship was to be in Valparaiso for only another three days—even though at twenty and earning approximately ten shillings a day he could have no hope of achieving her in any sense whatever—nevertheless he felt swept along in an exalted state of feeling which appeared to have no connection with his humdrum everyday self. In the end Hale had agreed to postpone his run down the Calle Taraje. He had resigned himself to another evening's 'poodle-faking', so they had all gone to the Casino. The Delbauts had organized some dinner and afterwards they had danced.

'I don't suppose I'll ever be as near to you as this again,' Marsh said to Lisette, 'there's so much I want to say and no words to say it with.'

She pressed his shoulder gently so that she seemed to draw him down into herself.

'You mustn't try too hard,' she said. 'It's not the time for you yet.'

'Nor for you?'

'How can it be?' she answered softly. 'Look how it is with our lives.'

'But . . . oh! Lord,' he groaned. The ship, his bunk, his little office, the mess, the quarterdeck, the routine and the feel of his life on board suddenly presented themselves to him in a kind of compressed vision of slavery as he danced with the scent of her hair in his nostrils and her brown, clear skin an inch or two from his mouth. 'Won't I see you again?' he asked desperately. He could not bring himself to say he was madly in love with her: it would sound so extraordinary and anyway, what was the use? She said nothing for a while and they continued to dance with each other as though lost to the world. Then she leant back a little and looked in his face.

'*Mais c'est curieux, quandmême.*'

'What is?'

'To know so much and to look so young.'

'You're not so very old yourself,' he said with a touch of indignation. He hated being told he looked young.

'Ah! yes,' she murmured. 'But then I know how it is with you and with me.' She gave a little shrug of her shoulders. 'And there is nothing we can do.'

'Nothing at all?'

There was a lump in his throat and his eyes were hot and stinging.

'You have to wait,' she said, and again he could feel her body alive, wonderfully alive, so near to him, moving so gently, so sensitive to his own aching touch.

'I don't know why I feel as I do,' he said at last. 'I wish I were dead—I know it sounds silly.'

'Oh! no!' she murmured softly, 'to feel in this way is true. It is always sad.'

Now it was his turn to be silent for a while.

'You know, you're extraordinary,' he said in the end.

'How—extraordinary?'

'I don't have to explain it in words. I've known you five minutes and it might have been twenty-one years. How old *are* you?'

'Seventeen.'

'I don't believe it.'

'Ah! you must understand,' she said with a kind of quick annoyance, 'out here we grow up very fast. That is why next year I go to Paris. Otherwise by twenty-one I am finish. Oh! yes!' She nodded her head vigorously. 'If you live in Chile you see for yourself.'

By the end of the evening the Delbauts had exhausted the small talk and the even narrower common ground which a different language and a different generation allowed them. They had done their best with their weary duty. So, too, had the faithful Hale, looking across the dance floor at an oblivious Marsh, with Lisette in his arms, while dance after dance Hale himself partnered a rather blown Chilean beauty, the daughter of a brewer, and the only makeweight to hand on the spur of the moment. He was itching to get down the Calle Taraje into a smoky dive with some real people, but he had said he would stick it out for the sake of Marsh and his popsy and this he did. But at last it was time to go. The bill was signed, the wraps collected, Monsieur Delbaut's huge chauffeur-driven Cadillac was brought to the door and the goodnights were said. The pressure of a hand, the promise of tomorrow and she had gone. Marsh followed the back of the car into the darkness, as the cicadas cricked and chirped, and the feeling of exaltation gradually died.

'My God! that was heavy sledding,' said Hale. 'Come on, let's get a taxi and go somewhere alive for a change. You've had your fun. Now it's my turn.'

By the time the ship reached Patagonia, their experiences in Valparaiso had sunk into perspective. Marsh was not the only one to get emotionally involved. Grey-Bennett, Peter Osborne and Cravenby all continued to receive mail with heavy Chilean stamps, and even Augustus Spratt was 'in tow of a little widow woman' as Meldrum described it for the benefit of the wardroom.

'It strikes me we left in the nick of time,' Collard observed as he smoked his pipe and sat on the club fender surrounding the wardroom fire. This was his favourite position. His ample back soaked up the heat, and by this time it was mid-winter in the southern hemisphere, so that scuttles and cabin doors were kept shut to give the electric fires a chance.

'Then perhaps the Senior Engineer will give us his recipe for keeping out of trouble in big South American cities,' said Spratt. 'We still have Buenos Aires and Rio de Janeiro ahead.'

'Trouble?' said Meldrum. 'You call Consuela Maria de Taragonada y Aleman trouble? She had money didn't she?'

'She had other things, too,' Spratt answered. 'We won't go into all that again.'

The large widow's pursuit of their pocket-size Navigating Officer had already taken its place in the ship's mythology. It was a classic music-hall situation and Spratt was aware of its and his own absurdity. Terrible jokes were made about his 'consuelation prize' and her feverish frustrated wooing came in for some dark comment each time her Buick appeared alongside the ship to fetch the Navigating Officer to her palace. She was a well-stacked lady with a repertoire of hats, and by the time the ship left Valparaiso the wardroom had affectionately adopted her as some kind of pet. Now that the mists and fogs of Tierra del Fuego swirled round the ship, she had become a legend, 'a kind of Chilean Brünhilde' as Spratt himself put it, 'emerging from an outcrop of the Andes every time a British warship comes into port—that is to say approximately once every three years.'

After leaving Valparaiso they had called in for five days at Puerto Corral, the port of Valdivia, and had then proceeded due south past the Chonos and Taytao Archipelagoes, the Gulf of Peñas and the Madre de Dios Islands to the Strait of Magellan. The days had shortened. They now wore their winter blue uniform. On the bridge they stamped their feet and nursed steaming cups of cocoa, and now after a voyage of some 1,600 miles they were anchored at Magallanes or Punta Arenas as the charts had it—the last town in the world. It was no holiday resort and it seemed to Marsh that the bare, cheerless landscape was a perfect counterpart to the bleakness he had felt in himself since saying good-bye to Lisette.

He did his work listlessly, almost glad of the routine. He turned out of his bunk in the morning to gaze at the cold, grey sea with distaste and an emptiness at heart. Breakfast in the gunroom, a cigarette, divisions, and then the day's work in the office, Requestmen and Defaulters, attending on the Captain, listening patiently to the Master-at-Arms, allowing his leg to be pulled by Able-Seaman Clarke, all the happenings and incidents of the ship's life both big and small which touched him now had a coated, dull, deadened taste. He wanted Lisette: he ached for her in the most intimate parts of his body and he knew perfectly well he would never see her again.

By this time it was May 1939. The last few months of peace lumbered on slowly like a great cartwheel over the potholes of a country road. The by now familiar ding-dong, pendulum rhythm of hope and despair continued to dominate their lives, and now that HMS *Antigone* had been in commission for over a year, she was no longer the Navy's newest and fastest cruiser.

'She's just a lonely old lady lost in the snow,' said Hale as he and Marsh took a constitutional on the quarter-deck, 'and I must say I won't be sorry to see the fleshpots of BA and Rio heave into sight. This kind of windy pur-gatory's all very well for the penguins, but Flash Annie's a good-time girl.'

Yet the little community at the end of the world re-ceived them with exceptional warmth. Chilean in nation-ality; Scottish by descent, the majority of their hosts were sheep farmers. There was whisky and beer in abun-dance. Great fires were kept in the houses and the Inten-dante gave an official banquet to the officers. Football matchs were played in the biting wind. The Concert Party and the Harmonica Band both performed to packed houses and enormous enthusiasm. The weather and the life in Magallanes reminded them of Scapa: but it also had much of Gibraltar in its appeal to the lower deck.

As if to underline this likeness their next port of call was a British possession, the Falkland Islands, some six hundred miles east of Tierra del Fuego. It took them forty hours steaming at their economical speed to reach Port Stanley with its English cathedral, its substantial Town Hall and the Union Jack flying proudly over Government House. Here they really did feel at home.

'Fancy being able to go ashore, talk English and have it talked back at you,' said Able-Seaman Clarke to the Master-at-Arms, 'no jabber-jabber-jabber and none of that dirty paper money we've had in Peru and Chile.'

'It's a bit of home all right,' the Master-At-Arms agreed as he watched a boatload of libertymen setting off across the choppy harbour to the bare, treeless land. 'Though it depends what part of England is home to you,' he added. The Master-at-Arms had been born in Torquay.

But home it was, though the clouds might lour and a wind straight from the South Pole might cut its way into their marrow. They looked at the wild marsh grass, at the peat bogs and the grey stone buildings, they gazed at the metallic waters and at the storm clouds racing up from the empty south, and they all felt the same absurdly powerful emotion. It was a little bit of home. England might be eight thousand miles away to the north but these small, forgotten, disputed islands were peopled by the same kind of folk as themselves, speaking the same language, clinging as tenaciously to their barren rocks and grimly forging their lives against the spite and fury of the elements with the same steady courage, the same underlying principles and the same gritty, threadbare decency as the crofters of the Orkneys or the cockneys of Wapping. Shortly after their arrival in harbour Trevesham sent for his Gunnery Officer and his Captain, Royal Marines.

'When we discussed the cruise programme in Bermuda,' Trevesham said, 'I mentioned the defences of the Falkland Islands and the Navy's responsibility for them. As you know, these defences consist of a single six-inch gun, mounted by *Ajax* and *Exeter* some three years ago—a fairly solid piece of Royal Marine Base Defence work to judge from the report.'

The idea of this armoury of one single gun struck them all as funny, and though none of them put it into words the same mixture of defiance and absurdity filled their minds as they considered Port Stanley, its geographical position and the possible role it might be called on to play in another war.

'Ours not to reason why,' Trevesham continued. 'The gun is there and the local inhabitants are very proud of it. The Governor is anxious for us to try out his fowling-piece and if we think its emplacement could be improved to do something about it. That's primarily a Royal Marine commitment, Taw-Street, but of course you and Brasson must work together. I stipulate only one thing. Since the gun is meant to cover the harbour and as it is some time since it was last fired, I should prefer you not to blow up *Antigone* in your practice shoot. If need be I'll take the ship to sea until the experiment has come to a conclusion.'

After this meeting with the Captain, Brasson and Taw-Street repaired to the wardroom for a gin.

'An intrepid assignment,' said Taw-Street, reflectively stroking his moustache. 'The Old Man's eagerness to get the hell out of it to sea while we explode this cannon, simply fills me with confidence.'

'One thing's certain,' Brasson remarked firmly. 'My Chief Ordnance Artificer is going to inspect that breech block microscopically before a single round goes into the gun.'

'Yes,' said Taw-Street, 'and then everyone will stand well back and pray.'

As it turned out their fears were baseless. *Ajax* and *Exeter* who had built the emplacement and mounted the gun, had done the job well, and it seemed to have been properly maintained by the local defence volunteers. When the gun had been fired and its performance checked, Taw-Street ordered its protective covering to be replaced.

'Well,' he said with relief, 'it works, though what possible use it would be against a warship the Lord alone knows.' Yet even as he said it he realized that at certain moments in history a single, lone rifle might turn the entire course of a war.

.Their sojourn at Port Stanley marked the half-way point of their cruise. They had come a great distance since leaving Bermuda in February but they were once again in the Atlantic and soon they would be headed north up the east coast of South America on his way back to their base. In the meantime Port Stanley did them proud. The total population of the Falkland Islands is slightly over four thousand and Port Stanley contains well over half of these. During the whole of the ship's visit the little town was *en fête*, the warmth of its hospitality contrasting sharply with the gale-swept, grim surroundings in which the islanders lived with their thousands and thousands of sheep.

'I've asked his Excellency what would give the local inhabitants the most pleasure in returning hospitality,' Trevesham told Hatchett towards the end of their stay, 'and he thinks a children's party on board would really knock them for six.'

'That's exactly what the ship's company have asked for, too,' said Hatchett. 'So if you consent I'll go ahead with "Aunty's Gone to the Funfair"—say for Friday?'

Trevesham nodded. 'We ought to lay something on separately for the parents as well. I don't feel a South American type cocktail party is quite what's wanted here.'

'Well, sir,' said Hatchett, 'the Pay's asking to try his hand at a bumper high-tea on the messdeck with perhaps some beer in the wardroom for the non-tea-drinking men. Shall I tell him to go ahead?'

'Yes,' Trevesham agreed, 'I think that's about the mark.'

In 1939 Port Stanley was definitely a 'ship's company port' and this could be said, in those days, without any overtones of class conscious snobbery. Officers and ship's company took things as they were. There were people in Rolls-Royces and people in clogs and it was no part of *Antigone*'s function to try and right these inequalities. Lima and Valparaiso were one thing, Port Stanley, and the Falkland Islands another. *Antigone* wove her way in among them all without preconceived ideas of how people should be. It was the same warship in the same role but the changing audience called for a little variety in the playing.

HMS *Antigone*'s Grand Fête and Maritime Gala Party was, indeed, something never seen before within a thousand miles of the South Pole. The quarterdeck was enclosed with canvas screens and every radiator that could be pressed into service played its part in getting up the right fug, as the gunroom had it. Inside this sizable marquee, strings of bunting, coloured lights and modified Christmas decorations turned the place into a kind of grotto-cum-funfair. There was a Mystery Tunnel chute from 'X' turret to the quarterdeck, the after capstan had been turned into a roundabout with wooden horses on the end of the capstan bars and Stoker Danny Evans in charge, there was a Pirates' Cave from which CPO Bowling would erupt with a striped jersey, a patch over his eye and blood-curdling yells. There was a lucky dip, a seesaw and a swing. There was a treasure hunt in the wardroom and conducted tours of wide-eyed children to the boiler room, the bridge and right inside a six-inch gun turret.

The children arrived in boatloads. However dour their parents, however rough and strenuous the lives they were destined to lead, however simple their homes—this was a party, and their squeals of delight soon drowned the music from *Snow White and the Seven Dwarfs* which was the Royal Marine Band's *pièce de résistance* for the evening.

As Hatchett had forecast, the Paymaster-Commander let himself go. There were pyramids of sandwiches, plum cake by the yard, Diggony Doughnuts, cream buns, chocolates, fizzy lemonade and even a giant Galley Cracker containing a sticky sugar snowball which the children fell upon with delight, a folly which was regretted in the ship for weeks afterwards.

The noise was appalling. Even cynics who had forecast a flop were convinced within half an hour that it was a thundering, clattering, yelling success. Outside the short day was already at an end. The wind from the Antartic blew gustily and relentlessly in the dark. All around, the waters of the harbour lapped against the ship's side, black and choppy, ice cold and forbidding, but on board the lights blazed, the fires glowed and some hundreds of children tore about the ship, each chaperoned by an adopted 'uncle' in bell-bottomed trousers, all intent upon the best party they had ever had in their lives.

The First Lieutenant, who had a particular way with children, was the favourite 'Uncle' of them all. He led them in Hunt the Slipper, he took them on an exploration of the ship past humming fans, through watertight doors, down vertical ladders, into the chain lockers, the steaming galley, and the spotless electric bakery. He showed them the torpedo tubes and let them train and elevate the pom-pom guns, specially floodlit and screened in against the wind. He carried them pick-a-back on his shoulders and when one little boy was sick over his cap he never turned a hair. Somewhere in his mind was a picture of the cottage at Liphook, eight thousand miles away, with its calm, longed-for wife, and his own three children, but he did not let it come too much into his consciousness. He threw himself wholeheartedly into the party and without intending it in any shape or form attracted the admiration of the Captain, the Commander, the Midshipmen (who became his enthusiastic Lieutenants at the party), and the entire ship's company who saw him at one time or another festooned with children, a kind of fifteen stone nautical nursemaid.

'We've had a lot of different parties in this ship,' said the Gunnery Officer as he and Collard watched the launch setting off for the shore crammed with exhausted children, 'but personally this has been the best yet. We ought to get a putty medal for this.'

'Yes,' said Meldrum on the other side, 'polite Anglo-Spanish small talk over cocktails is going to look pretty tame after this even in Buenos Aires and Rio de Janeiro.'

'The Chief Gunner's Mate tells me the controls in "Y" turret are completely stickied over with coconut icing, chocolate and chewing gum. A rag doll was found in the ammunition hoist and Torps says someone tied a wee knitted bonnet to one of his starboard torpedo tubes. I wonder what Admiral Sturdie would think about that.'

They looked out across the harbour to the shore. Somewhere in the darkness lashed by the wind and the rain stood the memorial to that victory in 1914 over von Spee, which had put the Falkland Islands into the history books of the world.

'Yes, I wonder,' Collard said thoughtfully, 'and I wonder if we'll ever be back here again.'

The last of the children had now left the ship and the duty part of the watch was at work unrigging the quarterdeck. The electirc fires were switched off, the capstan cover was back in its place, and soon the side screens would be taken down so that the quarterdeck could revert to its normal windy condition. Already the Midshipman of the Watch was walking about with his telescope under his arm, occasionally blowing on his fingers. The Bosun's Mate was piping for Able-Seaman Donovan to report to the regulating office. Down below, marine servants were turning down beds and laying out their officers' clothes for dinner, and the wardroom stewards were steadily getting the mess back into its proper shape. The Commander had drawn a hot bath and was wallowing in the steam. Forward in the galley tiddy-oggies were being served out for supper, and the cooks of the messes were exchanging jokes about the party as they queued up for their turn. Able-Seaman Clarke finished running off the Daily Orders and as usual clucked in resignation at his purple-stained fingers.

By now the launch would have disgorged its last load of children ashore and would be on its way back to the ship. It was blowing up for half a gale and later that night they might have to hoist in the boats. Collard and

Brasson turned to go down below as Meldrum spoke to the Duty Stoker Petty Officer about a detail of tomorrow's routine. The quarterdeck awning flapped and rattled in the wind and the Yeoman of Signals crossed in front of them with the green signal log from the Signal Distributing Office. There was no smile on his face and this suddenly struck a chord in Collard's mind.

'Any news of the *Thetis*, Yeoman of Signals?' he called out. Mellish stopped and saluted.

'No, sir,' he said, 'no good news, that is. It's beginning to blow up in the Irish Sea and the salvage people don't think they can hold her where she is.'

It was 2 June, 1939. The day before HM Submarine *Thetis* had submerged on her trials in Liverpool Bay. Her stern was out of the water off Great Orme's Head but hope of extricating alive the ninety-nine men was hourly dwindling. Eight thousand miles away from Liverpool the Captain and ship's company of HMS *Antigone* thought grimly about those ninety-nine brother officers and men in the doomed submarine as they went about the business of their ship. No one said it, but all were vividly aware that in slightly different conditions it might so very easily be their turn next.

CHAPTER TEN

'During the summer,' the Commander-in-Chief in HMS *Berwick* had signalled, 'I intend cruising in company with *Ajax* and *Antigone*. The following alterations in the cruise programme will therefore take place . . .'

They had received this signal at the Falkland Islands. It meant little change in their own arrangements. Instead of a lone cruiser visiting the great ports of the eastern seaboard there would now be a squadron of three warships and an Admiral's flag. They would be sharing the limelight. A few days later they reached Buenos Aires.

The three cruisers made a splendid picture as they lay alongside the northern docks, their light-grey paint gleaming in the sunlight. As at Valparaiso they were once more in a great city. The bleakness of the Falkland Islands and the remoteness of Chile were forgotten in the clatter and bustle of Buenos Aires with its skyscrapers and modern concrete buildings. But there were differences between Chile and Argentina which became more and more obvious the longer they stayed. Chile was poor: the Argentine rich. Buenos Aires was a capital city with ten times the population of Valparaiso. It seemed to be, as indeed it was, very much more in touch with the civilized world. Its people were more European, more cosmopolitan. Behind Valparaiso rose the Andes with the peak of Aconcagua crowning them all: behind Buenos Aires stretched five hundred miles of flat prairie richly stocked with the cattle upon which the prosperity of the country depended.

There was a sharp difference, too, between their naval hosts in the two countries.

'I don't know why it is,' said Spratt as he and Meldrum left one of the lavish official receptions, 'I felt at home in Chile, I don't here at all. They're too sleek and well paid. I don't trust them. There's a jealousy of England, a sort of oily dislike of us which never seemed to trouble the Chileans, the Peruvians or the Venezuelans.'

'Then of course there's always this business of the Falkland Islands,' Meldrum put in. 'Drop a hat and they start sulking about their blasted Islas Malvinas. Did you know they solemnly appoint a Governor of them every year who sits here in BA twiddling his thumbs?'

'Well, anyway,' said Spratt, 'I wish I had Argentine Naval pay and allowances.'

There were a lot of undercurrents in Buenos Aires in June 1939. The large Italian community and the not inconsiderable German colony openly resented their presence. 'Vayan gringos ingleses' and similar exhortations appeared in whitewash on the dockyard walls. 'Abajo imperialistas' were shouted at the troops as they marched to a ceremonial parade and 'Mierda británica' was found to be stencilled on certain stores delivered to the ship.

'The Mayor is very anxious to impress upon me that only an infinitesimal part of the population is anti-

British,' the C-in-C told his captains, 'but the Ambassador has a somewhat more realistic approach. I want ship's companies warned once again that incidents, rows, arguments of any kind ashore must be avoided at all costs. There are loyalties of every sort in this city and most of them are beginning to boil. It's our duty to keep entirely clear.'

Antigone took this very much as a matter of course.

'Appeasement! that's what it is,' said Able-Seaman Elcock to one of the Three Fat Men of the Sea, 'so don't you start none of your arguments about whose turn it is for cook of the mess. Go on, now, appease me.'

'Remember *who* you are, *where* you are and *what* you've at stake, you *wart!*' said Midshipman Mottram twisting up Watling's arm till he yelled for the thousandth time that commission.

Three cruisers in company brought their own compensations as well. They became a little naval community on their own. The squadron's daily life was administered by the Admiral. Duties were shared. Ships' routines had, of course, to continue as before, but in non-working hours there was now a guard ship, which they took it in turn to be, and which provided duty medical officers, boats, boarding-parties, guard and band—indeed all the frills and fittings of naval life which *Antigone* had had to find within herself for the last four months.

Another pleasant aspect of being in company in a foreign port was that they could exchange hospitality with each other. This was more important to officers than ship's company. Trevesham kept a close eye on his officers' wine bills as the regulations enjoined him to do. He was not an 'easy' Captain. Fossingham, the Torpedo Officer, had been the first to find this out, and any wardroom officer approaching his monthly wine bill limit of five pounds was sharply warned to show an improvement for the following months. But at Buenos Aires, as at Bermuda, Trevesham recognized that it was better for the ship and better for the Service if wardroom, gunroom and warrant officers were encouraged to see as much of their opposite numbers as possible. *Antigone* was a happy ship, and in the late forenoon her officers' messes were filled with visitors both from *Ajax* and *Berwick*, and also from the British community ashore.

'It's extraordinary,' Hale said to Marsh as they strolled round the Calle Florida in search of souvenirs, 'but now that we're here in BA I feel our trip down the other side —Magellan—even the Falkland Islands, might have been another commission in another ship. I know it's illusion. I know we're over six thousand miles from England. But I still feel we're back in circulation again—if the balloon goes up all of a sudden.'

Marsh nodded, his thoughts elsewhere. 'It does seem a long time ago.'

'Have you heard from Lisette?'

'Yes,' Marsh said reluctantly, 'she's supposed to be coming through BA on her way back to France.'

'Will you see her at all?'

'I don't think so,' he said, and then to forestall further questions: 'What do you think of these ponchos? Would an Indian blanket go down well at home as a present?'

He hated talking about Lisette. He knew it was silly. He recognized the hopelessness of feeling as he did but he couldn't help it. He had fallen in love and the further away it went in time, the deeper its hold seemed to go.

'You'll get over it,' Hale said, lighting his pipe.

'I dare say I will.'

In the old days he would have defended or excused his feeling. Now it seemed to be somewhere in his being like a dark, bottomless pool. It had made him far more reserved. Things mattered less in ordinary, everyday life. He had become obsessed with Lisette. He nursed it to his most private self, not facing the fact that events were all wrong, that in all likelihood they would never see each other again.

'I wish I could help in some way,' Hale went on, puffing at his pipe and looking at the pavement, 'but there never is anything anyone else can do.'

'Is it that obvious then?'

'Perhaps not to others. The Commander told me he thought you'd gone a bit sour. You were such an eager beaver in the early days.'

'Oh! well,' Marsh said, 'I suppose we all get over the first fine push of excitement about the buttons and braid.'

'Something made you join the Navy,' said Hale. 'You

can't be a good Naval officer and a happily married man. The two things just don't go together.'

'I know, I know,' Marsh said with a touch of irritation. 'It doesn't help, though, to see what you're missing. And another thing'—he went on as Hale started to speak—'it's not a blind bit of use telling me I ought to go and have a good thump in a brothel. Maybe I should. Maybe I will— but it's got nothing whatever to do with Lisette.'

'Hm!' said Hale, 'you have got it badly indeed.'

Meanwhile the different levels of life in ship and squadron continued to revolve against the darkening background of June 1939.

'Perhaps after all they're really on the defensive,' the Admiral told a meeting of his captains, commanders and navigating officers in the flagship. 'I don't believe it myself but that's neither here nor there. What has arrived and what requires your urgent attention is a set of new Convoy Instructions from the Admiralty. These you can take away and read at your leisure, but this morning I want to go over with all of you the organization for sailing and routeing convoys which will come into being if the Fleet is mobilized and war is declared.'

There were about a dozen officers in the Admiral's day cabin aboard the *Berwick*. A blackboard and easel had been set up and now the Staff Officer (Operations) was drawing a diagram of the pattern of operations which they might soon have to apply. Trevesham looked at the sharp, concentrated face of his Navigating Officer and the square, reddened features of Hatchett, both intent on the blackboard. He looked round at the other officers from the flagship and from *Ajax* and then out through a scuttle at the busy, bustling life of Buenos Aires. He wondered when and how it was going to come. He wondered if they would see Buenos Aires again, and which of them there would survive. He thought back to other and similar conferences he had had as a junior officer in the Great War. There wasn't much difference. The faces had changed: they used to wear winged collars and narrower caps, beards were then more in fashion, but it was the same Service doing the same job and it looked like being the same enemy all over again.

When the SOO had finished, there were questions and

the meeting turned into a general discussion. As Trevesham listened, as an occasional point presented itself to his mind it struck him that this little gathering of officers was typically, unmistakably British. He supposed the Germans, too, must issue and discuss their orders down the scale of command, but this friendly respectful informality would be missing. They thought of everything, the Germans. Once the plan was decided upon, not a detail would lack. Here, though, details had been given only where they were absolutely essential and sometimes not even then. The Germans would call it laziness: the British flexibility. Yet, what was this technique of success? The Royal Navy had had it a very long time. It was something unwritten. He had heard it called a 'mystique', whatever that meant, but it was there in the smallest and pinkest Dartmouth cadet and the oldest and crustiest Admiral of the Fleet. They were certainly not conscious of it as such. But Trevesham saw it even in the way Spratt and Hatchett stood up after the meeting. The way they moved, the way they stood, the way they talked. There was a wary, watchful confidence in their being. They were conditioned to sudden disaster yet somehow or other they had always found out the way to win in the end. As they walked along the jetty back to *Antigone* a new whitewashed swastika had appeared on the wall facing the ship.

'Our friends are closer than we thought,' said Hatchett looking at the sign.

Although it was now winter in the southern hemisphere, their cruise programme took them steadily nearer the equator. The ship was once more full of sunlight and by the time they reached Rio de Janeiro they were in white uniform again. Except for the lavish hospitality of the British Community, Buenos Aires had not been a success. Protocol and etiquette had been scrupulously observed. The right parties had been given and attended. But they all felt a hostility under the surface. They were none of them sorry to sail across the River Plate to the more friendly Uruguay and its fabulously expensive capital.

It was mid-July by the time the squadron had exercised for a week in the South Atlantic and had then sailed the twelve hundred miles north to Rio de Janeiro. By now the tension was beginning to mount. Marsh found more and more of his nights disturbed by the arrival of cypher messages in the ship. Taw-Street, who as Captain, Royal Marines, had custody of the ship's Confidential Books, put in some hard concentrated work correcting them and bringing them bang up to date. Spratt, aided by the Chief Quartermaster and Midshipman Watling, did the same on his charts and the paraphernalia of navigation. Hale and the Paymaster-Commander speeded up the normal mustering of Central Stores and again checked over with the various departments in the ship the state of their Permanent and Temporary Loan Lists. The engineers and shipwrights went through their mounting Defect List of work on the ship which would need to be done when next they docked. Brasson and Fossingham surveyed the state of their respective armaments and Grey-Bennett the maintenance of the floatplane. All of them knew there would be changes in their work, in their stores and equipment and in the complement of the ship if war should break out, but in the meantime they all seized the opportunity of an official spring-clean.

The visit to Rio, therefore, was both an experience and a break. The three cruisers, led by the Commander-in-Chief in HMS *Berwick* steamed slowly into the huge land-locked bay at about 0830. Even before hands fell in for entering harbour the upper deck was crowded with 'goofers'.

'Didn't I tell you?' said Able-Seaman Clarke to Kavanagh and Rillington. 'This beats even the scenery what the Colour-Sergeant painted for the Concert Party.'

'I had a basin of this in a commission I done in *Dragon*,' another seaman remarked. 'Just the same it was. Cor!'

'Now this place,' Marine Parker observed to the ship's postman, as he screwed and fidgeted with his waxed moustache, '*this* place has what I might term a bit of formation in it.'

Soon the ship's company were in long tidy lines standing at ease and marvelling at the spectacular scene passing slowly in front of their eyes. The Sugar Loaf Mountain, sticking up like a thumb, the bare granite slopes of the other mountains rising abruptly out of thick green forest, the Gavea with its flat-top and the Hunch-back Mountain with its huge statue of Christ on top, the white houses, their verandas splashed and dotted with bougainvillea and flame-of-the-forest, the curve of Copacabana Beach with its skyscrapers, and above all the vast, majestic and calming proportions of the city and harbour of Rio de Janeiro all combined to make their entrance into port that July morning an experience none of them would ever forget.

Large crowds had gathered at the dockside to watch the British squadron arrive. Against such a setting, the spectacle of three warships slowly berthing one astern of the other, their decks lined with immaculately dressed sailors, the White Ensigns fluttering proudly in the breeze, the gay bugles sounding out the Attention, the Royal Marine Guards and Bands on the quarterdeck, the puff and thunder of the saluting guns on board and ashore, the sudden glint of sunlight on gold braided caps, the businesslike snaking ashore of berthing lines—all the differing sights and sounds of the Navy's arrival provided ever-increasing crowds on the jetty with as much to compel their attention as Rio itself to the sailors on board.

Antigone was at the stern of the line and as she secured alongside a spontaneous cheer went up from the crowd as though a ballerina had just executed a particularly difficult movement.

'Look, Mum, no hands!' Spratt muttered to himself on the bridge as Trevesham brought the ship to rest in an effortless fashion. You could not take a cruiser alongside with the panache of a destroyer: on the other hand Trevesham wasted no time. He never dithered. His judgement was exact, his orders crisp: there was none of the 'Give-her-a-touch ahead' School about Trevesham. He was all to the point. He radiated confidence. On the bridge no one chattered and everyone around him became equally alert. Stripped of all uniform and badges of rank, you would nevertheless have picked him out instantly as Captain of the ship. He had the aura of command, and, however closely packed they might be on the bridge, he was always in himself a little apart.

There was an American Naval Mission in Rio and the Brazilian Navy did not exhibit the German and Italian traits of their Argentine *confrères*. Rio, too, seemed gayer than Buenos Aires in a hotter, lazier, looser-limbed fashion.

'It's rather like leaving Barcelona for Paris,' Fossingham observed. The Torpedo Officer was the only person aboard with that actual experience.

'Or like arriving in Edinburgh after a spell of Glasgow,' Spratt added, 'for those of us unconnected with the world of the *wagon-lit*.'

'Anyway,' Hale summed it up after their first run ashore, 'Rio's the hell of a fine city and they seem to like us all right. It hasn't taken the troops long to discover where the women in cages hang out.'

'Or you for that matter,' Crawford put in. 'I saw a Central Storekeeping Officer weaving his way through the Market.'

'Did you, now?' said Hale, unruffled as usual. 'Well, you can always price up a joint without making a purchase.'

'Trust a purser to think of it that way. No romance, no poetry.'

'It didn't strike me that Able-Seaman Elcock of the Top Division was over concerned with romance or poetry when I saw him last night. Anyway, what were you doing there!'

'Oh! sightseeing,' Crawford said airily. 'I fell in with a Brazilian NO who wanted to show me the town.'

For a short time they all relaxed. They forgot the strenuous exercises they had just carried out in company: they forgot the news from Europe: they forgot the anxious letters they were beginning to receive from home. Rio had everything cheap or expensive which a sailor could want, and with some two thousand of them in port, they seemed to be everywhere at once.

Hale and Marsh, who went ashore in each other's company more and more these days, took a trip to the top of the Corcovado Mountain. They caught a tram from the wide treelined Avenida Rio Branco and rattled along to the Cosine Vellio station.

'I suppose we should have stood ourselves a taxi,' Hale grumbled, 'but the longer this cruise goes on the shorter and shorter I get in cash.'

'There's no option for me,' Marsh said, 'I've been broke for months.'

In 1939 officers of the Royal Navy still felt a little

guilty about using public transport, especially when abroad. Both Marsh and Hale had been brought up to understand that Naval officers always travelled first class, and on South American tramway systems that was a little difficult. It was one of the many unwritten customs of the Service. Third-class travel did not accord with the style and address of a naval officer. Junior officers might just be excused in England for short journeys in uncrowded trains but it was never encouraged.

'And personally I think it's all balderdash,' Marsh said as the rack railway took them up to the summit of the Hunchback Mountain. 'I rather enjoy bumbling about in trains.'

'Well, I don't. Put my pay up to a living wage and you'll never get me out of a Rolls again.'

'It's not that so much—I think NOs are fearfully snobbish. Look at Grey-Bennett or Crawford, or Cravenby. They're so arrogant you'd think they were Princes of the Blood.'

'I concede you that point,' Hale said looking down the two thousand feet to the harbour, 'but the Old Man isn't a snob. Neither is Stubby. Neither is Number One.'

'What about Brasson?'

'Ah! well Honest Tom's a Gunnery Officer. They rank with, but after, the Deity himself. He's certainly a nob for the Service, but he's not socially.'

'And Torps?'

'As I see it, Fossingham's never grown up. He's still a playboy. He doesn't count.'

'Of course he counts,' Marsh said indignantly, 'he's one of the few officers on board with private means. He treats the Navy as a Club. Besides he's in the zone. He'd fall over backwards for his brass hat.'

'Well he won't get it,' Hale said. They left the train at the top and walked round the vast statue of Christ one hundred and thirty feet high which looks down on Rio with outstretched arms.

'It wouldn't surprise *me* if he did.'

'You're the Captain's Secretary,' Hale said drily. 'You type out all our Confidential Reports—so you know and I don't. But for my money he's not efficient. Neither is the Torpedo Department as a whole, despite Mr Partle's best efforts. At least Brasson's one hundred per cent. I loathe

242

his guts but if we ever have to fire our muskets in anger, I'll be damned glad we've got him. Torps is always passing on the baby. It's never ever Fossingham's Fault.'

'I think we should concentrate on the view,' Marsh said, 'there's nothing we can do about our elders and betters.' He paused and looked down through the haze at the three tiny warships in the harbour. 'But there are times I'm glad I'm still in the gunroom,' he added.

It was a superlative view. As they stood with their walking sticks and panama hats, Hale with his inevitable pipe and Marsh smoking a cigarette, the petty jealousies and squabbles of the ship slipped away from their consciousness. They felt calm and unhurried. They leant on the parapet contemplating the scene in its immense, proportional majesty. Marsh thought of Lisette and again felt the old familiar ache in his heart. But now he was almost detached. Now he was very nearly able to watch himself and the emotion as though he were someone distinct and separate. He glanced across at Hale, whose face even in repose seemed set in a determined scowl. He was a rigid man, identified with the mould which had formed his outlook, but with his broken tooth and sudden clear smile Marsh had a great affection for him.

'I suppose we haven't done too badly,' he said presently, 'to live in that tin can of a ship for over a year without any major disaster. I mean when you think how close together we all have to live . . .'

'Well, good Lord,' said Hale, 'that's our job isn't it?'

'I know it is. Still there's nothing quite like one of HM ships for packing a lot of high-pressure personality into a tin of sardines.'

For a while neither of them spoke, each meandering back in his thoughts.

'I think we tend to forget how other people look at us,' Hale said in the end. 'We must seem awfully alike to outside eyes. We aren't, of course, but people say "Oh! he's a typical Naval officer" simply because we all wear the same uniform. We react in the same polite formal way to outside events and we've had all the corners rubbed off. At any rate most of us have by the time we've got two stripes on our arms. There's damn little privacy to be anything other than a "type" on board *Antigone*. When I go along to the wardroom bathroom in the morning and I see the Commander (E) and his paunch in one bath, the Paymaster-Commander's scraggy frame in the next and the Surgeon-Commander's whiskified features peeping out of the third—I think what a sacrifice privacy is. It doesn't matter to us. We can splash about in the steam like overgrown schoolboys, but when you get into your forties and you still have to be just another ant in the antheap—well, I suppose none of us *can* deviate very much from the norm or the type. We have to *be* the roles we've chosen to play. The uniform and the ship almost express their lives through us.'

'That's the hell of a speech for two thousand feet above Rio de Janeiro,' said Marsh. 'Let's get down and have a drink. I think the height must be going to your head.'

Rio was the last great port they visited before the outbreak of war. The squadron was to leave for Bermuda on 27 July. It was to call briefly at Pernambuco and then after further exercises *en route* was due to arrive at Bermuda on 10 August. But during the last two days of their stay in Rio news was received that rioting had broken out in the oilfields of Trinidad. The Governor had asked the Commander-in-Chief for the assistance of a cruiser. This was the 'buzz' and it whipped through the wardrooms of the three cruisers like a contagious disease as pink gins were called for and certain bets were made as to which of them would be selected for the pierhead jump. They were not left long in doubt.

'HMS *Antigone* is to raise steam for full speed immediately and report when ready for sea,' read the 'By Hand of Officer' signal from the flagship.

'Here we go gathering nuts and may,' said Stubby as he read the message in his cabin and handed it back to the Captain's Secretary. 'Has the Chief seen it yet?'

'No, sir. I'm going to him next.'

The Commander picked up his cap and telescope and rang the buzzer for his messenger.

'Sir?'

'Ask the First Lieutenant to come and see me at once.'

'Aye aye, sir.' The seaman boy sped away, followed by Marsh. Stubby put on his cap and rammed his telescope under his arm as he had done thousands of times before. But now he paused and looked out through his scuttle at the jetty and at Rio behind. The note had been sounded, and soon the intricate machinery of naval power would begin to revolve. Soon the postman, the wardroom messman and the few ratings who were normally ashore in the forenoon would be back on board. Soon the brows would be out, the wires slipped, the ship's company fallen in for leaving harbour, and then *Antigone* would quietly ease away from the jetty and glide out across the great landlocked harbour to the sea. There would be no fuss and the minimum of ceremony in the farewell they took of Rio. They would leave their two sister ships behind and no doubt already the Commander-in-Chief, the Consul and the Ambassador were preparing statements to the press and to the public explaining the sudden curtailment of *Antigone*'s stay without revealing her destination or her purpose and without in any way starting up a more general panic. They had expected the balloon to go up for war. This was almost a piece of routine work—of police work on the side. Hatchett smiled to himself. Soon he would be immersed in detail, seeing the Captain, giving the familiar orders to prepare the ship for sea, checking this and belaying that. But for a moment before it all began, there was a sudden absolute calm. Outside through the haze and the heat, he could hear a tram clanging on its way and the sounds of a great city about its normal business. The balloon had gone up for *Antigone* alone. There was a small job of work to be done. Their days of showing the flag were at an end.

'Well,' Stubby told himself as he stumped out to the quarterdeck, 'that's that. It was fun while it lasted. I wonder what happens next.'

It took them very nearly six days steaming at twenty-eight knots to reach Trinidad.

'I must admit that until I looked at a chart I didn't realize it was the best part of four thousand miles,' said Spratt. 'Flash Annie's really seeing the world.'

This time they did not go to Port of Spain. They went straight to the oilfields. They had received a further signal from the Governor *en route* saying that the rioters were temporarily out of hand and were holding the refinery against the police. There had been five deaths and a few dozen broken heads.

245

'So you'd better arm the launch with a couple of machine-guns,' Trevesham told his Gunnery Officer, 'when we land the Marines.'

It was a busy time for Captain Taw-Street and Colour-Sergeant Forrester. They had to plan for a number of unknown possibilities. Their job was to contain the trouble and prevent it from spreading.

'I don't suppose the rioters are armed,' Trevesham said at a conference held two days before they reached Trinidad, 'but we may come up against the occasional homemade blunder-buss. It's possible the authorities may not want us to interfere at all. The Trinidad Police and the Volunteers can usually cope, so the Governor told me before, but a cruiser in the bay is a great boost to morale.'

'Do we know what it's all about, sir?' asked the Gunnery Officer.

'No,' said Trevesham. '*Ajax* was sent here two years ago over much the same trouble. There's always a grouse about pay and working conditions, but this is political. There are half-a-dozen trained agitators at work in the islands. They always make trouble in the oilfields when they run out of other ideas.'

It turned out almost exactly as Trevesham had forecast. They anchored in the bay and at once sent an armed party ashore to contact the police and the company manager. A condition of stalemate had been achieved. Certain parts of the refinery and pumping station were still held by the strikers, but no food was getting through to them and the more active rioters had drunk themselves into a stupor on illicit rum.

'It's very comforting to see you here,' the chief of police told Trevesham, 'as you steamed into the bay I thought it must be the *Ajax* again. You're sister ships aren't you?'

'Yes,' said Trevesham. 'What do you want us to do? I'll send you ashore with a landing party of Royal Marines and I'm holding a second seaman landing party in reserve.'

'I think the Marines are all we need. My chaps are pretty whacked: they've been at it nearly eight days. If you could take over security of the refinery and the harbour, it would relieve us to concentrate on finding our six bad men who have all gone underground again. I don't think there'll be any more violence here: it's mostly a job of clearing up to be done. The workers here are basically loyal. They're just beginning to see they've been tricked by their so-called leaders. They won't argue with the Navy.'

Although it was a serious matter, the departure of the Royal Marines on their first job of work provided the ship's company with inexhaustible mirth. They all appreciated that this was no exercise, no make-believe, yet the sight of a boatload of bullocks 'armed to the teeth and bent on slaughter' struck the ship's company as irresistibly funny.

'Got your little Union Jack, have you?' asked Able-Seaman Rillington of Marine Parker. ' 'Cos I shall want you to wave to me as soon as you're safe ashore.'

'Are you sure the Colour-Sergeant's got his hot-water bottle?' another seaman asked as the Royal Marines, their groundsheets, their rifles, their camp equipment and their fierce, erect Officer Commanding the Detachment went down the port ladder to the waiting launch.

Once ashore they set up headquarters and established communications with the ship by semaphore. Then sentries were placed and step by step the refinery was brought under control. Not a shot was fired. Indeed Trevesham had made the state of affairs very clear to the landing party before ever they left the ship.

'This is a domestic quarrel,' he said, 'and we're not here to take sides. These are our own people. They're all British subjects. They have exactly the same rights and privileges as we have however black their skins. We're here purely and simply to keep the peace. Before we got here five people were killed in an outbreak of violence. It is your prime job to see there are no more casualties in restoring law and order.'

Colour-Sergeant Forrester attacked this assignment with his customary vigour. The Royal Marines, whose splendid record stretched back through the centuries, had a small isolated chance to prove themselves again. This was to be seized upon and exploited as a golden opportunity for displaying their efficiency.

'Permission to speak, sir?' said Forrester as he and his Captain stood watching the troops clattering ashore.

'What is it, Colour-Sergeant?'

'This *is* a Royal Marine assignment, sir, is it not?'

247

'At the moment, it is.'

'Thank you, sir.'

Taw-Street looked at his Sergeant, stiff as a flagpole, and smiled to himself.

'You mean we don't want any seamen mucking us about?'

'Exactly, sir,' said Forrester, his eyes gleaming. 'Seamen are all very well aboard a ship: when it comes to operations ashore—in my opinion, sir, they lack the training and the knowledge of the Royal Marines.'

'Well,' said Taw-Street, 'better not let the Gunnery Officer hear you. However, the Commander told me this was to be our show—unless we found it was more than we could manage.'

'It won't be, sir,' said Forrester sharply and turned to bawl out a Royal Marine rank for sagging when in charge of a case of ammunition. 'Smarten up there!' he shouted. 'You haven't got a fainting woman in your arms. Get a move on, now!'

By this time it was August and they were within ten degrees of the equator. The heat was heavy and humid. The sun blazed down on them during the day interrupted only by tropical rainfall of a suddenness and solidity which brought no relief and drove them all to take shelter while the storm seemed to pour straight down out of the heavens.

'I don't think this expedition of ours is much of a problem,' Hatchett remarked to Trevesham after they had inspected the organization ashore. 'How can you have a really effective riot if everyone knocks off for three hours in the middle of the day?'

The day was one thing, the night another. Night in the tropics, with its chirruping cicadas, its glow-worms and its blessed release from the heat of the day, was normally that part of the twenty-four hours when white people felt at their best. It was a time for Planter's Punches on club verandas, a time when energy and life, pressed out of you during the day by the sun, seeped slowly and pleasantly back into your body. But out against the jungle with a rifle in your hands and your back to a valuable refinery which unknown persons were anxious to destroy —that was another matter altogether.

'Makes you feel kind of creepy, don't it?' one of the

younger Marines confided to Parker in the guardroom one night. 'When you're stuck out there alone.'

'The situation has what I might term hallucinatory factors,' Marine Parker replied with a sniff. Marine Parker's bible was a Manual of Popular Psychology by Karl Hackenheimer. The messdeck had discovered this with delight and 'Hackinbush's Handbook' had become part of the ship's folklore. But Marine Parker with his rigid dignity, his waxed moustache and his ideas of 'formation' had survived all the jeers and the laughter. He was a strong man and backed by psychology he knew he would win in the end. And he had. They still poked charley at his pompous way of talking but they had never got him down. In the early days they would ask what Hackinbush was tipping for the three-thirty but now Marine Parker with his badly printed paper-backed manual had achieved the position of a minor prophet. No one understood a word of what he said but it sounded magnificent.

'Go on,' said another Marine in the guardroom, 'give us the Hackinbush on it, Nosey.'

Parker twirled his moustache and ignored the nickname.

'Hackenheimer would say our task in Trinidad has marked Oedipus Initiatory Factors redundant in it,' he said in the manner of a famous Harley Street psychiatrist. 'In other words, we have to ask ourselves, are we merely reacting to circumstantial evidence as our fathers would have done?'

'Well my Dad's a bobble-maker in the upholstery trade,' one of the Marines piped up. 'I don't think he's ever had to look out for an oil refinery before.'

'Then it's no good falling back on him, is it?' Parker replied, blandly disposing of the question. 'There are more things in heaven and earth, Horatio, than what are dreamt of in *your* philosophy.'

'He's away!' said one of the others, sucking his teeth. 'Good old Nosey!'

But there was more to Marine Parker than met the eye, splendid though that was. He was an alert and efficient Royal Marine and he was chiefly concerned in the only incident of note during the ship's stay at Trinidad. The police forecast had been right and with the disappearance of the agitators, violence died out of the strike. But there is always the unexpected, the unplanned individual action and there were still known fanatics at large whose avowed intention it was to destroy the refinery.

'Now sabotage can only be effective at certain key points,' the Colour-Sergeant had explained, 'and those are what we have to watch our for—that's why we're here. Oil was to flow or be pumped from Point A to Point B and, put in language you'll understand, if it doesn't the whole bag of tricks jams up solid—like you had that Lewis gun on Tuesday, Marine Wilkes.'

The whole detachment knew of the trouble Marine Wilkes had been having with his Lewis gun. It was not a particularly fair simile but it gave them a vivid understanding of the whole operation. They were shown the control room where sabotage could be really dangerous, and this was patrolled on both sides the whole of the twenty-four hours.

It was during the middle watch of their fifth night when Marine Parker had paced out his beat for the forty-fourth time that he knew someone was watching him. Marine Parker believed in getting a bit of formation into the way he patrolled his beat. He may not have been guarding Buckingham Palace but an outside observer might have been excused for thinking it equally important. Yet underneath the stiff, formal movement Marine Parker was very much alive. He had seen nothing, but he knew someone was there.

There were only two lights on the outside of the building, which was separated from the barbed-wire fence by a wide stretch of gravel. Beyond the fence lay the undergrowth of the jungle, and from it came those intermittently repeated tropical noises which at first sound so eerie but to which you so soon become accustomed. Marine Parker's beat was in the shadows just inside the barbed wire fence and the noise he had heard was of the click of cutters on wire. It was a single sound some way behind him and prudently he did not stop his pacing. With luck he would meet his opposite number at the end of the beat and could tip him off. Silently he slipped off the safety catch on his rifle and continued round the corner of the building.

The other sentry was not in sight and it would take perhaps another minute to find him. It would also mean leaving his beat. Marine Parker turned back and with the same deliberate pace retraced his seps. Once more he turned the corner of the building and suddenly from out of the shadows he saw a black man running at him with a knife.

'Halt!' he cried. 'Who goes there?'

But there was no time to complete the challenge or to fire. The negro was on him. Parker threw his rifle on the ground, dodged the first lunge of the knife and grappled with his assailant. 'Help! Help!' he yelled before a huge black palm covered his mouth and he felt his head being wrenched slowly back. The knife had missed its first mark but he had received a terrible gash across the shoulder. He had hold of the negro's right arm, the one with the knife, and for a few moments they wrestled in silence. Then he managed to force the negro to drop the knife and as his mouth was again free he yelled once more for help. By this time they were facing each other and the negro brought his knee up sharply into Marine Parker's groin. The pain was agonizing and for one moment he thought he was lost. Yet somehow or other he managed to hang on. He had no strength left to wrestle but he threw his arms round the negro, like a hoop round a barrel and although there was another paralysing jerk up of the knee it missed its point of aim.

By this time the alarm had been raised and he heard footsteps running across the gravel. His grip had slipped down and he now felt himself being dragged to the barbed wire fence. He hung on desperately. He was only partially conscious, and this was just as well since his enemy had got him to the fence and then with a sudden jerk had thrown his whole weight on the wretched Parker so that he was forced to spreadeagle on to the barbs like a carcase impaled on a bed of spikes. But at last help arrived. The negro was set upon by three other Marines and in a few moments overpowered. At this point, too, Marine Parker lost consciousness, his shoulder ripped, his back torn and bleeding, a ghastly pain in the groin, and with no 'formation' at all left in his being.

Both Marsh and his cabin-mate Darbigh went to see Marine Parker in sick-bay. His back was in such a state that he had to lie on his side, but as soon as he had recovered from the shock, he tried to regain his stiff, imperturbable manner. His waxed moustache looked as splendid as ever.

'Very sorry you've been put to inconvenience, sir,' he said looking up at Marsh from the sick-bay cot. 'I'm afraid seamen ratings, sir, won't never comprehend the laying out of officers' clothes.'

During the operations ashore Darbigh and Marsh were both 'looked after' by a morose seaman from the Quarterdeck Division. Although they wanted to talk to Parker about his fight at the refinery, it appeared that Parker himself was far more interested in how his officers' cabins were being kept.

'Don't worry, Parker, we manage all right. It isn't the same but you'll soon be back on your feet.'

'Yes, sir,' said Parker, a severe look in his eyes. 'I expect I shall have to take the cabin in hand.'

It had long been the privilege of Royal Marines to be wardroom attendants and officers' servants. Parker did not care to have his territory poached on by a seaman even though the service reasons were unimpeachable. The Royal Marines have never mutinied in their whole history. In all warships where they are borne their messdeck is next forward of the wardroom. They stand between the officers and the lower deck, and for centuries they have been in an especial position of trust. This was part of the established order of things and in Parker's view, you never really knew where you were with a seaman.

Most unexpected of all his visitors was the Captain himself. It took Parker quite by surprise and there was nothing formal in it. Trevesham had been talking to the Surgeon-Commander about him.

'He's in no danger, sir, but he has had and will have considerable pain. Normally I'd suggest putting him in a hospital ashore but the sick berth Chief PO tells me he had very strong views about staying on board and has put in a special request not to be moved out of the ship.'

Trevesham had just drafted a report of the incident for the Commander-in-Chief. It commended Marine Parker's courage. His negro assailant had been a common criminal who had long been on the run and was now to be tried for complicity in the murder of three other people.

'Can we look after him all right on board?'

'Oh! yes, sir, but it's going to be a fairly long and tedious convalescence.'

'I'd like to see Parker,' said Trevesham, 'do you want notice of that, PMO?'

'No, sir,' said the Surgeon-Commander, sending up a special prayer. It was highly unusual for the Captain to visit any part of the ship except on his Rounds. This was as it should be. The lower deck was the lower deck and the Captain the Captain. Each had privacy. The Commanding Officer of one of HM ships may theoretically have had the right to inspect any part of his ship at any time whenever the spirit moved him. In practice, though, this right was rarely exercised. It would not have been fair. You loved and respected your monarch. You were pleased when he took an interest in your personal affairs, but you did not expect to find him suddenly in your kitchen. In the fifteen months *Antigone* had been in commission, the Captain had never once broken this unwritten custom of the Service. Yet now here he was in the dog watches standing beside the Surgeon-Commander in the sick-bay while all round other half-clad patients, improperly dressed sick-berth attendants and the usual free-and-easy traffic of messdeck life during non-working hours suddenly scurried away with a jolt of surprise. But it was Marine Parker who suffered the greatest surprise of them all. He had been dozing uncomfortably since he still had to lie on his side, and his sleep was always disturbed, when the sick-bay Chief gently shook his shoulder; therefore, he came back to consciousness with annoyance.

'What's it this time?' he asked.

'Marine Parker,' said the Chief, 'visitor to see you.'

Marine Parker opened his eyes and found himself looking into those of his Captain.

'Blimey!' he said and instinctively his fingers gave a quick twirl to his moustache.

'Well, Parker,' said Trevesham, 'how are you?'

'All right, sir. Thank you, sir. Up in a few days, sir.'

He caught his breath as a stab of pain went through him but his face remained mute and expressionless.

'I don't know so much about that. The Surgeon-Commander thinks you ought to be sent ashore to a hospital but *I* understand you don't want to go.'

'No, sir,' said Parker anxiously, and then with a kind of risky hesitation: 'I—I shouldn't be happy away from the ship, sir.'

His voice broke as he spoke and to his everlasting shame and embarrassment his eyes filled with water. He did not dare look at the Captain any more. He did not move.

'Beg pardon, sir,' he said miserably. Thank heavens the Colour-Sergeant and the Captain of Marines had not seen him like this.

'Well . . .', said Trevesham with a glance at the PMO and the sick-berth Chief Petty Officer, 'if we can look after him all right on board, I don't see any reason to land him. You've had an unpleasant experience, Parker,' he went on gently, 'but you did your duty as a Royal Marine should and we're all very proud of you in the ship. I'm writing today to the Commander-in-Chief commending you and the detachment.'

'Thank you, sir,' Marine Parker murmured. A large drop of what Hackenheimer called 'saline liquid ordinarily serving to moisten and wash the eye' now seemed to be rolling down his nose. It was most unfair. He felt a disgrace. He would never dare look anyone in the face again.

'I hope you'll soon be out of pain and back to normal,' said Trevesham briskly, and then, as he turned away, continued to the Surgeon-Commander, 'patch him up quickly, PMO, and keep him on board.'

The strike ended and work was resumed in the oilfield in another ten days. It was now mid-August. War was scarcely any longer in doubt. Thanked by the Governor and cheered as she left, HMS *Antigone* sailed to Bermuda at twenty-eight knots. She was to dock, have her bottom cleaned, complete with war stores and generally prepare herself for long days at sea and sudden action with the enemy.

A great change was to come about in the ship's life. Soon they were to feel they had never known any other background than the sea: soon in their imagination they would turn from heaving Atlantic and scudding wind to thought of warm, sheltered harbour and the smell of the land. But at present their outlook was the other way

254

round. A few days at sea, even at twenty-eight knots, were a pleasure and a relief.

The passage to Bermuda took three days. It was the hurricane season but there had been no warnings and the weather was peerless. Dolphin and flying-fish kept station abeam from time to time. The sun beat down upon the white, quivering quarterdeck and, in the evening, set across the rim of the horizon in a riot of purples and greens. The ship was in three watches—the normal sea-going routine into which the ship's company dropped with almost a feeling of relief. It was a good rhythm of work, relaxation and sleep. It felt right. Even though three days is a short enough period of time, it gave them the pause and the break they all of them needed. It was a restless speed and there was an urgency in the air. Yet when they arrived at Bermuda, when they saw the familiar *Ajax* and *Berwick* against the white buildings of the dockyard, it was as though they had only been away for a holiday and had returned to familiar surroundings immensely refreshed.

Change was in the air for them all. Soon they were in dock. The barnacles were scraped away; parts of the machinery were stripped down; stores and equipment poured on board as they had done at the time of Munich and now, also, the additional complement authorized for war was appointed and drafted to the ship. Change was about them in everything they did and this time they knew it meant war. This was no feint, no exercise. This time they all of them knew it was the real thing at last.

'We're all in a state of flux,' Marsh wrote home to his mother, 'and soon I expect our letters will be censored and I shan't be able to tell you where we're going or what we're up to. Don't worry too much. I expect old *Aunty Gone* will survive. Thank God some of our war complement have joined, and I now have two paymaster sub-lieutenants RNVR to help me with the cyphering. This is a boon but I still feel a bit chocker and sleepless. I suppose somebody knows what it's all about—but to me it's just one damned signal after another, and already the gay cocktail parties of South America seem a million miles away. But you're not to worry. I couldn't go to war in a finer ship—although all we expect to see of the struggle is one dreary convoy after another. I've made my will and you and Father are my executors. Please note I have £15 17s 11d in credit at the Bank so the Death Duties should not be crippling. Don't start knitting submarine sweaters (like Mid Watling's mother) but some more un-holeable socks would be a blessing. Oh! and by the way, if a French girl called Lisette Champlain shows up at Number 23 please be very nice to her indeed. I'm afraid she won't, though, worse luck! Cheer up, you two! It's all going to be all right. I'm due for my second stripe in Oc-tober and when Hitler learns that, the gunroom expect him to call the whole thing off . . .'

CHAPTER ELEVEN

War found *Antigone* at sea. Sunday the third of Septem-ber 1939 was a bright day in the north Atlantic, but a sea was running and the wind getting up. After divisions and prayers on the quarterdeck they all returned to their messes to listen to the Prime Minister's thin voice with its momentous news. Then half an hour later 'Clear lower deck: everybody aft' was piped, and Trevesham came down from the bridge to address the ship's company.

'All right. Break ranks and come in closer,' he said as he climbed on to his usual grating by 'Y' turret. Some five hundred officers and men crowded round their Captain on the swaying quarterdeck as the wind whipped off the tops of the waves and powdered the ship with spray. It was colder. The ship's course was steadily north. There was a sharpness, a bite in the air, and the green sea, their age-old friend and enemy, looked grim and foreboding.

'You've all heard the news.' Trevesham began speaking slowly and distinctly. 'We're once again at war with Ger-many. This is the purpose for which we've all of us been trained these many years: this is the responsibility—our special chance as professional sailors. What does it mean?

And how is it going to affect us in this ship?' He paused and looked at the grave upturned faces. 'This is a time for drawing together—a time to get things in perspective. I want you to try and understand the changes that have taken place and that will take place. I want you above all to remain what you already are—a first rate body of fighting men in the pink of condition. None of these things are accidental. I know the hard work that's gone into them; the hard work they'll continue to need—and I haven't brought you here on a windy forenoon to pay you extravagant compliments. We have a job of work to be done. No doubt we shall be a year or two doing it. So, now, I want to tell you exactly where we stand in the general picture and what our duties are likely to be.'

Again he paused thinking how magnificent his ship's company looked, mustered together on the quarterdeck, and how extraordinary it was that he, Colin Trevesham, should be their Captain.

'We're now on our way to pick up our first Atlantic convoy,' he went on. 'Our job is to cover and protect that convoy against enemy surface or submarine attack. That's our immediate task. Once that is done our second job is to keep our mouths firmly shut about it. That means nothing whatever in your letters home and not a word about it when you next go ashore. This is likely to be our employment for many months to come. Remember the enemy is cunning. The German never has been a fool. He knows pretty well the strength of the Royal Navy. What he doesn't know is where our warships are from day to day. If he did it would make his task—and our own destruction—very much easier. So it's a matter of plain common sense and I know I can rely on all of you for that.'

A cloud scurried over the sun and the ship's motion seemed to increase perceptibly. They were heading into a storm and dark clouds were piling up ahead.

'Our lives have changed a great deal in the last couple of weeks,' Trevesham continued. 'We've had a full and interesting fifteen months: we've had a luxury cruise round South America: we're over half-way through our normal commission. Now we have to forget all that side of life. The way to do that is not to look back on the "good old days". Put them out of your mind. It's our job now to be at sea, to find the enemy, to bring him to battle and de-

257

stroy him. That's what we have to think about. That's what we have to bend our best endeavours into doing.'

Despite the wind and the spray Trevesham held his audience completely absorbed.

'As you know, the Fleet is being mobilized. At home reserves, volunteers, retired officers and men will be thronging into barracks, being trained and then being sent to sea. It's an immensely critical time while the Fleet expands and it all gets sorted out. In the meantime—we— the fully trained sea-going Royal Navy have to hold the fort until others can relieve us. This is a time when every ship and every trained man in that ship is worth his weight in gold'—he paused for a moment, and looked round—'and I suppose that applies even to Able-Seamen Rillington, Kavanagh and Clarke.'

This unexpected dig at the Three Fat Men of the Sea produced a roar of laughter from the ship's company.

'So put out of your minds any thought of leave at this time,' Trevesham went on, 'even should we take this convoy the whole way through to the United Kingdom. This is a time for manning the ramparts, not for snoozing in front of the fire. And that brings me to what all of us are most worried about at a time like this—our wives and our families at home. I realize that nothing I can say to you here in the middle of the Atlantic can possibly remove that source of worry, nor can it alter the basic facts of the situation. However, once again we can get those facts into proper perspective. *We* can't do anything about it but the Government can. If large scale air-raids on our cities and ports take place—as we all expect them to take place— then *our* wives and families will be among the first to be evacuated to the country. The Admiralty wish this to be known and understood in every seagoing ship of the fleet. Any doubts you may have, any questions you want to ask should be discussed with your Divisional Officers and not bottled up in yourselves. That's what your Divisional Officers are for and that is where your duty lies in this matter. A worried man is no use to me as a fighting man. Now that *Antigone* is cleared away for action in earnest, we can't afford a single weak link in the chain. So remember that your officers are there to help you: if they can't, I will: if I can't, the Commander-in-Chief will and so on through the Board of Admiralty to his Majesty himself.'

He paused, wondering how much of his meaning had really got through. 'All right: that's all for the present. I would like you to know, though, how glad I am that we're all still together now that the war has come and how proud I am to have such a splendid ship's company under my command.'

Then something unrehearsed and quite unforeseen took place. As the Captain stood down and before the Commander took his place to dismiss the ship's company, Chief Petty Officer Penniwick jumped on to a bollard and shouted. 'Three cheers for the Captain: hip, hip, hip . . .' The resulting hoorays drowned the wind and the spray. The force of their spontaneity sent a thrill down five hundred spines. Then a little abashed, they found themselves dismissed, shuffling forward along the port and starboard waists, the officers going down the quarterdeck ladder to the wardroom. HMS *Antigone* was at war.

'Blimey!' said Able-Seaman Elcock. 'Hitler can't know what he's up against.'

Soon the seagoing routine of war completely absorbed their lives. Soon it was as though they had never done anything else. Soon each individual in the ship was immersed in his own trough of work. The changes were great but once made, once the inertia was overcome, once the increased discomfort and fatigue were accepted as normal, then HMS *Antigone* continued to hum around in her new role as effectively as she did in the old and more leisured days.

'And after all,' said Hale as he and Collard perched on the club fender after dinner one night, 'it's considerably easier for us than it is for a chap on shore. We go to war in our home. We don't have to give anything up except dressing for dinner.'

It was indeed a much 'matier' kind of workaday life. There was no longer time for the frills. Yet there were exceptions even to this. To the delight of his messmates the Paymaster-Commander continued to put on a boiled shirt and his mess undress uniform each night for dinner even though nowadays the dinner was always 'running' and was never conducted with the formal etiquette of a President, Grace, the King and the rest of the peacetime drill. But then the Paymaster-Commander was one of the old school. He still wore winged collars with his monkey jacket, an optional detail of uniform which automatically gave him a Great War look. Now in the evening he would find himself eating his soup slowly and meticulously from a linen covered table, instead of the polished mahogany and sparkling silver and glass which had been his especial joy for the last twenty years. He would find himself seated next to Grey-Bennett about to take the first watch on the bridge, whose seagoing attire pressed informality to its furthest limit and who reacted to the Pay's audible sniff with a remark about the ship's passengers having an easy life. The Paymaster-Commander had no night watches to keep and although Action Stations would, of course, get him on the move with the same alertness as his brother officers, he was the 'King of the Daymen' and thus greatly despised by the majority of watchkeepers whose lives were an unchanging one-in-three routine. To counter this the Paymaster-Commander saw it as his duty to keep up appearances wherever possible—hence the stiff shirt at dinner—and for this he was nicknamed 'White Carruthers of the British Raj'.

Everything now was simplified. The work of six hundred officers and men had been streamlined. This extended from cleaning the ship to the returns and reports which had to be forwarded. Now there was time only for essentials. There was no sitting around in the mess. There seemed paradoxically to be more work than ever to be done and less time to do it. Nothing could ever be deferred.

For those above the watchkeeping level, whether engine room, communications or upper deck there was now never any uninterrupted period of rest. The Senior Engineer and the Commander (E) were always, it seemed, climbing out of their bunks, into their white overalls and then through closed watertight doors which had to be laboriously unclipped and clipped up again behind them, down to the engine and boiler rooms to consult, advise, check and judge on matters which if glossed over or left would sooner or later take charge on their own.

Peter Osborne seemed almost to live on the W/T office and Augustus Spratt, red-eyed and laconic, was never more than a yard or two from the chart table on the bridge. The Signals Officer and the Navigating Officer kept no watches. They were there on hand virtually the whole of the twenty-four hours. Marsh, too, seemed never to be away from the cypher office. It was true that he now had two assistants. The two RNVR paymaster-lieutenants had just caught the ship at Bermuda. They were of invaluable help. They were trained, and although fresh from the beach knew what had to be done. But both of them, like Marsh to his continuing shame, were seasick. They could not be left on their own and so Marsh and Hale, occasionally helped by the Chaplain and the Instructor-Lieutenant, appeared to have taken up residence in the small oblong office well below the waterline.

Yet the strain to which in their different ways they were all being subjected was nothing to that of the Captain. He carried them all. It had to be thus and neither Trevesham nor the ship's company wished it any other way. His 'luxury liner' days were over. The vigil, the long nights of testing had begun.

To do this everything in the ship was subordinate to his single will. There was one point, one aim. Their daily routine work: the extra spurts they were called on to make: their intelligence, their specialized knowledge, their skill, had perhaps a more diffuse, general aim of serving King and Country, family and home. In *Antigone* there was a closer focal point—their Captain. Their ranks, their duties and the daily impulse of effort they put into them soared sharply to the narrow apex of a triangle. There, clear and firm, stood their Captain.

'I don't want the Old Man worried with detail,' said Hatchett to a meeting in the wardroom of heads of departments. 'So far as administering the ship is concerned, you'll come to me. I want this taken in the spirit and not the letter. It's time we forgot our peacetime rivalries. This applies also to Requestmen and Defaulters. We all know the Regulations—or if we don't the Captain's Secretary will put us right—but where KR and AI can be stretched to save bothering the Captain then stretched it will be. Is that understood?'

They understood it without being told. Even so dry and meticulous a stick as the Paymaster-Commander, one of whose secret pleasures had been to go and consult with the Captain, leading him by precise reasoning to foregone conclusions, proving time and time again that in administrative matters he was entirely bound by the Regulations and was thus no more than a consent-giving figurehead—even the Paymaster-Commander understood the wisdom of their new directive.

'The delegation of powers in wartime is fully covered by Regulations,' he observed pontifically. 'We have but to interpret the Book.'

They picked up their first convoy a hundred miles out from Halifax, Nova Scotia. They were approaching a period of equinoctial storms and the rendezvous was made in foul weather. The convoy was composed of forty-two 'fast' merchant ships with an average speed of twelve knots and a close escort of two destroyers and a sloop. These were primarily to give anti-submarine protection—not yet more than a potential menace in that part of the Atlantic. It was *Antigone*'s job to cover the convoy against German surface raiders.

'Roughly speaking that means the two pocket battleships *Deutschland* and *Graf Spee*,' said Trevesham to a conference in his sea cabin of the Commander, the Gunnery and Torpedo Officers, Grey-Bennett, Osborne and Spratt. 'Both were known to be at sea before the outbreak of war together with two supply ships. Both of them, I need hardly remind you, mount eleven-inch guns to our six-inch, but at ten-thousand tons displacement their armour can only be light, and we should have the edge on them in speed.'

'What about the *Scharnhorst* and *Gneisenau*?' asked Brasson. Germany's only two capital ships were the great stalking menace to a cruiser of *Antigone*'s size and the convoy she was covering.

'Reconnaissance puts them both in German ports,' Trevesham answered. 'I think they can safely be left to the Home Fleet for the present if they do try and slip out. Our problems are much more likely to concern armed merchant-raiders, the two pocket battleships, and the three eight-inch gun cruisers, such as the *Hipper* and *Prince Eugen*. However,' he concluded, folding up the chart and handing it back to Spratt, 'for the present our main task seems to be our old friend the Atlantic.'

It was indeed some of the worst weather they had ever experienced. Mountainous seas and winds of seventy to eighty miles an hour caused the convoy to reduce speed and turn into the storm. Riding out the gale was no sinecure even in as good a seaboat as *Antigone*. The merchant ships with twenty thousand tons displacement took it well enough but the smaller ones were in trouble, and the destroyers and the sloop were at times rolling over forty degrees. Their narrow beam and their 'greyhound' lines were of no help to them now, and life on board must have been a nightmare of seesaw and corkscrew movement without respite of any kind.

It was bad enough in *Antigone*. One of the mushroom ventilating heads on the foc'sle split open in a particularly violent sea and water flooded the messdeck below. Further aft a locker took charge and crashing across into Number 15 mess pinned Ordinary-Seaman Matson underneath it and broke his arm in four places. In a moment of folly Leading-Steward Warnham opened the scuttle in the gunroom pantry during what he took to be a lull, and a few seconds later that too was awash. It was a wild, singing gale and it carried away anything it could on the upper deck and the rigging. Inside the ship it smashed any articles at all loose or not properly secured.

To Marsh it was like a long illness. Although his own queasiness had slightly improved, he lived in a haze of fear and insecurity that another bout of it would start. He seemed never to be away from the cypher office for more than a couple of hours at a time. Then, as soon as he could, he got flat on his back wedging himself in his bunk as some small relief against the fury of the sea. He never went on the upper deck. He scarcely found time to go along to the Captain's office. In any case ordinary paper work was unthinkable in a gale like that, and when a large bottle of ink broke loose and launched itself against the bulkhead in a spatter of black, he gave it up as a bad job and retired to his cabin. There was something absurd in trying to write up the Captain's Request and Alteration Book in a gale.

Forward on the seamen's messdecks life was even more uncomfortable. Food, mess traps, ditty boxes and sleeping bodies all contributed to the slithering, swaying, teeming mêlée which conducted itself in what Able-Seaman Clarke described as a cold, wet fug. But Clarke was lucky. He used the messdeck only for eating. He slung his hammock in the Commander's office and the ship could have turned turtle without a single movable article falling out of its place. It was indeed a very tiddly office. Clarke had brought to bear on its arrangements years of practical seafaring allied to an inventive mind. The result was that each shelf had its own numbered lashing, bent on expertly as soon as the ship went to sea. The old typewriter—scarcely an instrument for touch typing after eighteen months of Clarke's pudgy fingers—was bedded on chocks as though it was a new and delicate weapon. Ink, paper, books, the duplicator were all locked into place with ingenuity, and the whole set-up compared most favourably with the Captain's office where Marsh and his messenger seemed always to be taken by surprise when the ship went to sea. There was always something which had been overlooked to the subsequent chagrin and distress of the Captain's Secretary. Clarke, who kept a humble and fatherly eye on Marsh's endeavours, would then volunteer to clear up the mess and would suggest ways and means of avoiding the next catastrophe. But Marsh usually forgot until it was too late—all over again.

Up on the bridge the Captain sat for hours on end on his high wooden seat, occasionally varying the vigil by walking about at the back of the chart table with its canvas hood into which the Navigating Officer seemed always to be stuck. Trevesham wore a short watch coat, half-wellington boots and a pair of well-washed chamois leather gloves. The bridge itself was cold but comparatively dry. Seas breaking on the foc'sle spent their force on 'A' and 'B' turrets, although one particularly violent wave had broken a glass screen on the bridge. All the instruments and fittings were soon caked with sticky salt, and at the height of sixty feet from the water the roll was enormous, yet the bridge was the best place to be and as the gale gradually blew itself out and the convoy resumed its course, Trevesham let his mind dwell on those above and below who worked the ship for him under far less enviable conditions. He supposed the stokers in the boiler room, the artificers in the engine room and the action personnel in the transmitting station were all comparatively favoured. But what about the stoker in the shaft tunnel, as the ship heaved and thrashed about in the storm, with the screws racing every time they lifted out of the water, and a few feet away from them a stoker crouching alone in the compartment amid the indescribable noise? What about the lookout in the crow's nest whom they had to bring down at the height of the gale half numb with cold and fatigue? Even the ratings on the searchlights and the signal deck had it hard—yet as Trevesham thought about the sloop wallowing a mile on their starboard quarter, as he watched the two old 'V' class destroyers rolling their guts out nearer the convoy, he knew that the big ship conditions of *Antigone* must seem like impossible luxury to the smaller vessels.

'I suppose that once the convoy comes under the protection of the Northern Patrol,' said Marsh to Hale on the ninth day out, 'they'll have finished with *Antigone*. Then they'll tell us to carry out the same service for an outward bound convoy.'

'They usually disperse outward bound convoys once they're past the known U-boat areas,' said Hale. 'You're quite right, though, they won't let us sight England again. That would be far too pleasant. They'll have some other shock in store for us—you see.'

They all longed for a sight of home. It was nearly eighteen months since they had left and, although they were all tempered to a two-and-a-half year commission, it was one thing to accept this fact the far side of the Atlantic, quite another to find themselves steadily drawing nearer the British Isles with every prospect of being diverted within a stone's throw to another assignment elsewhere. Trevesham had told them to put any thought of leave out of their heads but this was easier said than done. A year and a half away from wives and families, the war, uncertainty and change had them all on tenterhooks, their hearts restless and yearning. Yet even in imagination, home meant different things to them all.

'*I* could do with a few pints of Brickwood's mild and bitter,' said Able-Seaman Clarke after listening for the hundredth time to Elcock's kiss-by-kiss picture of how he would spend the leave they would none of them get. Able-Seaman Elcock's sexual prowess was a byword in the ship, but for Clarke a good time meant home cooking and wallop. The First Lieutenant thought about the cottage at Liphook and the daughter he had never seen who would now be over a year old. Stubby let himself picture how pleasant it would be to settle down in front of a fire with madame, a bottle of gin and the gossip of eighteen months to hash over. Even the stucco front of Number 23 Colebrook Avenue took on a misty attractiveness to Marsh as he sweated away endlessly among the lead-covered cypher books.

It was all imagination. A Secret and Immediate signal arrived addressed to *Antigone* repeated CS8, Flag Officer Northern Patrol and C-in-C Home Fleet from Admiralty. 'Leave Convoy HC3 at 2200 Thursday 15th. Rendezvous with homeward bound convoy from Gibraltar position . . .'

'So that's that,' said Marsh to himself as he typed out the message on the pink signal form and then climbed up wearily to the bridge to show it to the Captain.

'Usual distribution,' Trevesham grunted and returned to his study of the convoy through his binoculars. He did not encourage Marsh or anyone else to hang about on the bridge. He had noted his Secretary's depressed appearance in passing. No doubt when they broke company with the convoy tomorrow night and turned south there would be other disappointed faces in the ship. Well, he had warned them not to build up false hopes. If they did so, there was nothing he could do about it all. He was stiff and tired. He could have done with a few days at Drakeshott himself but there it was—another convoy to be met from Gibraltar: another vigil: another job of work to be done in a war which was not yet a month old. His mouth set in a hard line. It was time the ship's company learned the facts of life the hard way.

That evening they lost their first ship. It happened at dusk on the far side of the convoy from *Antigone*. It was a tanker carrying aviation fuel and she must literally have exploded as the torpedo struck her. There were no survivors; only a large patch of oil burning on the surface of the sea, its acrid smoke blowing in and about the convoy. The sloop immediately began hunting the submarine while one of the destroyers circled in a vain search for survivors. On *Antigone*'s bridge hardly a word was said. It was their first earnest of the war. Cravenby, who was Officer of the Watch, Spratt and Trevesham watched the glow die down as the convoy made a sharp alteration of course and a pattern of depth charges, dropped by the sloop, exploded throwing up huge mushrooms of water.

'Poor bastards,' Spratt murmured, rubbing his red-rimmed eyes, 'poor wretched bastards.'

'At least it was quick,' Cravenby added in a quiet voice. 'They can't have known much about it.'

Trevesham said nothing. He sat on his high seat, his arms on the coping of the bridge, staring at the horizon in a calculating manner. The Admiralty had warned them that four U-boats were known to be in their area. Attacks were to be expected. The close protection of the convoy and the hunting of U-boats was a matter for the destroyers and the sloop. *Antigone*, as a cruiser, was not even fitted with Asdic and was thus at this slow speed as much at the mercy of the stray submarine torpedo as any of the convoy. Moreover, she was a more valuable target. He tapped his fingers in irritation. Their job was to deal with surface raiders. It was time they were on their way. Now that their next task had been given them, he did not relish another day's 'strolling' about this part of the Atlantic with nearly two million pounds' worth of warship under him as a sitting target. It was highly unhealthy.

There were a number of false alarms during the night. These achieved nothing except to build up the tension. They consumed time and a vast quantity of nervous energy. They left a residue of frustration which seemed to harden and swell like a boil. Perhaps there had been a submarine—perhaps the Asdic echo was caused by a shoal of fish. You could never be sure. The convoy would be behind on its schedule but the danger remained lurking and undefined. This was the familiar atmosphere of a convoy which they were all coming to know so well.

It was a fast convoy as convoys were graded. They averaged twelve knots. This meant that the U-boats would lack the speed to shadow them. Once they were through an attack, therefore, they were likely to be safe until they ran into the next one. And in these early days U-boats still hunted singly or in pairs. The pack with its Focke-Wulfe guide and observer was yet to come.

But it was an uneasy night, each cycle of tension spiralling into the next. It would begin with a signal from one of the destroyers of the close escort: 'Am investigating contact'. This meant that the 'ping' of their Asdic had suddenly been echoed back. Something might be there. In *Antigone* and in every ship of the convoy this was an alert to danger in their immediate presence.

A few minutes later another signal, 'Contact confirmed,' would step up the nervous strain. Now there could be no doubt that there was something solid near the convoy under the sea. Asdics could not reveal the shape of a target, so the confirmed contact might still be a fish or a piece of wreckage. Then perhaps at the other side of the convoy, perhaps closer at hand the deep underwater clonk of depth charges exploding would strike through *Antigone* as though the ship's side had been hit by a heavy hammer.

Then followed a period of dwindling excitement shading off into the anti-climax of 'Have lost contact. Am rejoining convoy', from the destroyer. For every real attack—in itself almost a relief—there might be a score of false alerts. Each time this happened there was a growing feeling of insecurity in the ship, especially among those working below the waterline. Each time there was a confirmed contact the convoy would alter course away, thus losing more and more time. It all added up to a troubled night.

Trevesham brooded on the bridge for hours at a time. There was no moon and the convoy was all but invisible against the dark rolling Atlantic and inky sky. He had a sense of foreboding he could not define.

He kept this entirely to himself. Indeed, he had seemed day by day to grow more taciturn, as this long crossing continued. Something was in the wind. All his life he had had a vague, tantalizing awareness of events to come. Diana was the only other person who knew of this sense. They had tried in vain to apply it to the Derby and in other practical directions. He knew it with people and he knew it with things. It was a trace of consciousness from another level: undisciplined, rare and quite unpredictable. He had it now.

Yet the night eventually passed without any incident directly involving *Antigone*. The sun rose on the long grey swell with the convoy still steaming along in its business-like formation, with the destroyers ahead and the sloop astern, the white and blue and the red ensigns fluttering gaily in the wind another day nearer home for all of them except *Antigone*.

'Ask the Commander (E) to come and see me when he's free,' said Trevesham as he left the bridge to go down to his sea cabin for breakfast. He had had a total of three hours sleep in the night and nothing to show for it all except another night of anxiety survived. He shaved and put on a clean shirt. Then, without appetite, he set about the bacon and egg and the coffee which was his invariable breakfast. There was a knock at the door and the Chief, resplendent in white overalls, gas mask and tin helmet, stepped into his cabin.

'You sent for me, sir?'

'Yes, Chief,' said Trevesham, going on with his breakfast. 'I suppose we *will* be all right for fuel, won't we? It strikes me they're running us awfully fine.'

'We can make Gibraltar with fair comfort, sir. But if we have a lot of mucking about on the way then it might become critical.'

Trevesham looked at the bulky figure of his Commander (E) and again thanked his stars for having sent him a good one. He knew that the Chief was just as anxious as he was after the long Atlantic crossing with the prospect of another thousand miles to the south before they could top up again. The Admiralty and the C-in-C knew what they were doing—or they must be presumed to know by *Antigone*: they knew the cruiser's capacity and they must also know within narrow limits how much steaming she had done since leaving Bermuda. But some Commanders (E) would have been pestering their Captains in similar circumstances to send a signal reminding the powers-that-be, clearing their own yardarms in advance, generating another and possibly needless worry for their commanding officers to bear. It was certainly the prime duty of the Commander (E) in any warship of *Antigone*'s size to keep a most wary eye on his stocks of oil fuel and to warn his Captain long before any danger mark was in sight. Trevesham knew that his own Chief could well have been up on the bridge worrying him before now. He appreciated his forbearance.

'Thank you, Chief,' he said with a nod. 'We'll see how we get on. We can always start burning the furniture and the fittings.'

269

'Yes, sir,' the Commander (E) agreed. 'I've had an offer of the quarterdeck planking already from Hatchett. It would be a pleasure to take him up on it.'

In the late forenoon they saw a picture they would never forget. Out of the mist on the eastern horizon on an opposite course to the convoy came HMS *Hood* with two attendant destroyers sweeping out on either bow. She was a magnificent sight. The world's largest warship at forty-two thousand tons embodying all the lessons of Jutland, mounting eight fifteen-inch guns, ten five-point-five-inch and eight four-inch guns, she raced towards the convoy at dramatic speed. Her 144,000 horsepower could take her along at some thirty knots—and she was not far off that speed at the present time. She passed down the convoy 'hell bent on Carl Peterson' as Spratt observed, 'like a vast nautical Bulldog Drummond'. The buzz got around the ship like lightning and the watch below came tumbling up on deck to cheer the great battlecruiser on her majestic course. It did them all good. It was like a Langmaid picture in the *Illustrated London News*, the kind of picture of a vast warship at speed which they had all grown up with since childhood, a comforting reminder that Britannia really did rule the waves. Not a soul on board *Antigone* could have believed then that a single lucky shell would send her to the bottom two years later at a range of twenty-three thousand yards. Tearing past the convoy now she looked immense and unsinkable, the epitome of naval power.

'Oh! boy!' said Stoker Johnson sucking his teeth appreciatively, 'just let the *Graf Spee* run slap into that lot.'

As the day wore on Trevesham's malaise increased. Their next assignment was known only by him, Hatchett, the Commander (E), the Navigating Officer, and Marsh who had decyphered the signal. The rest of the ship's company imagined that with each passing hour their chances of seeing England again were increased.

It was a grey, overcast day. The sea was rising and another storm seemed to be chasing them up from the west. It was going to be a dirty night and Trevesham almost welcomed it for the respite from submarine attack it would bring. *Antigone* continued to make her long diagonal sweeps ahead and almost out of sight of the convoy. It seemed to Trevesham as they dawdled along that they

270

had never been employed on anything else. The sight of the *Hood* that morning had made him restless. She was out after something and even if it proved to be a wild goose chase that was better than endlessly mooning around a convoy while U-boats picked off a tanker here and a liner there. He drummed his fingers on the coping of the bridge, telling himself sternly that he had no business to allow such thoughts into his head. This was their job. The Admiralty, always short of cruisers, had considered their convoy important enough to be given *Antigone*'s protection. It was not for him to fret or complain.

No one else on the bridge, except possibly Spratt, guessed what was passing through his mind. They simply saw their imperturbable Captain with his lined face sitting in his usual position on the high chair the chippies had specially made for him, or walking up and down at the back of the bridge to keep his circulation going. Mellish, now a Chief Yeoman of Signals, watched him like a shadow. Perhaps he, too, felt a foreboding, but with Trevesham's example in front of him all the time, he put it away from his thoughts. Your resistance got weakened after long days at sea. Depressions, fears, illusions found it easier to prey into your mind unless you kept doubly on guard. There would be plenty of this sort of thing, he thought to himself. The sooner they proofed themselves against it the better.

At dusk *Antigone* took her usual place in the centre of the convoy, immediately astern of the commodore. A moderate sea was running. In such conditions a U-boat attack was possible but unlikely, the more so since there would again be no moon.

The first watch passed without incident. Sub-Lieutenant Darbigh was Officer of the Watch and Brasson the Principal Controlling Officer. This somewhat imposing title was the wartime equivalent of Duty Commanding Officer. The PCO had complete command of the ship whenever the Captain was away from the bridge either eating or sleeping. He could alter course on his own initiative. If attacked he could fire the guns. Brasson enjoyed every moment of this brief authority. He wished the Captain would never return to the bridge.

On the next deck below, the Instructor-Lieutenant was working the Plot. As usual the convoy would be zigzagging through the night. This was done to an irregular but pre-arranged pattern, with alterations of course carried out according to a set time scale. On alternate hours the general trend of the zigzag carried the convoy away to port or starboard of its mean course.

Since the convoy was completely darkened, since over forty ships were steaming at twelve knots at a distance from one another of not more than three cables or six hundred yards, since there was no moon and since radar had not yet made its appearance—the accurate keeping of the Plot and the alterations of course it decreed were of vital importance to *Antigone* and to every ship in the convoy.

It was a weird feeling to be in the middle of forty ships you could not see in a roughish sea and a pitch black night. At the prearranged intervals, silently and eerily, all forty ships changed their course according to the zigzag pattern.

The eyestrain on the bridge was intense. The risk of collision through a single wrong order—or an order carried out at the wrong time—was a constant nightmare to Trevesham and the other captains in company.

The thought of what could happen was a nightmare to Fossingham too. The Torpedo Officer had a middle watch as PCO with Cravenby as Officer of the Watch and the Surgeon-Lieutenant working the Plot in place of Schooly. Unlike Brasson Fossingham did not enjoy his turn of duty as PCO. He was secretly afraid of responsibility and his night vision was poor. He did not admit to fear as such but before the bar closed in the wardroom, he had a couple of quick doubles to help him along. Whisky always made him feel a little more cheerful.

After all, he consoled himself, the ship practically ran itself. The Captain would be there a large part of the time, Cravenby was alert enough and he could bully the midshipman into keeping his eyes doubly skinned. The whisky was a good idea. He soon felt very much better. By midnight as he climbed up on the bridge to take over from Brasson, the prospect of four hours in this black, windswept purgatory was not so much a nightmare as a bore.

They had zigzagged to port at midnight so that at 0100 their next alteration of course would be to starboard. Trevesham saw the watch turned over and for the next quarter of an hour stared out at the blackness. There was a Belgian ship to port and for a moment or so they had lost her dim shape when making the turn. That meant that either she had turned early or *Antigone* was late.

'I should think Belgian time is a couple of minutes fast,' Spratt had observed, adding for Fossingham's benefit: 'on the next zig she'll be turning towards us so if she's early on it again don't be surprised if she looms a bit close.'

But Fossingham hated being given advice.

'Bloody Belgians,' he said, 'they can never do as they're told. Serve them right if they had a good scare.'

No one commented on this puerile statement. It was typical of Fossingham, Spratt thought as he went down below leaving instructions to be called fifteen minutes before the morning watch. Trevesham took a final look round and then he too went down to his sea-cabin.

'Call me if you're in any trouble station-keeping or if the sea gets up any more—otherwise at 0150.'

He never allowed himself much more than an hour's sleep when the ship was in such difficult conditions. But this was their seventh night with the convoy. He was deadly tired. He always felt uneasy at leaving the ship in Fossingham's hands, but this was purely an instinct. The Torpedo Officer had never let him down yet but Trevesham felt he very easily could. Since he had no factual reason for this, he told himself he was being unfair and thus gave Fossingham rather more benefit of the doubt then he would have allowed to Brasson, for instance.

As soon as the Captain had left the bridge Fossingham told the midshipman to make cocoa and afterwards to watch the clock down in the Plot. The eye takes time to adjust itself to darkness and the PCO, the Officer of the Watch and everyone on the bridge needed their best night vision in the middle of a darkened convoy. Alterations in course, therefore, were called up from the Plot at the appropriate time and were taken by the bridge as correct.

The first hour went by easily enough. They had run up slightly on the Commodore's ship, her shadow suddenly appearing close and immense. That had given them all a shock but it was the sort of thing which frequently happened with slight variations in speed in such wretched visibility. The Belgian ship, too, had veered away to port and disappeared for three whole minutes before taking up her proper station once more.

'*Bloody* Belgians,' Fossingham said again when the scare was over, 'can't even steer a steady course.'

Cravenby, who had proved a good listener on many occasions before, was again being regaled with some of Fossingham's amorous adventures on the China Station. By this stage of the commission everyone knew everyone else's stories by heart, but Cravenby had found from experience that it was no good trying to stop Fossingham. He was determined to go on talking. The best thing was to grunt occasionally in a sympathetic fashion and pay no attention at all. Cravenby was worried by the Belgian on their port side. She seemed to be a flighty customer. In one of the darkest nights yet, it did not help to have an unreliable ship six hundred yards on your left.

At two minutes to the hour the midshipman called up the usual warning of their zigzag. Fossingham acknowledged this curtly but was deep in a highly spiced account of how he had had to ride through Hong Kong in a rickshaw without his trousers. Thus it was that when 0100 came and the alteration of course was ordered, he never noticed that he had ordered a fifteen degree turn to port instead of to starboard. Nor for the first thirty seconds did anyone else on the bridge. Then—

'The Belgian's early on it again,' Cravenby said as the shadow of the fifteen thousand-ton ship seemed to loom suddenly closer, and—

'*Bloody* Belgians!' said Fossingham, who had seen nothing amiss so far. *Antigone* and the Belgian ship were in fact converging on each other at a combined speed of about twenty knots.

Suddenly the shadow was closer than it had ever been before.

'Christ! she's coming at us!' said Cravenby.

'Captain, sir!' Fossingham yelled down the voice pipe, 'Captain, sir, can you come on the bridge?'

Two decks below in his sea-cabin Trevesham leapt off his bunk, electrified out of his sleep and started climbing up to the bridge. But he was already too late.

'Hard a-starboard!' Fossingham yelled as the Belgian ship came steadily closer. They were now in acute danger of being rammed amidships. The Belgian must have realized that something had gone badly wrong at much the same time. Her tall bows which had been coming straight at them now began turning away to port. But all the time momentum was carrying them closer and closer. As Trevesham arrived coatless and capless on the bridge it seemed as though the ship was on top of them.

'Hard a-starboard!' he called out urgently.

'We are already, sir,' Fossingham said, his voice trembling with fear. Although both ships were turning away, nothing but a miracle could save them colliding.

'This is it,' Cravenby said aloud, instinctively gripping a voice pipe against the coming shock. The two ships were now all but alongside each other, and a huge wave caused by this rapid approach rose up three-quarters aslant from the foc'sle, drenching them all on the bridge.

'We may just make it . . .', Fossingham breathed and at that moment there was a tearing rasp somewhere up near the port bow. The ship lurched heavily away to starboard. Then a sudden flash lit up the darkness of the night and almost at once came the clanging concussion of a minor explosion.

'Sound off "Emergency Stations",' Trevesham shouted, and as the alarm sounded throughout the ship, 'Collision forward port side'. Then in the hope of avoiding a further collision aft as the sterns of the two ships swung round. 'Midships. Hard a-port. Stop both.'

Now a lot of things were happening at once. The Belgian ship was still near enough almost to jump across and Trevesham watched anxiously for another bump. But this time they were to be lucky. The Belgian, who had evidently not reduced speed, began drawing ahead and *Antigone* was soon out of immediate danger from her. But they had now lost their position in the convoy. Other ships would be bearing down on them from astern.

'Keep a sharp lookout aft,' he called to the two bridge lookouts, and went on to warn the flag deck to stand-by their signalling lamps. To burn any light now might give the convoy's position away but would be justified if it saved a further collision.

'Shall I tell the Commander (E), sir?' Fossingham suggested. He wanted to ingratiate himself quickly now that the disaster had happened.

'Tell your grandmother to suck eggs,' Trevesham

snapped, striding over to the starboard side. Now that *Antigone* was stopped she was like an unlit rock in the middle of the sea, a terrible danger to oncoming ships. He did not know what damage had been done nor what had caused the explosion, but it was evidently well forward. 'Half-ahead both,' he ordered. 'Plot! What course should we be on?'

Voice pipes and telephones began sounding on the bridge.

'Main deck to forebridge. Fire on stokers' messdeck forward of Number Fifteen Bulkhead.'

' "A" turret to forebridge. Flashtight doors in "A" handing room jammed. Number One magazine flooding.'

Hatchett had been turned in asleep when the emergency began. Now in his striped pyjama trousers and a monkey jacket he was forward at the point of disaster. The lighting circuits had gone, and now that the fire had burnt itself out he was dependent on torches to find out what had happened. A few moments later he was on the phone to the bridge.

'Commander speaking, sir. We're holed below and above waterline. I think between three and eight bulkheads port side. Numbers fifteen to twenty-one watertight compartments are flooded. Fire on stokers' messdeck under control.'

'Any casualties?'

'Two stokers dead so far, sir. I'm afraid it's a bit of a shambles. I can't get for'ard of Number Eight bulkhead and that's leaking badly. I'm clearing everyone aft of Number Fifteen in case Number Eight bulkhead doesn't hold.'

'Very good,' said Trevesham, and put down the phone.

'Stop both!' he ordered. The hole in the bows would need to be assessed and a collision mat placed before he could drive the ship on into this rising sea. At that moment a merchant ship of ten thousand tons overtook them from astern at a distance of about thirty yards. The language shouted down from the merchantman's bridge was the ripest opinion of the Royal Navy they had yet heard. A lot of people were due for quite a scare before *Antigone* could drop out astern of the convoy and patch herself up. And now—most humiliating of all—they would have to break W/T silence and tell Admiralty what had happened.

'Chief Yeoman,' said Trevesham, 'make to Admiralty repeated C-in-C Home Fleet, C-in-C Plymouth, Flag Officer Northern Patrol and CS8. Immediate. In collision with merchant ship. *Antigone* holed above and below waterline port side forward. "A" magazine and handing room flooded. Intend proceeding with convoy.'

Trevesham never forgot that night for the rest of his life. They gradually dropped astern until they were out of the convoy. When dawn came they were alone. They were no longer in danger of further collision but they became almost a sitting U-boat target.

It had taken Hatchett about an hour to bring the situation below decks under control. Number Eight bulkhead was shored up with baulks of timber. The dead were laid out and the injured dealt with in sick-bay. Up on the foc'sle the First Lieutenant had eventually got a collision mat in place over the hole below the waterline. This had entailed passing a bottom line under the ship, an exasperatingly slow evolution in the darkness. But the shambles was cleared up and the ship's life continued. One of their four turrets was out of action, their speed was reduced, but otherwise the ship could be fought in the normal way.

In the first cold light of day Hatchett came up on the bridge to confer with the Captain.

'What caused the fire?' asked Trevesham.

'A couple of drums of white spirit, sir, in the paint shop,' Hatchett replied. The flames had seemed to dance round the twisted messdeck as though someone had set a light to a huge badly opened tin can.

'There are four stokers and three seamen in sick bay being treated for burns,' he went on. The fire had not been dangerous, but it continued to feed itself on bits of hammock and mess table. However, the fire main was intact and the dark, smoky compartment had gradually been dampened out.

'I'm afraid we've had a third casualty—Ordinary-Seaman Perkins,' said Hatchett, 'and Able-Seaman Williamson of the Foc'sle Division is missing.'

'Gone overboard or what?'

'No one seems to know where he was, sir. It's just possible he's forward in the chain lockers but, if so, he'd no business to be there and we've no way of finding out if he's still alive.'

'What possible reason would he have for going for'ard like that?'

'Well, sir,' said Hatchett, 'I understand that before we left Bermuda he brought a kitten aboard.'

'Who gave him permission?'

'No one did, sir. In fact as soon as the Master-at-Arms heard about it he ordered it to be drowned. But Williamson's mess-mates seem to think he didn't obey the order but hid the cat forward in the chain lockers, where he slipped away to feed it from time to time.'

'Well,' said Trevesham tersely, 'if that's where he is then he's in for a cold and dangerous trip.'

Early the next day they were told to make for Devonport and put under the control of the Commander-in-Chief, Plymouth.

'HMS *Whittington* is being detailed to stand-by you from 1000 to-morrow,' signalled the C-in-C, who could not have been best pleased at having to detach another of his over-worked destroyers to nurse the damaged cruiser home.

'I suppose we're in for a monstrous rap over the knuckles,' Spratt observed sardonically to Darbigh, who was Officer of the Watch during the forenoon when the destroyer rendezvoused with them as ordered in a splendid flurry of bow wave, 'but at least it means a few days at home—and oh! brother, could I use a good night's sleep in a steady bed!'

They buried their three mangled corpses at 1100 under scudding clouds and a louring sky. The Chaplain read the simple service of burial at sea as the ship's company, bare-headed in the high wind, watched the shrouded bodies of their three shipmates consigned to the deep. No one spoke. There was nothing to say. They had been together eighteen months and now three of them, sewn up in White Ensigns, slipped overboard almost as though the sea was claiming them as part of some half-understood bargain which *Antigone* had made with her fate.

Off Land's End they were bombed from the air for the first time. The crippled ship must have been an easy target, but perhaps out of respect for *Antigone*'s high-angle guns the bombing was made from a height, and the pom-pom crews had no chance of engaging the close-diving Heinkel they had expected. But it was their first mild experience of action. The shots they fired now were meant to bring down an aircraft out of the sky, not merely puncture a drogue towed for practice.

The bombs all missed but one was within thirty yards of the ship and the spray it threw up drenched them all on the bridge and upper deck. It was near enough to be uncomfortable. Trevesham, too exhausted to be afraid, nevertheless ducked down instinctively with the others on the bridge. It took him back to his destroyer at Jutland when for a few brief unpleasant moments they had come under fire from a dreadnought's heavy armament. Their speed had saved them then. But while the salvoes fell around them there was that same feeling of inevitability. They would be hit or they wouldn't. The ship would survive or it would be sunk. It was as simple as that.

As a trained Naval officer he knew the steps he must take, the small range of action available to him in any circumstance. The Navy had a routine for everything big or small. You could almost stand out of yourself and watch it going on. This was a momentary process and it operated now.

There was *Antigone* and there was the German aircraft. Bombs were aimed from the sky. Shells sped up into the sky. Both sides had been specifically trained for a purpose now being carried out. They were both using their maximum skill and the balance was chance. Chance made up of apparently calculable things like the force of the wind, the light, the state of the sea—and then blended with quite incalculable additions such as the queasiness of a rangetaker's stomach or a speck of dust in a bomb-aimer's eye. There was always Chance to neutralize the thrower and the thrown. And now as Captain of the cruiser which was the prime target of it all, Trevesham could merely watch and wait. Like so much of the war they were coming to know, this encounter was inconclusive. The bombs dropped, the AA shells appeared to be near their target, but the ship went on undamaged and the aircraft made off to the east apparently whole and in one piece.

To sail up Plymouth Sound, even shabby and damaged as they were, was an enormous thrill after eighteen months abroad. There had naturally been no advance news of their arrival. Indeed, until *Antigone*'s appearance off Plymouth Hoe only the Admiralty, the Commander-in-Chief and possibly the German High Command knew she had been damaged. But the Hoe has for centuries been a good point from which to observe the arrival of HM ships, and as tugs took her up harbour to the Dockyard the 'buzz' darted round Plymouth as only it can round a naval port. *Antigone* was not Devonport manned, but she was a major warship and her light-grey paint alone proclaimed her foreign service. She'd been in a bit of trouble and although censorship might prevent anything appearing in the papers, 'Guz' would want to know all about it.

Trevesham watched the tugs expertly nosing her into the dry dock, keeping tenderly away from her damaged bows, pushing and pulling with that economy of effort which gives the tugboat trade its fascination. He felt tired and sad. It was already as though the ship was no longer his. The dockyard, he muttered to himself, the sacred dockyard with its sullen, disaffected mateys, its bowler-hatted self-important foremen, its inefficient undisciplined delays and its inevitable, resented role in naval seagoing life.

'Well, there it is,' he said to Spratt as they went down from the bridge, 'now we're somebody else's baby for a while.'

'Some lap to sit in,' said Spratt with a sniff. 'Still, we are home again.'

When Trevesham reached the quarterdeck, the Commander was talking to a young Lieutenant RNVR wearing flag-lieutenant's aiguillettes. They both saluted and Hatchett said:

'The C-in-C's sent his car and his Flag Lieutenant, sir. He'd like you to wait on him at once.'

'Very well,' said Trevesham stepping into the cabin off the quarterdeck which he had not seen for a fortnight. They were really home.

A little later as the dock was pumped out they were able to open the chain lockers forward of where the ship had been holed. There, numb from exposure and lack of food, scared but still alive, was Able-Seaman Williamson of the Foc'sle Division. Tucked inside his jumper as they brought him out was a small dead kitten.

CHAPTER TWELVE

The Dockyard estimated four weeks to make good the structural damage.

'Leave!' said Able-Seaman Elcock, a light in his eye. 'Fourteen days' flipping wonderful flipping leave for each flipping watch. Cor! love us. It's a flipping miracle.'

The entire messdeck knew of Able-Seaman Elcock's intentions on leave, which were mostly concerned with the big double bed. But they each and everyone of them had plans of their own. It was indeed a fabulous break, the more keenly appreciated for being so unexpected. The ship emptied itself of half of its ship's company that same forenoon, and in the dog watches those not on long leave went ashore to drink good West Country beer and feel that rare, heady pleasure of walking about their own country among their own people, hearing their own language spoken in the soft Devon drizzle which had fallen continuously since their arrival and which had a peculiarly English magic all its own.

There was a reverse side to this, and Trevesham knew it as he went up to Admiralty House. There would be an inquiry and probably a court martial into the damage HMS *Antigone* had sustained. From what Hatchett had told him, from the flooding of 'A' magazine, he knew quite well that there had been a slip up over watertight doors. This might well have cost them the ship. It was bound to come out when the damage was surveyed. There would certainly be a 'rap over the knuckles' and possibly worse. It was small comfort to argue that had they been struck further aft the results would have been infinitely graver, watertight doors or not. The point was that the damage was greater than it need have been. The ship was out of service at a time when every cruiser was vitally needed. It did their pride and reputation no good whatever and although Trevesham knew the Commander-in-Chief as a friend, although in the vast expansion which naval mobilization spelt to one of the three manning ports, the little matter of a cruiser's underwater damage might be glossed over for more immediate and pressing problems, it lay heavy on Trevesham's own weariness and the exhaustion resulting from fourteen days of Atlantic vigil.

His reception by the Commander-in-Chief was therefore a pleasant surprise. It was some time since Trevesham had been inside Admiralty House. The impact of the war and its vast increase in Staff and Staff work was immediately obvious. Trevesham's four straight stripes still commanded attention from sentries and orderlies, but inside Admiralty House, commanders and captains seemed to be two-a-penny, and Trevesham felt an unreality in the scene. There could not have been a greater contrast with those long night watches in the stormy North Atlantic. Trevesham did not disparage the Staff. He had been a Staff officer himself for too long not to appreciate intimately the work they did. But their problems were no longer his. He had command of a ship at sea. It was a different order of worlds.

A coal fire blazed in the Admiral's office with its intensely English atmosphere of a well-mannered country house drawing-room. A pile of dockets and papers lay in both the In and Out baskets and a glance at the Admiral's Secretary, a grey-haired Paymaster-Captain with three rows of medals and the gold aiguillettes on his left shoulder, took Trevesham back to his own days on a Commander-in-Chief's Staff, so that behind it all he was aware of the immensely intricate machine of command revolving out of sight all around them. The Admiral nodded a dismissal to his Secretary and walked over to shake Trevesham's hand.

'Well, Colin,' he said, 'it's a pleasant surprise to see you again. I'm sorry about the spot of bother you had. We'll talk about that in a moment.' They looked each other in the eyes in the way of old friends each on his different level, each respecting the state and condition of the other.

'It's good to have a breath of sea air in this frowsty room once again.'

It was a few stolen moments for both of them. Time out from the hurly-burly of their daily routine, the different jobs they both found themselves doing. Trevesham was moved by this warmth and friendliness, this recognition that whatever mistakes or accidents had occurred, it was the seagoing Navy alone that mattered and that Trevesham as Captain of one of HM cruisers was a very special person indeed—entitled to a special respect even in the august presence of a full Admiral with the broad gold band and three stripes on his sleeve, with all that those marks of rank had standing behind them, even though he was aware that soon that same Admiral would be ordering his own court martial.

'I envy you, Colin,' said the Commander-in-Chief, 'I wish I were twenty years younger myself—at sea in command at a time like this. . . .'

'Well, sir,' said Trevesham, 'I'm afraid *Antigone* hasn't been a great help to the war effort so far—but it's good to be home again even as things are.'

'I'm going to send you on to the Admiral Superintendent in a moment,' said the Commander-in-Chief, 'but I'll expect you back for lunch. I . . . hm!' he hesitated and coughed. 'My wife happened to be talking on the phone to Diana last night. Nothing to do with your arrival, of course, but she should get here by lunch time, I think.'

The court martial was held two days later. Since the facts were known and the blame admitted, the proceedings were largely formal and the results almost a forgone conclusion. Trevesham came out of it with an expression of Their Lordships' Displeasure, the Officer of the Watch received a Reprimand and Fossingham, whose wrong order had directly caused the accident, was Severely Reprimanded and Dismissed the Ship. With this court martial went his last chance of promotion.

Alone, therefore, out of the six hundred men eager to be gone on leave, Fossingham was to quit the ship under a cloud, knowing he could never come back. It was a rare, sad feeling. Compounded of shock and bitterness, he knew he had failed. Inside himself he had never admitted to failure but it had been there all along. He saw it now.

Nothing seemed to matter any more. All the things he had wanted, the enthusiasm, the passion he considered he had poured into making the Torpedo Department the most efficient in the ship, all his selfish insistence on priority, his determination to succeed, to dominate, to achieve his brass hat—now seemed a little childish and absurd. Yet even now his pride would not leave him alone.

'It could have happened to any of us,' Collard had said sympathetically, offering him a gin in the wardroom after it was over. 'It's just fearful bad luck.'

'Don't worry. I'll survive,' Fossingham had answered curtly and strode out of the mess. He could not bear to be pitied and when Mr Partle had knocked at his cabin door to say how sorry he was, he shook hands briefly and sent him away without allowing any opinions to be expressed.

He had always thought himself charming and popular. A man of character, certainly, but with Nelsonic qualities a degree of arrogance can be excused and once Fossingham had got his way, he would always make up any previous disagreement with a smile, a drink or a generous gesture. It was, therefore, a double shock to overhear two of his own torpedomen discussing him outside his cabin, imagining him not to be there.

'Flipping stuck up sod,' said one, 'never listens to nobody but his own flaming conceit. Deserves double what he got—that one does. Flipping arse licker.'

'It would be '*im* get us all in the rattle,' said the other, ''im and 'is charm! Cor! Good riddance of bad ullage, I say.'

Before, Fossingham would have dashed out of his cabin and taken the two sailors straight up on the quarterdeck in front of the Officer of the Watch. Now, however, he paused. He caught sight in the mirror of his thin face, mottled by alcohol, blotched in the yellow light of his cabin. His mouth set in a hard, bitter line. Well—if that's what they felt about him after all he'd done to help them along—his own Torpedo Department—then he would leave them to their own devices. As soon as he had packed he would be gone. Then when his successor arrived, they would find out just how much they had misjudged him all this time.

He went up to say good-bye to Trevesham. He had

meant to apologize formally and leave it at that. But facing the man who had been his Captain for eighteen months, the one man in the ship whom he really admired in his secret being, a sudden humility struck him.

'I'm sorry I let you and the ship down, sir,' he said.

'I'm sorry for your sake,' Trevesham answered, looking him in the eyes. 'It's yourself you've let down.' He felt a compassion for Fossingham now. He looked whipped. 'You were unlucky—in that the accident happened to you . . . however, your life's not over yet. It's a lesson. We all learn in different ways. Perhaps this is your way, Fossingham. I shouldn't let it get you down too much. There's usually a second chance.'

Then without further ado they shook hands. Five minutes later Fossingham had left the ship for ever.

Just as war had changed their lives on board, so now these few days of brilliant, compressed leave were different from anything they had known before. Fourteen days is not a long time. But the quality of unexpectedness lit them, fired them, made them blaze brilliantly against the darkening mood of the home country in the autumn of 1939, when the excitement of going to war was being progressively dampened down by rationing, controls, air raids, magnetic mines, the comparative stalemate on the Western Front and the unfocused indeterminacy of the 'Phoney War'.

The majority of the ship's company lived in or around Portsmouth. It took them a mere half day to get home and another to return to Plymouth, leaving them thirteen clear, blessed days in the tender arms of their wives, the shy adjustment of children who had not seen their fathers for eighteen months, the self-importance of mothers-in-law and the renewing of old friendships at the local. This time was interrupted by the sirens, by fumbling with gas masks and tin helmets, and by that intimate problem posed always in the depths of the night of whether to stir up and go down to the shelter in a rather self-conscious way or whether to cuddle closer body to body and let the bombs rain down as they chose. At that time air raids were spasmodic and not very effective. For England the full horror of the blitz lay a year ahead, although the word itself had entered the common coinage as a result of Hitler's success in Poland.

To Collard they were the richest few days of his life. The pleasure he took in being with his plump, comfortable wife shone out of his eyes and seemed to illuminate his being. The daughter he had never seen gurgled at him and was just beginning to walk. The two boys were let off school and seemed never to be more than a yard or two away from their vast, broad-shouldered, gentle father with his slow smile and the rum-scented tobacco he smoked in his pipe. It was a time of unblemished enjoyment. He did odd jobs in the cottage, he washed up and helped in the kitchen and once to make a break for his wife he arranged for a neighbour to come in as baby sitter and took her in to Portsmouth to a music hall. She enjoyed this, as he did, but mostly because he had taken the trouble to fix it all up without telling her, as a surprise. After it was over and they came out into the Pompey blackout both were glad to trundle back home to Liphook in the Austin Seven, back to the home which she knew he loved, which she had made and kept for him and which had never been far out of his thoughts whether in Gibraltar or Peru during the year-and-a-half he had been away.

Hatchett spent his leave with madame at a hotel in South Kensington. Alice had greeted the war with a private whoop of delight. She saw an end to the boredom of being a lonely, childless Naval officer's wife with her husband on a foreign commission, and a beginning to a series of exciting jobs somewhere near the centre of things. She had come to London on the outbreak of war and had joined the Kensington Red Cross. She did not think she would last long at that, but all sorts of possibilities were opening up. She had her eye on the Foreign Office but her ignorance of shorthand and typewriting was at present a barrier to the Personal Assistant job she was after. She was delighted to see Stubby again, but he was in process of becoming a part of her world instead of the other way round as it had always been before. Stubby did not resent this. He bought a couple of bottles of gin and they sat in their impersonal hotel bedroom drinking them in front of the hissing gas fire with its broken bars. The impersonality of the room seemed to reflect the state of their lives but neither minded very much. It was like a meeting of two old friends, each now operating in different lines of country, with a lot to talk over and much pleasure to be taken in each other's company, but with a mutual detachment curious and possibly sad to an outside observer but completely and unsentimentally accepted by both of them as part of the natural order of things.

'I got us single beds, dear,' Alice had said, when she had first taken him up to the room. 'I thought you'd probably want a jolly good sleep more than anything else in the world.'

Marsh returned to Number 23 Colebrook Avenue rather as if he had come back from school for the holidays. Excitement, eagerness to pick over all his old things, pleasure in being at home, in his mother's cooking and in his wide, comfortable, old-fashioned bed, the satisfaction of arriving legitimately in uniform and of being the focus of his parents' admiration—all these factors which had before worn out their power in a couple of days this time promised to last through the full span of his unexpected leave.

'Fancy your being collided with!' said his mother, as though he were admitting to a loss of virginity. 'I suppose they'll make it up to you in some way.'

'Oh Mother!' he wearily explained, it seemed for the fortieth time. 'I keep telling you I scarcely even knew we'd been hit. I was in my cabin over the screws—nowhere near it at all.'

'The Navy's always been modest,' his mother said in tones of unshakable admiration. 'I expect it was a whole lot worse than you say.'

'Mother dear, I've explained *ad nauseam* that I'm a *pay-master* in a very humble position in the ship. I just sit in a well-protected steel box cyphering and being seasick.'

But it was no use. His parents smiled at him in that loving tolerant way which before had seemed to clog him but which now he had come to accept as inevitable. To two people at least Derek Lysander Marsh was a hero.

The main pattern of leave for those who were married and for those who were single did not vary much in essentials. Mr Partle had a long talk with the headmaster of his son's school. Chief Petty Officer Penniwick 'secured' his house in Cosham against air-raids and the black-out

287

and scarcely moved outside for the period of his leave. Able-Seaman Rillington re-enacted for the benefit of his family the role of King Neptune which he had carried out on the equator. Meldrum and Susan had a second honeymoon, even though it was at her parents' home in Wiltshire, a period of idyllic peace unruffled by frustration or disagreement of any kind—even though both admitted one evening that it *would* be pleasant if Augustus Spratt should happen to drop in for a drink.

But Spratt was up in Cheltenham in the austere, military home which never changed, helping the General, his father, to stick pins in a map of Europe. Chief Petty Officer Bowling gave advice on the rigging of a three-masted barque which his son was making. Captain Taw-Street had the loan of a horse and got in some riding in the New Forest. Petty Officer Cook Jenkins stormed back moodily to South Wales, venting his spleen at the propertied classes in general and his own officers in particular. Hale, whose home was in London, went to all the theatres that were open and firmly resisted his mother's plea to make peace with the Catholic Church and go to confession. Able-Seaman Elcock slept with five different women on five separate nights and Able-Seaman Clarke, whose uncle kept a pub, helped in the bar and contented himself with as much beer as he could hold. Grey-Bennett had his hair cut in Jermyn Street and haunted the Ritz bar, Midshipman Watling fell in love and the Master-at-Arms attended a Naval funeral in his frock coat and the dignity attaching to his position. For each and all of them the background was changing, but just for a moment it was as though they were being offered a final digest of their home lives in the form which they had known for so long and from which they seemed to have spent so long away.

'I wonder how it's going to be next time they give us a go of leave,' said Stoker Johnson reporting back at the regulating office on his return. It was a thought dodging about restlessly in all of their minds.

The dockyard kept to its schedule. Four weeks after their arrival at Devonport they were ready for sea, with freshly riveted plates where they had been holed and the inside of the ship built up again as new.

Hatchett's first action on return from leave was to tighten up the routine all round.

'Last time we were lucky,' he said, 'and we got away with it. Next time we may not be. No one can help an accident but we *can* make sure the drill's carried out as it should be. And by hell it will be.'

He was preaching to the converted. The shock of the collision coupled with the leave they had been given seemed to have stiffened them all. Their fighting spirit was excellent. To get home had been wonderful: to return on board was better. None of them would have felt like this in peacetime. But now there was a war on and they had a seagoing job.

There was nothing sentimental in this. They did not look on themselves as heroes or as being especially in the forefront of the battle but there was a job of work to be done which only they—and chaps like them—could do. That put them in a special position. So when *Antigone* was oiled and stored and provisioned, when 'A' magazine was restocked with cordite and shells, when the ship was inspected and passed as ready for further service at sea, there was not a man aboard who was not privately rearing to go.

Trevesham had thought about the ship almost all the time he was on leave. Drakeshott was in process of being taken over by a London school. The house and the gardens were still immaculate, but two of the gardeners had joined up and except for Diana's personal maid, her crone Annie, the domestic staff too were leaving piecemeal. It was a strange feeling. He had thought so deep and so often about his home during the past eighteen months. Now that he was there it seemed to be no longer part of him. It was an outside thing, a background from which he had become uprooted and disconnected.

During the five days he was there, on walks through the drifts of fallen leaves on mellow afternoons, taking a shot at the abundant partridge and pheasant so far undisturbed this year, drinking his favourite Amontillado in front of the drawing-room fire—in all the activities and scenes which comprised the word 'Drakeshott' he carried with him a picture of the ship. The forebridge, the rolling sea, the charts, the signal log proffered by the Chief Yeoman, his short dynamic Commander, the tall cadaverous

Chief Quartermaster, the archaic looking Paymaster-Commander, his fat confident Chief, his pale worried Secretary, the sound of the wind in the signal halyards, the hot thick cocoa in the deep night watches—the ship and its complement seemed to be stained into his being, and although exhaustion had made him long for leave as it does to all sailors, now that he was at home he felt lost. Something was missing, something was incomplete. When it was time to go back to Devonport, he was actually glad.

He found the Drafting Office had been active in his absence. With experience suddenly at an immense premium Trevesham knew he must expect a certain dilution in his ship's company. He did not envy the harassed Depot Drafting Commanders at a time like this.

'Tell me the worst,' he said to Hatchett when the latter brought him the list.

'A new regulating petty officer, the chief shipwright, the chief ERA, Painter Dawson, two petty officers, one of the supply chiefs, a leading-signalman, four leading-stokers and twenty-six able-seamen. Not a bad combing for Barracks,' Hatchett commented tersely.

'What about the CW Lists?'

These were the daily lists of Officers' Appointments issued by the Admiralty. Hatchett put his fingers to his lips.

'So far, sir, not a thing except of course for Caspar, the new Torps. The Second Sea Lord doesn't seem to be quite so quick off the mark as the Commodore of the Barracks. If we get away tomorrow, we shall be quite all right.'

'Hm!' said Trevesham, not caring to dwell on the incredible good fortune of still having his team intact, 'I'd like to see Caspar right away. Is that really his name?'

'Yes, sir.'

'Well, it should give the ship's company wags plenty of scope.'

The torpedo workshop had already been renamed Caspar's Cottage, although one look at the new Torpedo Officer convinced the ship's company that this old Caspar was most unlikely to act out the verses of the famous poem. John Caspar, in fact, was of a very different calibre from his predecessor. Still a lieutenant, he looked alert, intelligent and full of fire. He impressed Trevesham from the moment he stepped into the cuddy to be presented by Hatchett. He radiated the one essential quality Fossingham had lacked—a kind of humorous confidence.

'You're lucky in Mr Partle,' said Trevesham after discussing with unusual frankness the background into which his new Torpedo Officer must fit.

'Yes, sir,' Caspar answered with a smile. He liked Trevesham, and he knew Trevesham was making a special effort to welcome him as a member of the family. 'Let's say I'm lucky all round.'

Had Fossingham said that it would have sounded servile. From a junior officer it would have been merely impertinent. From John Caspar, however, it expressed without putting into words what he himself knew in his bones and what Trevesham had instantly seen—his new Torpedo Officer had 'star quality'.

They had expected to sail the following day but their orders came through before Quarters that same evening. 'Being in all respects ready for sea . . .' the well-known wording began, and steam was raised by the Engineering Department in record time. Their refrigerators were full of fresh meat, the canteen was stocked to its roof, the wardroom wine-store had been replenished and just before they slipped from the jetty a panting welfare-officer from Devonport Barracks staggered up the gangway with bales of 'comforts' in the form of balaclava helmets, mittens, sweaters, socks and a case of books for the ship's library.

'What—no little Wrens tucked away in that lot?' asked Able-Seaman Clarke as he signed the chit on behalf of the Chaplain. 'That's the kind of comfort we could do with in this ship.'

The Wrens were a new phenomenon to the great majority of the ship's company, and at one time it was thought that Able-Seaman Elcock had brought one back, tucked up in his hammock, for the general benefit of Number 18 Mess. But as the brows went out, the wires were cast off and *Antigone* drew silently away from the jetty, turning and gliding out into the swept channel as dusk fell, they all realized that England had been nothing but a brief interlude, unexpected and welcome but none the less for them, as they were at this stage of the commission, an alien luxury now finished and done with. They were once more at sea.

In the first months of the war the *Deutschland* and the *Graf Spee* had been ordered to keep away from trade routes in case Hitler could patch things up with the Western Powers after overrunning Poland. But this idea failed. In October the two pocket battleships were ordered to the attack. During the following six weeks the *Deutschland* had scant success. She sank a British and a Norwegian ship and made a prize of an American one. Then in mid-November she returned to Germany by the route to the north of Iceland. Her total harvest had been three ships.

The *Graf Spee*, however, did better. She captured a ship off Pernambuco, next transferred her attention to the Cape route, sinking four ships, and then to embarrass British strategy still further made a foray into the Indian Ocean south of Madagascar.

To the Admiralty the searching-out and sinking of these two raiders became a desperate operation of hide-and-seek. To counter the German eleven-inch guns we could dispose only cruisers with eight- and six-inch guns and there were grave doubts of their ability to prevail in battle. It was true that the aircraft-carrier *Ark Royal* and the battlecruiser *Renown* were based on Freetown, Sierra Leone, to seek out and destroy the pocket battleships once they were found. But these two great ships could not be everywhere at once. The likeliest encounter would be with one or more of the British cruisers patrolling the world trade routes in their traditional fashion. During October and November 1939 HMS *Antigone* took her place in this secret and honoured company.

This took them to Gibraltar, Freetown and the Cape on one side of the Atlantic and to Halifax, Bermuda and the Falkland Islands on the other. They settled down into long, eventless periods at sea.

It was a curiously remote kind of life. Except for an odd couple of days in harbour at the end of a patrol, when they oiled and provisioned, they were out of touch with the world. They took in the daily press bulletins and listened to the nine o'clock news, that extraordinary wartime institution, whenever the longitude was right, but otherwise for two months they kept company with the lonely sea, the winter gales in the North Atlantic and the summer calm in the south. They had been caught out on their first patrol of the war. They were not to be surprised in that way again. Now most of them could have gone to action stations in their sleep, if need be, they had done it so many times that by now their response was automatic.

But they still thought it odd to be so long on their own. Most of them, when they had visualized war at all, had imagined *Antigone* as part of a cruiser squadron dashing off into battle at high speed. It might not always be Jutland but that was generally how they saw themselves, smoke pouring from the funnel, guns blazing and the tattered white ensign riding high above the roar of cannon and the smell of burnt cordite.

'Cor! blimey,' said Able-Seaman Elcock, spinning his range-taker's wheels in the director control-tower, as they stared at the empty sea, 'this isn't *war*! This is peace with the frills knocked off, that's all. Where's the rest of the squadron I'd like to know? Hogging it in Bermuda, I shouldn't wonder, leaving poor old *Aunty* to sweep the Seven Seas on her own.'

As day after day passed at sea with nothing positive to show for it all, it was indeed hard to feel useful. Trevesham had explained to the ship's company that the German fleet, as a fleet, scarcely amounted to a headache. It had neither quality, nor numbers. But as commerce raiders, operating alone, striking where least expected they could gravely interfere with supplies reaching the United Kingdom. So the protection of trade was a paramount task. It might be monotonous but it was vital and that was exactly what *Antigone* was doing.

The ship seemed always to be crowded. Their war complement was up by about fifty, and on passage from Gibraltar to Freetown or down to the Cape there was usually a soldier, an airman or a grey-haired civilian pressed on board at the last moment at the urgent insistence of higher authority. *Antigone* made her guests welcome in the Naval Tradition and indeed was glad of their company as windows into the outer world, but with extra bodies in the mess and with the difficulties in getting about the ship which meticulous observance of the watertight door routine now entailed, it all added up to a feeling of compression and overcrowding.

Marsh had got his second stripe and had now left the gunroom for ever. Occasionally Darbigh or one of the Midshipmen would invite him in for a drink but now that he had diffidently taken his place in the wardroom, he looked back on his 'apprentice' days rather as he had looked on school after joining the Navy—as a time of testing and endurance which for some reason he did not know had to be undergone before he could claim his birthright.

The days turned into weeks and the weeks to months. They saw not a trace of the enemy and they suffered no attacks from sea or air. Round England, they knew, the magnetic mine was closing up our coastal shipping routes and by late November the Port of London had been brought almost to a standstill. Only the Clyde remained as yet out of range, open and free. How odd it must be, they thought, as they threshed about the South Atlantic, visualizing the misty reaches of the Thames empty and paralysed. But to the officers and men of HMS *Antigone* as they scanned the bare horizon it was a tale from another world.

If submarines and mine-laying aircraft constituted spheres of almost 'private' warfare so far as the Fleet proper was concerned, the 'surface' war suddenly became more ominous with the escape from Germany of the *Scharnhorst* and *Gneisenau* late in November 1939. These two battle-cruisers were a very different cup of tea from the *Deutschland* and *Graf Spee*. Against such capital ships no cruiser would stand a chance. Unless the Home Fleet could bring them to book, no cruiser dared risk a fight. A ship of *Antigone*'s size would be at the receiving end of eleven-inch salvoes long before getting close enough to open fire herself. With the sinking of the *Rawalpindi*, therefore, the odds against running into trouble shortened.

Then on Saturday, 2 December, an event took place which presaged the first great Naval victory of the war. The SS *Doric Star* was intercepted and sunk by the *Graf Spee* between the Cape of Good Hope and Sierra Leone on latitude 20° south. She was sunk as had been all the other victims of the German pocket battleships without option and without warning. This time, however, there was a difference. Before being silenced for ever, the *Doric Star* was able to report her position and the identity of her attacker. From that moment on the net began to close in.

The next intentions of the German could only be guessed. The Cape route might be getting too hot: they had skirmished into the Indian Ocean: it might well pay them to attack the rich traffic of the River Plate. Apart from anything else the River Plate was a long way from a British base.

To the north between Sierra Leone and Pernambuco the *Ark Royal* and *Renown* were on patrol; down at the Falkland Islands HMS *Cumberland,* an eight-inch gun cruiser, was undergoing a self refit, *Antigone* herself was patrolling to the north of Rio de Janeiro and a thousand miles to the south off the mouth of the River Plate, that focal point of maximum danger, a British cruiser squadron had been assembled in company under the command of Commodore Harwood and consisting of *Antigone*'s two sister ships the *Ajax* and the *Achilles* (manned by New Zealanders), and the eight-inch gun cruiser *Exeter*. These dispositions were of course unknown to *Antigone,* and they were thus on just another routine cruise though at any rate on the 'right' side of the Atlantic when the *Graf Spee* ran slap into the British squadron awaiting her off Uruguay at 0600 on 13 December.

Immediately contact was made the Admiralty drew the net tight so that even had the *Graf Spee* not entered Montevideo she could no longer have escaped. The British cruisers had an edge on her of nearly six knots. The *Ark Royal* and *Renown* were both being oiled at Rio de Janeiro, and *Antigone,* working up to her full thirty-two knots, made off south as the result of a 'Most Immediate' signal.

The battle itself, in the finest traditions of the Royal Navy, developed along clear, simple lines. It began when the *Graf Spee* was on the point of sinking her first non-British victim, the French liner *Formose*. While approaching this ship her mast-head lookouts sighted the mast of a warship well over the horizon. This was HMS *Exeter*. At this point the whole advantage lay with the *Graf Spee*. Her six eleven-inch guns mounted in their two formidable turrets were trained and elevated to their maximum range and a few moments later the first salvo of shells each weighing six hundredweight were speeding high over the horizon to their target seventeen miles away. The Battle of the Plate had begun.

This encounter was a gunnery triumph for both sides. The *Graf Spee*'s first salvo fell short: the second directly astern: the third and fourth just missed: the fifth scored a hit and the seventh a direct hit. This last salvo nearly took *Exeter* out of the action. It killed outright eight of the fifteen Marines manning the forward turret, and it wrecked the bridge immediately above. The Captain, in the centre, was unhurt: the two men on either side of him were killed.

HMS *Exeter*, her battle ensign flying, immediately closed. This was the brave, almost instinctive action of a British warship getting the worst of it in the early stages of a battle. Outgunned and partially crippled, HMS *Exeter* came steadily towards the pocket battleship and was soon within range of the latter's secondary armament. She returned shot for shot until only one eight-inch gun could be fired, and that by hand. Numerous fires broke out but were kept under control by gallant men throwing the burning material over the side, and between decks where the outbreaks were most serious by the staunch determination of the fire parties. The steering gear was damaged by shell fragments, and for forty-five minutes the Captain conned the ship from the after control just forward of the mainmast, using a boat's compass. This was done through a chain of ten sailors, orders being conveyed from man to man to the after steering control and to the engine room until the ship was no longer of use as a fighting unit and fell out of the action.

The *Exeter* thus drew the fire of the German ship mainly upon herself and this heroic deed enabled her two smaller sisters, the *Ajax* and *Achilles*, to herd the enemy in against the Uruguayan coastline and by means of brilliant manoeuvring, the clever tactical use of smoke, and a Nelsonic audacity in closing on either side of the German to within a mile, managed to inflict hit after hit with their lighter six-inch armament.

All day long, as *Antigone* tore south, the action continued in and out of territorial waters with the German ship trying to escape, twisting and turning through her smoke screen and continually frustrated in these attempts by the terrier-like tenacity of *Ajax* and *Achilles*. As the sun set and the last shots were exchanged it was obvious that Captain Langsdorff was seeking asylum in Montevideo, and at 2042 the action was broken off.

It took *Antigone* just over thirty hours to reach the mouth of the River Plate. She arrived at a critical time. The rules of international warfare allow a warship to take shelter in a neutral port for twenty-four hours solely in order to make the ship seaworthy after damage in battle or by the elements. Guns, armour, and fighting equipment may in no circumstances be touched. If a stay of longer than twenty-four hours is made then the ship must be immobilized and the crew interned.

'Those are the rules,' Trevesham explained to a meeting of his heads of departments. 'They were set out in the Hague Convention of 1907. Germany flouted them as she chose in the Great War. I shouldn't be at all surprised if she did it again. It remains to be seen. We shall take station with *Ajax* and *Achilles* just outside territorial waters and wait for *Graf Spee* to come out and give battle. Her twenty-four hours should be up at about eight tonight.'

In the meantime the great engagement was causing immense repercussions. Hitler was personally on the phone to Captain Langsdorff. A diplomatic war of sudden intensity opened up in peaceful Montevideo. The Germans wished no time limit set on their stay: Mr Millington Drake, the British Minister, and Monsieur Gentil, the French Minister, both protested in the strongest terms. The Uruguayan Government sent a naval commission to inspect the damage to the *Graf Spee* and as a result a stay of seventy-two hours was allowed the ship. But few skilled artificers could be found in Uruguay who would work on the German ship. The main ship-repairing firm in Montevideo was managed by Uruguayans of French descent. They declined to touch the *Graf Spee* or to supply materials, their shipwrights and riveters categorically refusing to 'work for Hitler' as they put it.

Across the River Plate in Buenos Aires the British community, with tremendous energy and that Anglo-Saxon genius for working together effectively in emergency, had fitted out a hospital ship, staffed it with the principal surgeons and nursing staff from the British Hospital in the city and sailed it to the Falkland Islands whither the crippled *Exeter* was making her slow, lonely way. Commodore Harwood was knighted and promoted Rear-Admiral. The Captains of the three gallant cruisers were awarded the Companionship of the Bath. Ashore in Montevideo the *Graf Spee* buried her dead with full military honours and a wreath from British sailors dedicated 'to their brave comrades of the sea'. Waiting outside the mouth of the river, the *Ajax*, with two of her four turrets out of action, was relieved by *Antigone* but remained in company. Further in the shadows but ready for the kill stood-off the great *Ark Royal* and the even mightier thirty-two-thousand-ton battlecruiser *Renown*, whose fifteen-inch armament could have engaged and sunk the three German pocket battleships at once. Those were the dispositions and thus they waited, silent, still and unobserved, till the tragic climax of the story came.

It was an extraordinary time to all of them aboard *Antigone*. Trevesham brooded on the bridge as the ship rolled gently in the swell. Although they had missed the battle it was strangely comforting to be once more in company with their two sister ships the *Ajax* and *Achilles*. As the hours ticked by the slow tension mounted, no longer prickled by the personal danger of battle but powered by the watchfulness of a cat waiting for a large wounded rat to emerge from temporary shelter.

The hours went by, measured off by the eight bells of a watch, divided into darkness and daylight yet oddly enough scarcely tuned to the calendar. To Trevesham it was time out as he paced up and down the bridge and read the signals brought to him by the Chief Yeoman and by his Secretary. Just in sight lay the funnel of the River Plate—familiar waters, familiar land beyond. How would the story end?

The Republic of Uruguay, though rich, is the smallest Latin American State. Its population is just over two million, its Navy scarcely a factor in world maritime power. The *Graf Spee*, therefore, was far more powerful than any naval force the sheltering state could bring to bear upon her. If the Germans had so chosen they could have maintained their pocket battleship in Montevideo, oiled and capable of navigation, inviolate against authority until the moment they selected to slip out once more into the Atlantic Ocean as a fighting unit. Uruguay was neutral and there are differing ways of interpreting neutrality, as the Norwegian Government was demonstrating nearer home in the use it was allowing of its own territorial waters. The Germans had lost the diplomatic battle right from the start, but there were still ten thousand tons of battleship in Montevideo. What was it then that took the *Graf Spee* out of harbour to her doom at ten minutes past five on the afternoon of Sunday, 17 December 1939?

Marsh asked this question of Hale as they sat in the cypher office when the news burst in on them that the *Graf Spee* was weighing her anchors. Hale quickly flipped through the log and passed over a signal for Marsh to read. 'That's why,' he said.

'It has been learnt through diplomatic sources,' the Admiralty had signalled, 'that the Uruguayan Government has invoked the Monroe Doctrine and has appealed to the United States of America, to Brazil and to the Argentine. In the event of continued German defiance of Uruguayan neutrality, it is understood that immediate help has been promised and the necessary naval forces to implement this decision have been alerted. HM ships on patrol off the River Plate may assume therefore that the *Graf Spee* will either be forced to sea when her period of grace has expired or that a combined North and South American Fleet will compel her internment and ensure the disablement of her engine and her armament.'

'It looks as though she's chosen to come out and fight,' said Hale, as 'Action Stations' sounded-off throughout the ship. 'I'd give anything to be up on the bridge at a time like this.'

But the *Graf Spee* had another fate awaiting her. Before an immense crowd of people she got under way in the inner harbour at 1725. Her attendant tanker, the *Tacoma*, went alongside, and to this ship the bulk of the *Graf Spee*'s crew of over a thousand men was transferred. At 1819 the battleship left the inner harbour on her final cruise, followed by the *Tacoma* and six launches.

Just outside the three mile limit, HMS *Ajax*, *Achilles* and *Antigone* lay waiting, their guns and torpedo tubes cleared for action and trained on the *Graf Spee*. Scores of telescopes and binoculars followed her movements, and there was something like a sigh of disappointment on the bridge of *Antigone* as she turned west towards Buenos Aires on clearing the entrance to the outer harbour.

'She's going to make a dash for another hole,' said Spratt. 'She's on the run.'

This event had been foreseen by the British squadron. To reach the deep-water channel to Buenos Aires the *Graf Spee* would have to leave the protection of territorial waters. That could be the moment of the kill.

Then a little later she confounded her watchers by again turning east towards the river mouth and the open sea. At 1900 she stopped just off the fairway leading to Montevideo. The six attendant launches came alongside and the rest of the crew including Captain Langsdorff were taken off. At 1930 the first explosion was heard. A train of other internal explosions followed and at 1955 came the one which sank the great ship. She went down in only twenty-six feet of water. While this was happening, escaping oil fuel caught fire and the flames raged round the superstructure for nearly two hours. The ship had been sunk on Hitler's personal orders as an obstruction to navigation and as a petulant reprisal against Uruguay's strict neutrality. As she settled slowly in the channel, her Captain saluted from a launch, the tears streaming down his cheeks. Three days later he shot himself.

A great event acts like a magnet pulling into its orbit people, energy and things. The River Plate action attracted world attention upon itself: it drew a small fleet of warships to its area and it paralysed the movement of merchant shipping. When the *Graf Spee* scuttled herself, these forces dispersed. Maritime commerce, like blood in the world's body, began once more to circulate in the trade route veins. HMS *Ark Royal*, already sunk twice by Dr Goebbels, and the battle-cruiser *Renown* returned to their base at Gibraltar. The *Achilles* went to New Zealand in triumph to refit and give leave. The *Ajax* and the *Exeter*, after temporary repairs, arrived back at Plymouth where they were accorded a civic welcome and were met by the Board of Admiralty led by Mr Winston Churchill. 'The brilliant action of the Plate,' he said to the assembled ships' companies, 'came like a flash of light and colour in this sombre dark winter when, apart from the Navy, we have been at war and yet not at war . . .'

Meanwhile HMS *Antigone*, somewhat wistfully cheated of a share in the battle, was ordered north to Bermuda. Christmas 1939 found her on patrol between Halifax and Iceland. 'Appropriately seasonable weather,' said the Paymaster-Commander as he inspected the ship's vast plum pudding being stirred in the galley, while outside on deck those on watch stamped and blew on their fingers in ten degrees of frost.

They were back into a seemingly endless routine of long days at sea, punctuated by brief boiler cleaning periods in harbour when the miracle of their mail catching up with them occurred all too rarely. But the short rest and the long vigil at sea was now the established order of their lives and on 23 February 1940 when their comrades of *Ajax* and *Exeter* were being honoured by the City of London with luncheon at the Guildhall, it was appropriate for Mr Churchill to remind his listeners and the country that 'for one stroke that goes home, for one clutch that grips the raider, there are many that miss their mark on the broad oceans; for every success there are many disappointments. You must never forget that the dangers that are seen are only a small part of those that are warded off by care and foresight, and therefore pass unnoticed.'

The officers and ship's company of *Antigone* felt a personal meaning in those words as they fed their boilers and cleaned their guns and stared out at the grey Arctic waters of their Northern Patrol.

CHAPTER THIRTEEN

April 1940 lifted the curtain on six months of world history without parallel in its sequence of disasters for the free nations. It was almost as though every debt made in the last twenty years had suddenly been presented for settlement without grace or mercy.

It began with Norway and ended with the Battle of Britain. By the time that hot, peerless summer had come and gone, the pattern of European power had completely altered. Norway, Denmark, the Low Countries and France were all under Nazi occupation. Italy in disreputable haste had come in on Germany's side. Pearl Harbour and America's entry into the war still lay eighteen months in the future. This was the time of endurance when England stood quite alone.

After a winter spent mainly in northern waters, *Antigone*'s next action began on 6 April 1940. '*Antigone* is to rendezvous with *Renown* in position 66°7′ N9°2′ E . . .' read the signal.

'Battlecruiser protection!' Spratt observed laconically as he showed the position to Trevesham on the chart. 'I wonder what's cooking in the Lofoten Islands.'

They were soon to find out. Three days later the 'real' war had begun.

On 9 April 1940 Denmark and Norway were 'invited' into the German orbit, the invitation being presented by an invasion force in both instances. Denmark collapsed without bloodshed. Norway, despite Quisling and his hotch-potch of traitors, resisted as best she could. Aided by the Royal Navy and the Royal Air Force, she made the lunge across the Skagerak as expensive to the Germans as Admiral Raeder had feared it might be.

The eight-inch-gun cruiser *Blücher* was sunk in Oslo Fjord, the light cruiser *Karlsruhe* torpedoed and sunk by a British submarine off Kristiansand and the *Könisberg* sent to the bottom of Bergen Fjord by aircraft of the Fleet Air Arm working from Scapa. Moreover British and Polish submarines, harrying German transports in the Skagerak, torpedoed and seriously damaged the pocket battleship *Deutschland*, now renamed *Lützow* for superstitious reasons by Hitler.

In return the battleship *Rodney* had been hit amidships by the heaviest type of bomb then in use but which mercifully failed to explode. Further north, however, there was far bigger prey at sea, and for the first time yet *Antigone* was in on it from the start.

She covered the five hundred odd miles to the rendezvous position overnight and during the following forenoon. There was something both comforting and impressive in coming upon *Renown* out of a slight mist exactly in the position ordered.

'Another ten minutes,' Spratt had said, with a quick glance at the course, 'that is to say I *hope* we shall see them in another ten minutes.'

They did. Almost to the minute the tall tripod mast came into sight over the horizon. They were visually challenged and gave the reply. Then at once came their patrol instructions and the news that the *Scharnhorst* and *Gneisenau* were at sea. These were Germany's biggest ships. Their eleven-inch guns could not match the *Renown*'s fifteen-inch armament, but the ships themselves were faster, as fast indeed as *Antigone*. They were formidable warships. Although the calibre of their main armament was less they mounted nine guns against the *Renown*'s six. In addition they were known to be well armoured.

They patrolled for the next two days without incident. The weather steadily deteriorated and the day Norway was invaded, they found themselves sweeping into a blizzard. After a long winter in the grey North Atlantic, another gale came upon them almost as second nature. They had all spent many, many hours with the rain stinging into their cheeks, with the hailstones flattening the surface of the sea yet somehow increasing the roll of the ship against a background of dark storm clouds racing across disagreeable skies. This Arctic tempest was familiar indeed. When the lookout in the crow's nest, therefore, first spotted the masts and upperworks of the *Scharnhorst* faintly appearing and disappearing through the driving rain he did not believe his eyes.

'Gawd!' he said as his lonely observation post rolled through its regular forty-degree arc: 'It can't be. It isn't . . . Gawd! I believe it is.' He pressed the buzzer and yelled down the voice pipe to the bridge. 'Lookout to forebridge. Ship in sight bearing green 32. Green 32. Tripod mast and . . . I think it's them, sir,' he finished off in most unorthodox excitement. Almost at once 'Action Stations' sounded-off throughout the ship, and down on the bridge a dozen pairs of binoculars strained out through the pouring, solid rain. A few moments later the readiness reports began to come in from all over the ship. The transmitting station down in the bowels of the ship was already calculating the range and deflection, the pointers flickering hovering like sensitive fingers, a sense of new urgency in the hands that spun the wheels and the eyes that concentrated on the dials. Up in the director control-tower rangefinders were lining two images together, the range-takers thrusting at the pedals and automatically sending their observations down to the transmitting station to be averaged and passed on to the turrets themselves. 'All guns load', came the order and as this was being put into effect, the first salvo of eleven-inch shells left the *Scharnhorse* and sped toward *Antigone*.

'Port thirty!' said Trevesham, and then as the ship leaned over steeply into the sea, 'Make smoke!' A few moments later dense clouds of black smoke began pouring from the funnel. It was far from suitable weather for laying a smoke screen but *Antigone*'s role was to play for time. Her salvoes, compared with the *Scharnhorst*'s, were puny. Except by a fluke she could not hope to survive, but just out of sight beyond the horizon lay the thirty-two-thousand-ton *Renown*, and already a Most Immediate signal had reached the battlecruiser from *Antigone*. 'Enemy battlecruiser bearing 052°—16 miles steering 350 speed 25 knots my position 69° 05'N 10° 16'E.'

Well—this is it, thought Trevesham as he braced himself against the bridge coping. This is the moment—after all these years.

Antigone was working up quickly to her full speed. They must be grateful for the blizzard. The *Scharnhorst*'s first three salvoes fell short and well astern. They were slow salvoes, too, Trevesham noted with satisfaction. *Antigone* could double that rate of fire. If only she could manoeuvre into closer range then her lighter armament might yet have effect. It was possible the Germans might run for port as they had done before—as undoubtedly they would do when *Renown* came on the scene—but for the present *Antigone* must offer too tempting a target; the odds were too heavily on the German side not to entice her to continue the action, to try and redress the River Plate victory and to put the 'saucy British cruisers' in their place.

Now for the first time in her life *Antigone* was in action against a surface enemy. 'And this time it had better be good,' Spratt muttered to himself as *Antigone* turned

304

back behind the smoke screen, 'or there won't be another time.'

Now the ship was functioning as smoothly as a watch. She tore back through the greasy smoke, every one of her six hundred officers and men at his own particular Action Station, tensed and ready. Trevesham picked up the telephone to the Gunnery Officer.

'Another two minutes, Guns, then we'll turn back into the smoke. As soon as we're through I'll turn to port on to our original course—then it's up to you.'

'Aye, aye, sir.'

Brasson sounded taut and confident. Trevesham pictured him up in the director control-tower poised and waiting. Tom Brasson was a type of Naval officer whom Trevesham had always disliked throughout his seagoing career, but whose aggressive ability could not be questioned. It was in the great tradition. Above all things he could be relied on now. He looked across the forebridge at Spratt. Honest Tom's antithesis, as Navigating Officers so often were. They were two opposing cogwheels enmeshed together by the Service to produce a required result. The ship was full of such contrasting personalities.

There was a sense of inevitability in everything that happened. Trevesham had never felt his brain clearer yet he seemed to be conscious in two separate halves—one receiving reports, judging, assessing and giving orders, a tall figure in a watch coat with a pair of binoculars slung round his neck, linked automatically to the ship and in tune with the constantly shifting situation in which they now found themselves; the other somehow watching himself, aware of all that was going on in his person and in the greater unseen self around him which the ship comprised. This second self, detached and wary, was something new to Trevesham. How odd! he thought as the ship suddenly emerged from the smoke and heeled over in a steep turn. There are two of us going into battle—one outer and one inner; and the inner one of him was also down in the boiler rooms, up in the crow's nest, handling an ammunition hoist, watching a propeller shaft and standing by in the wardroom flat ready for the fires which a hit might start.

They were now much nearer the *Scharnhorst*.

'Stop making smoke,' said Trevesham. *Antigone* had

305

now picked up her original course. The smoke screen drifted and blew behind them. It remained their only escape. Now they were approaching the enemy obliquely at a combined speed of some sixty miles an hour. 'Lookout bearing green one-five,' said the Spotting Officer into his telephone, which connected with the four turrets. 'Table tuned for deflection,' came the report from the transmitting station, far, far below. Then came a moment of dreadful calm—a long careful moment of silence. 'Broadsides!' said the Gunnery Officer in a sharp command and then the executive order 'Shoot!' Chief Petty Officer Rigby, the Chief Gunner's Mate, pressed the fire gongs, and with a blinding roar Antigone's first salvo sped on its way. In another seven or eight seconds the 'gun-ready' lamps glowed again and 'Up ladder—Shoot!' said Brasson. The action had begun.

Meanwhile the Scharnhorst had now ranged again on Antigone, surprised at her terrier's nerve in dashing out of the smoke to attack when she could have continued to dodge in safety behind it. The slow German salvoes began creeping closer. 'Any time now,' thought Spratt. The rain stung his cheeks, his ears became deafened by the noise of Antigone's guns and his mind dealt with and docketed almost mechanically the large alterations of course the Captain was making.

The German gunners might slowly be getting Antigone in such a position where a lucky salvo could blow her out of the water, but in the meantime 'Brasson's Benefit' was proving surprisingly accurate. 'Straddle,' the Spotting Officer said exultantly, and then a moment or so later: 'Straddle again.'

'A hit!' said Trevesham. 'Well done, Guns!'

But this word of praise carried away on the wind. In any case Brasson was too absorbed in staying on the target now that they had clamped on to it with such uncanny speed. 'Down two hundred—Shoot!' he said, then as the 'gun-ready' lamps winked on in order, 'Shoot!' again, and then again, 'Shoot!'

A near-miss salvo from the German guns fell uncomfortably close. A huge column of water enveloped the ship and as it fell away, the starboard torpedo tubes had obviously been damaged by shell fragments.

'Hm!' said Spratt to himself, 'a little trouble for Caspar.'

But *Antigone* had a ruse up her sleeve and now Trevesham decided to use it. It had been worked by *Ajax* and *Achilles* in the River Plate action with great success and even if by now the Germans had tumbled to it there was still very little they could do to avoid its consequences. The deception was simple. It consisted merely in dropping depth charges in the wake of the ship, timed by the flash of *Scharnhorst*'s guns to go off when their salvoes should arrive. The column of water thrown up by an exploding depth charge and a salvo of shells is similar. The German spotters were thus confused and led to correct their aim away from the ship or too far ahead of it. It was a simple game but Trevesham played it with relish and once more it worked. By the time the Germans realized that something was wrong *Antigone* had scored another hit and Trevesham was headed back once more into the smoke screen.

Then a few moments before they disappeared back into the smoke, the Spotting Officer called down in great excitement 'Renown's engaging the *Scharnhorst*.' She was indeed. Though invisible over the horizon, salvoes from her great guns had begun to drop near the German battlecruiser. At the same time she signalled *Antigone* to break off the action and resume her patrol. Somewhere not too far away the *Gneisenau* was lurking. Her sister ship could safely be left to the *Renown*.

But *Scharnhorst* herself had already broken off the battle and was drawing away. From the German point of view this was elementary wisdom. *Antigone*'s hits had caused damage enough: a fifteen-inch salvo could sink them. It would have been satisfactory to have crippled or sunk her smaller adversary but by some lucky chance the British cruiser had remained intact. This was a pity but to wait now and fight it out with a larger and more powerful battlecruiser would be foolhardiness. As soon as the *Scharnhorst* appreciated the situation she made off at top speed, pursued by *Renown* until the driving blizzard swallowed them both. Thus ended *Antigone*'s first full action against the enemy.

The starboard torpedo tubes would not bear, but otherwise *Antigone* had sustained no damage. The ship reverted to cruising stations and continued her pursuit of the *Scharnhorst*. Not, however, for long. The Commander-in-Chief, Home Fleet, signalled that the destroyed *Gloxinia* had been in action with the *Admiral Hipper* and urgently needed assistance. *Antigone* was to proceed and stand-by with all despatch.

It took two hours at full speed to reach the scene of the battle. The weather, though it had not appreciably worsened, was still squally with a fair sea running. On the way they were twice attacked by German aircraft without conclusive results on either side.

'It looks as though things are hotting up, sir,' said Spratt grimly after the second attack. Trevesham grunted. None of them talked very much on the bridge. Things were indeed hotting up. If the *Gloxinia*, a fourteen-hundred-ton destroyer, had been mauled by a German eight-inch-gun cruiser, the aftermath was going to be tricky. The ship might still be afloat but disabled. She would be difficult to take in tow in such a sea. If she had sunk, on the other hand, the outlook for survivors was poor.

It was dusk when they reached the signalled position. There was no sign of *Gloxinia*. Trevesham doubled the lookouts and began to search the area methodically in the fading light. Nothing more had been heard from the destroyer since her distress signal, but *Antigone*'s job was simple and specific. She had to find the ship or if the ship had gone down her survivors. Then as night came on, the inevitable question would have to be faced. Should he continue to risk a valuable cruiser by burning searchlights off an enemy coast or was the quest to be abandoned? Trevesham was not a religious man in the formal sense of the word, but during those anxious dog watches he prayed continuously.

They found the first boatload of survivors within ten minutes of the end Trevesham had set to the search. Around in the sea were other men in life jackets, and a little further away a Carley float to which more oil-soaked men were clinging. *Antigone* got out a scrambling net and down in the port waist, Hatchett and Collard supervised the rescue of their shocked and wounded comrades. It was not an easy operation. *Gloxinia*'s whaler, the only seaboat not shot away in the battle, was filled with eleven wounded men, most of them stokers scalded when one of the destroyer's boiler rooms had been hit. Others covered with oil fuel, coughing up their guts, or numbed by cold and exposure into a dangerous apathy, could scarcely hang on to the net, let alone climb up it. They were a pitiful sight yet Hatchett, as he watched and gave his terse orders, knew that this was no moment for pity. The cruiser was stopped in enemy waters, a magnificent target for lurking U-boats.

The rescue party worked quickly and efficiently, helping up the net those who looked like falling and securing life lines round those who needed to be hauled on board. There were only two officer survivors, a warrant engineer and a sub-lieutenant. The rest had been killed in action or had gone down with the ship. Twenty-seven only remained out of a complement of a hundred and sixty-eight.

The Surgeon-Commander and the sick bay staff had rigged up an emergency dressing station forward of the port waist. One of the messdecks, too, was made into a dormitory where those not wounded but suffering from exposure and shock could be wrapped up in blankets and kept warm.

Gloxinia had been a Portsmouth ship and the sight of these few survivors covered with oil fuel and numbed from immersion in the cold North Sea, provoked a feeling of deep anger in *Antigone*. They had taken survivors on board before, but these were Pompey sailors, their own depot, chaps they might find themselves next to at a Slop Issue or in a pub on the Hard. To *Antigone* this was something personal and very near home.

'When you see this lot,' said Able-Seaman Clarke to the Master-at-Arms as they went about listing the survivors' names, 'you wonder what we was up to during the winter. Makes you want to get right into Germany and *do* all them squareheads good and proper.'

'What makes me maddest of all,' said Hatchett to Collard as he slumped into the next seat in the wardroom when once again *Antigone* was under way, 'is that the *Hipper* just left those poor bastards to drown. They saw the ship sink. And they did nothing about it at all.'

'Well,' said Collard moodily chewing the supper he could scarcely make himself eat, 'I suppose that's why we're fighting this war. They don't seem to change much, do they, over the years?'

'Comradeship of the sea!' muttered Hatchett. 'Wait till I get my hands on a German officer. They aren't fit to *be* at sea.'

The next day it happened again. During the night *Antigone* was ordered south to the Stavanger Fjord area to bombard German positions from the sea. She arrived in time to pick up survivors from another destroyer, the eighteen-hundred-ton *Ghatma* which had been sunk after vicious bombing from the air. This time they could not accuse the enemy of failing to stop and help rescue survivors. This time it was worse. The exultant Luftwaffe had circled after the kill and had deliberately machine-gunned sailors swimming in the water. It was a grey overcast day. The weather had moderated, and as a new batch of half-drowned sailors crawled up the nets on board—like sick bees into a hive—*Antigone* rolled gently in the swell, her lookouts doubly on the watch for a tell-tale periscope, her Captain and Commander, one on the bridge and one down in the waist, both revolted at the carnage, both alive to the danger *Antigone* was in thus stopped in enemy waters, both filled with a deep feeling of disgust at such inhumanity.

It was therefore a curious relief when three Heinkels suddenly appeared from the east and attacked *Antigone*. She was a splendid sitting target, but the feeling on board was not primarily of danger but of cold, cynical rage. The cruiser's eight high-angle guns went into action together.

From *Antigone*'s point of view the attack could not have been worse timed. The rescue of the *Ghatma*'s ship's company was half completed. Trevesham had to decide whether to sit where he was and fight it out or abandon the remaining survivors for the moment and use his speed for evasion. Had *Antigone* been a smaller ship—and thus a more difficult target—the problem might not have been so acute. But she was 555 feet from stem to stern and some fifty-six feet in her beam. It took Trevesham no more than a couple of seconds to determine his duty. He must not risk the ship.

'I'm sorry, Commander,' he called down to Hatchett, 'we must leave them until we're clear of this attack. Tell them we'll be back.'

He did not let himself think of the men in the water as he rang down revolutions for slow speed and then when

310

there was no danger to the men from the screws, full speed ahead. He did not know until afterwards that those still in the sea, some of them wounded, cheered *Antigone* as she drew away.

The German aircraft wasted no time. It seemed from the ship that some of *Antigone's* four-inch shells must surely have hit. Yet the attack was pressed home with a courage and a speed which Trevesham could not but admire. There was no sun for them to dodge into, so with practised skill they attacked from three directions at once. As they came within range the multiple pom-poms on either side of the ship opened up, and to a roar of triumph from the crew one of the Heinkels was observed to be on fire. None of the bombs scored a hit on *Antigone* though all were uncomfortably close. Two of the aircraft sped away along the surface of the sea until they were out of range, then they climbed for the second attack. The third aircraft was soon out of control. It flew in a lame way for about a minute and a half, then suddenly its petrol exploded and it disintegrated in the air. Meanwhile the other two were returning to the attack.

'This is our last chance to bag the lot,' said Brasson to the guns' crews, 'they only carry two bombs. So let's make it a hat trick.'

Trevesham tipped his tin helmet over his eyes and watched the two aircraft approaching. The sharp crack of the four-inch guns was deafening and once again it looked as though the aircraft were attacking through a loose curtain of exploding shells. They came on just the same. This is no mean enemy, thought Trevesham as he put the ship into violent alterations of course. These are cold fanatical fighters and they're going to take a long, long beating before they give in.

There was something evil and fascinating about watching those two aircraft return to the attack, like seeing a look of sudden violence on the face of someone who practises a secret vice. There is always something obscene in physical danger, thought Trevesham, a sudden coming to light of sides of us which are normally buried and unobserved.

'It must be pretty hot up there,' said the Officer of the Watch as the two aircraft came in on their final dive, through a barrage of fire.

311

'It's pretty hot down here,' said Spratt as the ship made another turn of sixty degrees to starboard.

Then two things happened in quick succession. One aircraft released its bomb which missed the ship. The aircraft itself, though, must have had its controls shot away since it failed to pull out of its dive and continued with tremendous force into the sea. The other aircraft was luckier. It came with suicidal directness but apparently unscathed through a fountain of fire from the multiple pom-pom; it released its bomb which struck the foc'sle a tremendous clonk just forward of 'A' turret and then made off to the east. The bomb itself failed to explode. It lay, ugly and dented, up against the mounting of the turret, an unexploded threat to the ship. Trevesham reduced speed and spoke to Brasson up in the director control-tower.

'We've got an uninvited guest on the foc'sle, Guns. It seems to be knocking up a friendship with "A" turret. You'd better go down and take a look at it.'

'Will it explode later on?' asked the Midshipman of the Watch, but no one saw fit to answer this embarrassing question. Trevesham turned the ship on a new course and spoke to the Commander.

'We're going back for the rest of the survivors, Commander. In the meantime clear everyone aft from the foc'sle until we dispose of this bomb.'

'Aye, aye, sir.'

It was not a large bomb but it had dented the deck, and now rolled back and forth with the movement of the ship. Something must have jammed in its percussion fuse, but for how long it would remain that way was entirely a guess.

'I'd like to take it back with us and present it to the backroom boys,' said Brasson to Mr Legg, the Gunner who had climbed up from the transmitting station to look at their new passenger. 'But the vibration might just trigger it free. That cap looks properly jammed. I don't know —I suppose we might get it off.'

'It's not likely to have a booby trap in it, sir, is it?'

'I shouldn't think so,' said Brasson, 'it was designed to be dropped and go off on impact—not lie around and lurk like a mine. Get a strop round it and anchor it to that bollard. I'll report to the Captain.'

When Brasson appeared on the bridge Trevesham knew

312

instinctively the question he was going to be asked. His first impulse was to tell the Gunnery Officer to pitch it over the side. Every moment the bomb remained on board, there was a potential threat to the ship. On the other hand it might offer new data—something might be learnt from it of value to the country. He looked at Honest Tom's red face and his hard blue eyes and then turned away to the sea.

'Have you ever taken one of these things to pieces before?' he asked.

'No, sir. But I know how they *should* be put together.'

'What about you, Torps?'

John Caspar stood beside Brasson, exuding the same determined confidence.

'I think we ought to have a smack at it, sir.'

'I'm not asking you that.'

'No, sir. I've never actually handled one but I know the theory.'

In a few moments, thought Trevesham, we shall be stopped once more picking up the rest of the *Ghatma*'s survivors. We shall be a wonderful sitting target all over again, and now we have a bomb on board which might well blow off the bows.

'The detonator unscrews and lifts out, sir,' said Brasson in the nearest tone of voice which a Whale Island Gunnery Officer can get to pleading. 'I can do it myself with a wrench. Besides, sir, we should have to handle it over the side. It might explode then or when it fell in the sea—unless we work it aft and then crane it into the water.'

Trevesham turned and gave Brasson and his Torpedo Officer another long look.

'Very well,' he said. 'I can't risk you both—and it's against my better judgement.' He nodded briefly at Brasson. 'Good luck with it.'

'Thank you, sir,' said the Gunnery Officer. He saluted and left the bridge with almost indecent haste. I suppose he thinks I might change my mind, Trevesham reflected, and then with a wry smile: Perhaps I won't have a mind to change in the next few moments.

Then followed a period of rare anxiety. During the next hour they were liable at any moment to be blown sky high. Mr Legg had secured the bomb firmly but the cap was jammed in such a position that Brasson could

313

only move it a millimetre at a time. As he worked away on it very much alone on the foc's'le, *Antigone* arrived back among the survivors and, once again bristling with lookouts, stopped and began getting them aboard. On the bridge no one spoke. It was as though everyone held his breath, as though they were all tiptoeing thrugh a huge, shadowy cathedral, hardly daring to let their hearts beat for fear of attracting attention.

Then towards the end when Brasson, swearing and sweating like a three-badge stoker, had succeeded in shifting the detonator about a quarter free, when the last of the survivors were coming aboard and Hatchett could see the finish in sight, when Trevesham brooding on the bridge had decided that the strain to which they were all being subjected was so incongruous as to be ludicrous—a German fighter suddenly appeared at high speed out of a cloud, dived on the ship and raked the deck with machine-gun fire. The anti-aircraft guns opened up again but they were all so tensed up that this attack took them by surprise with its daring.

'Jesus!' said Spratt, who had ducked with the others on the bridge, 'that chap's got a nerve. They must know what Honest Tom's up to.'

But Brasson had been hit. It was the nearest to sudden death he and all of them had yet come. A bullet nicked his shoulder an inch from the detonator as he worked on it and then ricocheted off the armour of the turret. It did not feel bad. He found he could still work on. He was bleeding quite a lot but the end of the job was in sight, and anyway, as he strained and worked he thought of the *Ghatma*'s survivors coming aboard. The Surgeon-Commander would have his hands full with them. This lack of an option seemed to give him new strength.

Twenty minutes later with the rescue complete, *Antigone* got under way again. Trevesham had ordered everyone to remain aft of 'A' turret both above and below decks. But now with no news from Brasson he sent Mr Legg to investigate. From the bridge Brasson's legs could just be seen as he worked in the lee of the turret, but there was no response to Trevesham's hail, and no movement. This was understandable. When Mr Legg came round the turret he found the Gunnery Officer lying in a pool of of his own blood, the detonator in his hand, in a dead faint. But there was no longer any danger to the ship from the bomb.

Norway was to be *Antigone*'s background for the whole of that disastrous April. No sooner had she landed her survivors at Newcastle-on-Tyne—together with a protesting Brasson—than she was ordered to embark a battalion of troops for Aandalsnes.

At this stage Hitler's lightning thrust into Norway had established German power firmly in Oslo and also at the country's main ports—Kristiansand, Bergen, Trondheim and Narvik. But as yet there was no land inter-communication between these ports. The German garrisons were maintained by air and by sea. The Germans were advancing along the two valleys connecting Oslo with Trondheim, but it was thought that if Allied landings could be made to the north and south of Trondheim, this valuable port could be denied to the enemy and Central and Northern Norway could then be held by Allied forces.

Thus landings were planned at Namsos to the north and Aandalsnes to the south—each port being about a hundred miles from Trondheim.

This was the first time *Antigone* had acted as a troop transport. It made a change from the endless patrols. The messdecks were filled with seasick soldiers—'A lovely lot!' said Able-Seaman Elcock. 'Makes you *almost* like the Marines!'—who within twenty-four hours had neverthe-less endeared themselves so much to the ship's company that they felt genuinely sorry to reach the end of the Molde Fjord where they disembarked the soldiers with-out opposition. At that time no one could foresee that in another fortnight they would be withdrawing what was left of them after total defeat.

German supremacy in the air was already apparent. This was the new overriding factor which was altering the whole balance of the war. *Antigone*, once located by Ger-man reconnaissance, was continuously attacked, although the Luftwaffe showed respect for her four-inch high-angle guns and no close attack could be pressed home. The ship at least had teeth she could bare and which occasionally she could snap on to a victim. The troops they landed at Aandalsnes, however, had no such protection. Bombed

315

to a standstill during the day, they could only work and move at night and then most of their effort lay in making repairs. It was an experience soon to be shared by the British Expeditionary Force in France and Belgium, but as *Antigone* drew out of the Fjord and left the military to it, the main feeling in the ship was one of helpless sympathy for their mates in khaki.

'It's all right for *us*,' the Chief Yeoman remarked to Vincent, as the Norwegian coastline disappeared astern, 'we can get on out of it and give back as good as we get on the way. But those poor bloody pongos,' he sucked his teeth reflectively, '*I* don't know—they all look a bit out of date somehow—like they were playing a game where someone's gone and altered the rules.'

The Germans had not merely changed the rules: they had kicked them once more into the gutter. Hitler respected nothing but greater strength and at that time only the Royal Navy enjoyed more ships, better material and greater power than their German opposite numbers. The British Army and the Royal Air Force were struggling with insufficient and often inadequate equipment. They were grossly outnumbered and in all the countries which fell into the German grasp that summer they were continuously in danger of a sudden stab in the back from the Quisling fifth column. It was, as Mellish had remarked, a much easier matter for the Royal Navy. The odds were still on their side. A German submarine in a feat of splendid daring might penetrate into Scapa Flow and torpedo the battleship *Royal Oak*. Later that April in the withdrawal from Central Norway, the aircraft carrier *Glorious* might be caught by the *Scharnhorst* and *Gneisenau* and sunk with all her fighters aboard—but these were still small pinpricks in the great shield. The Senior Service had this prestige and its accompanying aura of success which the RAF did not acquire till the Battle of Britain that autumn and the Army not for another two years at Alemein. But in *Antigone* none of them took their luckier position in arrogance: instead it generated sympathy for the other two services who were 'having it rough'.

All through April they ferried troops and equipment to Central Norway. Then after the 26th they began taking them out again. It was a sorry, dispiriting game. The snowcapped Norwegian mountains came to represent in their minds the background to a kind of recurring failure. It was not the Army's fault, nor could blame be laid on the token Royal Air Force units which were sent. It was simply that both services and indeed the Allies themselves were badly overtaken by events. With Central Norway lost and evacuated it was decided to transfer the Norwegian Government to Tromso and to renew the siege of Narvik, at that time cut off and still out of the range of heavy bombers.

So as the days lengthened *Antigone* moved north. Operations were based on Harstad. An airfield was constructed. Shielded by the Home Fleet, British and French troops were landed in safety, and the Royal Navy likewise prevented any German reinforcement of their far northern garrison. This continued through May until the 28th. Narvik fell to the Allies and fighting ceased among the wreckage of British and German destroyers which were littering the harbour. It was a moment of peace. But this lasted no more than a few days. Then once again the heavy bombers began to arrive.

By the end of May, too, disaster was threatening in France. The German invasion of France and the Low Countries had begun on 10 May with spectacular success. The much-treasured Maginot Line proved to be the white elephant it had long been suspected. Things were going very badly indeed for the Allies. The day Narvik was captured, King Leopold of the Belgians surrendered his country to the Germans and the day after, the heroic evacuation of the British Expeditionary Force began through the Dunkirk Beaches.

With the RAF heavily committed in the south: with the Third Republic of France rocking to its doom three weeks later: with Narvik eight hundred sea miles direct from Scapa Flow and considerably more when setting course to avoid the Norwegian airfields: with the *Scharnhorst* and *Gneisenau* based on Trondheim it was decided that Norway must be abandoned.

Once again *Antigone* was called upon to evacuate troops. This time there was no rearguard action. It was all ordered and calm. Nevertheless no one could dodge the fact that it was another withdrawal, another tacit defeat.

The King and Government of Norway left Tromso sadly
and reluctantly. They arrived in London on the night of
10 June 1940. Earlier that same day Italy had declared
war on Great Britain and France.

CHAPTER FOURTEEN

Antigone's next important assignment was at Cherbourg
just before the final evacuation on 22 June. This was to
be their last job of work in home waters.

'Nothing but a transport—that's all we are,' griped the
lower deck. 'Pongos, Norwegians, pongos, RAF, pongos,
French, Poles, Czechs, pongos, civilians, pongos, pongos,
pongos!'

But although the ship was always bursting at the seams
and correspondingly difficult to work, they were glad to
have visitors aboard. By this time *Antigone* had been host
in peace and war to almost every imaginable visitor rang-
ing from West Indian negroes to French Cabinet Minis-
ters, from Peruvian aristocrats to Norwegian fishermen,
from wealthy Americans to disillusioned Danes.

After the two anxious months in Norwegian waters,
ferrying across the Channel came as child's play. Brasson
had returned to the ship, his shoulder healed. Trevesham
was glad to have him back. He did not tell him that a
recommendation for the DSO was on its way from
Commander-in-Chief to Admiralty. Now that *Antigone*
was being attacked continuously from the air, Brasson
strengthened his anti-aircraft guns at the expense of the
main armament. The four-inch high-angle guns and the
pom-poms were never long silent these days, but there
was no sign of a surface enemy for the six-inch guns to
engage.

They were sombre trips. Cherbourg itself had not
greatly changed although each attack from the Luftwaffe
brought down a crane here and a warehouse there. It was
the shocked and broken French whom they ferried to

Portsmouth, on whose faces the full tragedy was written. It was there in the shrug of the shoulders, the drooping Gauloise from the lips, the almost feminine disdain of Anglo-Saxon toughness. It lay in the dead eyes, the air of utter desolate hopelessness and their almost virulent dislike of being taken out of France and over to England— even though no one could come aboard *Antigone* unless he was a proved volunteer. The general contrariness of the French defeated every attempt of the ship's company to cheer them up, to help them or even make them feel at home.

'Talk about biting the hand that feeds them . . .', growled the Master-at-Arms as he watched their French military passengers brusquely refusing the pea soup and toad-in-the-hole so popular on *Antigone*'s lower deck. That was the general attitude. But some of them such as the Captain, Collard, and Marsh could see that what sickened the French had nothing to do with *Antigone* nor even with England. It was their own fatal collapse that had felled them. It so happened, though, that the ship was the first 'point of reaction'—the first place where their misery could be expressed—where they could grumble and grouse and behave abominably by English standards and yet still be suffered and protected.

'There's not a speck of gratitude in the lot of them,' Hatchett remarked to Collard as they watched their passengers shuffling down the gangway on to English soil, 'and personally I never did trust 'em.'

Collard glanced down at his stubby, compressed-looking Commander, the gold-peaked cap at its usual jaunty angle, the telescope aggressively rammed under his arm. He did not really trust the French either but it made him smile to see how completely incompatible they were to Hatchett. The Commander was yelling down now to one of the French officers on the jetty who was lighting a cigarette.

'*Ici* no smoking, *Capitain*, *pas fumer—Angleterre*.'

But the Frenchman was strangely deaf and in the interests of the entente Collard took the Commander across the quarterdeck to ask his advice on a modification to the depth-charge rails which had been giving them trouble. There was enough misunderstanding between the Allies as there was without souring things further.

It was part of Marsh's duty to keep a tally of the passengers they had aboard on these trips. He enjoyed going about the ship doing this. Even rough and ready as things were nowadays, *Antigone* was still a great cruiser in full commission. There was a pride in mothering their hapless refugees and in doing it out of strength. The ship's routine might have had to bend somewhat to events, but they were still one of his Majesty's major ships of war. England now stood alone, under daily threat of invasion—but she was still a great power and a whole one.

In receiving these ragged people on board, therefore, officers were of course properly dressed, the side was still piped and the quarterdeck saluted. Orders were obeyed at the double and Royal Marine buglers and sentries still had that smartness of bearing as they stamped about the deck, carrying out their harbour duties with the 'click and finish' of guardsmen outside Buckingham Palace.

Their French visitors might jeer at formality in times such as these. But as they were politely stationed about the ship, shown which heads to use and where to draw hot soup, asked to extinguish their cigarettes in sand-filled spitkids instead of stamping them out on the deck, asked by dozens of kindly sailors, 'Issy Bonn? OK? Got everything you want, chum?' and similar inquiries—it stood out a mile that there was still an active heart and intelligence behind the Royal Navy. The English might have their backs to the wall, but aboard *Antigone* there would be no slouching about the decks.

On one of their last trips came a coincidence which to Marsh made nonsense of the whole débâcle. They had nosed into Cherbourg again and soon another flood of refugees was pouring on board. In the early stages *Antigone* had restricted her hospitality to Allied soldiers and airmen with an occasional 'proved' civilian. Now that total French collapse was only a few hours in the future, they took all-comers who wanted to get away. There was now a preponderance of civilians, women and children. On this occasion Marsh had been down in the cypher office and had delegated the collecting of names and identities to the Chief Writer of the ship's office. He had been up most of the night and was exhausted himself. When the Chief Writer came to see him, therefore, with the long haphazard list, Marsh only groaned and said:

'I'm going to get my head down, Chief, for a couple of hours before starting in on that.'

'Yes, sir,' said the Chief Writer with the trace of a smile, 'but one of our guests has a special message for you. She says—perhaps you remember a Lisette Champlain from Valparaiso.'

'Good God!' said Marsh, jumping up so fast he banged his head a fearful clout on a low bulkhead. 'Where is she, for heaven's sake?'

'Well, sir, her father's got a diplomatic passport so naturally I put them in the Captain's day cabin in accordance with——'

'Yes, yes,' said Marsh in a ferment, 'don't go into all that.'

'But seeing as she's an old shipmate of ours, sir—in a manner of speaking—I did manage to extricate her from the others and put her in your cabin, sir, after asking the sub-lieutenant's permission.'

Marsh grabbed his cap and sped along to his cabin, his heart beating more wildly than he had ever known it in his life. The ship was already under way and overhead he could hear the anti-aircraft guns in action again. It was a slow business unclipping the watertight doors and clipping them up again afterwards, and it gave his progress a kind of breathless syncopation. Moreover, although he had stepped through these doors countless times in the past two years, now he was so agitated that he barked his shin with a searing pain which made him swear, but which he forgot all about as at last he slid open his cabin door and found her standing by the bunk, smoking a cigarette and looking him straight in the eyes.

'Lisette!' he cried and in another moment was hugging her desperately, rocking her gently in his arms, kissing her ears, her throat and her mouth in a sudden fever of pent-up longing.

'*Antoine! Pauvre petit Antoine!*' she said softly. 'Is this the correct greeting from the Royal Navy? No formality? No protocol? Here is my father!'

It was only then that Derek Lysander Marsh became aware of a thin, grey-haired Frenchman standing by the other bunk with a look of tired amusement on his face.

'How do you do, sir?' said Marsh formally, and then gave his attention back to Lisette. They looked into each

321

other's eyes, their arms round each other's waists as the guns blazed away and somewhere behind them in Cherbourg the bombs continued to fall. At that moment the ship could have blown up and sunk. It would not have mattered to Derek Lysander Marsh.

But if Fate had thrown a giddy gift into his lap, it allowed him no time to enjoy it. There was no leave at Portsmouth. They were to disembark their passengers and set off again for Cherbourg. Although *Antigone* had not taken part in the Dunkirk evacuation, these ferry trips to Cherbourg were beginning to have much the same kind of smell.

Lisette and her father left the ship at South Railway Jetty. Marsh watched them from the quarterdeck. At the foot of the gangway, Lisette turned and waved. But that was all. She had promised to send him her address as soon as they were settled. It would surely be London, she said, since her father was a diplomat. He would need her to look after him since her mother had died earlier in the year. But as Marsh watched them being swallowed up in the emergency immigration machine, he wondered sadly if Fate was offering him something with one hand to snatch it out of his grasp again with the other. It was an extraordinary summer, both on a national and a personal scale. The suddenness with which the little countries had fallen: the total collapse of their great ally, France: the unheralded arrival of Lisette aboard, which to Marsh was as though he had been groping in the dark and had accidentally found the light switch—and now, once more, the return to sea: the getting on with the job.

When France did finally surrender, the blow was so numbing that their personal lives were swallowed up in it. They had been ordered to stand off the French coast near the naval port of L'Orient when the news came through.

'I simply can't believe it,' said Meldrum as the signal was put up on the wardroom board. 'It just doesn't make sense.'

Through the wardroom scuttles they could see the blue waters of the Bay of Biscay strangely calm and sunlit. No one in the ante-room felt like talking. They brooded, each one alone in his thoughts. Marsh went along to his cabin, leant his arms on his bunk and suddenly found himself

crying. This emotion took him quite by surprise. He did
not know why he cried. He thought about the Germans
strutting through Paris, the brutalities of the blitzkrieg, the
stories the refugees had all had to tell. But it wasn't any of
those things. It was simply a physical feeling which possessed him. France has fallen, he kept murmuring to himself, as the tears poured down his face. Poor France—
poor France. He was glad this thing had not caught him
with the others in the mess. He did not understand why
but it was a terribly personal loss.

Within hours of this catastrophe, the fearful consequences began to emerge from the shadows. The French
ports were now enemy held. It was incredible but true.
Not since Napoleon had England been in such danger of
invasion. The Germans were now only twenty miles away
across the Strait of Dover. At once U-boats began slinking
into the Channel and Biscay ports, fuelling and then striking out further and further into the Atlantic. The RAF
might make things hot for visiting German warships but a
port was still a port.

The most tragic effect of all, though, was the destruction of the French Fleet. This was desperate, urgent and
almost unbearably poignant. It was a Naval matter and
it fell upon the Navy to carry out this sombre Cabinet decision. Attempts had been made in the last hours of the
French Government's life to get the fleet ordered to British
ports before concluding an armistice with Germany. But
this failed. The armistice terms declared that the French
Fleet was to be immobilized and disarmed under German
supervision. French politicians might talk themselves into
believing that this would be done, but no one who looked
back on Hitler's previous promises could be other than
cynical, and the British Chiefs of Staff could not afford
that in July 1940. A disclaimer from a ruthless enemy—a
promise from a broken Government no longer in power—
these were not good enough when England was quite on
her own, fighting as she had never fought before to save
herself and the free world.

On 22 June there had been a number of French warships at British ports. There was a squadron, including
eight-inch cruisers, at Alexandria. These were put under
restraint and most of them later on continued the war on
the allied side. The main battle strength of the French

Navy, however, lay at Mers-el-Kebir, near to Oran. This consisted, in the main, of the battlecruisers *Dunkerque* and *Strasbourg*, and three battleships of the 'Bretagne' class. These ships, added now to the Italian fleet, could have materially altered the balance of power against the Royal Navy. Their disposal had become a problem of the first urgency.

'HMS *Antigone* is to proceed forthwith to Gibraltar with all despatch:' read the Admiralty signal, 'she is to form part of Force H until further orders.'

'And what is Force H?' asked the sub-lieutenant RNVR as he and Marsh decyphered the message.

'I don't know what it consists of at present, but it's the main striking force under Admiral Somerville at the western end of the Med. It's usually made up of a battlecruiser, one or two battleships, an aircraft-carrier, part of a cruiser squadron and a destroyer flotilla. I wonder what's up this time?'

They were soon to find out. Force H at Gibraltar was almost exactly as Marsh had described it. On 1 July *Antigone*, her funnel salt-caked but otherwise in perfect trim, arrived under the shadow of the Rock to find herself in company with HMS *Hood*, the most powerful warship in the world, the battleships *Valiant* and *Resolution*, the famous *Ark Royal*, *Antigone*'s sister-ship the *Leander* and another cruiser. On 3 July, this squadron, shielded on either flank by a destroyer flotilla, arrived off Oran. It was a formidable fleet.

The long parley began. As the several alternatives were placed before the French Admiral, any of which he could have accepted with honour, the British Fleet patrolled slowly off the harbour mouth. Trevesham, hunched as usual on his high stool on the bridge, looked round at the familiar ships. He felt a kind of nausea in the pit of his stomach. It was like waiting in the ante-room of a law court while somebody's fate was decided.

It was a clear calm Mediterranean day with the sunlight hard upon the water. The Fleet moved slowly, protected against submarines by the destroyer screen, each ship's company closed up at Action Stations, waiting, waiting, waiting. Trevesham had never encouraged chatter on the bridge but now the tension was so great he would have welcomed it if Spratt had recited the multiplication table. Even an aircraft attack, he thought to himself looking across at the fighters and torpedo bombers on the *Ark Royal*'s deck, even that would do something to help. But they were far out of range of German and Italian aircraft, and nothing disturbed the brooding heat of the day.

Then at last Vice-Admiral Somerville signalled the tragic news. 'The French Admiral refuses all British proposals. Take action as previously ordered.' At the same time the *Dunkerque* was observed to be putting to sea.

Antigone was not called upon to open fire. She was there to give chase and to shadow if need be. She thus had to stand by and watch the great guns of the *Hood*, *Valiant* and *Resolution* open fire on the French Fleet. It was a ghastly, gruesome, shocking spectacle.

One or two ships returned a feeble, ineffective fire but quite clearly the French, dispirited and disaffected as they were, had also been taken by surprise. The British were thought to be bluffing. They would never fire on the French who had so lately been their staunchest allies. How wrong the Admiral at Oran had been, proved, thought Trevesham, as he watched the huge salvoes dropping on their target, in turn starting fires and explosions. And how easy it is to go wrong, another voice inside him murmured, when the two giants of Pride and Vanity are at work.

'Pity it can't be the Jerries at the receiving end,' the Navigator remarked. 'But I suppose that's too much to hope for in this year of grace.'

Meanwhile England was now under daily threat. The Battle of the Atlantic had gone gravely against us. The Battle of Britain bringing its saturation raids on London, its wholesale evacuation and its burning heroism from the 'very few' was opening up. Things were black indeed. The Mediterranean, too, had become a critical area. Friendly or neutral since the outbreak of war, it was now barbed and hostile. Malta was at risk. The Mediterranean Fleet, dispersed to more essential uses, was now reformed and convoys to Alexandria were given Fleet protection.

This now became part of *Antigone*'s duty. After Oran the ship was ordered back to Gibraltar and then picked up the first through convoy to Alexandria since Italy entered the war. This was a Fleet operation. Two battle-

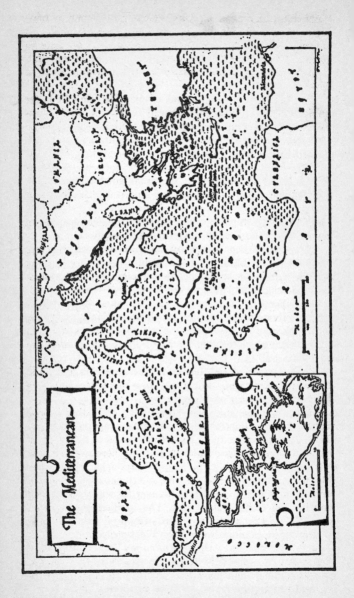

The Mediterranean

ships, the *Royal Sovereign* and the *Ramillies*, the cruisers *Leander* and *Newcastle* and a destroyer flotilla took the convoy safely through to Malta, and then handed over to another Force from the Eastern Mediterranean.

Malta was glad to see them. The Italian raids were becoming more frequent and the long siege had begun. It seemed to Trevesham far more than two years since they had worked up in Grand Harbour, since strident dghaissamen had last waited off the stern for shoregoing officers, since the smell of decayed goat and the tintinnabulation of bells came wafting across the water.

'They say you always come back,' Spratt remarked as they secured alongside at breakfast time. 'I can't say I ever wanted to very much in peacetime. It's a bit different now.'

As he spoke the sirens went, the anti-aircraft gun crews closed up and a few moments later firing began.

'Well, Pilot,' said Trevesham, as he went down off the bridge. 'They've given us all of three hours in harbour to freshen up on our memories. I'm going to give a hot bath and some bacon and eggs.'

Trevesham felt continuously tired these days. There was every excuse for this but it still disturbed him. As he shaved he studied himself in the mirror, trying to see exactly where he had aged. Two years of running the lives of six hundred men and two million pounds' worth of warship had deepened the lines on his face. Diana would notice more wrinkles where his eyes had creased up through the long night watches on the bridge. It seemed to him nowadays that he was always a little deaf from the sharp crack of the four-inch anti-aircraft guns. He wiped the shaving soap off his face and gave himself a last critical look. His hair was now grey all over and soon at this rate it would be white. 'Yes,' he murmured aloud, 'you're getting to look like an old, old man.' How odd it was! It seemed such a tiny time since he had been a cadet at the Royal Naval College in his 'bum-freezer' and dirk, worrying about his seamanship and his chilblains.

He rang for his steward.

'Sir?'

'Ask the Commander if he would care to breakfast with me—and if he's had his breakfast, then to come and see me in fifteen minutes.'

'Aye, aye, sir.'

With so much time spent on the bridge these days, Trevesham seized every chance of consulting with the Commander on the day-to-day administration of the ship. After a long patrol at sea, when his life was spent entirely on the bridge itself or in his sea-cabin immediately below, he felt strangely out of touch with the ship. It worked and worked well, but in a curiously detached and independent way. Now, in these three hours which they had suddenly been allowed at Malta, there was a chance to draw the family bonds together again. He wanted to see his ship's company again, a good solid mass of sailors, mustered together on the quarterdeck. And this morning there was an especial reason to do so. It was a piece of news Marsh had brought him in the night and which he had ordered to be kept secret till now.

'Guns has been given the DSO for that bomb,' he told the Commander as they tackled the small Spanish eggs from Gibraltar. 'That should buck us all up and it's about time the ship's company and I had a look at each other again.'

'That's an excellent bit of news,' said Hatchett. He thought about this award for a moment or so and then went on: 'When you talk to the ship's company, perhaps you can ease their minds a little about the bombing at home. They're all a bit restive over their families and the blitz. For that matter so am I. Alice has got herself that job in the Foreign Office.'

'I'm glad about that.'

'It's what she wanted. A kind of independence at last.'

Trevesham thought how impossible it would have been to talk like that about Diana. He realized with a sudden pang the isolation and sealing-off of people's inner lives. He did not know how much it mattered to Hatchett. Perhaps it didn't matter at all.

'I gather things are pretty sticky in London.'

'It's put up the gin consumption in Whitehall pubs quite a lot, I believe. Alice says when the raids are at their worst they all dart across the road to fortify their nerves. It's a costly business, she says.'

After they had had breakfast they got down to a blitz of their own on the business of the ship. Both of them rather enjoyed these combined attacks on outstanding work. Marsh was called in, the Gunnery and Torpedo Officers, the Commander (E) and the Paymaster-Commander each had a session. At sea routine reports, inspections of ship's books, etc, could all be sent up to the Captain's sea-cabin for signature. But this was an intermittent and chancy business. Occasionally, too, on quiet patrols Trevesham would find time to discuss departmental problems with his officers.

But in a cruiser the size of *Antigone*, wartime administrative problems generally took a back seat when the ship was at sea. Little things piled up which did not merit a chit to the Captain but on which an opinion, a decision, a word of advice could perhaps do all that was wanted. So Trevesham's and Hatchett's three hours in harbour were spent separately and together in purging the ship of her troubles, in seeing Requestmen and Defaulters, in talking things over with people at all levels in the ship. While they did this two more air-raids were made upon Malta. The AA defences of the Dockyard went into action and the ship's high-angle guns also opened fire.

It was also during this short time at Malta that *Antigone* received the Admiralty signal determining her fate. 'HMS *Antigone* is to be detached to the UK in order to pay off, arriving 3 October at Belfast. She is then to undergo a two months' refit at Harland and Wolff's yard in Belfast' read the Most Secret signal. Trevesham passed it over to Hatchett.

'So the end's in sight,' he murmured. 'Peace or war, nothing alters the Admiralty's refitting programme.'

He was aware of a sudden relief mingled with keen regret. Once a limit has been set to a thing, its whole context changes. He noticed that Marsh, who had brought him the signal, seemed scarcely able to contain his excitement.

'Well, Secretary,' said Trevesham. 'It looks like a new job of work for us all.'

'Yes, sir,' said Marsh but his thoughts were all on Lisette. He nearly jumped out of his skin, therefore, at his Captain's next remark.

'I suppose you'll be asking for a transfer to the Free French forces,' he said with a smile.

Hatchett handed the signal back to the Captain's Sec-

329

retary. It would go to the other Heads of Departments but to nobody else.

'What about the ship's company, sir, can they be told?' asked Hatchett.

Trevesham thought about this for a while. He thought how the news would be received on the messdecks. He thought about the security grading of the signal and then he thought about the blitz on London, the wives and the families at home.

'I think I can tell them we'll be home this year for Christmas. They needn't know the exact where and when.'

For the rest of July and the whole of August, *Antigone* was employed in Fleet operations in the Mediterranean, covering the passage of convoys to Alexandria. At home the Battle of Britain raged to its climax. Behind this daily avalanche of destruction and still oppressed by the threat of invasion, the Prime Minister, Mr Churchill, had taken one of the most courageous decisions in the whole history of warfare. This was to send out to Egypt and the Western Desert the only three armoured regiments ready at that time for service, together with their last precious hundred and fifty tanks. If these were sunk then for the present there could be no more.

These tanks were sent round the Cape. The Prime Minister wished them to be convoyed through the Mediterranean, but the First Sea Lord would not accept this risk. Although German dive-bombers had not yet moved down to the Mediterranean, Italian high-level bombing could proceed almost without interruption, and valuable ships which were not sunk by this means might nevertheless be damaged and slowed down to the point of having to drop out of convoy. Once this happened they could be finished off at the enemy's leisure.

In *Antigone*, of course, they knew nothing of these matters except what they saw with their own eyes. Trevesham, with his Staff experience, could guess a little deeper than the others by reading between the lines both of signals and of the broadcast news. But, except for intelligent deduction, *Antigone* was no different from any other constable on the beat. They were still at the job which had consumed the bulk of their previous year—the convoying and protection of merchant ships with their valuable cargoes. Like painting the Forth Bridge, Spratt had once described it: you no sooner finished one end than you started back on the other.

But, now, this autumn of 1940, with the knowledge that soon they would be returning to England to pay off, their approach to their daily tussle with the sea and the intermittent hazards of war seemed appreciably to lighten. They fed on hope. As the bombs fell out of the sky into the blue Mediterranean waters from aircraft far out of *Antigone*'s range the gun crews shouted abuse, but they shouted defiantly without a trace of despair. Soon they would be home. Home for a spell of leave after two-and-a-half long years at sea. Bombs, mines, torpedoes, shells—let them all come. *Antigone* would soon be flying her long paying-off pendant, her duty for the moment done.

So it was, at the very beginning of September, on a dark squally night that *Antigone* left Gibraltar on her last convoy to the east. She was in distinguished company. Two light cruisers had come out from England to join the Mediterranean Fleet. They were exactly what was called for at that moment. Their main armament had been removed and in its place their decks bristled with anti-aircraft guns of every type and size. There were two fifteen-inch battleships, and more important still, HMS *Illustrious* was in company. This was the Royal Navy's latest aircraft-carrier, and the first one to be fitted with radar. This great ship with her new and more deadly aircraft was in herself to alter the balance of power in England's favour until the Germans came down into the Mediterranean in 1941.

But *Antigone* knew nothing of this. The next day the anti-aircraft cruisers were studied with interest and the *Illustrious* with awe. 'Very handy for deck hockey' said Chief Yeoman Mellish as he examined the flight deck through his telescope, and Grey-Bennett aired his technical opinions on the aircraft she carried. 'Frankly,' he observed, 'it's an honour to be in her company.'

'Frankly,' growled Spratt, 'you airmen are all in love with yourselves.' For Spratt the Fleet Air Arm and the Gunnery Department ranked equal bottom in popularity. He imagined what it would be like trying to take the *Illustrious* into Portsmouth Harbour in a high cross wind.

He patted the compass repeater affectionately. 'Good old *Aunty*,' he muttered. 'No longer the newest but still easily the best.'

Yet even Spratt had to admit an excitement in opening up the Mediterranean again with such a fleet. After this passage, convoys were to be regularly run from Gibraltar to Malta and on to Alexandria until control of the Mediterranean was lost to us in March 1941. During the two days that followed they were attacked in the usual way by Italian aircraft flying high out of gun range, but now *Illustrious* sent up her fighters and four out of the six bombers fell crashing into the sea. The other two lumbered back to Italy to spread the bad news. They were not attacked again until Malta lay behind them. Then a force of nearly thirty bombers rained down their bombs on the sea astern of the fleet and the convoy. Radar was already proving its value. This time the fighters were airborne when the Italians arrived and nine of the bombers were shot down.

Then came the signal from the Commander-in-Chief Mediterranean to the Senior Officer of their Group which they had all been hoping to receive. 'There are indications that Italian Battle Fleet has left Taranto and is at sea. Detach two cruisers and destroyer escort to patrol Ionian Sea in area Zante to Cape Matapan.'

So it began.

In the early stages it was like any other of the countless missions they had embarked upon without success. The convoy, the escort and the rest of the covering force disappeared over the hard rim of the horizon, and *Antigone* was left in company with *Aurora*, another six-inch cruiser, and two destroyers. After the presence of *Illustrious* and the battleships, they seemed to be very much alone.

'An odd thing really,' Spratt observed, 'when you think of all those months we spent quite by ourselves in the Atlantic and Pacific.'

HMS *Aurora* was of slightly smaller displacement than *Antigone*. She mounted six six-inch guns to *Antigone*'s eight, but otherwise her potentialities were much the same. Even so they were no possible match for a capital ship. They had but one slight advantage over any Italian battleship they might encounter and that was speed. Their role was clear. They were the sprats cast into the Ionian Sea to catch what was hoped would be a shoal of mackerel. They spread out on a twenty-mile sweep at a speed of some twenty-eight knots. At this speed, and zigzagging as they were, although it was not possible for the destroyers to operate their Asdics, the risk of submarine attack was small. Thus through the afternoon they continued to sweep the empty sea.

None of the four ships was fitted with radar. Therefore the keenest point of intelligence at that moment aboard stood perched up in the crow's nest. These lookouts were changed every two hours. The rest of the human machinery on board, closed up as it perennially was at cruising stations, relaxed as best it could. Their time would come later. But upon the look-outs aloft, each of them an able-seaman in his early twenties, the fate of the ship depended and, indeed, at one remove possibly the fate of British power in the Mediterranean sea.

So afternoon turned to night and the night passed. With dawn came a signal from the Commander-in-Chief ordering the two cruisers to part company. *Antigone* was to sweep south-west from Matapan and *Aurora* to search in the Ægean north of Crete. If the Italians had not doubled back to Taranto, if they were again edging away from an encounter with the British, then possibly their purpose in being at sea was to reinforce Rhodes.

Now with her single destroyer escort *Antigone* was more than ever alone. Once they happened upon a fishing boat, but otherwise it began to look from the bridge and masthead as though this was just another abortive mission. Soon, no doubt, the search would be called off and they would rejoin the convoy on the last stage of its voyage to Alexandria.

Down below the ship's routine turned and repeated as it had done for over two years. In the galley bacon rashers and sausages for six hundred men were being cooked by PO Cook Jenkins and his staff. Hammocks were being lashed up and stowed by 'Guard and Steerage' watchkeepers. Able-Seaman Clarke was scrubbing out the Commander's office. Marsh, feeling as though he had scarcely had a wink of sleep, was on his way down to the cypher office for the forenoon watch. In the engine room Meldrum was taking a quick look round, relishing his first smell of steam and oil before going up to the wardroom for breakfast. Hatchett was shaving in his cabin and the Paymaster-Commander was putting on his winged collar, affixing it round his neck with the same stiff fingers he had used for twenty-five years. The Surgeon-Commander was taking a breath of fresh air on the quarterdeck. Guns was in the wardroom heads and Midshipman Mottram was writing a letter home.

Up in the plotting room the Instructor-Lieutenant finished drawing his weather map and then took it up to the Navigating Officer on the bridge.

'There's a new depression not far to the west of us,' he pointed out, 'and it's coming up at some speed. There was no trace of it in the last report.'

'What's the glass doing?'

'Falling.'

Spratt considered the implications of this. They were heading almost directly into the weather and already there were banks of clouds on the horizon. It meant a new factor in their day's search. It meant rain, a rising sea and bad visibility.

'Thanks, Schooly,' said Spratt. 'I'd better tell the Old Man.'

Trevesham was having breakfast in his sea-cabin. It had been another night of constantly interrupted sleep leaving him dulled and without appetite. He had a depressed feeling that now they would never make contact with the Italians.

'Captain, sir.' Spratt called down the voice pipe.

'Yes?'

'Schooly's just brought up the weather map. We're running into a warm front. In about an hour's time we can expect visibility to close, some rain and wind freshening from south'ard.'

'What's the weather like now?'

'Still shining at the moment, sir, but it's clouding up to windward.'

'Very well,' said Trevesham, and returned to his egg. The weather was certainly not going to make things any easier for them.

An hour later, as Spratt had forecast, they were well into the warm front. Rain clouds swirled about them and the sea was getting up. 'Spend your Holidays in the Sunny

South,' Spratt muttered as a gust of rain drenched his face. 'The Blue Mediterranean Welcomes You.'

At that moment through a gap in the rain, the masthead lookout caught sight of a tripod mast on the horizon. Two seconds later 'Action Stations' sounded-off urgently in every part of the ship.

CHAPTER FIFTEEN

Antigone's first duty was to report the enemy and this Trevesham did straight away. But this initial sighting had been snatched out of the bad weather which was now closing in on them more and more. The scene had suddenly darkened and events were now scarcely predictable. Anything might happen and indeed could do so with startling rapidity.

Trevesham had no idea if the Italians had sighted *Antigone*. From the bridge visibility had perhaps been eight miles. From masthead to masthead the distance might have been anything up to twenty-five miles, and nothing but a glimpse of the enemy's mast had been seen from their own masthead. The enemy's course was unknown. They might at this moment have lost touch altogether or they might be running slap into each other at an alarming rate. It was impossible to know.

'Reduce to twenty-five knots!' Trevesham ordered. In such obscurity it was instinctive to reduce speed. Yet his immediate task was to close the enemy and establish contact. By now everyone on the bridge had binoculars trained into the driving rain. Up in the director control-tower rangefinders were sweeping the horizon hoping to find a sudden clear patch. On the bridge the Torpedo Officer, the PCO and the Officer of the Watch glared hopelessly into the darkening clouds. To surprise the Italians by even a couple of minutes might mean the difference between success and a total defeat, not only for *Antigone* herself but for the Mediterranean Fleet. A lone cruiser was in desperate danger had she run into the Italian Battle Fleet in good weather. Masked by a squall, invisible but with the possibility of a tip-and-run appearance in the heart of the Italian formation, the odds were dramatically shortened.

Trevesham paced up and down on the bridge. He analysed the possibilities in his mind, working out the immediate courses of action he would take for each variant. The bad weather gave him a dazzling advantage. It gnawed at him. He must seize the initiative while he had it. No weather conditions hold for very long in the Mediterranean. The present driving rain would soon be followed by a cold front and the return of sunshine and a calmer sea. It was now or never. But he *had* to know where the enemy was and where she was going. He had to know those facts and know them now.

'Prepare to launch the float plane,' Trevesham told the Officer of the Watch. 'Tell Lieutenant Grey-Bennett I want to see him at once.'

Everyone on the bridge knew what this meant. It put the situation into brilliant perspective. Visibility was now little more than half a mile, and the rain seemed to cut into their faces. It would be tricky enough to fly off the aircraft. The chances of recovering it were nil. Even if the weather changed *Antigone* would not be able to stop and hoist the machine back on board. So, to gain the information he needed, Trevesham was forced to sacrifice two men and a valuable seaplane.

'Poor old sod!' Spratt muttered to himself as he watched Marcel in his flying-kit being briefed by the Captain. He wondered what was going on in Grey-Bennett's mind. He wondered how he would feel himself had he been ordered to shadow the enemy battle fleet till his fuel ran out and then make for the Greek coast, with almost no chance of survival.

Down by the catapult Mr Partle was making his usual checks. The Commander had come up to see his last launching of the aircraft and in a matter of moments it all seemed to be over. Grey-Bennett and the telegraphist air-gunner climbed into the machine, the engine roared, the thumbs-up sign was given and the launching charge was fired. One moment they were there, the next they were a speck swallowed up in the mist.

Both Hatchett and Mr Partle saluted them as they went. A few seconds later the mist had closed in again and there was nothing to be seen. The little group round the catapult remained in silence, staring after the vanished machine. Then Hatchett nodded briefly to Mr Partle and went below. They both had other jobs to be done.

Grey-Bennett himself flew through the squall with a confusion of emotions chasing each other through his consciousness. He was acutely aware of the danger. This was an event he had long anticipated. He knew he was expendable. He knew he would be one of the first to be risked simply because it was on his eyes and on his flying that the ship depended in the early stages of any engagement.

He had worked it all out many many times before. Yet now that it had actually come about, he could scarcely believe it. He was very afraid. He hoped he had managed to conceal it when the Captain was telling him what he wanted. He felt pretty sure he had carried off the interview with his usual nonchalance. Only he wished he had not been so embarrassed when the Captain unexpectedly shook his hand. But now as he flew through the clouds and sped on to where he thought the Italians would be, he found himself helplessly in the grip of fear. He flew the aircraft automatically, groping in his consciousness for the self-control he knew he must find, if he was ever to survive.

Ten minutes later *Antigone* received her first sighting report from the aircraft. 'Two battleships "Cavour" class, three cruisers "Zara" type, four destroyers course approximately 290°. Am closing to verify.'

This was the last that any of them heard from Grey-Bennett. A few moments later a burst of anti-aircraft fire penetrated the cockpit killing both Grey-Bennett and his observer a fraction of a second before the aircraft itself exploded in mid-air. Thus the ship sustained her first casualty before being properly in action with the enemy. It left her once more eyeless in the mist, and as minute dragged on into minute, the wireless silence told them all only too clearly what must have happened.

'So that's that!' Spratt thought as the drizzle continued

to swirl round the bridge and *Antigone* drove on in search of her prey.

But the one message which had got through contained the vital fact of the enemy's course. Trevesham had only a rough idea of their position but at least he knew where they were going and that was obviously back to Taranto.

This fact, set against the weather, was electrifying in the possibility it suddenly presented *Antigone*. For a moment Trevesham was unnerved. This was an opportunity —albeit fraught with the most appalling risk—which he knew instantly would never recur. Step by step he reasoned it out.

He thought first of all of the standard rôle he was ordered to play. This was to locate, report and shadow the enemy. He had command of one small cruiser in contact with the whole Italian Fleet. Under normal conditions it would be folly to engage the enemy. His chances of inflicting any but superficial damage were slight, the odds on his own total destruction were staggering. This was not a matter of courage but of common prudence. The Commander-in-Chief would expect him not to endanger his ship.

But the enemy had turned back for home. There was no possibility of the main Mediterranean Fleet overtaking them now. Nor, under such weather conditions, could an air strike be flown off from *Illustrious*. But the clouds which prevented this also provided *Antigone* with something like a magic cloak in which she was invisible. Yes, thought Trevesham, invisible for the moment, but how long will it last?

Nevertheless, there was the enemy and there was *Antigone*. This was a classic situation—David and Goliath, a Drake versus the Armada—and Trevesham's whole being tingled with the knowledge that here was a chance which comes to a Captain not once in a decade but once in a generation. Whatever the outcome, however paralysing the odds, this was the one great opportunity of his life. He had seen it for what it was and now like the closing of some vast electrical circuit his mind was made up.

He decided to try and work round the enemy to the south. The wind had veered to the south-west and thus, if he should succeed in getting ahead and to windward of them, he would be in a position of tactical advantage, and would have the benefit of attacking out of the weather.

So far so good, thought Trevesham. The Italians would be heading approximately into the squall and would almost certainly have reduced their speed. They did not build heavy-weather ships. The Italians believed above everything else in speed. The weather would slow them down. However, the odds were still vastly on the enemy side. Trevesham was well aware that not only did the 'Zara' class of cruiser mount eight-inch guns to his six, but that also they had an advantage in speed of nearly seven knots. Once caught, therefore, in fine weather there would be little hope for *Antigone*.

By this time, though, the wind which had been steadily freshening was now blowing the best part of a gale. *Antigone* was taking it comfortably enough, but her attendant destroyer was washing down dangerously. At any other time Trevesham would have reduced his speed, but now it was essential to get ahead of the enemy without a moment's delay.

An hour and fifteen minutes later they were suddenly in contact with an Italian destroyer. She appeared dramatically ahead on their starboard bow through an unexpected gap in the weather. She was stern on to *Antigone*, a bare half mile ahead and steering almost a parallel course. A few seconds later the visibility closed in again and blotted her out.

The moment she was sighed the Gunnery Officer came through from the director control-tower.

'Permission to open fire, sir?'

'No!' Trevesham snapped curtly. His immediate action had been to haul away to port. It was still possible that *Antigone* had not been observed. He was not going to allow his plan to be sprung at half cock by one wretched destroyer.

Trevesham remained in his usual position in the starboard forward corner of the bridge, his arms hunched on the coping, his eyes peering into the mist. He knew his thinking was right. Just as he had sacrificed the aircraft to glean the first essential fact of the enemy's course so now this glimpse of the destroyer gave the enemy's approximate speed, which Spratt estimated at eighteen knots. Trevesham calculated that the destroyer was part of the normal arrowhead screen crusing ahead of the battle fleet. By altering course to starboard, therefore, he would find himself right in among the Italians in a matter of minutes.

By this time he must assume that the enemy was aware of being sighted. But they would be in a state of confusion. The Italians might well presume that they had stumbled accidentally on the British Mediterranean Fleet. They would have no idea of what was threatening them through the swirling mist. The thought of what actually was threatening them brought a sudden smile to Trevesham's face. But at the same time he knew that he still had the initiative. And that was a priceless gift. *Antigone* might be able to dash in, aided by surprise, and create havoc in their midst.

He leant over to the voice pipe down to the plotting room.

'What's the barograph doing, Schooly?'

'It looks as though it's stopped falling in the last half hour, sir.'

'H'm!'

He turned to Spratt, his judgement poised.

'It looks as though this thick weather isn't going to last much longer, Pilot.'

Spratt nodded quickly. They stared into each other's eyes, both of them for a moment still, both withdrawn into their thoughts.

'It's as thick as anything now, sir, perhaps'—Spratt paused for a fraction of a second wondering if he should give his advice—'perhaps this is it, sir.'

'Yes,' said Trevesham almost to himself, 'this is it—our great golden chance.'

Then the decision taken, he called out sharply:

'Chief Yeoman!'

'Sir?'

'Make by lamp to *Vitriolic*—"Am going in to establish position of enemy battle fleet. Intend to attack with torpedoes. Follow me at best speed. Be prepared to fire torpedoes on either beam as opportunity offers".'

Then as the signal lamp began winking astern to their hard-pressed destroyer, Trevesham turned *Antigone* to starboard and increased to thirty knots. The squall in which they had been immersed seemed now to be rising to a climax. Both Trevesham and Spratt were aware of

340

the significance of this. It meant that a cold front and better weather conditions were almost upon them. They had very little time.

Events, however, now crowded upon them as swiftly as the weather. Unseen they had slipped through the destroyer screen and were now in amongst the Italian Fleet.

'Christ!' said Spratt, 'we've arrived!'

Through the murk at a distance of not more than half a mile an Italian battleship loomed before their eyes. The ship was flanked by a cruiser and for a second or two it looked as though *Antigone* would pass between them. Both the battleship and the cruiser had their main armament trained fore and aft. This meant they had been caught entirely by surprise. At almost point blank range *Antigone*'s six-inch guns opened up on the cruiser. The second and third salvoes scored direct hits and the cruiser turned away on fire without replying to *Antigone*. Still concentrating her guns on the cruiser, they drew rapidly closer to the battleship. The first round was unquestionably theirs.

Antigone had certainly created the panic which Trevesham had planned. They had perhaps a minute, perhaps two to three minutes while the initiative still lay completely in their hands. Trevesham noted that the Italian main armament was now being brought to bear, but such must have been the confusion on board that the guns were first of all directed diametrically away from *Antigone* instead of towards her. But already the weather was beginning to clear. Their time was running out. It was now or never. This was the zenith of their one unrepeatable chance.

'Stand by to fire to port, Torps,' said Trevesham.

'Aye, aye, sir.'

John Caspar peered motionless down his sights, waiting for his moment to come, only his fingers ceaselessly altering and lining up the sights, scarcely breathing with the intensity of his concentration. They were now no further than eight hundred yards from the battleship, tearing towards each other on nearly opposite courses.

'Here we go, Torps,' said Trevesham and swung *Antigone* to starboard away and towards the protective rain. At thirty knots this violent alteration of course made the ship heel over steeply to port, a magnificent bow wave pluming

341

away as she turned. The Torpedo Officer rapped out 'Fire One!' then, as the first torpedo leapt plunging into the sea from the port waist, 'Fire Two!' and then a moment later, 'Fire Three!'

For the next forty-five seconds, time on *Antigone*'s bridge stood absolutely still. At such a short range they could scarcely miss, but that interval while the torpedoes were streaking underwater to their target held them paralysed with tension, their hands gripping anything solid on the bridge, praying, staring transfixed at the battleship as she drew further and further aft and her guns began almost lazily to open fire.

Then suddenly came the first deep underwater 'WHOOMPH' followed two seconds later by another one. Two out of their three torpedoes had got home. The enormous tension on the bridge as though in sympathy with the explosions released itself at the same time. Spratt jumped up and down, the Officer of the Watch thumped the Torpedo Officer on the back, the Chief Yeoman did an absurd little dance and everyone on the bridge let out a huge yell of delight. Trevesham, too, was swept up in the raging exaltation of success.

'Bloody wonderful, Torps!' said Trevesham with a sudden, wide grin. 'Wonderful! Wonderful!' then without pausing he went on: 'Full ahead both! Make smoke!'

Now they must escape. Now to survive *Antigone* must indeed 'get like a bat out of hell'.

'Give her everything you've got,' he called down to the Chief. This was the critical time. They had scored far more than he had dared to hope possible. If their luck continued to hold they might just get away with it—just —and no more.

There was no longer any doubt that the weather was clearing.

'Hurry up with that smoke,' Trevesham said sharply. A smoke screen would neither hold nor be of much protection in such a wind but anything was worth trying at this juncture.

Now *Antigone* had her stern to the Italians and only the two after turrets would bear. Yet their wild success had put them all on the top of their form. The Gunnery Officer kept up the pressure and another two salvoes found their mark. They began to zigzag. The ship was working up rapidly to her full thirty-two knots as, desperately, they fled the finer weather racing up astern and the delayed revenge they could scarcely pray to escape.

By this time the Italians had recovered from their surprise. One of the other cruisers unmolested by *Antigone* had opened fire. The second battleship, too, lobbed a heavy salvo into the sea about a hundred yards ahead of the ship. The Italian cruiser's gunnery was rapid and accurate, its aim obviously directed by intelligent anticipation of the few courses *Antigone* could take.

All the time visibility was improving. The rain and the clouds—their celestial protection—were being chased away by the cold front which conditioned their fate. For a couple of minutes a rain squall blotted them out and filled them with hope. Then with sinking hearts they watched it blow itself away. The clear weather came. The enemy range-takers adjusted their sights.

On the bridge no one spoke except to pass orders or essential reports. But the Torpedo Officer, Spratt, the Chief Yeoman of Signals and Trevesham himself—all knew in their hearts that they had left their escape a fraction too late. Nothing but a miracle could save them now.

Hatchett and Penniwick were making their way aft along the Marines' messdeck when *Antigone* received her first hit. A salvo of eight-inch armour-piercing shells struck her just below the catapult abaft the funnel on the starboard side. They entered on the slant, penetrated both boiler rooms, exploded and blew out a section of the ship's port side plating. *Antigone* gave a convulsive shudder. This was instantly followed by the deafening scream of escaping high-pressure steam.

But Hatchett and those with him heard none of this. A shell had exploded almost directly beneath them. The messdeck on which they had been standing was torn apart and in the moment of explosion those who were there, together with the stokers in the boiler room, were all of them shredded to death.

The lights failed and the ship lurched unexpectedly to port as the sea began pouring in from the hole in the side. The Commander (E) who was on his way up from the boiler room had his skull cracked open. For a few seconds a form of consciousness persisted in him. He clung to the twisted ladder and began to scratch the paint

343

off the bulkhead with his nails. But this was a purely muscular reaction. In point of fact he was already dead.

The Senior was in the engine room when the ship was hit. As the lights died out he saw one of the seams in the forward bulkhead gaping and through it an increasing torrent of water pouring in. The turbines changed their note. Although there was still power to drive the screws, *Antigone* began losing steam at a disastrous rate. He reported this to the bridge. His Captain's voice, remote and metallic, yet strangely human and reassuring, came back to him:

'Try and keep her steaming,' Trevesham told him, 'try and give me some electric power.'

'Aye, aye, sir,' he said automatically, but there was nothing he could do. *Antigone*'s fate had already been settled. There had only been two casualties in the engine room itself, but water continued to flood in from the torn bulkhead. Artificers and stokers looked at each other in the dim emergency lighting. All of them knew that a loss of speed meant an easier target for the enemy. The ship was listing to port. The chances of a sudden end down there below the waterline were now frighteningly high.

Other information was now reaching the bridge. The Quartermaster reported he was using thirty degrees of starboard wheel yet the ship was still falling off to port. A fire was raging along the main deck aft towards the wardroom. Collard and two seamen, all of them badly hurt, were trying to quench it, but pressure was dying out of the fire main, and the angle at which *Antigone* was listing made progress between decks almost impossible.

By this time the ship had turned in a slow arc so that now she lay stern on to the wind. She had been making smoke when the shell had struck. This smoke continued to pour from the funnel and now enveloped the bridge in acrid, partially burnt oil fuel. Blind and choking, Trevesham and the others struggled into their gas-masks. The ship was still continuing to turn slowly, and soon the smoke would be carried away to starboard. In the meantime they were totally out of control.

From the director tower the Gunnery Officer reported that turrets no longer had hydraulic power. So the guns could not be trained except laboriously by hand. On the

344

bridge itself the Chief Yeoman had been killed by a flying splinter, and on the flag deck below only one young signalman remained alive. Forward the ship was undamaged. As far as Trevesham knew all four turrets could still fire but only at a very slow rate. By striking into the heart of the ship and depriving them of power, that one unlucky salvo had done them the maximum damage.

As water poured into the ship, *Antigone* heeled over further and further to port. She did this in a series of jerks as watertight compartments filled up and new levels were found. Salvoes from the Italian cruisers continued to harass and near-miss them. It could only be a matter of time before they were hit again.

Some distance away there was the sound of another heavy explosion. By now the bridge was clearing of smoke. Trevesham wiped his smarting eyes and looked round for their attendant destroyer. He was just in time to see the stern of the destroyer lift in the air, remain poised for a second or two and then plunge quickly beneath the surface of the sea. So *Vitriolic* was gone, and now *Antigone* would enjoy the undivided attention of the whole Italian Fleet.

By now the ship lay stopped and beam on to the wind. This gave her a most uncertain movement. Each time she rolled it occurred to Trevesham that she might suddenly go. Although the weather was moderating, there was still quite a sea running, and this made things continuously difficult for the crippled ship.

Down in the cypher office Marsh lay unconscious in a pool of blood. He had been standing when the explosion occurred. The force of it had thrown him to the deck semi-stunned. In one of the subsequent lurches a steel chest containing the cypher books had broken loose and a corner of it had struck him on the crown of his head, splitting it open and depriving him of consciousness.

Aft in the ship's office the Paymaster-Commander had been trapped by the fire which was working its way along to the wardroom. He, too, had been slightly concussed and at one stage in the darkness he thought he would be suffocated by the smoke. But forethought and discipline came to his aid. As his consciousness returned he remembered that he always carried a torch. He crawled over the heaving, slanting deck feeling about till he found it. Miraculously the bulb was intact. So far so good. Then he remembered his duty. Should it be necessary to abandon ship the ledger and other important documents should be placed in a watertight cylinder and thrown overboard. There was no one to do this but the Paymaster-Commander himself. Or was he confusing it with the Great War? He did not feel quite himself. One side of his wing collar had sprung away from his neck and his glasses were broken. He found to his astonishment that he could not keep his train of thought for very long. He began to put the ledger into its container, then came a gap in his consciousness and next time he was aware of what he was doing he found himself laboriously taking the ribbon off the ship's office typewriter. This struck him as odd but try as he might he could not remember what he had set out to do. He abandoned the typewriter and sat down with his head in his hands. The smoke from the fire outside made him splutter and choke. The torch fell once more from his clutch and this time the bulb broke as it struck the steel deck.

Outside in the flat Collard, too, lay asphyxiated. He had been caught off balance by one of the ship's lurches. He had slipped and fallen where the smoke and the fumes were densest. The fire had burnt itself out by now but Collard had no means of knowing that the ship's refrigerating machinery had been punctured and a mixture of its escaping gases and the fumes of the explosion, heavier than air, were creeping aft through the ship.

His left ear and the skin of his neck had been burnt when the fire had first begun and this caused him a lot of pain. But it was the smoke he was afraid of. He decided he had better get up on deck. He began struggling to his feet but at that moment the ship lurched again and he fell slithering across the compartment. For a short while he flapped helplessly like a fish on a slab. Then oblivion came. Three minutes later he was dead.

Up on the bridge they had one consolation. The Italian battleship they had torpedoed was obviously in difficulties. Like *Antigone* she, too, had heeled over to a dangerous angle. Like *Antigone* she had suffered a fire. But unlike *Antigone* she was still able to steam. Gradually she drew further and further away, leaving the British cruiser to the attentions of the rest of her fleet.

At that moment an Italian salvo straddled the ship. There were two hits in quick succession, one on the after super-structure, the second penetrating between 'X' and 'Y' turrets on the quarterdeck. This was the shell which finished them off. It entered 'Y' magazine, which in turn exploded. An enormous mushroom of yellow-red smoke raced up into the sky—a spit of red, then saffron, then darkening off into a sinister grey-black. *Antigone* gave another long, anguished shudder. The power of this explosion told Trevesham all he needed to know. Now there could be no hope at all. The ship began settling down by the stern at an alarming rate, and this was understandable since the force of the explosion had blown off the whole after part of the ship. The quarterdeck, the screws, 'X' and 'Y' turrets, his own cabin, the wardroom, gunroom and warrant officers' messes, most of the engine room—all now had gone. Little more than half his ship was still left precariously afloat. There would not be much time.

'Prepare to abandon ship!' Trevesham ordered. She was sinking by the stern. The speed at which she went would depend on how the lateral bulkheads stood the increasing pressure.

'Wheel jammed hard a-starboard,' the Chief Quartermaster reported to Spratt.

'We no longer have a rudder,' Spratt answered down the voice-pipe, 'better come up on deck, Bowling. It's prepare to abandon ship.'

Even now when the fate of the ship was no longer in doubt, there was no element of panic. Forward—a part of the ship completely undamaged—men poured out of turrets and up on deck from the foc'sle. The Gunnery Officer came down from the director control-tower. Sub-Lieutenant Darbigh climbed down from the high-angle director. Cooks filed out of the galley. A few stokers and artificers came up from what remained of the engine room. The Surgeon-Commander left his sick bay. Royal Marine bandsmen clambered up from the transmitting station.

On deck Carley floats were being heaved into the sea, followed by wooden gratings and anything which would float. Trevesham watched this activity for a while. Then

347

he gave the executive order 'Abandon ship!' The scramble into the sea began.

Down in the cypher office the shock of the second explosion brought Marsh back to consciousness. He was just in time to hear a distant voice calling, 'Abandon ship!' He crawled out of the cypher office, dazed and afraid. He was below the waterline and it was very dark outside in the flat. He had no idea how long he would have and at first the panic sent his mind spinning in small circles, out of control of himself.

Then with an effort he got his head above the level of his fear and with that effort came all the carefully taught Naval reactions. He knew what he must do. He felt his head. His fingers came away warm and sticky with blood but he was still alive and able to think. He still had a chance.

He crawled on all fours to the forward end of the flat, found and unclipped another watertight door but could not open it due to the angle at which the ship was lying. That was his only way of escape and he had no strength to raise open the door against its own weight.

Then cunning came to his aid. In the flat were rows of rifles used for arming landing-parties. These were stacked along a bulkhead. Marsh felt his way to this stack, took a rifle and inserted it between the door and its casing as a lever. It worked. A moment or so later he was through on the other side in a throng of men struggling to go up the ladder to the foc's'le.

From then on he was almost carried along on the human tide until he found himself slithering down the ship's side in the smoky sunlight, tearing his hands and his buttocks on the barnacles and ending up in the disgusting sewer-like oil fuel which covered the surface of the sea. His mouth filled with the stuff but by an effort of will he managed to hold it unswallowed until his head was out of the water and he could spit it out. The oil fuel seemed to sear across the open wound on his scalp, but there was no time to pay much attention to that. He began swimming with the others away from the ship.

The bridge was now leaning over into the sea at an angle of forty degrees. By this time the ship was well down by the stern and already the bows were beginning to lift in the air.

Only Trevesham and Spratt remained on the bridge. It must be clear to the enemy that *Antigone* was doomed, but they still continued to fire at her. As the Carley floats and their clusters of survivors drifted away from the ship —the boats had all been rendered useless—a salvo of eight-inch shells landed in the water close to the ship.

'Bastards!' said Spratt shaking his fist in a futile despairing gesture.

'Come on, Pilot,' said Trevesham. 'Time you went. She's not going to last much longer.'

It was, indeed, purely vicious of the Italians to continue shooting at the stricken ship. Already from the steepening angle of the bridge it was difficult to see but, as Spratt jumped off into the sea, there came an odd and extraordinary pause. The rate at which *Antigone* was settling into the water suddenly altered. One of the main watertight bulkheads must be holding, thought Trevesham. He had been on the point of following Spratt into the sea but now he hesitated. What remained of *Antigone* lay two-thirds on her port side. From where Trevesham stood wedged he could have leapt straight into the sea. Perhaps she'll turn turtle and float, he thought, the two turrets would fall out, and the air trapped in her bilges and lower compartments would give her a dubious buoyancy.

From the position he was now forced to adopt it was difficult to move. He decided to wait a little longer and see. The Italians had now ceased firing at *Antigone*. It must be apparent, even to them, thought Trevesham, that now it was only a matter of time. Poor old ship, he thought, it's been a short and crowded life. My first big command and here I am about to leave you for ever. He felt tired and numb. He shook his head impatiently. Feelings were always a bit of a luxury. He would need to shock himself out of this overpowering emotion he felt at leaving his doomed ship for ever. It had happened before. It would happen again. Yes—but not to *Antigone*— not to your first wonderful, strong and beautiful cruiser that now lay half at the bottom and half on her side like some obscene piece of meat hacked off a carcase and thrown into a canal.

Antigone gave something between a lurch and a wriggle. It passed through Trevesham's mind that he had left it too late. Perhaps now he was alone on board except for the drowned, the dying and the dead.

It was a moment of the most poignant feeling. For a time it had him helpless. He struggled to master it with tears in his eyes—he who had spent a lifetime under discipline, a centurion set under authority, a creature who had learned slowly but thoroughly to control himself and to drive this outer being with four gold stripes on its arm, now found himself mute and paralysed, overcome with emotion on the bridge of his sinking ship. He knew his duty. He knew—the driving part of him knew—he must plunge into the sea and swim as far away as he could before she went down. 'Leave her, Johnny, leave her, it's time for us to leave her.' The words of the old sea chanty kept on going through his head. But for once he could not make himself obey. He remained wedged against the coping of the bridge—that selfsame coping he had leant his arms on so many countless times these last two-and-a-half years—and try as he might, his will failed him and he could not make himself leave.

The ship gave another lurch and to Trevesham's amazement began slowly, grotesquely to right herself again. She was lower in the water now but somehow it was as though she too had regained her self-respect. She was going to the bottom in a consonant fashion, upright with her head in the air as she had been designed to sail the seas. She was going reluctantly but with the slow dignity of a funeral rather than the agonized writhing of a beast on the slaughterhouse floor.

Yet as the smoke began clearing away and Trevesham looked down at the sea, his tired eyes saw disgusting traces of the human carnage wrought in the ship. Little groups of survivors, swimming or clinging to rafts, were now some way from *Antigone*, but closer at hand as though drawn to the ship by some kind of magnetism were maimed headless bodies, arms, torsos, the intimate immensely pathetic pieces of human men who had been bodily torn apart by the terrible explosions and scattered like grotesque confetti over the surface of the water.

All those, thought Trevesham, were my sailors such a short time ago. Hatchett would be in among them and Collard, the First Lieutenant—there could be no hope for them. The Chief and possibly the Senior Engineer—they, too, must have gone. Taw-Street, the Captain of Marines, and his incomparable Colour-Sergeant. Perhaps the Three Fat Men of the Sea. His starchy Paymaster-Commander. Almost physically he forced his mind away from the picture of all those who must have perished. Now only he remained on board his ship, alone and alive.

From the position he was in he could not see the Italian Fleet, and now a great silence came on him and the ship. It irritated Trevesham that he could not see. Instinctively he turned to the Officer of the Watch to tell him to alter course and brace his ideas up. But of course that was absurd. There was no one on the bridge.

This tiny shock brought him to his senses more rapidly than anything else. He shook his head violently. It was like coming out of a cold shower. He looked sharply round. The nearest rafts were now some distance away. He must hurry. 'When they go, they go fast,' an old boatswain had told him in the Great War, and he had seen it proved again and again. This was no time to be mooning about.

He climbed down the ladder to the flag deck. That bright young leading-signalman lay dead in a mess of blood by the signal lockers, pinioned by part of the funnel casing. He was the one, Trevesham remembered, whom Mellish wanted to recommend for Accelerated Advancement. Now both of them were dead.

Just beyond, the sea lapped gently, thick with oil fuel and wreckage. He took a last look round at all that was left of his ship.

'Poor old *Aunty Gone*,' he muttered. 'Poor old ship.'

Then without further ado he jumped into the sea and began swimming away from the ship.

They could not see the Italian ships from where they were in the water. They lived on hope. Soon, they told each other, soon they'll be back to pick us up. In the meantime they swam about in the oily sea waiting. Even the silence now was oily. It never occurred to them in the water that the Italians would simply leave them to die.

Trevesham swam about among the survivors encouraging them and checking up on identities. The sea was still choppy but now the sun shone. It could have been very

351

much worse. *Antigone* or what was left of her was still afloat.

'It's all that hot air and flannel on the foc's'le messdeck what keeps her from going,' as one seaman explained.

'If she holds out much longer I'll go back aboard and bale her out by hand,' said another.

But for the main part they clung on to the rafts or swam about in silence waiting for *Antigone* to go. Brasson was among the survivors. So was Meldrum and so was Hale. There were two midshipmen, the Navigating Officer, Mr Partle and a warrant engineer, but the rest of the officers except for Trevesham and Marsh must have died. There was no sign of the Surgeon-Commander, the Torpedo Officer, the Chaplain or the Instructor-Lieutenant. They had jumped with the rest but some must have been blown out of the water, others must have drowned or drifted away. There had never been much hope for anyone abaft the flag deck and the funnel. The Commander, Collard, that phalanx of officers who had formed the heart of the ship—they must have perished at once, thought Trevesham. Yet he still wondered how it was they had gone.

In the event their cruiser sank without fuss or drama. Some compartment in the foc's'le caved in with a subdued rumble and then she began moving down fast, as though clawed to the bottom by unseen powerful muscles lying in wait under the surface of the sea.

They watched her go in silence. There was no honour they could do her, no final mark of respect. The hundred odd survivors in the water were numbed in themselves. It had all happened so quickly they had lost their sense of surprise.

'Well, she's gone and that's that,' said Chief Petty Officer Bowling, his saturnine face streaked with oil fuel, his two black eyes glowering out of the hollow cheeks. He thought about the curtained chief petty officers' mess with its leather cushions and Penniwick in his usual corner having a ziz. He had not seen the rotund Chief Bos'n's Mate among the survivors. He would have been aft with the Commander no doubt. 'Alas, poor Yorick,' said Bowling as he thought about his shipmate and his friend. It was a phrase he always used to express some particular sadness bearing down on him, the causes of which lay far beyond his control. Poor old Arthur, he thought, with his six children and his bright cheerful reaction to life—shan't see another like him. Chief Yeoman Mellish, too, he had not found him among the survivors. Petty Officer Vincent would have been near the after conning position so there could be no hope for him. But despair was of no avail. He stopped this train of thought abruptly and devoted himself to taking charge of his little group of survivors. It was more of an effort than ever, but then he had always been privileged to make greater efforts than were strictly necessary to the job in hand.

'Come along, lads,' he said, 'keep moving. It's a long swim to Malta—but we'll make it yet.'

Petty Officer Cook Jenkins was there. The left side of his face had been burnt through being thrown against the electric range so, in addition to the perpetual grudge he bore against life, he was now in considerable pain. But it was to Jenkins that Marsh owed his life. He realized this when he found himself being hauled up on a Carley float. He had lost consciousness through the wound on his head and but for Jenkins' strong arms would have drowned.

So the vigil in the water began.

For the first couple of hours they were cheerful enough. They talked about becoming prisoners-of-war and living off a diet of spaghetti and ice cream. They described in bawdy and irreverent terms the dusky Italian beauties who, the sailors thought, would no doubt attend their captivity. Then as the time passed and the sun began dropping down into the west, the first serious doubts started to build up in their minds. Were the Italians never going to pick them up? Was nobody coming? What about the *Illustrious* they had heard so much about and the battleships of the Mediterranean Fleet? Were they simply to be left, waterlogged and forgotten?

So the short Mediterranean twilight came and went and soon it was night. The sea was still calm, but if there are degrees of emptiness, then what was left of *Antigone*'s ship's company experienced them all. Exposure, too, was taking its toll. The delayed effects of shock, the deepening cold, the growing, growing sense of being abandoned and overlooked, the losing fight against lethargy, numbness and sleep—all these factors, the common lot of the ship-

353

wrecked sailor, took them in ones and twos as the night wore on.

The stokers and engine room ratings were the first to collapse. Most of them had rushed up from intense heat to plunge thankfully enough into the cooling sea. But the change had been too abrupt. Pneumonia began picking them off, and they lacked the resistance of their upper-deck comrades.

Trevesham, grey and all but spent with exhaustion, swam painstakingly from raft to Carley float, keeping his little band together, injecting them with new spirit and holding them still in what now seemed to them all the blessed bond of Naval discipline. Whence Trevesham himself received his energy he did not know—but although many times the little silver river of vitality dropped to a trickle, the link with some finer level of consciousness still held him in its stream and saved those who, with him, could reach into themselves for a last desperate response. And save them it did. When dawn came, only eighteen had died in the night. There were still nearly ninety of them alive.

Strangely enough this time in the water was the chance Leading-Seaman Battersby had long been awaiting. He knew that in exhaustion and stress the qualities of leadership shine unobscured. He had seen Petty Officer Vincent killed on board, and now in the water Battersby appointed himself unofficial Captain's Coxswain. He followed Trevesham wherever he swam. It was all he could do to keep up, but he was fascinated to see how Trevesham still generated his power of command. Since Battersby intended one day to be a Captain himself, he told himself that if Trevesham could do it then so could he.

Marsh had become delirious. He had always been lonely and inaccessible, but now the pain in his head drove him into some distant part of his being beyond all reach of help. He babbled in a maudlin way of Lisette and of some stoppage of leave the gunroom had suffered in Peru. Blood and oil fuel caked the gash on his scalp. He was seized by an ague and of all the wounded men on the raft he was most in need of care and attention. It was to this raft that Trevesham always returned after his slow journeys round the survivors. There was nothing practical he could do for his young Secretary except to watch over him in his bad time and see, if possible, that he came to no further harm.

Almost inevitably Nobby Clarke had survived. The Commander had sent him forward on a message just before the first shell had struck. So Hatchett and the Chief Bosun's Mate had been killed, whereas he, Nobby Clarke, had got away with it again. Now his domed shape floated with a kind of blue-skinned benignity like an unpuncturable rubber ball. The other two Fat Men of the Sea were also bobbing about elsewhere in the water, 'not having a nice time at all'.

At one stage towards dawn Nobby found himself next to Battersby and Petty Officer Cook Jenkins. The three of them had not been together in each other's company since that night in the Belfast Mail Packet.

''Ullo, gentlemen,' Nobby said huskily, looking from one to the other. 'This is like the night before we joined old *Aunty Gone*—but wetter. Remember crossing the Irish sea two years ago?'

To his astonishment PO Cook Jenkins managed a wintry smile and the nearest he ever came to a joke, in his sing-song Welsh accent.

'Could have saved ourselves a basin of trouble, then, couldn't we?' he said, 'by jumping overboard straight away.'

Taw-Street and most of the Marines had perished when 'Y' magazine had blown up, but Marine Parker, who had been down in the transmitting station, had survived. His waxed moustache, impervious to the assault of water, had nevertheless succumbed to the oil fuel in the sea. He clung to the raft on which Marsh lay babbling, keeping an eye on his officers as he had done for so many years of service, wondering how Hackenheimer would have psychologized the present events and determined, if opportunity offered, to get a bit of formation into his shipwreck before it was all too late.

The *Aurora* found them nearly twenty-four hours after *Antigone* had been sunk. They had drifted towards Crete, some considerable way from the scene of battle.

These were the most stirring moments they had experienced. When first the cruiser came into sight, they could scarcely believe it was true. Then while the ship was nothing but a mast on the horizon, there followed that torture of doubt, needle fine, that tearing uncertainty that perhaps they would not be seen. Perhaps the ship would disappear again like the wraith it seemed to be.

Some of them shouted pitifully with what strength they had, as though their exhausted voices could carry the several miles to the unknown ship. Some of them closed their eyes in order not to see their rescuers go away unheeding. Some, like Trevesham, prayed to whatever they understood by God to succour them then at that agonized moment, to draw help towards the men in the water, to beseech from the level of life a gesture of grace and mercy from above.

'O God, our help in ages past, Our hope for years to come . . .', he began, saying aloud the words of Isaac Watt's famous old hymn, and those around him, led by an elderly engine room artificer, took up the chant in a grotesque petition from the surface of the sea. It was a garbled and gabbled prayer. They could not remember the verses in order but they had sung the lines so many times bare-headed on the quarterdeck that it did not seem to matter. The intention came through. 'Our shelter from the stormy blast, And our eternal home . . .'

Then spontaneously they broke into that deepest and most compelling hymn of them all. 'Eternal Father, strong to save, Whose arm hath bound the restless wave—' there was no harmonium now to lead their singing. There was no need of it. That essential prayer from the sea quavered, hesitated and then caught up on its own emotion as they clung helplessly to the rafts—'O hear us when we cry to Thee, For those in peril on the sea.' They had sung this hymn every Sunday morning since the ship had commissioned and on all the other Sunday mornings in other ships stretching back through the years. Somehow and in some way it brought them strength. 'O Trinity of love and power, Our brethren shield in danger's hour—From rock and tempest, fire and foe, Protect us wheresoe'er we go—Thus evermore shall rise to Thee, Glad hymns of praise from land and sea.'

So it was that the cruiser *Aurora,* bearing the sweet

name of the Goddess of Dawn, who at the close of every night ascended in a chariot drawn by swift horses up to heaven to announce the coming of the Sun—so it was that HMS *Aurora* bore down upon the little band of survivors in the troubled sea, and the gentle, infinitely tender rescue of the few that were left began.

Bestsellers
from
BALLANTINE BOOKS